Arlinga

CONCERNING A MAN

Roan Clay

—for Wade

A NOVEL—
by Roan Clay

 FriesenPress

Suite 300 — 990 Fort St
Victoria, BC, Canada, V8V 3K2
www.friesenpress.com

Cover Painting Copyright © 2014 by Allan Livingstone
Cover Design and Photography by Ben Livingstone

ISBN
978-1-4602-5308-3 (Hardcover)
978-1-4602-5309-0 (Paperback)
978-1-4602-5310-6 (eBook)

1. Fiction, Fantasy, General

Distributed to the trade by The Ingram Book Company

To the reader...

Fear not, kind purchaser. These writings are transcribed in that dialect of the Indo-European language known by some as English. You need not learn any new tongue to understand them, nor make any special effort in the reading of the short passages I have included. Even the pronunciation of the names need not trouble you, although should you choose, you may learn the proper sounds of native speech from the text in the back of this volume.

But, as I say, those whose minds are not stirred by a love of languages should not trouble themselves over the strange Arlingan names. You may even imagine your own approximations for ease of reading.

My ambition in the crafting of this story was the amusement, edification, and general benefit of those such as yourself, who for some untold reason chose to open the cover and begin the adventure of exploration into a new land.

It is my sincerest hope that all who read beyond this page will taste of the joy that the writing of this book has given me, and I, of course, shall ever endeavor to remain

Your humble servant,
The Author

Post Scriptum

When the image of the Sheewa, with his long cloak, broad hat and walking staff came to my mind, it was entirely unbidden, like a dream out of half sleep. It was only some months afterward that a friend told me of the Czech Krakonoš, whose costume is practically identical. Whatever unseen wind of ancient legend was stirred up in the rhythm of my pen, its work lies before you. Farewell.

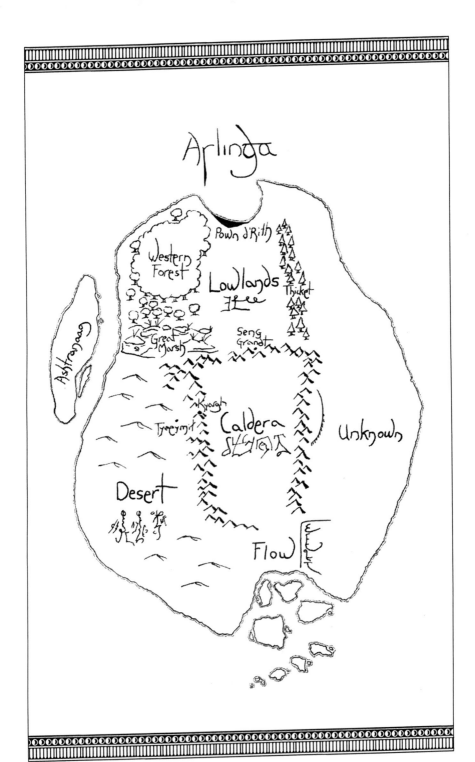

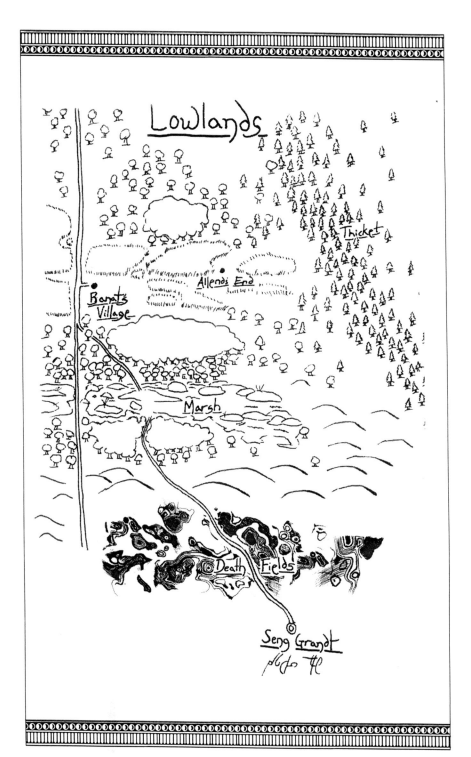

Arlinga

Chapter 1
The Trail

I'VE TROD THIS NARROW LAND ACROSS,
HAVE SEEN THE REALMS OF OLD.
I'VE WRIT THE BLOOD OF MIGHTY MEN,
WHO BUILT THEIR PRIDE ON GOLD.
STILL THE END OF ALL MY JOURNEYS SEEMS
TO LEAD ME FAR AWAY,
FAR AWAY AND BACK AGAIN,
HOME TO OLD SENG GRANDT AGAIN,
BEFORE THE BREAK OF DAY.

~Sheewan Striding Song~

From the rear of the column came a mulish bellow and a sodden impact, and a man cried out in pain. Hunter turned and saw that the rearmost driver lay on the ground, rolling back and forth in agony. It was not unexpected. Apparently the man had struck his beast in anger once too often. The foul driver had shown himself bad tempered from the very first, and now Hunter was thankful the man and not the mule had been hurt. Men he could replace, but mules were a precious resource, and especially such mules as these.

It was but the third hour of the day, the fifth day of their journey on a long and weary trail. As yet, they had not reached the broad forest and farmland that enveloped the Hills beyond the Plain. Their obstacles were currently smaller — the occasional wild beast or marauder might threaten the mules' safety, but they were of no great concern. The sea no longer lingered in the air, nor did the inherent stench of the city, but rather the sharp smell of dust mingled with that of the wayside flowers.

Four days had passed since they had left the coastal city of Pown d'Rith, and never had Hunter been so glad to be out of it. In truth, it could not rightly be called a city, for it had neither central administration nor any semblance of law. Rather, it clustered and spread around the broad harbor as though scorning contact with itself. He stopped there twice every trip, first to load up with grain for the Hills, last to drop off tea for shipment — that exquisite tea of Arlinga, changing character with every cup, first heady with spice, then smooth like sweetened cream. The leaves were harvested from plants bred ages ago for survival in harsh Arlingan winters, and they had lost nothing through the generations.

Of necessity, on this end of the Trail the mule train never ventured outside the high walls of Kroon d'Rith (the Fortress of the Harbor), that high-walled fort which marks the ending of the Great Trail running from the Hills to the sea. Once, a long time before he came to be leader of the caravan, one of the muleteers had strayed from the fortress into Pown d'Rith on the night when they had received their pay. Perhaps he had fallen in with villains, perhaps he had shown his gold too openly as he spent it. His body had been found in the morning, floating facedown in the scum below the docks.

Always remembering this, Hunter had made sure to keep his men busy during their stay in Pown d'Rith, the Black Cradle, and so had spared them similar tragedy. During his term of leadership, not one driver had ever gone out into the city. Once the merchandise had been carried inside and loaded onto the beasts, they hastened to put Pown d'Rith behind them amid a driving rain.

They now traveled down the Great Trail (a name left over from the days of Empire, when kings and generals made the track wide and kept it so). Now the path was tended but once a year in the spring, when local villages would set to work on it out of common consent. The Trail was used as a main artery for merchant caravans as well as for local traffic, and every kual[1] or so a small avenue branched off to connect local farms and villages.

The places they had passed thus far had not the look of farming communities so much as clusters of inns and public houses. As they passed farther out of reach of the Black Cradle, the buildings grew humbler, seen as they were a kand away against the flat horizon. Gradually the sweet smell of livestock and field grass built in the air, until at last they could be reasonably sure of safety from highwaymen and other miscreants. Nightfall was approaching, so when the next village came into sight they turned their mules along the avenue, and soon the town embraced them as a mother folds a weary child to her breast.

In every village along the Great Trail, there was a large enclosure fitted with stables to be used only by passing mule trains. Generally, they were operated not on a wage basis, but as a simple act of gratitude on the part of the villages, for the drivers, unable to spend their pay in Pown d'Rith, invariably scattered their gold coin along the Trail like a farmer

---

1   A quarter kand (0.65 miles/1 kilometer). A kand measures 2.6 miles (4.18 kilometers), or the distance between two ancient markers on the Great Trail.

sows seed, the fruit of which was a warm welcome wherever they stopped.

Not ten minutes had passed until the mules were squared away, and the small yard was emptied of drivers save for Hunter, Byorneth and the injured man, whom they had helped into the enclosure and laid out on his bedding. Barring any festering, the wound would soon heal.

Byorneth ambled stiffly over to a grain bag and sat down. He had been with Hunter as his leader when Hunter was but a mule driver, and now that he had handed the reins over to the younger, he was very useful as adviser and confidant. On occasion, when the column had been threatened by thieves or beasts, Byorneth's blade had been an added benefit, his gray hairs proving no impediment to the swiftness of his arm.

Hunter stood and looked at him. Each night, pairs of drivers took the job of guarding the grain and keeping watch over their fellow drivers, and the watch had fallen to Byorneth and Hunter. In spite of his strength, it pained Hunter to see an old man stay awake so late. "Go to sleep or join the others, old friend. I'll collar one of the others to stand watch with me."

"Ha! Which one? Harn? You'll be so busy guarding him, the men will have a free hand with this town! None of these urchins will be sober till morning, including him! Let me alone! I am not so old as to fail my duties! Get out!"

Hunter smiled. Far from taking offense, he saw the wisdom in his aged lieutenant's words. He knew too that even were Byorneth not relieved, he could easily stand guard all night. Hunter patted the old man's shoulder. "Right you are, old friend. I'll stand the third watch." So he left his counselor there in the corner, sword in hand, alert, scowling into his gray beard.

Hunter was always interested in the doings of his drivers in the villages. Their relationship with the Villagers was a tenuous one, and he wished above all to ensure continued friendly relations with everyone along the Trail. He stopped in at all the usual haunts — the requisite ale huts where they sold pungent drinks concocted from grain, herbs and other substances best not thought of, the hovels where enterprising yokels set up games of "chance" and "gambled" with silver gleaned from previous caravans. Every time the mule train stopped for the night, Hunter was a ghost among his drivers, silent and watching.

It was early yet for there to be any trouble. The men had not yet consumed enough *rashi* to become belligerent, and the Villagers had not yet won enough for his men to become resentful. All these establishments stood in a great circle around the village square, and so, confident any disturbance would awaken him, Hunter settled down beside the well in the center of the village within earshot of his men.

He had not slept an hour when that old familiar noise broke out, the sound of drunken anger. Hunter sprang to his feet and entered the hut from which the noise came, a dark place dominated by a central table at which sat three of his men and two of the Villagers.

The game had gone awry somehow, for Harn was on his feet, menacing the Villagers one by one with his blade, demanding the return of his money. Hunter moved quickly, and the man had no time to react before the handle of Hunter's knife knocked him senseless and he was dragged out into the street. Hunter thrust his head back into the tent.

"I apologize for his behavior," he said to the Villagers. "I've put him out for a while, and then he'll go back to the stable, so he should cause no further trouble."

A thin, ruddy countryman smiled up from the dice, which he had already resumed. "Think nothing of it, Captain. I have my life threatened every time a train comes through. It's the *rashi* before the gambling that does it."

The game resumed, and Hunter stepped outside again just as Harn got to his feet, so he grabbed the scruff of the fellow's shirt and walked him briskly toward the enclosure, advising him to sleep it off. The blow had taken the fight out of him, and he stayed where he fell.

All the village save the men running the games and serving drinks were asleep in their houses, the long peak-roofed dwellings opposite the dens of vice. Perhaps his most important responsibility this night was to ensure his drivers did not stray into these homes, for diversion was scarce along the Trail.

Soon the third watch came, and Hunter returned to the stables, reflecting not without remorse that he had taken the better duty, for now the wind had blown up violently and blasted chilly through the little village, signaling a bitter night. He found Byorneth as he had left him, squatting on the grain bag with the drawn blade lying across his brown knees. He arose stiffly as Hunter entered, bringing a cold blast with him, and gestured toward the sleeping form of Harn, nodding his approval. Then Hunter was left alone to settle into the warm spot Byorneth had left.

It was early the next morning when they got on their way again. It was not a happy morning, for the better part (or worse part) of the drivers suffered greatly from their libations the night before, as well as too little sleep. It was always worse at first, with the men eager to spend and the Villagers just as eager to sell. Many also suffered cramps and chills from having slept out in the open, where they had fallen or been thrown, at the mercy of the cold night and morning dew.

The sun rose on their left as they marched along, and the sky turned darkly purple, then orange, and finally light blue as the day matured. The dust soon rose and began to choke them, and every time a driver sneezed it was followed by a little groan. They were now one man short owing to the wound, and the extra mule did little to ease their day. Indeed, the mules fared better than the men, who invariably faltered as they went, each silently vowing abstinence. The beasts had been fed well, and as much as mules are not known for their agreeability, they seemed almost joyful by comparison.

The day grew hotter, and soon the men removed their coats. The going had been easy in the beginning where the land had been broad and flat, devoid of hill or any other feature, but now the earth began to buckle slightly, as if pushed against the sea from the other side. Hunter's heart rejoiced at it, even as the men suffered.

The danger was past inasmuch as Pown d'Rith was far to their backs, but the land was becoming more hazardous in that they passed hillocks on every side, perfectly suited to ambush. In this area lived that particular breed of farmer who, whenever the duties of farming pressed him less heavily, would wait beside the road to rob unwary travelers. Sometimes, when the caravan would stop at a village after a theft, they would find the stolen grain and mules in the possession of one of the Villagers, with no recourse against him.

For this reason, every hump and hillock they passed was viewed with suspicion, and each man stood ready to sound the piercing *"Chareer!"* that brings swords and daggers to the ready and circles the men about the mules and their precious cargo.

The breath caught in Hunter's chest when out of dull haze of distance and dust a lone figure appeared. They could not discern it in full until it topped the highest of the ridges, where it floated above the wavering ground for a moment before it dipped once again and displayed itself against the road.

It was a man, striding long and easy, as if he had covered many kaind already and could easily cover that many again. As he walked, a broad, dark cloak shifted from one side to the other, bellying with the breeze of his motion, fastened about his shoulders with a leather harness. Around his legs he wore short trousers that extended below the knee. He carried no weapon but a hooked dagger, and walked with a long, stout staff. The brim of a broad hat obscured his face almost down to his rounded, dark beard, and he wore a leather pouch under one arm. Hunter had never before seen such a man.

The approaching traveler raised his hand and Hunter ordered the train to halt. As is the rule, the drivers stood about the animals and waited, watchful in all directions, and only then did Hunter raise his hand in answer to the universal traveler's salute, and lifted his voice in the greeting, "Good trail!"

"And also for you!" came the reply. The man halted, and his broad cloak wrapped itself around him as he stood in the dust with both hands on his staff. "Have you any news of the North?"

"No, sir. There is no news. The town of the harbor is still the Black Cradle, and the villages bear no remark. Whence come you?"

"From far to the south." The lilt of his speech was peculiar, especially out of such a fierce face. "I am come out of the High City, Seng Grandt." The dialect was strange too in its fluency, greater than any man of the North would ever use.

Hunter blinked. "I know naught of such a place. Is it a new city?"

"Nay. It is a place much older than even this Trail." Then his shaded eyes fell upon Byorneth, and they widened. Then, as though reminded of forgotten business, he removed a roll of rough paper from his bag, pulled a reed pen from a side pocket, and dipped the pen somewhere deep within the recesses of his pouch. With quick strokes he scrawled something on the corner of the paper. Almost instantly all was put away, and with a quick nod to Hunter and a final stare at Byorneth, he was off again at his peculiar pace. His form was soon lost in the dust, and they saw him no more.

With much cursing and braying, the caravan moved again, and hour faded into weary hour until finally the sun stood at its zenith, and the mule train stopped under a small stand of aspen which shaded the roadside. The mules were tethered to the limbs of the gray trees to graze, and the men sat around to eat out of their ample packs.

Hunter walked to the farthest tree and sat next to Byorneth, the old man grunting in acknowledgment. The younger swallowed a few bites of the soft, greasy bread and dried beef, and washed it down with water out of his leather bottle. "That man on the road today. I've never seen such a one as him."

Byorneth only grunted again and filled his mouth.

"He recognized you."

The old man swallowed and nodded. "They know of me."

"They?"

"Yes. I'm surprised you've not seen one in all these journeys, although they do not often come this far north. They travel through the Island, writing as they go. When they've finished, they return to their mountain stronghold."

Hunter stared. "How do you know this? I've lived my life on this Island, and I've never once heard of them!"

"I was among them for a time." He shook the crumbs from his beard and fixed his companion with a steely stare. "This knowledge stays with you. I am not privileged to reveal it."

"Very well."

They sat in silence for a few moments. Byorneth produced a lump of curds he had been saving and offered some to Hunter. They ate in silence until an hour had elapsed, then Hunter went and stood by his mule, waiting until the men saw him there and pulled their mules into line again. Of all that Byorneth had taught him, this lesson had served him best — let men obey on their own.

For all the responsibility, danger and trouble, Hunter loved the work. He was never troubled by drink or loss as were his men, so the sunshine fell cheerfully on his face, and the twittering of the wayside birds, reviled by each *rashi*-soaked driver, aroused no ire in him. He found delight in the swing and push of the long journey. Years ago, he had experienced a welling impatience as he looked ahead, his nature rebelling against the long tramp between the train and the Hills. But there was a great difference between him and the boy he had once been. Now, he welcomed each day as it came, and did his best to make each hour work its hardest for him. His mule would stray away or shy at the wayside birds that burst out as they passed, but he pulled it back in line without thinking, well used to the constant struggle. The days passed with the easy pace of a familiar distance.

Suddenly, the Hills appeared, blue and far off. At first, one might have mistaken them for a low-lying cloud bank, but soon the white caps became clear, and they even fancied they could smell snow in the summer wind that blew in their faces. In the field by the road, a lone bird flitted and all at once fell to the ground, only to spring into the air again with a struggling serpent clutched in its mouth. Life thrived about them in abundance, and the train moved to its quickened rhythm.

Their way was often broken by rivers and stretches of aspen, ever so slowly giving way to low oak and scattered evergreens. Most of the bridges that spanned the streams and sharp gullies had long since decayed and fallen, but the men were well used to such struggles, even the mules having become somewhat resigned. They had just passed one of the few bridges left standing, rickety and uneasy, when Hunter raised his hand and the column stopped.

He crouched close to the ground, Byorneth beside him, and studied the tracks which crossed the Trail at an angle before them. They were of padded feet, large and round, with a claw mark at the tip of each toe. Their eyes met and Byorneth nodded. "Bear. A huge one."

"The sign is very fresh," Hunter replied. "This is close." He paused and spoke again, almost in a whisper. "I think we've met this one before."

"Yes. Two journeys ago. We lost a mule." They remembered it well, the sudden rush in the night, the booming grunt of the dark beast, high ears like horns. No mule driver soon forgets such things.

"Captain!" one of the men called out behind them. "On the pad of the left forefoot, is there a jagged scar running from toe to heel?"

Hunter looked. "Yes."

The speaker was a new driver, solid and steady, though now obviously frightened. "I was raised near here. This bear is the one we call Leen d'Arns — the Spirit of Arn." He came closer. "Years ago Arn, a murderer, was caught and killed in our village. The next day, this bear devoured the child of the man who had put Arn to death. Since then, it has grown in strength and cunning, and people say that the spirit of Arn inhabits the bear.

"That scar," he continued, his voice unsteady, "he received five years ago when he met my brother in the forest. He was a mighty man, and he gave Leen d'Arns that wound before the creature finally crushed his skull."

Byorneth, ever alert, stood up. "We should keep moving."

Chapter 2
The Slave

As they passed the cultivated fields of the villages, Hunter noted that there began to be more slaves working in the fields — Hillfolk, dark skinned and industrious, some lately taken from their people, others who had been slaves since childhood. They labored side by side with their masters, cutting and stooking grain or tending the bearded, scoop-horned cattle which gave life and status to the villages. Nearer the sea a slave is a rare thing, and may belong only to the very rich, but here his labor profits many.

The sun dipped slowly far toward the west, and the drivers had long since grown listless and dull, so Hunter led the train down the next reddening avenue and across a stream to a village. A few slaves still labored in the fields, while their light-skinned masters were out of sight indoors, settling down for the night. Hillslaves always sang as they worked, and so the mule train was serenaded all the way to the village in a strange tongue set to a strange tune.

The songs of the Hillfolk are strange to the Northern ear. The scale and rhythm evoked mountain passes and cold streams, and one almost fancied he could hear the faintest echo, as if the sound were reflected from a faraway cliff. Some Villagers had by this time begun to learn the songs themselves, but this was farther off the Trail, nearer the Thicket. Here, the people were just proud enough to keep their prejudice.

Hunter felt as though he were returning to his other home, already among the Hills while still in the Plain. The air seemed clearer, and by the time they were walking the mules down the dirt street of the little village, the language had fully revived in his mind. For this reason, when a dusky-skinned girl turned a corner and nearly collided with his mule, word came before thought.

"Staayg bkhtnaanharr hahcheerr." (Please forgive my beast and I).

Startled, she met his eyes with hers, large and smoldering, until she remembered the rule and resumed her downcast expression. She was wrapped in a dark cloak, but garments black as night itself could not have obscured such a face, for there was that in it that stilled the blood in Hunter's breast. The girl, still looking down, spoke haltingly as would a Lowlander.

"Hahcheerrbeenk sya'ntsnaanyeerr." (Your beast and you are forgiven.)

A harsh yell shattered the moment and the girl trotted down the avenue toward an irate, poison-faced man wrapped in wool. Heat shimmered up from the fields and hung in the air like lead, yet he was bundled to the ears, and a woollen cap was pulled low over his forehead. The bulk of his clothing gave him the look of a very fat man, but his cheeks and eyes were hollow. He cracked out another rebuke as she passed, and she jumped as though he had struck her.

Hunter stayed rooted in place until Byorneth jabbed him in the ribs, and he pulled his mule on.

They found the stables in the usual place, the end of the village farthest from the road. Most of the men had long since tired of late nights and grain beer, and so after the mules had been watered, fed and brushed, each man curled up in his bedroll and dropped off immediately.

Hunter had the first watch, and he sat in a corner and gazed over the western wall of the stockade as the dipping sun painted broad flashes of gold, then crimson, pink and violet across the sky. There was a high torch flaming in the center of the round space, but it did nothing to obscure the glory of the heavens above him.

He stiffened when the great broad door beside him swung noisily inward on its leather hinges, and before it had fully opened, he was on his feet with his sword drawn and at the ready. The slave girl whom he had met before came in, eyes downcast as before, showing nothing of the glory behind her eyelids. He put up his weapon and stared speechless, momentarily forgetting his manners, for she no longer wore a cloak, although the weather had cooled, and her wavy, shining black hair hung all down her back.

She shifted from foot to foot and spoke in the village tongue, never meeting his eyes. "My master desires that you be comfortable. I have brought food — bread, beef and corn. I will return for the basket."

Hunter sat once more against the wall, and motioned invitingly. "Come, sit with me if you have no other obligations. I would talk in Kyarrghnaal again before we reach the Hills."

She hesitated. "The fault will be mine," he said. "Come, talk with me." With an inward jerk, she came and sat beside him against the wall, absently smoothing the cowhide skirt across her thighs.

Hunter dug into the basket and brought out the bread (not heavy, greasy Plain bread, but a light, sweet loaf of the Hills). The beef too was not as he had ever found among the Lowlands, having been spiced and seasoned and then fried, not roasted plain on a spit over the fire as some farmers preferred.

He looked up and caught the girl's large eyes, delighted at his reaction to the meal. At his glance, her eyes fell and she blushed through her long hair, which, slave-fashion, had been arranged so as to at once obscure and reveal her face. During his travels he had seen many Hillwomen, but never any exuding such a smoldering wealth of beauty. This, together with her cooking, would have had her married off in the Hills long ago, and by now she would have had a child hanging onto her skirts.

"You cooked this all yourself?" She nodded. "And you expected to be away before I saw what you had brought." She bit her lip and turned away from him. Moved by an impulse, he caught her arm and turned her toward him, smiling what he hoped was a disarming smile.

"Friends should look at one another. Let's be friends, shall we?"

Once again, she granted him a glimpse of her eyes as she smiled a little more, and they sat back against the clay brick wall looking up at the appearing stars for a while in silence. Then Hunter's eyes fell on the pile of grain bags across the courtyard, and he heaved himself onto his feet to fetch one for her to sit on, which she accepted with surprise and a very experimental thank-you in her native language.

"Maiden." She looked up again at the unfamiliar phrase. "It is a miserable thing to eat alone. Will you share this with me?"

She agreed with another smile, and they divided the food equally. They had both labored hard that day, and it tasted quite as good as Hunter had anticipated, so he consumed it faster than he meant to. When the last bite came he chewed it slowly, appreciating every nuance of flavor that unfolded as it fell apart across his tongue. She blushed a little, pleased by his enjoyment.

"When were you captured?"

She had to think for a moment. "Ten years ago."

"How are you called?"

"Srstri."

He smiled. "Crystal. That's lovely." He had seen such crystals on occasion hanging from the necks of the Hillfolk, smoky and clear.

"But in the village they call me *Deesard*."

Hunter looked his perplexity. "*Deesard*? Mark of status?"

"Yes. Each year the men of the village take stock of their goods. Whoever is found to be wealthiest owns me until the next year."

Now he remembered. It was a custom shared by several villages along the Trail, where one girl was kept as the community's symbol of beauty, purity and affluence. She would remain forever untouched, as a prized work of art, a safe but solitary life.

"Is it because you are the prettiest?"

She shrugged. "They say that I am."

But all was suddenly forgotten when there came a noise at the outer wall of the stockade.

Hunter motioned the girl to stay back and drew his short sword, moving to the middle of the enclosure. His men were awake now and stood slowly from their blankets, their wide eyes following the sound which had worked its way along the wall. Then it was lost as the mules smelled danger and sent up a terrific braying, jostling and shoving one another in terror. Whatever it was had by now scented not only the mules but the grain they carried, and now hungry death might come from any direction. Srstri feared more than them, for she knew the legend of the bear, how Arn's murderous spirit had flown from his body, how it gave the bear strength and cunning beyond its flesh. She had seen one survivor as he was borne back into the village, one leg all but torn off, and she had tended him as he died, raving and terror stricken. Now, she wished above all for a sword of her own.

The walls of the enclosure were of dried mud bricks, as was the whole village. This may have been proof against the hand of man, but soon the whole structure, and even the ground beneath them, shook with the impact of a heavy body, and the very air about them sang a dirge. Once, twice the impact was heard above the mules, and each man fought the impulse to run, while mud and mortar fell from the wall like snow.

Then, with one final mighty impact the wall was breached, the broken pieces forming the impression of a great bulk before they crumbled away, revealing a nut-brown mountain. The creature shook itself and strode free of the mud, then reared up to its full height and grinned at them, positively grinned, Hunter would swear, its broad head bobbing as it sniffed all around and laid its tall, pointed ears back against its head. Towering above the high stockade wall, the bear was thicker and larger than a cedar tree as his heavy muscles flexed, one by one, under the quivering coat. He was of the species of the great Lowland bears, and he had a long tail that lashed as he gazed around intelligently, examining them all, until at last his eyes fixed on the mules in their pens.

He moved quickly, as bears will. Huge as he loomed, one long, loping stride brought him to the mules at once, only to be met by the drivers, including Byorneth and Hunter, all armed with drivers' short, sharp swords. With one broad sweep of his hairy paw, he threw them aside as he would so many children, and then made for the mules. He was buffeted for a moment by their hooves, then his attention was distracted as Hunter, who had not borne the full force of his blow, recovered and cried loudly, at which Leen d'Arns turned and grunted.

He reared up again as Hunter brought his blade back over his head to swing. From a towering height, the Great Bear of Arn threw his considerable bulk onto Hunter, who sidestepped and brought his sword forward with all his strength. The creature swatted to the right as it charged, and the momentum of that great body and the force of Hunter's blow buried the blade soundly in the offending limb, knocking the blunt side back into Hunter's forehead. His and the bear's hot blood mingled and flowed into his eyes, blinding him.

The bear howled in agony as it came down on top of Hunter, who, lying on his back dazed and stunned, was still aware enough to prop the pommel of his blade on the ground so the bear impaled itself on it with another scream. As the gross weight came down, the slave girl snatched up a sword from an unconscious driver and drove it with as much force as she could muster beneath the broad skull.

Leen d'Arns gave a great, sorrowful groan as his life drained away. He made a few feeble passes at Srstri, then the mules and mule drivers, but with one final effort he gave up his last breath into Hunter's face. Seconds later he was pierced with ten sword points, but it mattered not. Srstri had already delivered the coup, and the thing was done.

Hunter in his turn slipped into a hazy void as the sword slid through the bear's body and the full weight of the beast collapsed slowly onto him. Byorneth, Srstri, and the rest could hear Hunter's ribs breaking, and it took all their matched effort to roll the body free. The young man lay still as death, the wound on his forehead staining the earth below him a darkening red.

Chapter 3
The Forest

A MAN MAY BEAR A WOMAN FOR A KAND,
BUT WHEN HE FALLS, SHE BEARS HIM FOR TEN.

~The Arranin of Tagrri~

Ten times he clawed himself up through the fog, and ten times he slid back down to the bottom. The eleventh time he broke through, thrust his head through the gloom and opened his eyes.

He lay on a cot of animal skins under a roof of slender beams and marsh grass. As he stared, the beams receded behind the grass and jumped out at him again, sending Hunter far away once more. When next he awakened, it was to a pair of deep, soft brown eyes.

And scooped horns.

Srstri entered and gasped, then with a sharp cry she drove the curious cow back outside and into the fields. Hunter turned his head and looked over toward the far wall of the hut where a slab of beef lay sputtering over a fire. At the sight,

Hunter retched and turned over, groaning with the surge of pain and nausea the movement brought. When his stomach stopped revolving, he fell asleep again.

Srstri returned and sat by the bedside, feeling his bearded cheek with the back of her hand. His head was wrapped in a large poultice, and underneath, she knew, the scalp was laid open to the bone from the bridge of his nose to the dark peak of his hair. The blow had profoundly blackened both his eyes, and the earnest face was fixed in the serious scowl of the slumbering invalid, but still she smiled at the sight of him. She thought of the valiant showing he had made in protecting his mules, but mostly of the brief time they had spent in conversation over a meal, which had brought back to her sweet memories of a home all but forgotten. He might have been her brother, come home to eat after a day out on the hillsides.

The hazel eyes opened and he saw her. He would have smiled had he not been convinced the slightest emotion would throw him back into nausea. Instead, he reached out and took hold of her hand, and the returning grip brought back a measure of his balance.

A bundled figure entered suddenly without the customary knock on the doorframe, and Srstri snatched her hand away and folded it with the other one in her lap. The hulk stepped up to the bed and laid his hand heavily on the girl's shoulder, who jumped and averted her gaze, once more the fearful slave of their first moments together. Without the least smile on his hairy face, the man grumbled at what must have been his lowest register.

"I have a duty to honor you for your action." The words came as if by rote. "We all look forward to seeing you well and on your way. In the meantime, please consider my possessions yours." His duty fulfilled, he left, wrapping his furs around him against the balmy heat outside.

Hunter and Srstri sat silently together for a time before she spoke, softly as before, but with the hidden strength of the caretaker. Her eyes knew a boldness that had long been a stranger to her. "I've got some nice meat on the spit. Are you hungry?" His gorge rose at the thought and he held up his hand.

She nodded and bit her lip. "I should tell you. Your caravan has moved on." Hunter's eyes widened. "No, do not talk. I'm sorry, but they said your men had stayed too long, so my master told them to leave yesterday. They left a man behind — the eldest. He said he would not leave you."

Hunter relaxed again. If the mule train had moved on, so had his responsibility for it, and the one person he would have truly missed had stayed behind. It could only be Byorneth. The caravan had been owned by all the drivers equally, with each sharing equally in the profits, and so he had really lost nothing but his share.

He tried to lick his lips, but his dry tongue only rasped against them. Understanding, Srstri dipped a cup of water out of the basin for him and gently lifted his head to drink. Very slowly the warm, stale water crept down his throat and his body cried out in gratitude. Hunter had never tasted anything better, and he had never seen a fairer sight than he did now, with Srstri holding his head and leaning close enough for him to feel the heat of her body. She had tied her hair so the entire shining length of it hung down upon her breast, and he was absently fingering the soft tresses as once again he drifted away.

A few days passed, although Hunter had no knowledge of them. He awoke and it was light, and the next time it was dark, but the significance of these details escaped his bruised mind. He fancied it was always the same dream that came to him between times, always giving the same stale flavor, and he soon wearied of it, though he could never remember it afterwards.

At the end of five days, his color was better and reluctantly Srstri judged him fit to see a guest. When next he opened his eyes, he found Byorneth crouched beside the sickbed, almost smiling. The patient was still deathly pale, but by now he could manage to smile up at his friend and greet him.

Byorneth spoke softly. "The mule train is away."

"Who has the charge of it?"

"They chose Harn."

Hunter heaved himself suddenly upright, almost fainting, but Srstri was there immediately and eased his head onto the pillow again with a withering look at Byorneth. When the pain subsided, Hunter croaked, "Harn? He caused strife in every village we ever stopped at! He is an uncontrolled drunkard, a spendthrift! They would give him such responsibility? Put their lives in his hands?"

Byorneth shrugged. "It was their judgment. At any rate, I'll lay you a wager he will be a different man by the time they reach the Hills."

With a vacant sigh, Hunter lay back and slept at once. For fear of awakening him, and to avoid the rebuke of the slave, Byorneth slipped silently away into the sun.

⌒⌒⌒

Hunter stayed dozing for a good many days. In that time, the servant girl cared for him, including all the menial, demeaning little tasks the expression entails. All these things were done cheerfully, always remembering the considerate way in which he had treated her — not as a slave, but a young woman — and his actions in the fight with the bear. Her time with him was not like a duty.

Though Hunter could not talk much, when he did speak it was to an equal. During those days Srstri was transformed, smiling as she spoke, truly visiting for the first time, and with each smile she charmed Hunter all over again. She slept nearby just across the tent, and he watched her dimly as he drowsed, listening to her soft breathing. Her time with him was the liveliest of elixirs, for even in his bouts of illness, he never raised his voice or betrayed the slightest impatience, and this set him far apart from all the men in her village life. Whatever may have befallen her, she was above all a Hillwoman, long cut off from fellowship even with her fellow slaves, now unbound and soaring above the Lowlands, speaking the Kyarrghnaal tongue.

At the end of two weeks, Hunter felt he could stay in bed no longer, so he eased himself to his feet and tested his legs. They were like those of a newborn as he stumped unsteadily across the hut to the clay oven and leaned on it with a deep breath.

"You're up." Hunter turned toward the door and blinked through the sunshine. The shadow resolved itself into Byorneth. "Good. You've been lying about too long. We must be away."

Hunter blinked again. "So soon?"

Byorneth nodded. "Our welcome is wearing thin. Banat, Srstri's master, objected to your presence from the start, and now that you're well we'd best be away."

Hunter swayed for a moment, then followed Byorneth out into the hot air of the village. Once outside, his head and stomach conspired against him, and he clung to the doorway for a while, trying to hold himself together.

A pair of wool-shod feet intruded into his downward vision, and a familiar rumble followed. "I suppose you'll be leaving now."

Hunter pulled his eyes up toward the broad, glowering face, then straightened and replied, "Yes. Thank-you for your hospit—"

Banat turned on his heel and stalked off, and in that instant Hunter ceased to care. He walked slowly over to where Byorneth was packing their bags, and the old man stood and shoved one of the bigger bundles into Hunter's chest. "He says we must go, but we cannot leave without provisions. So, it follows that he should supply them." Hunter could not find it in himself to object. With customary abruptness, his old friend slung a huge bag over his shoulder and started off down the road.

Hunter glanced around, hoping to say a final goodbye to his nurse, but he did not see her, and it would not do to spend the time it would take to find her. He hoisted his bag and followed his friend.

As the last swirl of dust settled down behind them, a keen-eyed slave boy darted out from a corner behind the washhouse, hotfooting his way through the street so keenly that nary a master asked his business, no officious lady stopped him, and soon he vanished into a certain dwelling. Immediately, he flashed out again, closely followed by Srstri. She stood looking down the road for a moment until a procession of slaves passed by on their way out to the fields, and Banat came after and thrust a hoe and shovel into her hands. Quietly, she walked away ahead of him, and as she went her master threatened all manner of jealous violence upon her.

Byorneth and his friend had gone but a kand's distance, but owing to his injury and long rest, the ground wore hard on Hunter. His head pounded with increased violence, and at times the road seemed to ripple like a dirty river, until finally after a little more than a kand, Byorneth called a halt, and they sat by the roadside to rest.

Hunter stretched out on the slope of the road and fell immediately to sleep, and Byorneth let him rest for a whole hour, for there was no hurry now that they were clear of the town and Banat's jealousy. The sparrows sang in the trees above them as they lay in the sloping sunshine. Leaning back against the lush slope, Byorneth listened to his young friend's rhythmic breathing, and soon he too closed his eyes and drifted off to the bright chirping sound.

He was awakened out of light sleep by the crunching of leaves far off among the trees, and though his wrinkled eyelids remained closed, one shaggy gray eyebrow sank lower while the other sought his hairline. He focused his ears far into the scattered trees beyond the rough board fence not ten paces away.

Ah! Two feet, trying not to be heard among the dried twigs and dense undergrowth. They stopped, but Byorneth knew exactly where. They continued, more cautious, then stopped again, and crunched violently as if someone had climbed the fence and come down hard on the other side.

There was a gasp, and then quick footsteps headed straight to where Hunter lay. With a rapidity belying his years, Byorneth threw himself from a prone position into the offending form, and both rolled over and over down the grass slope before jolting to rest against the fence.

Srstri heaved herself up and away from Byorneth, who spluttered confusedly, freeing his face from the cloud of long black hair. His eyes finally focused, and after consternation had given way to irritation, he looked up the hill and saw Hunter standing there with drawn blade, wild eyed and swaying. With a cry the slave rushed up the hill toward him, catching him as he fell forward.

⌒~∧~

The three sat side by side on the edge of the road, two dusty from having rolled together into a fence, and one feeling close to death for having rolled to his feet in a hurry.

Byorneth was angrily giving voice, the conclusion of a tirade that had begun the moment he stood up from the fence. In the ebbing of his high-racing blood, the tone had turned to that of a scolding old woman, peevish where it had been violent. "Above all, it is discourteous to awaken one without first announcing one's presence! And when are you expected back, anyhow?" he concluded at last.

"I'm to be back at sundown." They looked at the sun. Not nearly enough time. Hunter had tired of all the talk so he stood, hefted his pack onto his shoulder and started off down the road. Soon, he let Byorneth take the lead, content to labor along behind.

At nightfall, Byorneth stopped and faced his companions. "To the mountains, then?"

They agreed. The mountains would be safe, and the trails there were less accessible than the open road. They left the Great Trail and took to the trees. Any pursuers might follow along the Trail that night, and perhaps they would not realize their mistake until morning. Perhaps.

The going became much slower now that they had fallen limbs, hanging moss and tangled vines to contend with. The growth was so thick in some places that they walked not upon earth at all, but high above it upon tangled serpentine tree trunks, twisted into unity through generations of growth.

Sometimes even a patch of wild flowers or berries could be found growing in a piece of earth, lifted on high by the growth of these giants, so that low-growing fruit flourished among the middle reaches of the forest. Their packs caught in the greenery and pulled them off their feet as growling clouds began to drop on their heads.

Behind in the village another party was making ready for a journey, a party bristling with weapons and dire intent, for a valuable piece of common property had been stolen, and it might still be within reach. Grimmest of these was Banat, full of ill-humor and impatience, generally making the proceedings miserable with constant reminders of his position in the village, and mostly of his greater loss.

But another party had been sent first — a party of one, with a ready message on his lips. He was no slave, but a Villager who received wages for faithful service, sent out with promises and compelling words.

They would come. Any who valued gold would come.

Chapter 4
The Challenge

"I HAVE LONG BEEN A REIVER,
BUT AS I AM A MAN, I WILL REIVE NO LONGER."
AND ALLEND THRUST HIS LONG SWORD INTO THE EARTH
AND VANISHED FOREVER INTO THE TREES."

-The Chronicles of the Last Kings-

It is not to be supposed that even in the deepest forest mankind has not established its presence. Neither Hunter, Byorneth nor Srstri knew it when they passed over the river flowing below the tree limbs over which they walked. It watered the entire forest, flowing through underground courses raised by a tier of bedrock until it showed through the undergrowth, housing all manner of fish and crabs.

People lived by the river beneath their feet, fishing and gathering, unknown even to their nearest neighbors except for idle rumors of ghosts and spirits in the forest. They knew the levels of the trees as a bird knows its sky, and melted in and out at will. Their fortunes rose and fell with the river, and the comings and goings of the Villagers seemed frenzied and senseless in comparison. So it was with the Folk of the Woods.

Farther along toward the east the forest thinned and then thickened again, edging toward pine and spruce, forming the beginning of the Thicket which ran like a wall from north to south, dividing the villages along the Great Trail from their forest-dwelling neighbors. The river ran there also, twisting and splitting in its own inscrutable way, feeding the earth, its level changing as the faraway seasons of the Hills dictated, running through marshland and back into forest again.

One branch of the river, a younger, reckless one, tired of the close-set trees and constant surveillance of its staid siblings, exited the forest and made for the open country. Along the way, it swelled and grew until it was nearly as mighty as its mother far away to the west, placid with experience. Wherever it was going, it would soon be there, and no amount of strife would hasten that end. It was along this wide stretch, set among wide fields and farms, that the village of Allend's End lay.

Allend's End was quiet as villages go, too far from the Great Trail to be used by the mule drivers and too high to be bothered by spring flooding. In times past, a barracks had been built on that spot for the Reivers of Allend, a troop of thieves employed by the Royal House to supply its expeditionary forces with rations. When the great Fall came, the buildings had collapsed into disuse and finally disappeared, to be replaced by the settlement which now stood about their graves. All that remained of the former times was a great stone soldier at the center of the square, protected from the weather by his stone canopy, but rounded at the edges by 550 years, constantly baring his great stone sword in defense of the peaceful colony.

Owing to its high origin, Allend's End was larger than many of its neighbors, but not so very different in its parts. Squat houses formed a narrow stone street, stained across at intervals with mud. At the center of the community there was a square, and every week saw a swell of people from all around, in carts and on foot, dragging their wares along with them. They were great occasions, and brought with them all the noise of 50 rainstorms.

But this was midweek, and the square was almost silent but for the man and his sons. For Elnaan, the day began a great deal earlier than for the townsmen. He was a man to whom the burden of labor was but a natural element of life, and he did not like to be caught idle. Not that any of his four brothers had any undue love for sleep, at least not any they ever indulged. Today, he worked with Teidin his brother, born on the same midnight nearly 20 years before.

Their father had freighted a cart of barley into town, and they worked beside him in the blazing day unloading it. The last bag fell off the cart and threw dust in their eyes. "One more load and that's the last," their father said, and they stood and breathed, blinking the sweat out of their eyes. "Let's go."

Teidin and his brother climbed up into the back of the cart, and their father took his place in the front, gathering the reins expertly. Once again it rattled down the lane, and then out into the countryside away from the river. The old man in the front was quiet all the way — a gregarious, pleasant man who had done a day's work already and was content with silence. The brothers could not help but admire his way with the team. There had been stories in the family of when he had come into the South, a mere child driving a team of six mules, and they knew enough to admire such skill.

The farm was as they had left it. The boy Ellarn was out in the garden with his mother and sisters pulling weeds. Iblar, the eldest, was still in the outer fields, toiling by himself.

Back they went in the cart, loaded and unloaded, until finally the day ended and the young men's hearts rejoiced. Their father drove it back out into the evening, and Teidin and Elnaan walked through the village to a certain barn, now open and filled with light. Allend's End being a town rich in young men, evening was always accompanied by the consumption of *rashi* and the constant trial of their strength, and every night found them in the same place.

Teidin left his brother outside to exchange pleasantries with a few gathered men, going and taking a table, drinking his first cup of liquor before Elnaan came in, shouldering his way through the gathered bodies up to the long sideboard that was set up every night, transforming the empty barn into a lively place for the youth of the village. Men and women greeted him as he passed, for everyone, young and old, had a strange affection for the tall pillar of a man. After a short conversation with the barman, he came over to Teidin's table with two drinks. "Ah, I see you already have one. My mistake."

"Yes. Your mistake. Sit down."

He sat down opposite and smiled at Teidin. There were no words, for they had worked together all day. Elnaan was only a few minutes the elder and a trifle taller, yet his deeds had earned him an air of legend that Teidin had never had. Stories about him abounded, many of which were even true, and there were few men who cared to challenge him. This suited Teidin, for he was happy to stand by and observe. Manhood need not be constantly proved.

"Good evening, Elnaan. Teidin. Where is your brother?" The voice came from the direction of the door.

"I expect he may be along." Elnaan pulled a stool out for Ordo, a lean young man with an impressive beard edging toward premature gray except for the growth on his lip, which bled dark brown down the gray chin.

"And your sisters?" he asked after a long drink.

The brothers smiled. Their sisters were acknowledged as being the fairest in the district. "No notion."

The door creaked open above the din inside, and their father entered to be greeted loudly by dozens of voices all across the barn. He started toward the brothers, then a cluster of his friends called him away, and with a shrug to his sons he went away with them to the end of the building.

The inevitable happened at that moment. A fight broke away at the other end of the room, and the men turned around to watch. Fights were children of the times, manifestations of the masculine spirit. Reasons were not important, only a man's conduct. They shouldered their way through the gathered audience, a dense circle around the combatants — three farm lads circling around a slender creature, their blows landing sparsely but heavily. Had the men been sober, they might have taken him outside to beat him in secret. It was hardly serious, and the men meant no real ill-will, but the smaller one, just barely a man, fended off their fists so weakly that Teidin saw what would happen.

"This is not right," his brother muttered under his breath, and Teidin moved out of the way, watching Elnaan take one of his giant steps and strike his first victim on the bridge of his nose. Teidin had seen this before, how his brother used his height and speed to devastate his opponents with a deadly martial dance. In an equally matched fight, he would always give his opponents an even chance, but here, where the many fought the few, he bobbed and flashed without mercy. The fury ceased only when two men lay on the floor, one holding his nose, the other nursing a wrenched shoulder, and the other had fled the barn. Elnaan faded instantly back into the crowd, and his brother and Ordo found him seated back at the table as though he had never moved, flexing his hands.

"I hear that a slave escaped from some village over to the west."

The other two sat down with him. "Yes, she went along with a mule driver, so they say. There is a large reward for her return." Ordo smiled into his drink. A slave was a pretense in the district of Allend's End, a tacit admission of laziness. No man ever admitted that any fight, whether it be a *rashi* brawl or the daily struggle for livelihood, was beyond his strength. The primary struggle of their lives was a dawn-to-dark toil for food, and more importantly, self-respect.

For this reason, one word gave them pause. There would be a reward, and it was well known that the villages to the west were very rich. They sat in silence a while, and then Elnaan raised his cup. "Who will go with me?"

Teidin reached his cup out and touched his brother's. "It is done, then!"

"Until such time as our fortunes are won!" Elnaan downed his glass.

"Even so!" Ordo sat back and watched them, smiling. He had too much to remain for, too many duties, but he would have enjoyed the spectacle, and truly wished that he was free to join in, if only to see lands beyond his own.

A man's word is all he has, indeed all he is, and so they were well and truly bound as they left early for the night. The day ahead would be full of the toil of travel, and so they slept early, awaking before dawn to bind on their swords, fill their water pouches, and step into their best shoes. Ellarn and their mother were at the table when they emerged, eating along with the sisters. They were all silent as the men sat down, shifting their scabbards back out of the way as they reached for the food. "Are you boys going away?" their mother asked, and the girls' looks echoed the question. Ellarn continued to eat, little concerned with the world of his brothers.

"We may not be back for many days." This was not unusual for them, but the way they avoided their family's eyes marked the journey as different. Even the bright-eyed boy sensed something strange in the air, and looked up from his breakfast sharply.

"Very many days?" Merna asked. Whether she or her mother spoke was immaterial — they were two women with one mouth. "More than last time?"

"Much more."

Their mother stood and turned to the cupboard. "Take some of this journey bread with you." She turned back with a large pan of sturdy cakes. There is no food like a mother's, and this mother's especially. The bread would be most welcome as they walked, little pieces of home to take with them.

Elnaan took them and stood. "Teidin, we'd best be away. Who knows how many others are upon this thing."

They were stopped once more out in the yard among the clucking hens by Iblar, their eldest brother, fresh from his bed and bound for the fields. "And where are you two off to this early? Not to the fields, judging by your clothes."

"We are on a long journey across country, and may be long away. You'll take care of the farm while we're away?"

Iblar nodded. Ever since they were young boys, he had treated Elnaan with care. At a young age and after a great deal of abuse, the younger boy had taken a large measure of pride out of his elder brother unexpectedly as he walked around a corner of the house. As Teidin told it, Elnaan had buried his fist to the elbow in Iblar's gut. Ever since then, the younger brothers had been treated with a careful respect.

Iblar had his own place to take care of, but though the sisters were more than capable, he still felt a responsibility to his old home. The two farms were hand in hand, the fields of one leading uninterrupted into the next, but none could say Iblar was aught but a mighty man, and the land would be well looked after.

As he watched his younger brothers walk away through the fields toward the south, he could not help but feel a measure of pride. The youths he had once known were now men, straight of back, broad of shoulder, direct in purpose.

He knew what they went to do, for he had been present when the stranger had come with his news, a stranger from the villages to the west with a star token strung about his neck. Standing in the square, he had proclaimed at the top of his voice that a slave had escaped, and all who wished could join in the hunt. Most would not, unwilling to leave their homes for such an uncertain business.

He might have known his young brothers would choose to go, and perhaps it was right. The family should be represented.

———

The two men and the woman had gone for about two hours when Byorneth called a halt and sat down on a tree limb to catch his breath. The others were grateful, for the night was darkening, and in spite of the moon they had difficulty seeing the path, even when it lay clear before them. So they sat, panting and shivering with the mounting night wind and falling mist. Hunter had improved vastly with the clear air, though his head still troubled him a little.

"Byorneth," he said, "you've been leading us on a path you seem to know well. Where does it end, precisely?"

Their leader sighed. "We're going to Seng Grandt."

Silence.

He continued. "It was my home." He turned to Hunter. "Do you remember that Sheewa that stopped us on the road?"

"Sheewa?"

"Yes. The wandering scribe." He reached out and broke a dead branch for a staff. "I told you that I was one of them once. I lived among them and traveled with them before I left to wander on my own.

"They may be unhappy to see me back, but Seng Grandt is still the safest place, if any were to follow." When they had gained their breath, they set off again through the shadowy limbs and hanging moss.

The foliage changed subtly as they walked along by the light of a waxing moon. Everything became steadily more damp, the moss longer on the branches and deeper underfoot. At times, Hunter had to support Srstri, often she helped him, sinking knee deep with each step. They were besieged on all sides with little birds that burst from their nests as they passed, and thick mist whitened everything beyond the reach of a man's arm. Earlier in the night, they had stepped gratefully off the branches of the forest and down onto the solid ground once again, which, even covered as it was with thick moss, felt more comforting.

All at once the ground was not there, and they half-ran, half-slid down a sharp slope, followed by a cascade of earth and rank grass, and as they did a terrific stench hit them and left them gasping. It was a familiar smell of waste and stagnant life, and when they slid to a stop, they were standing in water up to their ankles. They stepped back quickly enough, but still the thick fog that rose from the surface of the vile pond permeated their garments until the clean air of the Plain was foreign to their memory. The sun was rising, and although it remained invisible, its rays illuminated the foul air, along with every particle that floated upon it.

Their eyes were dazzled at first, but soon they began to discern long docks bestriding the broad Marsh. It was as if they had grown up from the water like foul weeds, and out of each one sprouted boats — long boats that pulled away into the deeper water in the body of the Swamp.

Each year, the rain fell and the snow melted high atop the great Hills, shedding water far below. Those of the Hillfolk who lived and cultivated within the Caldera used this flood for planting and growing, while it came to those of the villages as a swelling in their clean, bright rivers. The rest flowed down to be fouled by the Great Marsh, and it was this body that over-flowed their senses as they stood at its northernmost edge.

Byorneth scowled. To continue toward Seng Grandt, they must cross this bog, wading through the midst of the infested waters. He had thought to come out of the Forest in the shal-lows farther along toward the east, but now they were in the thick of the Chadeyzdeer, those outcasts who dwelled near the Hills and captured Hillfolk to sell to the farms and villages in the North, who gave to those Swampmen contempt along with their gold.

It was too late. They were seen, and already the men had turned their boats toward shore, quickening their poling so that in less than a minute, 20 of the Chadeyzdeer swayed in the filth before them. They seemed to be tall men, perhaps only the effect of their standing on top of the water rather than in it, clad in rags which had been so worked together that they fitted like a natural layer of scum. The leader swayed before them, studying the three with dull, gray eyes. They were dead, those eyes, but the eyebrows above them worked like inch-worms, rising and falling with each languid thought.

Finally, he lifted his hand in a signal to his men. They poled themselves toward shore as would an invading army and seized Byorneth and Hunter by their clothes, dragging them into the boats with small regard for their knees. Srstri was handled more carefully, and they set her down gently on the gunwale.

The dead-eyed man raised a long, shrill call across the water, and he and his men swooped their boats across the pond like carrion birds. When they pulled up to the docks, it was with such skill that the prisoners scarcely noticed stopping.

The shrouded figures hoisted them onto their feet and set them roughly on the docks. It seemed they might be free, and indeed they had determined to run as soon as they were loosed, but now they saw that among the thick-barreled trees and gray moss that surrounded them, there were hovels. Where the trees met at the bottoms, the gaps had been filled with these mud-daubed structures, thickly roofed with leaves and branches. One could not travel 20 paces from the lake without being forced to shoulder into one of these places, or else somehow scale one of the trees.

Thus disappointed, they waited for their captors to tie their boats, then walked with them, or rather were walked by them, down the long, narrow, spongy dock onto the land, where each inhabitant of the damp little city had already gathered in a long gauntlet as they passed.

A more silent group Hunter had never seen. The children, ragged urchins half hiding among their mothers' skirts, looked them up and down owlishly, dirty faced and puckered. The people, one and all, seemed sick, their skins thin and pale, eyes listless.

Finally, they stood at the feet of the trees and houses, and from the junction of two trees' roots where stood the grandest of the little mud shanties, stepped a man. He was the eldest of his people, a gray beard covered his chest, and a large leather hat obscured his hair completely in a shapeless mass of moss and dirt.

Somehow, this little individual managed a sort of aged dignity as he hobbled down the roots that formed the irregular stairs of his house, and when he was at their level, he proved a very short man indeed. Even with hair and hat, he stood well below Hunter's shoulders, and Hunter would have guessed he had seen 80 summers at least, every one of them cloistered in this putrid hole. The legs were bare and bald, and each thrust outward from his body at a different angle.

When he spoke, it was with an old voice, one that seemed older even than he, raspy and unsettling. The dialect too was strange — a variety of the Harniyen tongue of the villages, but corrupted and slurred by generations. "What for come you to our place? None of the Villagers travel never except by road, and our place is never came by others."

He turned his sunken eyes toward Srstri and the wrinkles around them twitched. "And what for come with you a *deeyaz*? None of its kind come here but with collars and chains, for to be driven down the roads for gold sold. In other, they are abominating, as by now it should know." He did not look Srstri in the eyes as one would a fellow human being, but spoke of her as inanimate, as is the custom of all but the kindest Villagers.

Hunter looked down into his eyes and spoke, for he had anticipated such questions and they had all agreed upon the answers. "This deez is mine. I found it in a village we passed and purchased it. I knew we would have need of it when we crossed the Swamp."

Their dwarfish interrogator turned aggressively toward him and shoved up close. "You lie. You do not go road, like traveler of honest. There is no so great sin as *deeyaz* thievery ever. We know this is stolen. Our villages Great Road beside, and messengers come with news of deeasard-thieving in villages one. We are gold promised for its return, and like all we know—" He turned to his people now and lifted his voice. "There is on the earth so precious nothing at all!" The people all around cried assent, and were as suddenly silent, only the screams of the creatures among the gray growth echoing their cheer.

The little man drew himself up to his full height and pronounced sentence. "Lock them all in *daz*fence. When Villagemen return, we give all as *deeyaz* and they give the gold!" Their captors roared again, and they rose up in a precipitous flood of filthy humanity, carrying Byorneth, Hunter, and Srstri like foam upon a wave to the steps of the highest house. It propelled them even through the dwelling (its scum-caked facade by far its most impressive part), and brought them down a set of crazy rootsteps to a large corral, spanning about half the length of the village, and a heavy door was swung shut behind them. They were left utterly alone in the sudden, sodden silence.

Byorneth rubbed his shin furiously and rocked back and forth (he had stumbled as they were shoved up the steps and barked his shin along the gnarled roots of the house), muttering in a furious whisper. Hunter's breath raced and his heart pounded. He did not sit until he had spent five minutes walking all along the walls of the stockade.

The columns of the walls were of living trees, and had over the long years interwoven themselves into one another so that nothing less than long and concerted chopping could set anyone free. At the wall's upper rim, there were fastened timbers slanted inwards and entwined with the trees, and before the doors had closed, Hunter had seen several guards taking up positions along the outside. At last, he gave a long sigh and sat with his back to the wall beside his companions, ignoring the cramps which tortured his rain-soaked legs.

Srstri laid her head against the rough tree behind her. She did not cry, for she was merely tired, defeated. Addressing no one in particular, she whispered into the dark, "I half expected to be caught again, but I had to try. I would have been the first to return to the Hills. I would have been able to come and go, to work for myself. Now I've brought you into servitude as well."

Hunter turned his head and looked at her, dark and beautiful. He studied the graceful slope of her nose, the large, sad eyes. There were no tears, but her sorrow was evident, and her dusky skin had turned pale. He took hold of her hand. "I am sorry, Srstri. We were your hope, and we have failed. But there may still be escape."

She shook her head. A few dark strands of hair came loose and fell across her forehead. "No. I think now that I must have known it was hopeless, but I have always needed this." She met Hunter's gaze directly, and his heart jumped in his chest. "A slave needs something like this, a wild leap into hope, however unavailing, however senseless. It—" her voice half cracked, "it makes the years ahead more bearable. I should be able to labor for a good many years now."

Byorneth snorted with impatience as he walked back and stood by Hunter, kicking him suddenly. "Well, my son. Is this where it ends? We who led a mule train, you who killed the

Great Bear, to be slain by the Chadeyzdeer or sold into servitude for the rest of our miserable days?"

The younger made no answer, but thought to himself about their time together on the Trail, the respect they had wherever they stopped. There was no regret, for he somehow felt that all this had been meant to happen, that it had been fixed long before. The flame of hope flickered, but it still retained life, and Byorneth saw it.

Srstri replied, "I have been in this place before. There is no escape."

"There is always escape!" said Byorneth with unexpected violence. "You have been rescued from nothing! You are still a slave!" He pointed at Srstri and said to Hunter, "That is how a slave acts. It sits and tamely accepts. I care not. She can be driven like a beast if she prefers, but I am taking you to Seng Grandt."

Then, to the woman, "Forget your slavery or be a beast!"

The Hillwoman's head snapped up at the sound of her native tongue, and she and Hunter watched as Byorneth's eyes crept along the top of the wall, then stopped as he pointed up to a section not far above their hands. Hunter and Srstri looked and saw a cleft in the lip of the wall. "Unless I am mistaken, there's a trough up there where a man could hide." He laid his hand on Hunter's shoulder. "You climb up there and take a look."

Hunter had perhaps only one-quarter of an idea what was in his friend's mind, but he jumped and grabbed hold of a branch, and with a grunt, swung a leg over. Byorneth said softly, "Be quiet, and keep low. If there's no lip on the outer wall to hide behind, then climb down."

Hunter nodded and swung himself up, dropping back down to the ground immediately with a grunt, knees bent.

"The trough is quite deep, more than enough to hide in. But what good would that do us? We would soon be found, and the guards outside would stop our flight."

Byorneth smiled broadly and clasped his best friend by the shoulder. "Panic, my son. The way out is through panic."

Chapter 5
The Sheewa

The sunset is not visible among the bogs and moss of the Great Swamp. The light simply fades, and suspended moisture ceases to gleam. Trees fade into shadows, and all manner of creeping things seek shelter under rocks and dank earth. In their places come the night-crawling beasts, many eyeless, and others whose eyes are terrible and luminous, shining brightly in the night. There are few even among the Chadeyzdeer who will venture out in the Swamp after the light's fading, for there are rumors of other fouler creatures that inhabit the dark forest, things long dead and now enlivened with dark light, folk who live in and are moved by the twilight mist, who will take the very heart from a man's breast and send him to their own domain in the fiery center of the earth.

Deep gloom had only just clamped down when one of the tree hovels vomited out a thin young man with a thinner excuse for a beard, who carried a wooden board full of a strange dinner. He unlatched the heavy wooden gate with one shaking hand and balanced the tray with the other as he nodded to the guards who signaled back, daring to make no sound in the dusk. Then they turned their attention back toward the forest, with only occasional glances at the fence.

Swinging the door outwards, the youth walked in cautiously, peering into the shadows for any who might jump out. But the corral was completely empty.

He dropped his load with a clatter and let out a cry, long and loud. The forest spirits had taken the prisoners, or the prisoners were spirits themselves, come to bring madness and torment. The houses opened noisily, one by one. People came running, and soon the whole village was dancing and jostling one another in the tiny square to look inside the corral. The more sensible ones had already started shouting orders, but in the confusion they were barely heard. The guards deserted their posts and joined the crowd.

Byorneth nudged Hunter with his foot, then started to crawl up over the ledge while Hunter and Srstri followed him. It was a dangerous business, for the stockade's walls had never been relieved of their branches, and the darkness was such that protrusions could hardly be seen. Hurry was of utmost importance, for none knew how long the Chadeyzdeer would take to collect themselves.

Their pathway was clear toward the dark forest by reason of the general fear, and soon they had vanished among the boughs and green, lacy curtains of moss. They pushed on quickly, narrowly avoiding deadfalls and snags, for the Chadeyzdeer would not be slow in following once the heart was put back in them again. Each went a slightly different way, doubling back and circling around, for they knew their pursuers would lose valuable time calling back and forth, dividing to follow false leads and regroup.

Soon, out of necessity and because the Chadeyzdeer lagged far behind, they slowed their pace, climbing where they had vaulted, trudging instead of racing through the snagging underbrush, following a straight line (no mean feat in the dark and dense growth).

Hours passed as quickly as the trees around them, and the half light of the Swamp slowly revealed a wilderness of rotting trunks and stinking pools. It was only when the sun shone palely through the thinning trees that Hunter realized they had been moving all night. Still, they could not stop. For the possession of a slave of Srstri's quality, the Chadeyzdeer would run almost any distance, and the Villagers paid highly for beauty. And there was the sun to give the slavers confidence in pursuit.

They had long been soaked, for every leaf was sodden with moisture and left dragging marks on the three until their clothes hung heavily on their shoulders. There had been nothing to eat since the village. All these reasons, along with their fatigue and hurry, left them unprepared for the Kaarnaan.

You of the Plain who read this must understand what manner of creature the Kaarnaan is. It is not akin to the smaller kaarn of your flat fields and riverbanks, this Great Lizard of the Swamps. The small dragons of the Plain, kept as pets by small boys, paying for their keep by eating vermin, live for about three years, whereas the great Kaarnaan lives, as a rule, for more than threescore, and every season grows larger and hungrier. His broad back is covered with stripes, each of which marks a plate of armor, and at least two rows of teeth line his festering mouth.

The Kaarnaan of this forest had lived a full 80 seasons. Hatched after the manner of his kind in the mud of the Great Swamp, he had wriggled, eyeless and soft, down into the water where he lived and grew half a season until his eyes formed and his legs strengthened. When at last he was ten seasons old, he fought and mated there by the water's edge. Finally, finding the females of his tribe fickle and rivals many, he retired into the forest, and there he abode in holes and caves of the earth, ever wandering, ever hunting, hungry and alone.

Now this old dragon of the forest awoke, for stumbling footsteps disturbed his slumber. Had they passed but two days earlier they would have gone unchallenged, but now the brute's belly waxed hollow, and he sensed his next meal passing near with cold-blooded excitement.

The three hurried on through the sparse growth of thin oaks and aspens, long bereft of leaves which now lay where seasonal streams had left them, some in meandering runnels, others mounted in heaps along the way. Hunter's belly ached with hunger, and he found himself falling harder and more often.

All at once, as they passed a great mound of leaves it reared up with a yawning groan, and slowly shook its covering loose to reveal russet and green stripes.

They stopped in their tracks and stared open mouthed as the great brute gave a hiss like the running of a mountain of sand. His cold serpent's eyes identified his meal immediately, all huddled together as they had stopped, anchored in horror. Kaarnaan knew this fascination. It would soon give way to panic and headlong flight, robbing him of his rightful dinner. Again he hissed, lowered his triangular head to ground level, and scurried after them, shaking the wet ground as he went. It was all so simple, and he was confident. One blow with his massive tail and then a feast, as had happened so often before. These two-legged creatures made good eating.

He swung his tail with a whistling speed, but his intended victims ran toward his hindquarters, so that the long whip curled itself around, never touching them. In each, there was the realization that at least one of them would die there in the forest. All their weapons had been confiscated by the slave traders and left behind in haste. Now, all they could do was to make their killer work for his meal. Hunter determined to throw himself in front of Byorneth and Srstri, if it came to that.

The monster straightened himself and prepared to roll over on his prey, but they ran clear. Kaarnaan hissed angrily, and with a mighty effort hoisted himself upright onto his hind legs and stood swaying, cold and awesome, forelegs outstretched. The prey was now certain. Whichever way they bolted, those sinuous limbs would scoop them into his maw just the same. Srstri came close to Hunter, but he pushed her away. "We'd better scatter!" he cried.

Suddenly, Kaarnaan screamed a strange screeching note up into the gray sky, and they saw that an arrow had transfixed the flap of tough hide covering his throat. His would-be victims scattered and cleared a space for the huge body to land in. He groped at his gullet, and cried again as another arrow lodged itself in the thick part of his throat, and then his frigid breath came out frothy with blood. With one final helpless screech, he tumbled forward for what seemed an age before he landed with an impact that shook the very ground and sent rotting leaves high into the air.

Yet even that was not the end, for in his death throes the beast sent the three rushing farther and farther away. He threshed down bushes and trees, and even flicked boulders out into the forest until a small clearing was cut all around him. Then at last with his final agony, he tore a great tree from its roots and it fell down across his pointed head. The long body twitched fitfully, and that was all.

Slowly, the three travelers rose from where they had thrown themselves. Srstri had scrambled up the wooded hill which bounded the little valley, crawling beneath an interlocking pattern of fallen trees. Byorneth had ended up farther to the south, behind a hump of dirt and scraggly shrubs 50 paces from where Hunter had found refuge behind a cluster of young saplings. High in the tree above there was a gash where a great stone had hit, and across the forest floor behind were scattered shards, even driven clear through some of the smaller saplings.

The young man arose, trembling with energy, relieved as he saw Srstri get up as well, wide eyed, brushing the leaves from her rough clothing. Silence reigned once more in the forest. Byorneth peered all around through the trees, his nostrils twitching speculatively. Hunter followed his eyes, and Srstri watched them both, none breaking the strange quiet.

Slowly, a tall figure in a broad hat stood up from behind a small wooded hill, and raised a recurved bow in greeting. Byorneth raised his hand in reply and cried a greeting in a tongue strange to Hunter's ears, and then Hunter remembered — the scribe on the road, the leather pouch, the staff, the broad hat, the short trousers. All but the short, formidable bow was the same. The man could only be a Sheewa.

The strange figure vaulted the rocks and ran down the leafy slope and across the glade that separated him from Byorneth, at the center of which lay the Great Kaarnaan. Byorneth ran forward and met him in an open space ten paces beyond the creature's body, and they embraced as brothers, each clasping the other's elbows, then walked up the hill toward the others, arm in arm.

"Hunter, this is Arneth. He must have been but ten years old when last we met! Arneth, this young man is Hunter, my particular friend, almost a son to me."

With a wide grin, Arneth greeted Hunter in the Lowland fashion, slapping him on his arm and wishing him well, which Hunter returned. Then the young Sheewa saw Srstri standing behind. For some unnamed reason, the way Arneth smiled at the girl disturbed Hunter.

"Hunter, is this your slave?"

"No. She escaped and joined us as we passed her village. We are taking her to her home in the Hills." He looked back in the direction of their pursuers. "Now a whole tribe of the Chadeyzdeer are following us. I would suggest that we talk as we go." And so they set off with Arneth and Byorneth in the lead.

"We go now to Seng Grandt." The old man spoke humbly, and Hunter was puzzled at the tone. "Will your people take us in?"

Arneth shook his head. "Were it yourself alone there were no fear, Byorneth, for your memory is still a fond thing to many. But we cannot have such trouble as a stolen deez will bring. You know our calling. We are to keep and compile the records, waiting for the emergence of the *Pagrâi*. We do not involve ourselves or Seng Grandt in the troubles of the Island."

In the distance, they began to hear the sounds of pursuit. They quickened their pace, for their trail would be very clear, marked as it was with the dead Kaarnaan. After some distance through the murky woods, Arneth sighed and said, "Very well. I will go with you to the High City, but I cannot answer for your welcome there."

Before long, they happened upon a road cut through the trees, and on this they continued until forest gave way to empty wasteland, with patches of grass and rock all torn asunder and forced together again. The road died as the daylight died, and the travelers set off through these obstacles until their feet hurt and they began to turn their ankles because of the darkness. Finally, because of the risk of injury and general weariness, they came to rest some distance away from the road in a deep ravine, about a kand away beyond the edge of the forest.

The gully cut through this wilderness as the only gesture of order in a hopeless waste of offending mounds and ledges, wreathed in a cold gray mist. A hundred or so paces down the ravine, a small stream flowed noisily as it tumbled down from the high ledge. It was evidently a well-established campsite, for the earth was almost bare between the sloping gray walls, and a scorched spot marked where generations of fires had been made. Stakes, old and new, still stood all around.

As much as they would have liked to build a fire, the air being damp and the wind whistling above their heads, their pursuers were too many, and perhaps too near. Regret was expressed that they could not continue through the night, but the terrain was deemed too rough to negotiate safely in darkness.

Arneth, being freshest and the most rested, elected to take the first watch and Hunter the second. The three travelers huddled in their clothes around the dead fireplace, Srstri nestling between Byorneth and Hunter, as a slave's clothing lacked any double layers. Hunter felt her shivering through the cloth, and he huddled closer to share his warmth. For some reason, be it her presence, the cold, or the fine mist beginning to fall, sleep did not come easily to him. They left Arneth to fill his canteens and watch in the night.

Just before sleep claimed him, something occurred to Hunter. "Byorneth, that word that Arneth mentioned. *Pagrâi.* What is its meaning?"

"It means 'king.'"

The young Sheewa sat by himself among the clay that made up the far wall of the ravine. It would have taken two looks in the dark to distinguish him from the dirt around him, and so he sat invisible until the sixth watch. Then he stood and stretched with a small groan, walked over and shook Hunter, who woke reluctantly and took his place, grateful at least for the residual warmth Arneth had left. He was not, however, so grateful when he saw him take the place beside Srstri that had been his, drawing near to her as he had. He turned away and focused far out into the night.

━ᴧ ᴧ━

The brothers had gone far in the last few days, and with greater, more constant speed than had ever been required of them before. Night had faded into day with very little sleep, and even upon them, well used to rising early and bedding down late, the long hours told. The travel also proved difficult, for they had decided on a direct route to the southwest so as to join the other slave hunters, and the two big men were unaccustomed to traveling through the dense scrub and trees.

Now at last the old woods were behind them, and with great effort they passed through the Swamp out into a stretch of trees, guided by the words of a disreputable fellow of the Marsh, who swore by three generations of his family that the pursuers had passed through farther to the west. Reluctantly trusting his word, they soon found the wide trail, and before long they met the first stragglers, those committed to the purpose, but without the will to follow too closely. They asked these fellows no questions, for there was little news at the end of the line, and the greatest rewards go to those who forge ahead. Soon the company grew thicker, and in the deepest darkness they came out into a barren wasteland full of such folk as they had never seen, squanderers and vagabonds, wealthy farmers and tradesmen, all tempted away from home by stories of easy wealth. As hereditary farmers, the land seemed to them a comfortless waste, without one plot where a man might plant.

In the near distance, the beginnings of a fire burned at the center of a group of men, and they boldly approached until they were told to stand still. A man stood up from the infant blaze, bundled thickly. "And whence came you two? I've never seen you before. What are you doing at our fire? Go build your own at the rear with the rest of the vermin. You're not needed here."

They were the guests, and it was only their knowledge of this that prevented the brothers from repaying his rudeness in full. A few paces away there was another fire being lit, and this time they were welcomed to the fire as equals. From the smell, there was at least one Swampman present, but they were in no position to judge.

"What cheer, fellows?" came a voice from across the fire, the source invisible through the flame. A hand reached across, proffering a water bag, but the brothers were already drinking from theirs, and so the hand was retracted. "You're not familiar to me. Are you from the Trail?"

"No, from Allend's End. We heard of your chase here, and thought a man might carve a little something out for himself."

The men chuckled all around, and at first the brothers thought they had become the butt of some jest.

"You've never met our fierce leader, have you?" A man off to the right laughed. A fringe of white hair grew around the rim of his bald pate, and this with his broad grin gave his face an unsettling, cadaverous look, but the voice seemed sympathetic. "A very great man, he is! If we value our living, we follow him, and these our slaver brothers have been promised great sums. I never have heard him guarantee aught to anyone else! You may have covered all this country for nothing, unless you have good reason for staying. Did you kill a rich man back home?"

They laughed again, and Teidin laughed with them. "Well, what say you, Elnaan? Shall we go back?"

"No. Come along with me for a moment." The elder drew the younger away into the night.

They walked together far into the darkness, away from other ears. The pervading scent of the Swamp, so long in their noses, could hardly be smelled now, but the valley had its own strange odor, one of old rain and a dearth of sunlight. "Teidin, you go back home if you want. I have no say in the matter. But if we stay at the front regardless of what the man says, we may be able to cut this slave out and have the reward ourselves. We are not of their number, and we need not be joined to them."

His brother nodded. "And who's to say that we can't hunt during the nighttime?"

They had water, weapons, plenty of food. The night was warmer than most, and the moon gave light enough for careful men, and so the brothers let the woolly man and his minions have their fires. From the way that the camps were spaced, and the very fact that the searchers were stopping for rest, it was evident that there was no clear idea of where to look for the fugitives. Anyone might have a chance.

"Hold on." Elnaan's hand came up.

"What do you see?"

"I do not know. Something different."

The darkness protected them as they crept closer, until at last they saw more clearly. Three people crouched around a fire that burned so sickly that it barely made a difference to the nighttime around them. Soon, they could see that the fire had been built small, not out of caution, but rather of frank inability, for two of the men abused the other between rubbing their hands over his feeble handiwork.

"I saw none of you fools rush forward to build one for me."

"We feared you might burn us." It was a mirthless joke, born out of misery and not humor. These were not with the searchers. Their dialects differed too widely, savored too much of the entire length of the Great Trail, to be that of ordinary Villagers. Villains fleeing enemies in the Black Cradle, perhaps, for why else would they make camp in such a place? From the stories Teidin had heard about the assassins of Pown d'Rith, he doubted it could make much difference.

"Hand over that leg." They were cooking a leg of mutton inch by inch over the smudge, gnawing at it as it browned, and the sight nearly turned Teidin's town-bred stomach. A rough-faced fellow they had not seen before sat away from the others, throwing a dagger into a big branch. One of the men cried out and snatched his bag out of harm's way, but did nothing more. The man's blade was too ready and his looks too dark. "I would that I had Harn at the end of this knife now," he muttered, his bitter voice barely reaching them.

His words might have seemed weak, seated as he was on the damp ground in a circle of aching men, but those words put another chill in the air, and even seemed to kill the fire. "If we had stayed with the mule train, you might have had your chance. Why did that fool ever lead us away from the Trail?

The Hunter never did. There was never any need to. That pack of beasts may have taken our lives away as well as his."

"He is a fool. Nothing more. We're all well rid of him." The speaker stabbed violently into the fire with a long stick with each sentence. The brothers could see these men were ill-equipped for a night in the Wastes, or even a night alone in the busiest part of the Trail. Their leader had taken them away from the Trail which, as the man had said, was foolish in the extreme. The motivation could only have been selfish curiosity.

"This is no business for an adventurer. It needs an aged man, one who hates travel, one who is happiest in the Hills or in Kroon d'Rith. It's better for all of us. Had I been in office, now—" The others bade him be silent, with threats upon his person. He was eldest of the drivers present, one who felt his age more acutely than a man should.

The angry one stood with his knife across his broad palm, pointed across the fire. "Shut up with your advice, old one. I would have no leader at all unless it were the Hunter. Until he returns, I will quit the business of driving, and serve no one unless it be him. These are my words, and upon my blood I say them." Stepping back, and delivering an impotent slash at the flames, which had seemed to rise with the heat of his words, he walked out into the night, leaving silence behind him.

Teidin and Elnaan turned away to confer together, facing outward into the darkness. "This is a cold trail we're on," Elnaan said, almost under his breath. "It's strange, though, that these men should be muleteers, the same as the man we seek. Could this Hunter they speak of be the man?"

"It seems likely to be. Hunter the muleteer, Hunter the thief. Why would he steal a Hillslave away with him and run off to the Hills?"

"We can ask him when we catch him."

On they traveled into the night, away from the distant fires, the cool breeze their only companion aside from the guiding stars. The path they followed placed the North Star toward their back. Their purpose was not spoken between them, nor need it have been, for these drivers must have been split from the Hunter's company several days past, and there had been no contact between them and their leader since.

The party they sought would light no fires, draw no interest toward themselves. That was why they very nearly turned off toward the east when the red fringe appeared along the top of the distant hillock. But Teidin held his brother's arm, and Elnaan understood. Honest curiosity compelled them, for this camp was likely to be another small piece of the lost body of mule drivers, led astray by their mad captain.

They were correct, but only in part. Mule drivers they were, but this was a larger blaze, circled about with a great many more men than the other, men who ate plentifully and drank strong drink. Although some rejoiced in their excess, Teidin could see that the *rashi*, the laughter, the jostling carouse, concealed and took the shape of a personal hurt. The one island of stillness in the center of the mob was a thin staff of a man, seated on a pile of grain bags, wincing at every touch. Now a reveler would spill his drink on him, now a spark would fall in his clothing, and he would jump only to come to an awkward rest again.

Little did he know that behind the fire, in the thick of the roaring drunkards, there were concealed three very earnest men in sober deliberation. At last there came a signal and the camp arose, their revels all forsaken, and rushed as one swarm across, bearing the thin man up as upon an ocean swell. He was held there for an instant as several men built the pile of bags up into a platform, and they placed the man upon it.

"Silence, all of us!" There had been very little noise, so grim and silent was their purpose. The eldest present had been appointed spokesman. "We see before us Harn, a man, one of us, who has been responsible for much, and let much go to ruin. As the rule tells us, it falls to the men, one by one, to give the hard charges. Do it."

Anticipating his words, five men had formed a line. The first stepped forward and raised his voice in a high trumpeting blast, almost a wail. "He led us away from the Trail and our rightful business!"

Out came the second. "He brought us out into a plain full of corrupted water, and we fell oppressively sick."

"He left the mules defenseless against the pack of rover wolves, and we lost them all, and much of their cargo."

"He ran from the terror in the night, when the last two of our precious beasts were slaughtered by the monster out of the darkness."

"He made himself so drunk that we lost most of our daylight, and had to stay another night in this foul valley."

There were such trials held in the Lowlands, albeit not often. With the absence of any law, men made their own and enforced it themselves. The abiding rule for a mule train is that the leader's rulings must be obeyed to the letter until such time as five of the drivers could bring compelling charges of abuse, corruption or endangerment. The drivers had been anticipating this moment long before they left the Trail.

As the charges concluded, the old man held up his hands to his fellow drivers. "What say we to these?"

"Out! Out! Out with him!" the men cried loud and long, over one another, for there were none dissenting. Several mounted the grain bags and bore the man Harn down, casting him to the ground by the fire. They held his garments as he fell, which tore violently from his body. Teidin could hear his brother's hard breathing, and knew his dagger was ready in his hand. But no one made any threat upon the wretch's life, and if the charges were correct, then this was justice, no more. Even death would be well deserved.

The men cast Harn's clothes into the fire, and others came forward with leather thongs in their hands. None hurt the naked man until he stood, slowly staring, only just beginning to whimper. Then a lash whistled onto his back and he began to run, a pale flicker in the night, hotly pursued by several men, beating him out into the darkness.

The rest settled down by their fire again, resuming their drink with a heavier heart than they had feigned before. A mule driver with no mules was perhaps the most wretched figure in any country, for there was no resource available to him, and most Villagers regarded their kind with a feebly disguised suspicion — one who has lost his mules could hardly be trusted with cattle.

Soon the others returned, tossing their thongs in a pile away from the fire. Together they sat, neither speaking nor sleeping, and the brothers left their unknowing company.

Chapter 6
The Fields

I KNOW WHAT MEN WILL DO TO MEN,
I'VE SEEN THE TRIBUTES FALL.
ALL THIS TINY ROCK ACROSS
I'VE HEARD THE EAGLE'S CALL.
MY HEART GROWS HARD AND STONY THEN,
AND I GO FAR AWAY
BACK TO OLD SENG GRANDT AGAIN,
FAR AND SAFE FROM BLOODY MEN,
UPON THE CLIFFS OF CLAY.

~Sheewan Striding Song~

Hunter was still alert when the others awoke in the morning, stiff and shivering. Along with the drizzle that had fallen earlier that night, a heavy dew blanketed everything, soaked the ground, even forming puddles among the folds of their garments. They gathered their belongings together without a word and climbed painfully up the ravine's steep wall, but once there they fell on their faces in the slick mud and crawled back down into the gully where they had slept.

The long, broken land was scattered with people. Both Chadeyzdeer and Harniyen traversed the Wastes, crossing back and forth, shouting faintly to one another. The Chadeyzdeer always went armed, and the Harniyen bore long knives and clubs.

Arneth let out a long, shivering sigh. "Your friends are motivated indeed, and quiet." He glanced at Byorneth and the others along the ridge. "You have offended two peoples enough for them to hound you across the Plain and into the Wastes. You who were once of the Sheewa." Byorneth said nothing, but bit his gray mustache, and a fresh pang wrung Hunter's heart. Hands shaking with sudden hunger, he took a mouthful out of his rations.

Arneth led them off in a low lope across the countryside, keeping to what little cover they had. They were grateful for the exercise, which warmed their limbs, but soon their feet sank even deeper into the mud, and the drizzle turned to persistent rain, and still the Lowland army gained on them.

They somehow managed to avoid detection for about a kual of slimy earth and unforgiving rock until they found themselves skylined unexpectedly, and a great shout arose from across the Wastes. They ran. Arneth addressed Srstri, his voice broken by his hasty motion.

"I have never known men to chase through the night for anything but gold. Why do they chase you?"

"I am Banat's *deesard*. I am important to him."

Byorneth cut in. "No man would follow this long, even for his *deesard*. Unless he loved her."

"No!" she cried, horrified.

So they trotted on in silence, keeping to the low ground as best they could. They stopped abruptly at the top of a particularly sharp hillock, so sharp that Hunter very nearly toppled down the far side. Before them stood two men, one a Slaver and the other of the Lowlands. Hunter knew them both — the one had ordered him plucked out of the water in the Marsh, and the other had been a hanger on at Banat's village. Both had blades drawn.

The little group stopped and raised their hands in surrender. *These men must be part of the advanced guard,* Hunter thought swiftly, *and the others would be at least ten minutes in catching them. If she could not tell us what the pursuit was for, perhaps these two will.*

"Good trail! It's a long way from your homes, travelers. Why would you come all this way just for us?"

The tall Swampman answered thinly. "They promised gold for us. The girl is ten slaves' gold worth. Now, we can sell you."

"Yes, but why would anyone offer so much for one slave? There are many at least as pretty, and Banat can soon find another *deesard.*"

The other shook his head slowly. "That our concern not to be. Our living on gold, and that is the thing what we gain."

"Yes, but what if I told you that you could double your profit on this transaction?"

The man blinked. "What?" with a sidelong glance at his companion.

Hunter pointed at the Villager, and Byorneth thought he would never be more proud of the young man, for he guessed his intention. "He must want something that the slave carries. What else would make the village pay that price for one Hillwoman? Are you going to let them cheat you when you could bring such wealth home to your people? They might make you a king."

Byorneth glanced over his shoulder at the advancing horde. Time was running thin.

The Villager, panicky and desperate, spoke louder than he meant to. "They lie, Kerny! Do not listen! We will pay you twice her worth!"

"Why?" replied his companion, now cautious. "You only could offer so much if she carried a rich something! What is it? Give it me!"

He advanced and menaced Srstri with his killing blade, but she only shook her head and folded her arms. To the Chadeyzdeer, the Hillfolk are objects to be bought and sold, and are even referred to in the neutral gender. This man would not hesitate to kill, and so as the blade rose high in the air and the Villager stood by, Hunter whipped Srstri around and searched her, violently and quickly, ignoring her blazing eyes. Finally, as he felt along her side, something round and hard bulged out. He held it up for all to see.

It was a stone, faceted and bright, gleaming in the fresh sun as he turned it around, and within it Hunter could see a forest of needles nestled in the green depths. It was polished on all sides, with a hole drilled through its length, and even this had been worked to a high shine, and it gleamed like a silver rod. Their interrogator grasped for it roughly and pushed the girl into the Villager's arms. "Here!" he cried in triumph. "Take it! Now we agree on the stone. This is better than anything ever in my eyes!"

The Villager's face contorted in rage. He threw Srstri to one side and rushed upon the other with drawn dagger, but the Swampman was ready for him. He spurned the blow with a clang, then drove a hidden dagger upward into his enemy's chest. Groaning helplessly he struggled, then with a final shudder he kicked out his last life on the turf.

The victor was never to have any joy at this success, for at the height of the conflict an arrow had appeared in his back.

The realization of death did not strike him at once, but he looked perplexedly all about, and when he saw Arneth's bow, he growled and lifted his blade. But before he could turn to meet the Sheewa, he slumped to his knees and fell forward in the rank grass. In a flash, Byorneth and Arneth were on the move with the others not far behind. Their pursuers were well within earshot now. As he went, Arneth stooped and picked up the bauble without breaking his headlong stride. The Lowlanders raised a shout of triumph, but by then their quarry had reached the cover of the long, low ledge of rock which marked the beginning of the Death Fields.

Once behind this dike, they kept low, and the Swampmen, unused to tracking over bare rock, balked like mules at the sight of the frozen lava which heralded the end of the habitation of men. In that land, what appeared to be innocent flat ground might have been no more than a bubble, hanging overtop a great empty space of jagged volcanic shards. Death traps abounded, and so the pursuers hung back in fear, the taste of death in their mouths.

—⌒ ʌ ʌ ⌒—

A mixed horde scoured a long, broken valley, bounded on the south by an immense lava flow. They searched the safe ground very thoroughly, but finally they stood, hesitating, looking over the hellish land ahead of them without moving. Banat soon arrived from the rear. He had not expected to be involved in the chase until the end, when there would be a jewel to recover and vengeance to exact. The chase had gone on far too long already.

"Well? Give account! What happened?"

"We followed them to this point, Banat. But we have not been compensated for this level of risk. We can go no farther."

"What happened to Hambaak? With him leading, you could never display such cowardice."

"We found him farther back, a dagger in his chest. The man who killed him had an arrow in his back." He spoke with obvious contempt. He and Banat had played together as children, but the man was not the man the child had been. "Perhaps if someone strong and fearless were to lead the way, we could do as you ask. But I see none of that stamp here."

In a land where men treasure their honor above all things, it was well known that Banat held sway not by noble character, but rather the good fortune of having a close relative in a position of power in the village. Out of necessity the men might obey him, but they reserved their respect. It was this above all that irked him, that and the two brothers who stood to the side, silent and watching.

Banat's shade turned darker, and he even loosened his long woollen scarf. "I have much gold in reserve. If we retrieve that girl, I will pay three times what you lost."

"That is more than we know. If we do not recover her by the end of the day, then you may go on alone, and the best of luck go with you."

Banat fixed him with a look of immeasurable hatred, tightened his belt with a jerk, and strode gingerly forward into the black, glinting landscape. Gradually men followed him, stepping where he stepped. Hour faded into hour, and the sun slanted and reddened as the men followed Banat in steadily advancing lines, trailing around through the few places known to be safe. Still, they found no one. They gazed through the translucent walls of caverns, searching for any movement, but the land had swallowed up all that had been given it, and left no trace.

Two brothers walked among them, treading as tenderly as they knew how. Tales of the Death Fields had frightened them as children, and it both excited and terrified them to be in that otherworldly place. They could not have known that even had they known the land, it would have made no difference to their search. They thoroughly explored every covert, yet none yielded their quarry.

Finally, at sunset, there came a tinkling crash as a body fell to a jagged floor far below. The news spread across the glass, and as one man, Villagers and Swampfolk alike began to file out of the roiled mess. Banat knew he could not detain them, and so he did not try. He simply picked his way out, his look blacker even than the ground on which he trod.

This would not hinder him for long. Come what may, he would find his *deesard* and wrest from her that which he loved above all else.

—◇◇—

Many years ago, a lone deer sought refuge in the Death Fields from a pack of rover wolves. Immediately it became lost, and venturing out onto a leaf-thin layer of obsidian glass, had plunged through and perished in agony. Now, all that remained was a pile of bones far below. With his death he had created an ideal place of concealment, for below the edge of the glass was a ledge which could only be reached by one who knew of it. It was here that four figures lay still, overlapping one another breathlessly.

Soon, silence returned. Men's voices grew small and distant. Before, where there had been shouts back and forth, sounds of slipping and angry utterances, there was now nothing to obscure the plaintive cries of the eagles high above. It was this sudden silence that awoke Arneth, and he nudged the others with a warning not to roll over into the pit. They stood, and Hunter's toes gripped the ground through his soles as he looked down below.

No one of the Plain willingly enters the Death Fields, as they are called in the Harniyen tongue. Even the sure-footed Hillfolk require a good reason. Hunter, a Plainsman born and bred, set his teeth as he looked across that brutal vista, with its sharp edges and blinding slopes, drop-offs and greedy black fingers.

Arneth led off at a quick pace — too quick, Hunter thought, for sanity. "Have a care," he said over his shoulder. "Walk only where I walk."

Byorneth showed no fear. Even as Arneth led them along a ledge barely a hand's-breadth wide, which fell away on the right side into a pit, the bottom of which glowed strangely red beneath the glass, he trod confidently. As they passed to more open ground, he fell back beside Hunter, and addressed him in a low voice. "I have seen you in danger, facing it like a man. I saw the way you handled those two men today. Are you afraid of this place?"

Hunter thought for a moment. A moment ago he might have answered yes, but now as Byorneth talked, the calm, sane voice drove unreason from his mind. He had a safe path to walk on, a skilled guide. He shook his head.

"Good. I have crossed this way better than a score of times on the way to my home among the slopes. Do not fear." He slapped Hunter sharply on the shoulder. From here on he would walk tall, for fear is for those without a way to go.

And so he stepped with confidence, though all around him were reasons for an imaginative man to doubt. Each side of their narrow, uneven path was thickly lined with deep, spike-lined pits in which lay the contorted skeletons of cattle, wild dogs, and even men — many of whom were only streaks of armor rust on the rocks.

They had long since left behind the blasted patches of grass between the flows, and now the four travelers walked in a wasteland entirely full of black and twisted glass, long cooled but hot with the blazing sun. The mist had receded and left the air incredibly clear, allowing the sun to broil them from above and bake them from below as the rocks reflected its heat. The water rose from their garments in clouds, and soon they began to shed layers, leaving only enough to keep their skin covered. They had a little water between them, and at Byorneth's insistence each drank only about half of what their bodies cried out for. Even with Arneth's full supply, they had just barely enough for their journey, and the old man was determined to arrive with plenty to spare.

The young Arneth had been on a mission to the Fisherfolk of the northwest coast, but even the sternest Sheewa would agree this mission took precedence. Even beyond the duties of hospitality, there was the consideration of the slave, for though the Sheewa never concerned themselves with the institutions of the Lowlands, they acknowledged their duty as protectors of the realm.

The heat of the day was now fully upon them, and when they came to a convenient overhang, Arneth and Byorneth laid themselves out under it and went to sleep. Soon Hunter and Srstri did likewise, and so they escaped the more brutal hours of midday.

When they awoke, the sun was a few degrees nearer the horizon, and already the air seemed cooler. The moon hung like a dim lantern over their path, and it gradually became the dominant light in the sky as dusk settled over the land. Then the light faded even further, and they began to stumble over the surf of glass. Srstri, as a slave unaccustomed to long walking, especially suffered. At last, she jammed her toe violently against a low ridge. She groaned quietly to herself as she leaned against a stone until the pain passed, and Hunter stopped beside her.

"Are you alright?"

She nodded, but did not speak. He called for the others to wait, and when she was ready, he held her close as she supported herself on his shoulder, keeping her weight away from her injury. When they caught up to Arneth and Byorneth in the fading half light, he insisted they stop for a rest, and so they sat by the road and dozed fitfully until the morning light.

They set off again in the chill breeze of dawn, and soon they could see patches of green peeking past the broken black fringes and shell fractures. Soon these expanded into full glimpses of verdant vegetation such as Hunter had not seen even in the fattest part of the Plain. As they walked on, they entered long grass between high black pillars, but it was not until they passed the last roiling ledge that they were treated to the full panorama of low hills covered in fruit trees and crops. They were foothills, extending in an even, cultivated wave to the first bastions of the High Hills, and the fresh and living scents of growth beckoned them in.

A great weight seemed to lift off Hunter's shoulders in the newborn sun, and soon conversation resumed, unstilted and free. Even Byorneth joined in, as much as that silent man could ever talk at any time to anyone but Hunter. One all-but-forgotten name conjured another, until Hunter marveled at his friend's joy in the old acquaintance renewed.

"Where were you born, Hunter?" Arneth turned at last to him, conscious of his neglect.

"I was born some distance east of the Black Cradle on the coast," he replied. "My parents were fishermen."

Arneth nodded, his eyes brightening. "I've long been interested in the Fisherfolk. They breed adventurous sorts of men, I hear."

"No more so than such travelers as you, seeing new things, traveling through the Island." The fruit trees blossomed thickly about them now, hanging with heavy perfume. "And to have such a royal home to come back to! I could easily envy you this life."

"And what of the boats?" Arneth, cheated out of his expedition and hungering for the sea, eagerly turned the talk back to Hunter. "What manner of craft are they? What fish did you catch?"

The young muleteer answered simply, even reluctantly, but Arneth never ceased his questions. With the thorough interest of a crow over carrion, he asked after Hunter's childhood, his parents, even his house on the hill by the shore. With each answer his envy mounted, until at last it overcame him and he asked, "And why ever did you leave all this to join a mule train?"

"My parents were both killed when a rogue wave swept them out to sea. After that, I went down to the Great Trail. Byorneth came by at the head of a mule train and took me on as a driver." His voice was neutral, flat and calm, without hesitation. There were no more questions, and Hunter was glad to walk in silence once more. He never saw Srstri as she looked steadily at him, eyes wide with pity.

They came to a new line of fruit trees halfway up the second hill, trees that had begun to bear fruit, the first of which shone crimson among their greener fellows. For the last few days, their hunger had been a constant, nagging companion, and of one accord they lay out underneath the interlocking branches and filled themselves with the bright little fruits that hung over their heads, fruits that satisfied their thirst as well as their bellies, leaving only crackling seeds and no pits. It was Srstri who disturbed that quiet moment.

"Give me the stone."

The tone was not angry, or even especially demanding, yet there was an authority behind it that came as a surprise to the men around her. She repeated herself, higher this time.

"Give me the stone."

Arneth had not spoken since his embarrassment, and he was still ill at ease. "Srstri, you cannot understand. Mine is a very ancient Trust, and this stone is now my responsibility. I cannot give it to you."

"If you do not give it to me, I shall take it. My Trust is no less old or binding than yours. I do not want to cause any grief, but believe me when I say that I will defend my Trust as you would yours." She paused. "Do not worry. I will not take it away. But it is important that I carry it."

Arneth looked to Byorneth, who nodded. Drawing the blazing gem from the folds of an inner layer, he handed it across to her. She put it back from where Hunter had taken it, smiling around at her companions. All was well.

So they set off again through the lines of trees. They went for some time, eating at their leisure, in no particular hurry. Hunter fell back with Srstri, letting Byorneth and Arneth go ahead. Before she could, he spoke quickly. "I want to tell you how sorry I am about what happened back there."

"About what?"

"Well, I — I searched you."

She laughed. "I think I can forget about that if you can. We are all still living, and that's worth a few liberties."

He lapsed back into silence, which he broke again with an effort. It used to be much easier to speak to her. "What will you do first when you get home?"

"I suppose I should find my family, but I cannot be sure. I've been without one for so long. Maybe I will be better off without them."

"I am sure it would be a joy to your people to have you back again."

They began to pass others, pickers and cultivators heading home after the day's work. These folk smiled at the travelers curiously, but after all, a good many Sheewa had always passed this way. These lands belonged to Seng Grandt, and the scribes leased them to a few farming families, who carried it from one generation to the next. Even strangers might be trusted if they traveled with the Sheewa.

Along they went, passing through the orchards, then the vegetable crops, then little pens full of small cattle and goats, beyond all of which a massive outcropping of ancient stone reared like a guardian giant, an apron of clay fanning out from its skirts. In the middle of this mountain lay a droplet of gray rock, part of the bowels of the mountain below, on which rested a great fortress. It ruled all lands below the mountain-tops, all-expansive yet separate, hospitable yet grandly aloof.

They walked past old landslides and small homes, until finally they stood at the foot of the narrow path which led up to the gates of Seng Grandt, the High City.

Chapter 7

The Tale

AND THIS HOUSE, ON THIS HILL, SHALL HOUSE
IN ITS WRITINGS ALL THE LANDS OF THE EARTH.

~The Dedication of the High City~

There is no city like Seng Grandt.

Hunter and Srstri stood in awe as they looked on it for the first time, a great pale ship on the tangled main. It did not taper toward the top, as one might expect, but rather the mighty walls sloped inward and then flared out again, so that it resembled a sash around a woman's waist. Yet there the resemblance ceased, for it was fluted all around like the bark of a red spruce, with runnels that would shed the wind from the city's sides. Between the runnels there were the balconies, each a miracle in itself, and even from where the travelers stood, they could see little figures standing on them, watching the world below. In the middle of the wide structure stood two vast arms, snowy white, spread as if in welcome, and at the center of these were the great doors. High above it all stood ten great towers, like linen sails in the sun, the greatest of which stood in the center with an unseen watchman safe in his perch.

They began the long climb up the single paved road, worn smooth down the center with generations of footsteps. All around them on the lower slope there were round hills and ridges of slick clay swarming with mud-caked children, sliding down the steep slope on their backsides, laughing and shouting back and forth. It seemed to Hunter that he was with them on those hills, living his childhood again, and it filled him with a wild, inward glee to see how Srstri's face brightened as they passed these innocent revelers.

Soon they left the children behind, and Hunter found that the slope was not all bare clay as he had assumed, but planted all around with low creepers so that no travel was possible but by the single steep path. At the end of the long and weary way, they stood at last at the foot of the great city, between the widespread arms of its outer walls.

Wordlessly and almost breathlessly, they mounted the ledge that marked the beginning of the structure's foundation, a white slab as thick as the height of three tall men. Into the surface there had been laid red granite in the shape of a sun surrounded by hundreds of subordinate stars, each one bordered all around with the flashing blue of birdwing spar.

Finally, they stood at the great oaken gates, plainly cut, thoroughly pitched and surmounted by a massive jutting lintel. In the stone above the lintel, and shielded by a scalloped overhang, some ancient hand had carved an inscription, deeply and permanently, in the Old Tongue which Arneth translated for the benefit of Hunter and Srstri:

Halt, oh traveler, and consider what a
Presence thou dost enter.

Arneth lifted his voice in a long, lilting hail in a strange language, neither Hill nor Plain. An answer came from they knew not where, and instead of the whole door swinging to, as Hunter had half expected, a small door opened off to one side, and a voice gave them an eloquently courteous welcome in both Kyarrghnaal and Harniyen. Arneth stepped through and the rest followed him.

They came, not into the damp, dark chamber that Hunter had anticipated, but into bright sunlight, brighter even than the day outside. The high vaulted ceiling was full of windows, strangely constructed so as to allow entry to the sunlight but not the rain. Before them stood a man, smiling and silent, clothed not in the broad hat and short trousers that Hunter knew, but rather white, light material, draped over his shoulders and fastened snug about his waist with a black sash. He smiled at his guests warmly, and then turned on his heel and walked across the broad, airy room, stopping only to open a thick black door and motion them in.

This time, they stepped through into a large, high-ceilinged hall dominated by a magnificent chair elevated by several snowy-white slabs. Why there was such a profound hush as they approached, or why his own breath was bated, Hunter could not tell. The chair was covered up, down, and on all sides with expertly worked cloth, embroidered with faces and stories of kings and princelings engaged in hunting and falconry. All was surmounted by a large canopy fastened to the back of the chair, deep blue and starred with white stitching. The entire frame was studded with golden buttons, and gold thread was worked into each scene, highlighting a princeling here or a star there according to strict symbolic rules.

Their guide bowed low before the throne, and Byorneth motioned for Hunter and Srstri to do the same. They were then led past the platform to a large wooden panel which the man opened with hardly a creak, disclosing a long corridor lined on the sunward side with booths bathed in yellow light. In each booth was a slanted desk, and at each desk sat scribes of both sexes, writing carefully and steadily on long sheets of vellum, bringing their pens around in the elegant loops and twists of the Old Tongues of Arlinga.

Not one of these silent scribes so much as looked up from their work as the guide led Hunter and Srstri past. The pair stared, for the written word was rare in their experience, and the whirling lines on the scrolls intrigued them. When yet another door was opened before them, they paused for a long time, taking in the ornately carved paneling and lavish tapestries woven skillfully in ages past. The ends of scrolls gleamed like circular ghosts in the walls, and against these a tall figure stood in black shadow, a figure that stepped forward when they arrived and revealed a tall man, gaunt with age but with eyes of penetrating flame. The guide, having fulfilled his purpose, vanished without a sound among the wooden panels.

The room was lit all around with a single lamp that threw wavering light in and out of the vacant shadows in the paneling and the old man's robes. His sash was of scarlet, and into it was tucked a long, hilted dagger. His hair was as white as his robes, woven in and out with a very few dark strands that curled all the way down into his long beard. His eyes darted up and down with all the curiosity of youth, the wrinkles around them curving upward into a dozen little smiles.

Turning, he spoke briefly to Arneth in the same tongue which they had heard before, but it seemed significant that he addressed Byorneth in fluent Harniyen, rather than the strange tongue of the city. "It has been long since we have looked on you in this place, friend Byorneth. And why have you brought these strangers with you?"

"We have come through great danger because of our care, Algorneth. I care for this young man, who has long been both my son and only friend. He seems to care for this woman, but we all care for a thing she carries."

Algorneth looked down at her benevolently, and sensing what was expected of her, Srstri only hesitated an instant before she drew out of her cloak the shining green jewel that had so inflamed the Swampman's lust. It glinted only slightly in the wavering light, but their tall host's breath caught and his eyes opened wide. Bending, he took a long look into the depths of the stone, then looked Srstri up and down again with an inquiring little smile.

"Perhaps you do not understand what you hold, my dear. If you knew, you could understand the immense debt of gratitude which we all owe to you. Perhaps it even partly excuses Byorneth's bringing you here." He turned to Byorneth. "Well, old friend, what are we to do? You know the sacred Trust by which we are bound, and how perilous talebearing can be. These people must be instructed as to their duties in this place."

"I can inform the boy. I agree, it is altogether essential that he understand. The girl will do no harm. She can go back to her people and leave the jewel—"

"No!" she cried and drew the stone once again into her clothing. "Let me keep it! I will return to the Hills and tell no one of what I've seen if you let me carry my Trust with me!"

The old man smiled. "You are quite right, my dear. I know something of the ancient oath by which you are bound, an oath older even than ours. Come with me, all of you." He moved to the door and opened it. "I shall explain all that you would know. I know your loyalty, my dear, and I trust your judgment."

They followed him through long halls, the walls of which were littered with the trophies of ancient wars, past long corridors lined with shelves of scrolls, far into the mountain and the deep gloom of rock and memory. They passed scholars translating by the bright, flickering glow of lamps, some making notes or reciting text quietly to themselves, in a place where the literature of ages extended dimly beyond the end of their sight, and every footfall repeated itself against the unseen distance.

Soon, the tall old man stopped and rested his hand on a shelf. "These are the chronicles of Arlinga, from the beginnings and our earliest legends until now. The time we are presently concerned with begins here." He drew a scroll ever so gently from its place, handling it as though he held a newborn child. "It was the time of the Great War, the last in written remembrance.

"The race which inhabited this Island was a dark one, like unto you, my dear. They were the Pengdyam, and they were ruled by the Children of Ambalyeth, whose fortress stood where we are now, this city, more than 500 years ago. In those years, it was a great nation, with a sound ruler in its kind and well-advised king. The rule of the Pengdyam extended all over Arlinga, even unto the Unknown Region of the East, which even at that time was wild and dense.

"Then," he continued, moving along the shelves, "a threat came from across the sea, a light-skinned race in tall ships. They landed and began to move across the country, killing and burning without mercy. They cleared a space for their own king at the Great Bay, where he landed and from which he waged an immense war of conquest against the peaceful inhabitants of this Island.

"There were many small battles, fought by bands of farmers and landowners in lieu of any army, amounting to nothing but containment and desperate delay. The invading king's counselors advised him vainly against war.

"At last, the day came when the Pengdyam forces were ready, and they met the light-skinned army in the Forests of the Plain against the advice of their own counselors. They fought back and forth for weeks, and then months, until all semblance of order was lost in a sea of blood and filth.

"In the end, nothing remained. Those few left alive had not the will to fight, and the royal houses of both nations were entirely cut off, the provinces left to their own devices. All that remained of the old order were the counselors and wise men, who of one accord left the Plain and retired, each side making peace with the other, to this great fortress of Seng Grandt. Here, we hid away our records, the history of both kingdoms, expanding the vaults and cutting new ones. We have continued our writings, and over the course of our existence have compiled all we could find about the languages and customs of this Island, even to the nomads and tribes of the Western Deserts.

"All this time, we have remained and waited for a king to emerge, one who will unite the Island and set up the nation, wisely using these records of past foolishness to make himself wise. We have seen evil things in these years. Men have no laws beyond themselves, and our chief city, that stinking Black Cradle by the sea, breeds by the hand of man every form of pestilence and degradation." His emotions had overtaken him, and a few tears ran down his face and into his snowy beard.

"When a man truly meant to rule emerges, we will turn over these our records as well as all our other treasures, for they are not ours, but belong to him and to his heirs. We will advise him as our forefathers advised, and he will give heed."

Srstri listened and looked at the scrolls as they went by, imagining all the stories the man was leaving out, all the human drama and tragedy which had brought them to the present day. She spoke when he had finished.

"But in all of this, where does my Trust fit in?"

The old man shook himself as if from a dream and fixed her with his bright eyes. "First, I am curious to hear all that you know of the history of this gem you carry, and the responsibility to which your family has so long been bound."

So she began her story, quietly, and beginning in Harniyen, but her memories of the forgotten past altered her speech, and soon the occasional word of Kyarrghnaal emerged like a budding plant. "My mother told me the story when I was a child, long before I came into possession of the stone. Before the Great War, her ancestor lived in the valley as a farmer. He was working in his fields one day when there was a great battle, some distance away through the trees. He was almost finished his work when a party of men in purple robes came running out of the woods. They gave him the stone, then made him swear he would keep it safe until such time as it should be called for. He swore and took it, and at that moment a company of fair-skinned men came out of the forest and fell upon the men in the purple robes. My ancestor hid himself, and when the men had finished their killing, they could not find him.

"He took all he had up to the Caldera to live among the Hillfolk, and there he took a wife. We've been there ever since, and the Trust has been passed down through the years until it became mine.

"My mother showed me where the jewel was hidden. One day, my mother and father were away on business and had left the house in my charge. I finished all my chores and went to look at the stone as I had so often, but as I took it out of its place, someone seized me from behind and dragged me away so quickly that I had not the time to put my Trust back in its place. Quickly, I slipped it into an inner pocket, and kept it there as the Stinking Men took me through the deep snow, then through the Swamp, and I still had it as I was sold and taken as *deesard*.

"It was safe until I fell into the hands of Banat, but I was careless one day and he saw the Trust. He coveted it immediately, and took it as his own, then set about making himself so rich that neither I nor the stone could ever be taken away from him. I took most of a year in finding it again, and then it only remained to await a chance to escape. And then one came.

"Hunter was kind, and I knew that if I left with him, he could protect me and my Trust from those who would follow. I got it back from its hiding place and followed after these men."

They were silent for a time, and in the stillness Srstri could hear the faintest echoing sounds somewhere away through the chambers. "Wonderful," said Algorneth. "You have done well, my child. Who could have suspected that so many generations would stay true to the last royal order ever given? Now, I will show you what you and your line have protected all these years."

He held out both hands, and Srstri hesitated for an instant, then gave him the stone. Cupping it carefully, reverently, he spoke in a soft whisper. "The location of this gem has been a matter of debate and study among us for generations, ever since it was lost so long ago. It was always with the king whenever he was away from his city. In the heat of that last great fight the stone was lost, along with the life of the king. Those who were sent to retrieve it never returned, and none knew of its fate until today. But the scrolls told of it, told of its matchless color and shape, its internal garden." He lifted his eyes and spoke even lower. "Come. I will show you."

He led them on, further into the mountain past vistas of scrolls, ancient and well tended, until at last they stepped into a vault, guarded by an armed man who stood erect as he saw Algorneth approach. The old man ordered the lamps lit, and a breathless silence fell over the group, at which he smiled in quiet delight, just as any collector should when a stranger beholds his collection.

The room was by no means large, but every inch of space on the walls was covered in treasure. An array of 20 inlayed and ornately inscribed swords and knives hung beside a broad breastplate, well used but still serviceable and even beautiful, set around the heart with five sharply defined star sapphires the color of the deepest ocean. At the center of these was a jasper of the royal kind, which by some wonder of nature had been patterned with a landscape of bright blue sky above and a familiar clay slope, bleeding into brown beneath, representing clearly to any Sheewa his royal home. A broad cape of now-flimsy silk was attached to its shoulders by two eagle claws of the rarest pink jade.

Hanging apart from everything else was one great two-handed sword, the pommel of which burned with the hot brilliance of a ruby deeply set into the metal, a ruby of the sort wrested from the white marble of the mountains, that glows in the sun like a living ember. Upon the right wall were the court accoutrements — arrays of cutlery, the steel Hammer of the Workmen, scores of small weapons, and then, in its own place, the scepter. It was of lustrous beaten gold, shining with hammer strokes and set above and below with banded red and yellow agate, shaped as a sheath around the long shaft. At each end of this was the representation of an extended hand, one open and the other closed into a fist. Set aside were the court instruments — flutes, viols, harps, all long disused.

In the center of it all on a white stone pedestal sat the crown, the Great Crown of the Old Kingdom, a wide, solid band of gold surmounted by a central tower of the same, set all about with turquoises and rugged chains. In the middle was the Gem of Kings, a fiery violet victory stone, the like of which no common man in the kingdom could possess and live. There was a plain gold diadem on a stand below the crown, used for daily royal life, but it was the crown that held their attention, for the setting directly above the victory stone was empty, with only a broken spindle left to show what had once been.

The old man held the green stone up to the place and beamed about, teary-eyed. "At last, at the end of 500 years, the Green Star has returned." His voice broke. "Your Trust is now fulfilled, and the brave men and women who died in its deliverance may now rest quietly."

He set the stone down beside the crown and sighed. "Thank-you, all. You must be tired. Arneth, will you show these people to their chambers? I will order the jewelers to begin their work."

Hunter was grateful to him. Ever since they had entered the cool depths of the Hills, his eyes had been fading in and out of focus, sneaking shut so that he barely saw the wonders before him. Srstri, relieved of her Trust and its constant responsibility, had begun to yawn and lean, and though Byorneth showed no fatigue, Hunter knew him well enough to see that even his strength was giving way.

They were led through the city, out into a bright expanse of window-lined corridor that branched off into their rooms — square, severe rooms cut into the native rock with beds piled high with furs. Byorneth took the first one, next came Srstri's, and Arneth was there to open the door, smiling and even touching her arm as she went inside. Hunter took the next room without comment, and so Arneth went on his way with a song on his lips, but Hunter slept with a heavy heart, berating himself for hanging back.

He made a solemn promise to himself as he drifted off. Whatever happened, he would be the first to greet Srstri in the morning.

It is curious that no matter how deeply and soundly we may sleep, the knowledge of pressing business will awaken us early the next morning. Hunter had traveled through the Swamp, the forest, and the Death Fields, almost without rest, but he awoke as he had intended — early and alert.

He was standing at Srstri's door in the bright stone hallway when she opened it. They had both been provided a change of clothing in their rooms, and when Srstri emerged, Hunter's breath caught in his chest. She had been attractive as a slave, but now, washed and in flowing garments, her wavy black hair flowing down the length of her back, she was a queen.

She flashed him a smile and her tone was like music. "Good morning! Did you sleep well?"

"Yes, I did. It got quite cold toward morning, but I had plenty of furs. How did you sleep?"

"Nicely, I suppose. I hardly ever sleep soundly in a new place until I get used to it, but I feel rested." She looked up and down the corridor. "Is anyone else awake?"

"I don't know. I've heard no one."

In fact, the day had started an hour before they had opened their eyes. Morning comes early in Seng Grandt, and those who would follow the Sheewa's path spend long days and short nights. Everyone along that corridor had been informed of their arrival, and had gone quietly in deference to their guests.

Hunter knocked at Byorneth's door, but got no answer. The training of the old man's childhood was too strong, and these surroundings brought it all back. Even in his years with the mule train, and at his advanced age, self-indulgence had no part in him. He had already washed and eaten, and now sat discussing yesterday's journey with Algorneth in his study.

Algorneth was the eldest and generally considered the wisest of the living Sheewa, and for this reason had long been the undisputed Keeper of the Slopes. He had studied all of the old scrolls, and knew many by heart. Having thoroughly learned the physical arts in his younger days, even in age he taught the younger students the finer points of the sword, dirk, bow, staff and unarmed combat. Now, he sat quietly listening to Byorneth as he concluded the story of Hunter and their travels together. One might have thought that he slumbered, but Byorneth knew better. Three hundred Sheewa moved all across Arlinga at his personal command, a vast web of clever, subtle men gathering subtle facts. Aged though he may have been, his elemental vigor had in no way diminished, and Byorneth could still see in him the young man who had been his comrade so many long years ago.

"He seems a remarkable fellow, this young man of yours," the Keeper of the Slopes said when the full story was told. "Wise and discreet for his age. Does he defer to your judgment?"

"Yes, and perhaps he leans on me too much. But he always had a firm control over the drivers, and never thought of his own comfort before their welfare."

"And you think he may be the one?"

"I am sure that he is the one. We have waited long enough."

This time, Algorneth was silent so long that Byorneth shifted in his seat. Then the old Sheewa continued. "Kingship is no easy thing. We know that Hunter can lead a train of mules from the Coast to the Hills and back again. He may even be humble enough to accept correction. But can he take absolute charge over scores of diverse tribes and govern them, establishing justice, dealing with offenders and managing trade across the sea? Even with our knowledge at his disposal, he must also have great wisdom."

"He will seek greater wisdom."

"I have no doubt that he will, but the most decent among us can be spoiled by power. We as Sheewa must be bound to our king, even as he must be bound to his people. Would you see your friend, your son, debased by his own nature in the gratification of every whim? Would you see the Sheewa and all Arlinga threatened?"

"He would never come to that. Hunter is not made as other men are. I know not precisely what separates him, but his mind does not entirely rule his actions. There is something else, something beyond himself. I suppose one might call it a spirit of authority."

"Ah. Is it so, then?" Algorneth was yet unsure. He knew and trusted Byorneth, though few others did. He alone knew of Byorneth's reasons for leaving, of his certainty that somewhere out in the Island he could find the man who would unite Arlinga, free the people from themselves. Still, one man's word is only one man's word, and Algorneth desired counsel in every matter. "We will train him as a Sheewa. He will study all of our arts, and then he will travel with you, Byorneth. Better no king at all than the right king too soon."

He bent to his scrolls again, and Byorneth rose stiffly and went out, taking care not to make any noise as he swung the door shut.

———

Far away in a place where old-growth giants and scrub pine meet, a fire blazed and its light flickered warmly on the wet branches above. To contrive such a fire in such a place had taken skill, and a supply of tinder kept dry in a leather bag. It was a larger fire than was needed for just one person, yet only one person sat at it, motionless as the ancient trunk he leaned against except when he fed the warmth from the pile beside him. The winter had almost begun.

When at last the cry came out of the trees to the east, he looked up quickly. It was a husky voice, and the tongue it spoke was strange, not to the Lowlands only but even to the Sheewa, who made it their business to know all language. "All hail, the Man from the West."

"Who comes?"

"One of his train. Who answers?"

"One who welcomes all who follow him. Come in."

A clump shifted back and forth, and out of the midst there stood a man so narrow across the shoulders that he might have been a child but for his height. Slowly, he picked his way through the low growth into the firelight. He had the look of a Lowlander. The Man from the West chose his agents carefully.

He sighed as he sat down like a man twice his age, and the man who had gathered the wood, cleared the ground, and built the fire snorted and offered his water bag. The drink the man took was long, and a little spilled down his front. "My thanks. I had great need of that."

"No trouble. At least, not much. You are just out of the West."

"Yes."

"I knew it the minute I heard you away off among the trees. If you had been running, you could not have made more noise. Take another drink. I see you carry no water yourself."

"I lost it out there somewhere. I praise the fortune that led you here to meet me."

The fire had begun to wane, and the man let it go. The night was not very cold, and he had no desire to be more than necessarily hospitable to this man. "It was not my choice. I was told to meet you here by messenger, which might have brought a great deal of suspicion upon me. I suppose you have no food with you either? Here, eat your fill. You can come to the house of my master tomorrow and get another meal there."

"We have but one master, my brother."

The man gave no immediate reply, but took the bag back, much lighter than it was before. As he leaned into the firelight the stranger from the West saw that he still wore the starred amulet. "We play a perilous game. To serve our master in the West, we must serve our masters in the East."

"Until our time comes to rise."

"If it comes. I've long ceased hoping for it."

The man across the fire shuddered at the words. He had been warned that he could easily lose sight of his mark with too much time spent in the East. Some few of his acquaintance had come back from the East to an imperial welcome, only to be slain for some chance comment the next day. It was the women, most likely. Women were the root of all trouble.

Still, the country was full of the loyal kind, as the Man from the West had long said. There must still be many who held fast, who had not become soft with the long years. Their race was too strong to fall so easily.

It must come soon. The land must be theirs.

Chapter 8
The Seed

THE FOOL WILL TEACH ERE HE HAS LEARNED,
AND HIS VERY SERVANTS SCORN HIM.

~Lowland Proverb~

The orchards and crops they had passed on their way to the city must have produced very well, for Hunter thought he had never had a more varied meal. He and Srstri were given immense platters laden with fruit preserves, bread and meat, which they ate together in a small porch which overlooked the valley on the right and opened to the mountains on the left. They talked but little, for Hunter was happy to be close to her, and every time he opened his mouth, it seemed easier to fill it with food instead. At last, he swallowed his final bite of apple and was about to speak when a rough hand was laid on his shoulder, and he turned and saw Arneth, the young Sheewa's warmth entirely missing. "Leave your plate. You're to come with me."

Obligingly, Hunter stood and was about to say goodbye to Srstri, who had never taken her eyes away from the view, but Arneth cut him short. "Come along! Now!"

With some trepidation, Hunter set off down the hallway a few paces behind Arneth. After many long bright corridors, they stepped into what appeared to be a throne room or reception hall, although it now stood empty and silent, with straw mats upon the floor. Even stripped bare, the room was magnificent, the walls all carved in floral designs and historical scenes, beautiful but meaningless to Hunter, and lining the high walls were cabinets, immense things containing all manner of decoration and furnishing, safe behind sturdy oaken spindles, engraved with the stories of kings and polished to a high shine.

Arneth stopped suddenly and Hunter collided with him. Before he could apologize, Arneth pivoted violently and swept Hunter's legs from under him, at the same time toppling him with a sweeping blow to the shoulder. There was no apparent malice in the action, only a relentless intent that angered Hunter more than anything else might have. Rage mounted hot inside him, and he shot himself up off the floor and into Arneth, but his adversary simply absorbed the force of the attack, fell over backward, and threw Hunter far behind with his feet.

Lying facedown on the straw, the haze of anger left Hunter and he could see clearly. The details of the room faded from his mind, and things assumed their true perspective. Instead of a fight, this was a systematic physical conversation, every punch an argument, every defense an objection. This time, he would let Arneth come after him.

High up on the balcony and hidden in the shadows, Byorneth sat, grimly watching. His son's training had begun, and even by Sheewan standards, it would be brutal. There was very little time.

⁓ᴧᴧ⁓

Among the Sheewa a boy begins training at the beginning of his 13th year, and it continues until his 21st birthday when tradition dictates he set out on his first journey. Hunter would be trained for no more than one year, and so you may imagine how hard that year was for him. Each day began with a severe rough-and-tumble session, which he both dreaded and enjoyed. Sometimes they worked with weapons, mostly without. As he progressed, he was also set against several Sheewa at once, first armed, then with only his hands to protect him. This was no polished fighting style, full of superfluous movement and sound such as some nations practise for sport. This was a genuine fight for survival. One day, near the beginning of his training, Arneth kneed him viciously in the groin, and even then the attack did not stop. He learned to fight heedless of pain, to keep his mind clear, to strike without hesitation or uncertainty.

There never seemed to be any rest. He was always sent directly from the gymnasium into a sealed room with a maddening old Sheewa who would only speak to him in an odd jabber of strange vowels and inflections. The room was lined and filled with a strange assortment of objects — cooking utensils, tree branches and leaves, food, tools, weapons. They would walk around, his companion pointing at one object or another and speaking in foreign sentences, and soon Hunter began to enjoy the game, repeating and imitating. He found he had a gift for mimicry, and it was not long before this strange tongue began to unfold its hidden secrets to him, albeit shyly. Some unknown emotion awoke and rejoiced as his knowledge grew, and his master could scarce contain his amazement at Hunter's quickness.

The fighting left his body sore and tired, and although this new game left his mind no less weary, he enjoyed it all the more, exulting in a newfound power. Once, when he met Byorneth for the midday meal in the great stone dining hall, he spoke in his new language in an attempt to mystify the old man, but Byorneth replied without hesitation in fluent and idiomatic terms so completely beyond Hunter that he went back to his studies, humbled but with redoubled hunger. The language was Huaynił, the tongue of the Western tribes, the Riders of the Desert.

After the noon meal, he would be put through his paces in the art of the scribe, the innate meanings behind the strange loops and curls of writing revealed and simplified. He learned of the tongues of the ancient royal houses, and the language of the Sheewa which had sprung up around them. More importantly, he learned to write them well, to make each stroke without hesitation and in the proper order, to inscribe each distinct language with quick grace.

In all his training, morning and evening, he learned other arts, for the foes a Sheewa may meet are not restricted to the ranks of mankind. In far countries, a fever may kill as easily as a sword. So with every injury, every sign of sickness, he was made to treat himself. They showed him plants, the roots, leaves and juices of which could be used for healing. He learned to pack them, to preserve them for times when they were not easily found.

In the midst of all his learning, he almost never noticed the girl, who with furtive looks skirted the edges of his life. Almost.

⌒⌒ᴧᴧ⌒⌒

It had now been two months since his men had left him, and since that day there had been no rest for Banat or for the few men who stayed at his side. The desertion of his Villagers served only to temper his purpose. Several of the men had remained, having nothing better to do and no life outside the search. They were jackals, happiest in the shadow of the cat. As for the two tall young men who walked slightly apart from them, they were of little concern. Diggers from the East. Nothing more.

Their progress was slow, for the Death Fields were large, and may be safely traversed only at a snail's pace, trying every patch of ground for soundness. Many times their lives were saved by a cautious tap and resounding crash. Each day took them through labyrinthine death, and each frigid night sent them to their blankets on some rigid outcropping, a sullen, mirthless company.

They had had a fire from the start, for the summer was waning and the rocks held little heat. This night, on Banat's orders, the blaze was especially high, and they could barely see him for all the cloaks he wore. Yet still, he shivered. He sat up alone, gazing grimly into the dying coals, and when his companions began to snore, he wrapped his scarf another turn around his neck and left them to sleep. He could not rest, much less allow himself to actually drift away. The Hill sow had taken not only his sole treasure, but his entire worth as a man, and he now lived for nothing else. Triviality had always angered him, and now, most of all, he hated his men for sleeping when he could not.

He walked, impatient among the low forms, a habitual scowl twisting his lips. Turning suddenly, he saw that not all of his men slept — one set of eyes, calm and steady, were ever on him, and wavered not a hair when their look was returned. Here was one Banat wished would sleep, and his inmost thoughts were betrayed in the almost loving caress he gave to the hilt of his blade. Still the eyes held to their tortured target. Only one hand came out of the blankets to grasp his own knife. Hesitating only an instant, Banat walked away with a loud snort.

The eyes did not close for a while. Rather, they burned out into the night, restless back and forth, the hand still clasping his weapon. It had been given to him by his father in the days when he still had time for his children, and he treasured it for this, but it had value even beyond sentiment. He loved it for its exquisite balance, the fine detailing of its steel and darkwood handle, but mostly for its blade, which would hold a keen edge through any mishap, and had even saved his life. Elnaan, like his brother, had been taught to value a reliable weapon.

In the morning they awoke, the worse for having slept the night on the hard lava, but the pains they felt had become old friends. Giving them only just enough time for a bite or two out of their packs, Banat ordered them away through the black land. They were glad to be out from under his presence, and some few had even gotten a taste for the desolate, glassy, ropy land where their leader was so sure they would find the body of a slave and his jewel, miraculously intact. The brothers went together out of comfortable habit, Teidin falling back and letting Elnaan go ahead when the trails were narrow. Over the course of their wanderings, they had destroyed many of the traps which made the land deadly, but still it behooved them to tread carefully. The cold magnified even the smallest of their injuries.

They mounted up on a high place, where centuries before a surge of lava had frozen in a high rounded shape. It was safe here but for ridges off to the west, and they breathed a little easier. This was the only place where the old heat of the Island's past remained, for upon the utmost summit there remained a fountain from which fresh red pools oozed, to form new layers of ruthlessly rough ground. Keeping their distance from the heat, the brothers sat together.

The momentum of the chase had been lost, and it had begun to disturb the young men. This Banat, although beyond any doubt determined, could never be called an imaginative man, and the Death Fields were still the Death Fields. Not a sign of the mule drivers or the stolen slave had been seen for weeks.

"Why need we stay with the woollen man?" Teidin said, half to himself. "We have sworn no oath, and are in no way obligated. Were we to find his slave for him, it would be easy to find him here and collect our gold."

Elnaan took a pull at the water bag. One sweated far too much under that sun, even after the chill of the night. "How would we know them? Suppose they've gone back among the Hills where there are ten thousand like her? Suppose they've already sold her?"

"Suppose we are missing them by staying in this place?" Teidin rejoined.

The land was hot, the ground hard, the company unsavory. Squinting off into the far distance, Elnaan nodded. He had learned as a small boy to trust Teidin's cool mind, and to admire him for it. It was far too easy to think of Teidin as the younger brother, and Elnaan had often regretted it. "Yes, I would love to feel the grass once again, if they have grass in that land. If nothing else, we will have seen things we have not known, strange folk and new lands. Let's go now. I am wearied of this place."

It is not to be thought that during all her time Srstri's keen attentions remained unoccupied. She had soon explored the entire city, had its highlights explained to her, saw all the work of the scribes, male and female. Seeing what the wives did during the day, writing, sewing and cooking, tending the crops and orchards, she had begun to be a great help in their work. Her experience down below in the village served her well, and she rejoiced as she worked the ground in freedom for the first time, but then even that was taken from her as the advancing winter began to wither the leaves and harden the ground.

There are many other pursuits in Seng Grandt for a girl of an active mind, and Srstri was rather more intelligent than most. She turned her attention to learning all she could, especially where Hunter was concerned, for it gave her a strange comfort to involve herself in the things that occupied him. Though she saw very little of him, she still regarded him as her protector, her guardian, this strange man who seemed to have forgotten her. And Arneth was not behindhand in his efforts to usurp his place.

As for Hunter, his mind was keenly focused, and he made his way back to his room each night strangely untroubled by restless thoughts. He had seen nothing of Srstri for a long time now, but his work had taken her place more than he would have thought possible. There was only an underlying feeling that he had left something undone, but whenever fear clenched him, there was always a diverting piece of history or some wild language to distract him.

One day, he sat alone at one of the desks in the archives, which they had passed on the first day of their yearlong visit. His teacher had left him alone to copy out a scroll which dealt with things long forgotten by all but the most dedicated of scholars in Seng Grandt. Being as it shed light on certain mysteries of Sheewan tradition, Hunter sat captivated by the story. In his absorption he forgot his training, and the footsteps echoing down the corridor toward him went altogether unnoticed until they stopped beside him.

He jumped and nearly knocked his lamp onto the floor. Srstri reached out and took hold of it as Hunter did, and their hands touched, but he did not move his away until the lamp was safely back in its place and she removed hers. She smiled down at him exactly as she had months ago, kind and somehow expectant.

"Hunter." She addressed him after the Sheewan form. "Are you well?"

He nodded, but made no other answer.

She looked down at the scroll laid out before him. "That is beautiful."

Hunter nodded again. In all his study, he had nearly lost the wonder of the art, a thing which even the highest scholars envy their children. Her words brought part of it back to him, and all at once there was no Seng Grandt, no Arlinga, only them and the meeting of their eyes.

He wanted to reply, "You are beautiful. You have bloomed in this place, even beyond the perfect loveliness of that girl I found on the Trail." Words, long pent up, rushed through his mind in high poetry, a form which had always eluded him, but now the tangled words in his mind resolved themselves into the very rhyme and meter of the rhapsodies of the ancient kings.

Then in a moment it was all gone and he looked away. He did not see her blush.

She spoke Kyarrghnaal now, their first language. "Hunter, I know you're very busy, but may I ask for your help?"

"Yes, Friend Srstri." And he managed another smile as he said it.

"I would like you to teach me. Teach me some of what you are learning. I feel I am without purpose here. In the village, I was kept constantly busy, but here I have no place. Teach me anything, anything I can learn before the time is gone forever." Her tone became desperate as it rose higher, and somehow it frightened him. Very slowly, he rolled the delicate scroll and replaced it on the shelf with the others. Then with the energy of sudden decision, he took her by the hand and together they flew past the centuries of scrolls and out of the huge chamber.

His teacher was drinking tea in his small drawing room when they found him, and when they told him of their intentions, he was well pleased with the idea. There is nothing that helps a student more than the chance to teach.

The next day found Hunter up at his usual early hour, and after his daily round of defending his life, he went to the schoolroom, where instead of the same maddening old man he found Srstri sitting on a stool, hands folded in her lap, waiting for him.

He gave no greeting, no indication of the wildness within him, but pointed to the stool underneath her and said, "*Fulja.*"

She had been told what to expect, a courtesy which had never been extended to him.

She repeated, "Fulcha."

He corrected, "*Fulja.*"

And so it went. He spoke, and she tried to mimic him, gradually learning to operate outside the realm of the sounds of the Plain. Having spoken two languages fluently for most of her life, a third was less difficult, and soon the strange consonants came easier. "*Fulja,*" she said.

He took her by the hand and stood her up, then lifted the stool above his head, still holding her hand. *"Seedhieueeshto auaqve vev."*

This puzzled her. If *"fulja"* meant "stool," then a form of that word should be present in this new sentence. Hunter had expected this, and very nearly smiled as her pretty brow wrinkled. Huaynił words changed their form completely depending on their use in a sentence, but he knew she would have difficulty realizing it. In the meantime, her perplexity made her even more beautiful.

The lessons progressed well. Almost too well, although Hunter strove to maintain a detached attitude over their days together. The girl learned quickly, and he found her intellect disconcerting, soon suspecting she had greater skill than he. Abstract constructions gave them trouble, and they found themselves cheating, using Kyarrghnaal or Harniyen words to translate ideas which they could not act out. The Sheewa forbid their number to learn strange tongues through translation, but they were all alone in the room, and their joy was strong.

The subject of their study interested them both, and although Hunter found that his young spirit was never satisfied by these exchanges, it was at least appeased by Srstri's proximity. They laughed together at all the little mistakes, so much so that he found himself hoping for them. Once she tried to say, "I will buy myself a tent," but instead insisted that she would purchase a grandmother, and her laughter rang like a silver bell as she leaned forward in her chair. He reached out to catch her, and just happened to brush her soft cheek with his fingertips.

Anyone might have done the same.

The society of the Sheewa was entirely elegant. They were a mixture of two distinct groups, but racial distinction had over time assumed its proper lack of importance. And this had a minimal effect on the language, for every Sheewa could converse in both the Harniyen and Kyarrghnaal tongues without hesitation or ambiguity. The two tongues had been folded into Sheewan so completely that one could speak exclusively in either language, and never step outside the bounds of Sheewan. In broader terms everyone, Hill and Plain, spoke in either dialect of the Sheewan language, though most had never heard of the High City, and hardly ever understood one another.

Srstri remained in the city, worrying both Hunter and Arneth. The violence of Hunter's combat sessions with Arneth grew in proportion to their contact with the girl, which the other young men saw and kept their distance, preferring to view the exchange from afar and seek other wives for themselves. They saw trouble coming by pure instinct, the elder by long experience. The dusky Hillgirl was trouble, and temptation may take hold of the best of men.

But Hunter soon learned that the angrier he became, the more often he would find himself on his back with Arneth pinning his throat. He learned to fight furiously but without emotion, viciously but without passion. In one flash he learned this, and at that moment, in the middle of his most violent exchange, he became a truly dangerous man.

That was the last fight he had for a long time. Now his masters allowed him to rest, even letting him sleep until midday, but Hunter found he could not help but rise early. He occupied his time with walking, running, anything to stave off the restlessness which had replaced his regular training. Every Sheewa he asked refused to train with him, until at last he saw a greater purpose behind their refusal. But he determined not to become the man he had once been, and so he trained alone, putting himself through harder experiences than his masters ever had.

His appetite for challenge grew the more he fed it, and soon he did things, explored places that few had ever explored before. He saw all the edges of the Death Fields, and even ventured into them along the trails. Soon he knew every passage of Seng Grandt, and he read scrolls that no one had seen for centuries. He would read of a battle, and then rush to see its representation in tapestry, or the scrolls would tell of a famous weapon, and he would go at once to see where it hung behind spindles or in a private cloister.

And he explored even beyond the knowledge of scribes. The folk of that city kept to the path as they went out and came in, but not he, not when his blood flowed with such a sparkling vigor and the distance called to him with wild, wonderful music. Exploring far out across the slope with a bag of food and a broad hat, he never heeded the clinging creepers and distance. He was at the edge of a high mountain, looking out over the land from a pile of tumbled boulders and scattered stones when he heard behind him the suggestion of a sound. Turning, he saw two other Sheewa, dark against the distance of the slope. He climbed down the hill and started back along the path he had cut in the vines, and when he was near enough to see their features one of them called out that he was required in Seng Grandt. Wondering what might come of this, he followed the two men, giving the land one final, loving look as he left it behind.

Today's bout would not be the commonplace beating and sparring he had undergone before. He knew it the moment he entered the old familiar hall and saw his adversaries. Fifteen of them stood in an open circle, hands behind their backs, and he thought he discerned wild aggression beneath their stance, passive though it seemed. The sun hurt his eyes as it shone through the high windows and reflected every detail of the lacquered paneling. A ploy to impede his vision, no doubt. They had chosen the right time of day.

Squinting, he walked into the center of the circle, to the very spot where he had suffered and bled for the past months. He was careful to keep his face passive as he stared into the eyes of a man across from him. A small fellow, with quick, nervous eyes. It was these eyes he watched.

Finally, the eyes widened, and Hunter turned to meet a vicious blow to the face, blocking and striking with the same snapping motion. The very moment the attacker went down, another came from the side with a long knife. It was blunted, but could still have searched his inward parts had he not side-stepped, twisted the weapon out of the Sheewa's grasp, and pushed him out of the way. One by one, they came out against him, some with bare hands, others wielding clubs or blades, and one by one they were disposed of. Where a few months ago his hands had been soft, now each of them found its mark like a stone from a sling. Where his reactions had been slow and deliberate, they were now automatic and unerring. His mind rode the center of the trail, darting left and right with each rapid strike and pull. Hands, knees, elbows, feet, all were used in short, simple movements that devastated his opponents. Above it all rose calm exultation as he began to comprehend that these men were holding nothing back.

The entire exercise lasted less than two minutes, but to Hunter the time stretched to great lengths as his mind raced, directing his body as a general commands his troops. At last, as he pulled a foe into his knee and threw him aside, the attacks ceased, and through the silence of the hall a voice echoed. "Well done, Hunter. Your training has served you well. You may retire to bed."

Hunter's pace was measured as he walked away, hands flexing, itching for another round. But he remembered his manners and stopped at the door to address his adversaries, some prone where they had fallen, but none badly hurt. "To my brothers, I am grateful. Unto you, I give respect."

High in the shadows of the upper hall, two old men sat. Hunter was impressive. He would never hear it from his teachers, but no one had ever progressed as he had. No one had ever learned so much in so little time. Necessity could account for that, but there was something deeper both men could see beneath every action. His motivations were different, somewhere far below the surface, even as Byorneth had said, and as the Sheewan ancestors had said of all the greatest monarchs, in the scrolls beneath their feet.

Byorneth eased back in his chair. "I believe he is ready now. He fights well, and neither of us has seen one so old master other tongues."

"Perhaps, my friend, but I have been wondering whether you are ready. Your vigor is such that I sometimes forget how near your age is to mine. The training could not have been an easy thing for you. Perhaps we ought to let you rest, live out your days in the city you ought never to have left."

Byorneth scowled but said nothing, and when Algorneth looked again the seat was empty. The old man rose and followed his friend out into the stone corridor that led to the archives, where Byorneth sat and leaned forward on a desk.

Algorneth shook his old friend by the shoulder. "What ails thee, Byorneth?"

Byorneth did not answer, but took a scroll down and rolled it out. Algorneth knew the impulse, the need to forget what was important before addressing it. At last, he rolled and replaced the vellum. "I have seen better than threescore and ten years, my friend, and I feel that for me there is very little time left. My days are running down like a diminishing tide, and there is no desire in me to perish in the High City."

Algorneth had never understood such feelings. A flamboyant, adventurous man in his youth, the eldest of the Sheewa had exhausted his wanderlust within five journeys, and now he wanted nothing more than to expire quietly in his sleep or over some ancient scroll. Men are the chanciest of all creatures.

"I am not so old that I no longer remember the Kyargh, Byorneth. It taxes the strongest of youth to its very limit, and even our ancient training will not put strength back into aged bones. You may harm Hunter should some ill befall you."

"Do you imagine that I have forgotten?" Byorneth snapped, then scowled to himself and gazed pitiably into Algorneth's eyes. "Forgive me, my brother. If I die while my son is so far away, I will utterly break. He is all I have, and I feel within my heart that much will hang upon our unity. I must go, whether the Keeper of the Slopes gives me leave or no."

He took down another scroll and read it for a time. Then, without looking away from the ancient words he said, "You know that Hunter has chosen his emblem?"

The Sheewan emblem is a family symbol worn by every scribe. It is passed down through the father and stitched into each Sheewa's tunic. Many are older than the city itself. Hunter, a new arrival, had the privilege of choice. "No, I had not heard. What image did he choose?"

"That of a falcon in flight with a serpent in its beak." A stranger might have thought the statement commonplace, but even Algorneth, who had attained a certain royalty by his years of waiting for the king, spoke slowly when at last he could breathe again.

"Did he know what he did?"

"No. The thing is unknown except by the highest order of scribes, as well you know."

Deep within the nether parts of the oldest levels of the city, there is a sealed cubicle within which is housed the secret scrolls. No one sees them but the few who have been bound to keep dark their secrets. The seal which emblazons the outer edge of one of those papers is that of the First Kings, a bird of prey carrying a snake. It had not been worn since those times.

The two graybeards spent the rest of the night in the bowels of the city, reading together. It was the only place in which they felt they were truly Sheewa, truly the advisers of kings. There they remained, and dreamt of glorious times.

The winter was fully upon them now.

Chapter 9

The Hunt

HOW MANY TIMES, WITH HUSHED HOORAY,
HAS TWILIGHT MET THE FALL OF DAY,
AND IN THE EVENING'S SETTING SWELL,
BADE RETURNING LIFE FAREWELL?

~The Meetings of the Morning~

Two men stopped to rest for the first time since the seventh watch. The sun stood directly above their heads now, and they were grateful for the cool breeze that rolled down upon them from the higher Hills. In the days since they had left the black Death Fields behind, they came through green meadows and up and down the rippling ridges that preceded the mountains themselves, every footstep strange, every feeling fresh. Teidin had not felt this way since the wildest times of his childhood, with the new discoveries of the old.

It seemed like presumption to enter the mountain range, so strange to their experience, so desperately cold that they bundled themselves up like Banat himself, but enter it they did. On their second day among the ranges, Elnaan shot a great red stag between two rocks, and they feasted gloriously beside their fire, the slave all but forgotten, Banat far away.

"There is snow up there." Elnaan pointed to the high peaks, white against the vivid blue. "And soon it will cover the flats as well."

"We might try to find a way around. There's the Great Trail, which they say runs straight up into the heart of the Hills. Why not go that way?"

Elnaan knew his brother was right, yet still he was reticent. The slave and her escort had come through the Death Fields toward the mountains, but the trail was long since cold, and they could lose nothing by going around. Still, it was good here in the mountains. The air was not yet brutally cold beyond the occasional whiff blown down from the High Hills, and there was a special beauty in the passes with their broad slants and upland pastures, the high ice and the bright little rivers quickly freezing over.

He stood so suddenly that he nearly spilled a little water from the bag, which he handed back to Teidin with a little smile. "Shall we go away to the West?"

They headed out of the Hills toward the easy ground. As if to hasten their journey, a bitter Hill squall came up and battered at their backs with driving snow, harrying them even as they walked out into the open once again.

But they still had the vast blue faces off to their left, strangely comforting companions to their travels, and as long as their austere bulks stood visible, there could be no doubt as to their place in the world. The lava fields began to impinge upon the right as they walked, and the contrast made them feel somewhat lopsided, beauty upon the one hand and shining death upon the other. The compromise came some distance later after a day had passed, and a night in the shadow of the mountains, where the edges of the Death Fields formed a vast network of lava worms, interspersed with the grass of the foothills, in which were all manner of little holes and caves where creatures might dwell.

For a long time, they walked together through the lava wasteland, jumping across narrow stretches of grass, watching for the little beings of the night that darted across the ground before their feet. Days passed, and as their hunger grew and their stock of stag disappeared, both men stopped to string their bows, continuing with a sharp eye for game. Twice, one or the other would nearly shoot at a flash of fur among the rocks, but new arrows are not easily made, and if they were to lose any, they preferred it were for a larger meal.

Then the snow mounted in a vast white pall over the mountains, and covered them over as they slept. From that moment, they were never entirely warm, and they saw the land through clouds of their own breath.

Then, gratefully, the smell of smoke and signs of clearing proclaimed the presence of man, and their bows were put away. But the wind was deceitful, and it was the better part of a day before they came upon the first of the little farms and houses where the last of the Lowlanders lived. Many were edified and defended by outer walls and ditches, remnants of a more violent time when marauders from the Upper Hills would descend and carry off whatever, and whomever, they desired. The brothers paid a little gold to a farmer in exchange for half a loaf and heavier coats, for they were anxious to reach the Great Trail before nightfall. They now had only a little gold left.

At last there came a long ridge of bare rock, and climbing it, they saw a thick lawn of grass prevailing all the way down the other side where the wind had cleared the early snow away.

A few goats trimmed the ground, tended by a little goatherd, alert and ready for trouble, who menaced them with his staff until they crossed, hands in sight, onto the Pass which lay before them. But surely this was only some side avenue, a prelude to the great and storied Trail itself. The Pass was a narrow one where the Hills split to admit the passage of travelers across the Sky Line, and in places the road was barely wide enough for two. Yet it was the Great Trail, and it carried the lifeblood of the Island, north and south in wave after beating wave, trampling the snow into a gray mess.

"Who could have known that this land held so many strange creatures?" Elnaan laughed as Teidin muttered the words under his breath. They stood at the edge of the Trail, reluctant to set foot in such a stream. "Do they walk out of the sea?"

"I suppose we could not expect them all to look like us." Allend's End was a large village as villages go, yet exceedingly small in its sphere. The brothers had barely ever seen a Hillman before, and these people dwelled in the border regions between the Hills and Lowlands, with the habits of both and the standards of neither being equally upheld. They would have seemed odd even to the folk in the Caldera, both in dress and manners. The speech too was strange, being a variety of Harniyen edging more and more toward Kyarrghnaal with every kand one walked toward the south. Nowhere in all the Island were there such conceits, for there between two worlds was such poverty and wealth that aristocracies had developed, as varied as the words they spoke.

"Well, perhaps they have food," Elnaan initiated, and led the way down to the Trail, drawing hardly any notice. As the brothers walked up the slight incline onto the beaten path, they found that only the intervening distance kept them from a clear sight of the sea far to the north. Not one traveler met their glance, no one so much as altered course to avoid them, but they were not men so easily to take offense. Southward they were bound, and southward they went, and naught but the gravest insult was likely to stay them.

Tea traffic, grain traffic, cattle traffic, and every other manner of traffic passed them by on the Upper Trail. Lowlands met Highlands in an uneasy, whirling pool. Now and again a cackling group of washerwomen would come by with bundles on their hips, swinging wide and speaking loud as befits women who maintain their own. Then would come a knot of soiled and stolid miners, heavy with toil and gold, and woe unto any that sought to waylay them, for each carried the curious spades and axes of their trade, and if the ancient walls of the mountains could not stay them, how much less could thieving flesh and blood? Especially wary of these creatures were those wealthiest of thieves, the landholders, who, loving the gold the miners carried, had all the more reason to shun them. All these traveled quickly to conclude their business before winter began in earnest.

The walking was easy, the forward view seductive, and the ground slipped away very quickly indeed. Soon enough, they came to a place where food was prepared and sold in a little meadow by the way. A man, woman, and a small child built and cooked delicacies upon an open grill, and a queue had formed which reached partway down the Trail. The smell had enticed them for a kual,[2] and they hurried to join the line.

Ahead of the brothers there stood a blister of boys, just past the age of concern, bristling and laughing at whatever they happened to see. These were Anandaans, the sons of

---

2   1/4 of a kand (0.65 of a mile/1 kilometer).

wealthy landholders, out for the day and feeling their elevated station. As such, they were not bothersome, for the brothers could remember a time when they had been much the same, secure under the auspices of a successful farm, swelling with pride and life. The line moved at its own pace, and soon the Anandaans were up to the grill.

"What seems good to you?" The man of the grill smiled broadly across the flames.

One of the boys, an extraordinarily sun-browned fellow in a thick cap, took three or four dainties from the side of the table in one fist and distributed them to his friends.

The man was affable yet. "Those cost two sections each."

With a grunt, the young man opened wide his mouth and put the whole piece in, then stooped, took up a handful of dark snow and dirt, and spread it evenly across the surface of the grill, spoiling every bite of food that lay ready to be eaten. At this, the boys in his train burst into extreme mirth, spitting out portions of the food they had stolen. "There are two sections of the Trail, my man. That should be good enough for such as you!"

The woman had already sent her son home, and now she stood beside her husband and the grill, her eyes wide, but glinting with steel.

"We wanted to eat here too." It was Elnaan's quiet tone, and Teidin set himself for trouble. "Pay the man."

Like one body, the youths turned to face the brothers, who were now all alone in the line. Slowly, the leader lifted his leg and almost negligently kicked over the brazier, spilling the glowing charcoal into the snow, where it sizzled and died. No sooner had he completed the motion than he was on his back, cradling his pouring nose.

Elnaan had already stepped over him and begun his rapid, deadly dance. Before the boy could recover, his friends decorated the Trail all around in various states of ill health.

The tall shadow of Elnaan fell across the boy, and the voice repeated, "Pay the man. If you're too poor, then you can work to redeem the debt."

At the affront, the rich man's son slapped Elnaan's hand aside and climbed to his feet. His fist swung around in a slow arc, but before it reached halfway Elnaan's darted in like a snake and crunched into the center of the indignant face. Once more, he lay in the dust.

Eyes streaming, the boy held his nose and groaned foul curses through his own blood. He might have quit the fight had he not seen the woman and her husband standing by their ruined venture, looking grimly on his ruined face. Once more, he came up with a low, mad cry and lunged with all the strength he could summon, intent on dragging Elnaan down with him.

It was as though Elnaan was back at work in the fields, as with one effortless movement he reached over the miscreant's shoulder, seized him by his belt and flipped him across his knee. A quick jerk had his breeches down, and with a long series of broad blows, he rendered the white backside ruddy and glowing.

Red at both ends, the rich man's son took one more ineffectual swipe at Elnaan, which sent him sprawling in the snow yet again. With that, the humbled youth ran away weeping through the snow, pulling his breeches back up between bounds, and the rest slunk away after him.

"This was all he carried." Elnaan gave the man ten gold pieces and scooped up enough raw food for himself and

Teidin, who had already helped the woman to set the brazier upright again.

Without a backward glance, they walked away together down the Trail.

⌒ᴧᴧ⌒

Seng Grandt had never been self-sufficient, nor had the Sheewa ever intended that it should be. The Hills above, beyond the swath of slope, were abundantly rich in meat and herbs, and any who felt inclined for a little exercise could make the journey. Over the centuries, a hard path had been worn up the great incline, and its entire length had been laid with flags of stone to ease the journey. It was inadvisable, and frankly forbidden, for any to venture this way alone.

There are any number of solitary places in the High City, but on this day there had come upon Hunter a burning need for unhampered steps where the soft earth would cradle his feet, and he cared not to share these joys with anyone else. Still, there were very good reasons for each rule given, and it was unwise at any time to walk into the mountains without a companion. Today, he was regretfully accompanied by a stony man, Hastraneth, who said not a word as he led the way up the long slope and finally into the rocky seclusion of the narrow Hunting Pass.

The Sheewan cloak suited Hunter well, thought of with the long traveler in mind, and perfected over 500 years. The lack of a sword, however, troubled him, and the mule driver in him missed the short sword. The hooked dagger was a fearsome weapon at close range, and useful for cutting brush, but even with the bow slung across his back, he felt unsafe with so small a blade.

There was no direct way from the city into the Caldera itself, and yet as they climbed into the sacred silence of altitude, he could not help but remember the journeys of his mule train, and how his heart would leap within him as they crossed the Sky Line into the old, true Hills. He had been happy to live in the city, to take joy in his lessons, and there had been no cause to regret his lot until this moment. But regret it he did.

Ever since his first sight of them, the Hills had beguiled him with the rough complexity of their peaks and gullies, their expressive, internal language. As they walked higher, Hunter stopped and turned to look at the city behind them, the broad belt of snow that covered the land so brightly, the tiny line of the distant forest. He even fancied he could see the Lowland farms, and marveled that two such worlds could be in such proximity, the inhabitants of one so unaware of the other.

Hastraneth never saw anything. His eyes stayed on the path, never straying to the Hills around him, never indulging themselves with the least little transgression against their sacred purpose. The man was oval faced, and his beard showed only a few small traces of frost in it, but one might have thought him in the twilight of life for all the joy he showed. At last, Hunter could stand it no longer, and halted on the Trail. "Why are we so hurried? There's no hot meal awaiting us, and the weather is warm for the time of year."

The man kept on at a testy gait. "Rest if you must. While there's daylight, we should travel. I like no place but the city."

It seemed years since Hunter had been in the free air, and his lungs craved it. They had provisions for three nights if needed, and he had experience of travel at the head of a mule train. The Sheewa spoke again, a little farther down the path.

"While there is daylight, we travel. Come along. We are out for meat, nothing else."

"Do you see no beauty out here? Are you not refreshed by the breeze? Come, let's go slower, at least. This Island is our home! The city has cramped me many months, and the Sheewa ought to rejoice in their journeys!"

The man never answered or gave any heed. Before Hunter's words were finished, he had increased his pace, but when next he turned and looked, the young man was gone.

The snow had fallen less thickly in the higher Hills than on the beaten path, but even the snow and its coat of ice delighted his steps. He climbed where he did not need to, pulled himself up using the rocks and evergreen bushes. His erstwhile companion had begun to call his name from the Trail, but the game had already started, and there was little difference between a scolding now and a scathing later. He had been told they were there to hunt, and he had his bow with him, so what harm could there be?

A cluster of white goats on a far-off hillside scattered when he appeared, and he marveled to see them so close, to smell the strange life of the mountains, so different from that of the Lower Plain, or even the High City. But his mind had begun to be troubled by his transgression, and for a moment he sorted through a string of plausible explanations for his unannounced leave. His path back to the Trail was still clear in his mind, and so finally he returned. He was bracing himself for the slide down the slanted stones onto the original path when he stopped and crouched low.

Hastraneth was where he had last seen him, now accompanied by two rough men, with another watching from the rocks across the way. From his position, Hunter could see the bow and shaft the high watcher wielded, but it was unlikely that Hastraneth could see it from the trail.

"We do not want gold. We do not need it. Undress." The man who spoke carried a long knife, almost a sword, with which he tickled the indignant Sheewa's beard. In the other hand, he held the bow he had taken away.

Their pedigree was plain to see — Hillmen who, whether by ill fortune or desperate preference, had turned to the trade of robbery.

"You intend to kill me. So do it."

"I would, Longfarer, but we need new clothes. I do not love work so much that I would sweat to undress your dead body. Take them off yourself." He shivered a little as he spoke, hungering after the Sheewan cloak and leggings as he would after treasure.

The scowling Sheewa did not hurry in divesting himself of his garments. The weapon was ready in Hunter's hands, and no one had seen him. If he were to shoot the man high up on the crags, the lower ones would kill their prisoner. If he chose the lower bandits, the higher would doubtless manage a shot before he could account for him. The man had very nearly finished undressing.

Smoothly, he pulled the bolt back and let it fly downward, his eyes fixed upon the mark. The instant it went, he knew it would fly true, and by the time Hastraneth had disarmed and killed the other, Hunter had already shot at the man in the rocks. But this one had already rolled out of sight even as he saw his friends go down. The Sheewa below pulled the knife out of the man's belly and called up, "Did you shoot true?"

"No."

"Well, run and finish it! It was all your doing, and if he warns his fellows, we may never again see the City! Go!"

In three mad, reckless strides Hunter reached the Trail, and hardly slowing he dashed up into the rocks. Now the ice hindered him, and his stiff toes struggled painfully against the climb. Soon, he stood where the bandit had lain, and immediately dropped as an arrow whistled by his nose.

"Get out there!" Hastraneth called from below, and with a groan Hunter rolled off the high ridge, running and sliding down the glazed slope in a low crouch. The ground was all but barren of snow, and the ice gave little sign, but Hunter's many hours on game trails served him well. The occasional bare patch among the frosty rocks, a bent plant here and a footprint there, showed his enemy's passage, and he covered the slope in a low run, darting back and forth against another shot. That last bolt had come too near.

Another arrow flew by, farther off this time, and he did not drop. In drawing aim, the man had exposed himself to view, and Hunter rolled the rest of the way down the hill as he saw him nock, ready to shoot again. As Hunter came to his feet the bandit moved again, darting from cover to cover, and Hunter dared not stop for a shot himself. As he came near, he dropped his bow and quiver and drew his hooked dagger, the point up. His adversary held to his refuge behind the great rock, and as Hunter climbed silently up, he saw the man crouching below, as silent as himself, but in great fear. Then the wretch saw him and raised his bow to shoot up, but Hunter was already descending upon him and knocked the bow away into the snow.

It was a brief, bitter struggle, for the man had a knife of his own which searched for a home in Hunter's chest. For a brief instant, his hazel eyes met the man's gray ones, fixed with the same desperation that must have been in his own. Hunter's training deserted him at first, but then his body remembered its paces and he rolled over, tossing his enemy across into the rocks with a fierce kick. Before the man could recover, Hunter was on him, plunging his blade into his heart up to the hilt.

The hook remained where it was for a time as Hunter sat and blankly watched the life drain out of the man. Unseeing, his eyes drifted away straight ahead, but it was only after he retrieved his knife and wiped the gore on the folds of the fellow's rags that his eyes rested on a very strange rift in the rocks which marked the end of the little tortured valley. Beyond the stones he saw a vista, very remote, blue with intervening sky.

Like a dead man, Hunter walked back to the Trail, weaving only a little, feeling neither cold nor sunshine. Precisely how he reached the Trail he would never know, but it was only then he realized with blank wonder that his nose had bled all down his front, and there was a large cut over his left eye. Somewhere along the way he had retrieved his bow, and now he slung it across his back and put the dagger back into its place. The fellow had bled all over his hands. The breeze nipped at him hungrily, and mechanically he flexed his fingers against it. The snow had begun to fall heavily.

When at last he drifted back down the slope, the sun had gone far down to the west. What had happened to the day he did not know. The feeling began to creep back into his soul again, shadowy emotions far off in the fog of his mind. It was only when he rested his shoulder against the dark stone of Seng Grandt's walls that the fullness of his pain came to him, and he cried out quietly to himself. A few tears froze his beard to the stones, and several hairs pulled out as he drew away.

He entered the ancient doors and walked the halls of the old sanctuary, feeling every eye on him, every look that seemed to read him like a scroll. A chief characteristic of a young man is his great and abiding fear of youth, of the exposure of immaturity. He had run off like a wayward infant, and the entire city must have known it. And the blood still covered his lower arms, spattered finely across his face.

He only barely made it to his chambers before he started to weep, sobbing into his bloody hands as he leaned against the closed door, heedless of the snow that melted into a reddened puddle all around him. He slid down the door and remained there for quite some time.

He slept on the bare stones that night.

⌒ㅅㅅ⌒

Far away, across a wild maze of passageways and echoing halls, an indignant scribe gave a report to Byorneth and Algorneth in a chamber far removed from all assemblage. The old men listened with an unchanging look, and as soon as his anger was vented, he was quietly dismissed, still fuming. For a long time, the old men said nothing.

"The fool ought at least to have stayed to see that Hunter lived. He left the boy alone to hunt the man down himself. He is an elitist cull."

"It was the boy's doing, the whole trouble." Algorneth was less sympathetic, less willing to blame a Sheewa of good standing. "He is undisciplined, he wandered away the moment his guide was not looking. This would never have happened with a man like Arneth."

"Arneth! That pasty fellow! Hunter has more of manhood in his smallest finger! He has walked a greater distance in his lifetime than any Sheewa. For nearly ten months now you have imprisoned him in this tomb, and you are all astonished when he, a man both older and younger than all of us, chafes at solitude. The time has come and gone when he should have been sent out on a journey. Turn him loose! Let him stride freely again!"

The elder Sheewa laughed slowly. "And you, my friend? Might not this reproof have a double edge? Often I have seen you pace up and down the long halls of a night, when reasoning men seek the comfort of their beds. When you came again into the city, I rejoiced to see my greatest friend at rest at last. But the cold bones of the Island are the only bed for yours." It was a tone that would accept no reply, and not even Byorneth dared give one.

All seemed well with Hunter as he drifted into the hall to eat, but all the people, young and old, spoke of him. He had not the strength to face any but Byorneth, and so it was there that he sat down. There were no words, no sounds besides those of chewing. All that might have been said was already on the lips of every Sheewa, and Byorneth knew that Hunter had not joined company this morning for words so much as for the comfort of silence.

All men who ever lived stood together in condemnation against him, and because of his childish selfishness there were none who would ever trust him. All these thoughts and more hung, mute and heavy, before his eyes, mocking him to his face. Foremost and brightest in vision was the darkest spectacle of them all — that of a small moment when a man had cringed as his heart was breached, spilling red life over Hunter's hands. Water could never wash the death away.

Byorneth took his last bite and got to his feet, and Hunter thought he had left when a hand clenched around the bones of his shoulder with a sudden violence that nearly made him cry out. "Come with me." There could be no debate. Hunter dropped the last of the bread on his plate and followed his friend out onto a veranda out of sight of anyone else. Once there, the old man closed the door and pushed Hunter back into the hard wall, and Byorneth's crooked nose almost touched his.

"Oh, villainy! Tell me all that happened out in the mountains, or by my word I will cast you from this place myself! You took to the rocks to foil the bandits, because you saw them coming to rob you! You fell behind and lost the tracks of your companion! Tell me anything, only tell me!" With each explosive sentence, he drove Hunter backward with a force that made his head ring, until an answer shook itself out.

"None! None of that is true!" Hunter gasped the freezing air. "I walked away! I went out among the rocks on my own, because I wanted to see new things! I ran back to the Trail, and the bandits were there! Hastraneth knows! Ask him!"

Byorneth released him, and began to look more sad than angry, turning and leaning his elbows on the stone rail as he looked out toward the west. "He gave his report, but I never believed him until now. No matter. If you had not wandered away, you would have been taken by those men yourself, and be lying dead instead of them."

There was so much more for Byorneth to know, how the man had died at his hand, not a target for his arrow, but close to him, and how he still remembered the silent plea of the man's eyes, felt the thick heat of the welling blood. The words silenced themselves in his throat. It was for him alone to know.

"You are very young, my son." The old man continued without turning around. He pulled the edge of his cloak up against the high wind. "The young do foolish things, even such as you. I may have done a few myself."

Here was a branch, and Hunter clung to it. "Which things?"

He half expected Byorneth to be annoyed at his insistence, but instead he sighed. "It was perhaps my 17th year. The waters had begun to run in the mountains, and the new wind blew life into the old city and subjugated the minds of young men. One day, I stood in this very place with two others like myself, and we saw that an exceedingly large pool had gathered right below. I said, 'The sun is hot, and this place is a tomb, but there is plenty of relief to be had only paces outside our gates.'

"The rush of the moment was full upon us, and we ran out to the first room and pulled off our robes. Out we dashed into the sunlight and felt the kind sun on our bare skin, chasing away the winter. The pool was cold. No one was there to see us. I thought I had never felt truly young before, and I am sure that I have never felt younger since."

The irritable lines around his mouth spread into an unaccustomed smile at the memory. "Wet, grimy, smeared from head to foot with clay, we ran barefoot across the clinging hillside, falling over the undergrowth with every step. We were laughing when we came once again to the gate, but we fell gravely silent when the door would not give. We beat upon it and cried our loudest, but no one heard. Some conscientious Sheewa had seen the door hanging open while on his rounds and locked it behind us."

Hunter's chin began to twitch, and he grinned at the image the tale conjured up.

"At last, we had to make the long walk down the slope into the orchards and ask the folk there for clothing. All that we met were matronly women, and one by one they laughed, and one by one, still laughing, they told us they had no clothing. When at last four big sacks were found and fashioned into tunics, every planter from the Death Fields to the Slopes knew, and I think that their mirth could have been heard even up to the High City. When at last we walked up the path, none of us could prevent the planters from trooping along behind us like a giggling army, and with their combined shouts at last the Sheewa heard and opened the door.

"We thought our troubles were over, but with the first wide-eyed scribe who saw us, they all began again. You think the Sheewa a staid, gray people, humorless and hardened? Walk among them nearly naked and smeared all over with clay and tell me that again!"

Hunter had not laughed in a long time, and it was long before he was finished.

Chapter 10
The Spring

HAVE I TRULY LET OUR SCRIBES UPON THE WORLD,
OR UNLEASHED ITS FINAL TEMPEST?

~The Keeper of the Slopes, Upon the Occasion
of the First Sending of the Sheewa~

He would always remember one day especially, toward the end of his training, when the spring had begun to touch the edges of the earth, and fuse the snow into ice. After an unending session of fighting in which he acquitted himself well, having been knocked down only once and fought his way to his feet again, he was allowed a day of rest. As soon as his teachers set him free, his steps naturally inclined toward Srstri's chambers.

She smiled when she opened the door and saw him. "Would you care to walk in the orchards with me?" he asked.

"I would, thank-you! Let me fetch my coat." She took it down from its hook and they walked together out of the city, down through the gardens and vineyards among passing workers, talking of nothing in particular.

Many of the workers, especially the women, were known to Srstri. Though they spoke in a strange dialect, they were of Hill stock, and Srstri had enjoyed cultivating acquaintances among them as they cultivated their crops. One woman in particular was friendly to her, and looked up from hoeing a garden as they passed, greeting them in a loud voice and smiling to see them together. Her husband was a Sheewa, and so she wiped away a sympathetic tear and returned to work.

They passed a grove of apple trees, the same ones they had seen on that first day. There was no fruit yet, only the wet new leaf buds fighting their way into the light. Although Srstri had long understood something big and dangerous was brewing inside this young man, her mind was closed and happy. The danger was nearer now than ever, but she ignored the warning note within her.

"You are going away soon?" she asked in comfortable Huaynił, somewhat formal in keeping with their royal home.

He was unwilling to think of their parting. "Yes. I'm going with Byorneth to the land beyond the Hills."

Anything beyond the Hills might just as well have been beyond the moon. Somehow, it distressed her that he should be so far away. "Why can't you stay? There is a good life for you here. I would think you'd had enough traveling."

"Do you want me to stay?"

"I only wondered. Why do you go about to change things if you are happy here?"

"Byorneth said that I should."

"Why do you obey him? You are free! Stay if you want, or go elsewhere. Anywhere."

"Yes, I am free. That is why I choose to go with him."

He took hold of her hand, and it seemed natural and right. "Srstri, I am free to choose whom I will follow."

It was wisdom such as is denied even to kings, and certainly Srstri had never considered it. There had never been anyone to teach her, for her parents had known nothing but freedom, and therefore knew nothing of freedom. Neither of them knew that in that moment, the new kingdom had begun.

Then they were quiet, and there followed a noisy silence filled with the sparrows' twittering and scattered singing of workers, busied with their labors. It was nearing the early harvest, and the winter fruits were just being picked. The snow was gone from the slopes in the heat of an early spring, and through the last stubborn crust there grew tiny flowers of yellow and blue.

They still held hands, neither venturing to part them. "Srstri," he said finally, and she met his eyes, which nearly undid him. "I hardly know you, and you hardly know me, but would you be very surprised to learn that of everything and everyone here in this place, I will miss being with you most of all?" He had taken her hand in both of his, clinging like a drowning man.

The trouble had come all at once, but she recovered quickly. "I think I know what you mean, Hunter. I will miss you too. You've become my greatest friend in this city. Please do nothing to change that."

He bit his lip and turned his head for a moment. Having staked all on one toss of the dice and lost, he put up a brave show and smiled. "I suppose I'll have to be satisfied with that."

They went on talking about other things, and Hunter replied, smiled and laughed as though he were alive, but Srstri was not fooled. His eyes never regained their cheer, and his tone retained a base note of sorrow even in laughter. Finally, at her suggestion they walked back home, and it was just as well, for the world was darkening as they strode wordlessly up the long path and down the long corridor that led to their chambers, dogged and mocked by their own weird shadows, so that they drew near to one another without knowing it. Too soon, they reached their rooms where they stood a moment in the hallway, unsure of how to part.

"I enjoyed our time today, Hunter." She stepped backward a little as she spoke, anxious to be out of harm's way.

"Thank-you. So did I."

He reached out once more and held her arm for a moment, at which she smiled. Then he gave her a simple goodnight, and she vanished behind her unforgiving door. Hunter closed his own and lay on his bed without undressing, staring into the gloom, savoring a new, exquisite pain. Finally, he slept without dreaming, but when he awoke the ache was still fresh.

—∧—

In all the broad Caldera, there could not have been a more desolate place. On hillsides all around there was lush lawn or tea, and higher up along the Hills great stands of timber, but here on this plateau there was only gray sand with a few feeble blades of green for company. After the long winter, Teidin found that these were not enough. He desired color, the tumultuous sounds of daily labor, but most of all food and company, though in these last months he had not managed to pick up more than a few words of Kyarrghnaal.

But this place did afford them the best possible view of the whole Crater, and the eyes of man are never full of the far sights. They felt like giants in the land, parting the clouds with their fingertips. Yet the distance they had come since they crossed the Sky Line was nothing to the vastness which lay off to the south.

"Do you suppose we ought to go home?" Teidin's mouth was half full of bread, purchased from a householder with money they had earned chopping wood. "We are looking for a dark woman in a Crater full of dark people."

"Well said." The other brother had finished eating, and stropped his knife on the sole of his boot. "Mother and our sisters will be wondering about us. Iblar is there to help them, but he has his own holding to worry about. Maybe he's suffered enough for us."

At last, they determined to return to the Pass another way, seeing all there was to see of the land, for the day was fair, and they were in no hurry. The people along their journey had been friendly, but not intrusive. It seemed one could make a decent living by simply traveling back and forth across the Caldera, accepting what was given. If only for this reason, they wanted to be back in the Lowlands, working on their own land once more. But until then the Hills were broad, the air bracing, the tea strangely delicious and exhilarating. It had been fully two hours since the farmer had served them three cups of his signature leaf and sat with them telling stories, but their thoughts still raced as clearly as the spoked sunbeams that touched the earth far below them.

Even through the winter, especially the few months at the end when they were both convinced the elements had conspired together to kill them, the Hillfolk took them in. Any one of the simple families would gladly have taken as many strangers into their house as they had beds, but the young men had not come this far to languish in a dug-out hut.

Even in the deep snow, the country was magnificent. The months had vanished with the killing winds, and now especially they regretted leaving. Neither led the way, but each wandered at his leisure out across the slopes, now thick with high grass. They kept one another in sight always, but that hardly hampered them since their sight could extend as far as a kual in such air. They were children again, running to and fro to see everything until hours were wasted in discovery. At last, the desolate plateau they had come from was but a thin pale line against the southern horizon.

Teidin called out to Elnaan across the vast sward, and he came running. The younger brother was sitting on the grass, which dropped off sharply like a bench, giving way to a lower bed of rock which curved into a tunnel straight through the heart of a mountain.

"Looks like the mountain's mouth."

"Let me have a piece of bread, will you?"

They sat for a while eating together (in their excitement at this new land, they had quite forgotten how hungry they were), and looked into the hole. The shadow of the rocks fell precisely across the cavern's mouth, and so nothing was visible as little as five paces into the bowels of the mountain. "Seems to be calling us forward," Elnaan said, and Teidin nodded. Its forbidding nature enticed the young men.

They did not discuss it, there was no indecision. They simply finished eating and walked forward into the rock.

The invisible, cool hands of the Hills touched their faces as they came forward, and soon they brought more clothing out of their gear and thickened their layers against the chill of the dank walls. The tunnel was smooth all the way through, cut many eons before by a flaming wash of lava before the Hills had been settled. The light of the world outside faded, and they walked painstakingly in the darkness until at last the sunshine from the other side grew clearer.

They came out into a different world. Nothing of its character was familiar, not a weed or flower to remind them of what they had left behind. All was a wonderful confusion of boulders and heaps of smaller rocks, filling the bottom of the little canyon. And yet it was not a canyon, for it was cut off at both ends, and there was no water but for a small spring which burbled down the sheer walls across from them.

Where Teidin would have returned to the Caldera immediately, Elnaan's heart leapt at the sight, and he set out across the rocks, gaining in the zeal of adventure as he climbed and slid through the tortured landscape. His brother sat down to rest and watch, satisfied to leave such a land alone.

All at once Elnaan disappeared, and when he did not reappear, his brother called his name. There was no answer.

He found Elnaan crouched in a space between the rocks, wider than the others, where a rare patch of grass still flourished. Where he knelt there was one boulder set apart from its fellows. While the other stones were bare and ragged at the edges, this was entirely smooth, and a coat of moss grew on its shaded surface twice as thick as that on the stones all around. Elnaan held a lump of this in his hand and looked at the marks he had uncovered.

The written word was by no means in constant use among the Lowlands, although the more learned, or pretentious, of the Harniyen might learn a few characters. These letters were nothing like the ones they knew. Elnaan stared as if he might force their meaning from them.

"Let's go back. It was much better over on the other side." Teidin laid his hand on Elnaan's shoulder, and the kneeling man started as though from a dream. They could have known the significance of the stone, or its placement. Translated freely from the Old Tongue of bygone kings, it was a dire warning against those who would disturb a tomb or sanctuary, threatening the vengeance of those long forgotten.

Even though Elnaan could read none of it, a measure of its reverence had touched him across the ages.

He might have continued exploring this valley, but he bowed to his brother's words. They hoisted their packs and started back toward the tunnel.

But the tunnel was not to be found. Where it should have been was only smooth rock.

This country was of a deeper character than they had thought. All around them were holes in the mountain, any of which may have been theirs. Cursing themselves for their carelessness, they began to explore in earnest, but at the end of an hour of separate searching, they met once more among the boulders.

"Have you seen the inside of that cavern?" Teidin pointed away toward the end of the hollow where it tapered away into a dark corner.

Elnaan shook his head. "Perhaps. I may have been in any one of them. We should start there and work our way all around the edges together, missing nothing."

The day was already waning, and now they searched with a redoubled will. Even Elnaan would have preferred to spend the night on a soft bed of Calderan grass. There had come upon him the old homesickness, the flash of childhood which may overtake any man in the darkening hours, when sleep calls and he cannot answer.

But the smell of this first hole was different, not dead and stale as the others had been, nor yet as fresh as the opening for which they sought, but bespeaking an even greater stillness, a death-in-life of living things, wanting of the open air. Elnaan would have gone on to the next, but Teidin stopped him. "Wait. There is something alive back there. How long has it been since we ate?"

His brother nodded, and silently they strung their bows and stepped into the darkness. As they ventured farther into the heart of the Hills, the smell became fouler, and their noses rebelled from breathing it in. Their steps inclined downward as they walked, farther toward the fires which they had been taught still burned in the bowels of the earth.

They had not gone but a few steps before Elnaan stopped in his tracks. "Brother, this place is dark, and we are but two. Whatever creature lives in this place, it has lived long enough to grow very large. I should not like to die for the sake of one meal."

Hunger argued against his words, but Teidin knew he was right. They turned about, and were almost in the light again when the wind changed and it whistled across the mouth of the cavern. As the piercing note faded away, there came another far behind them in the darkness, a lower tone like the moaning of the mountain itself, and an orange light flashed dully across the far stones of the passage, and then died again. Their first thought was that the mountain, sitting on a bed of fire, had groaned and shifted in its sleep, but then a puff of air breathed in their faces. They knew the smell of wood smoke.

Where there was fire, there was man, and all men ate. Once again they turned and walked into the chamber with greater confidence. They went into total darkness until there appeared a little fire in the darkest recesses of a large chamber, a fire which wavered between life and death and dimly illuminated a creature, huddled all by itself over the warmth in perfect stillness. A few strings of hair hung over its brow, and by its wrinkles and the state of its clothing, it may have been a preserved corpse, propped by the fire as a gruesome jest.

"It's been long to be waiting for you to come." The voice was slow and dusty with disuse. They wondered that it spoke

Harniyen, albeit a dialect so strange and mangled that at first they hardly knew it. Very slowly, the brothers came up to the fire, weapons still ready, but hanging by their sides. The man did not look up to see them as they approached, but remained crouched by the smoldering coals, staring across at the indefinite gray walls of the inner mountain.

"May we sit at your fire?"

The man never acknowledged their words, or even their presence. But they lived by a code of manners, even if this man did not, and knew better than to sit down until invited to do so.

At last he turned toward them and looked on their faces. "Do you know that I was hearing you from the first? Even before you were stumbling into my home. You were being very loud."

"May we share your fire for a while? By thanks we could help with the expense of your next meal."

A spark of life lit the man's eyes. "Keep you your gold. To me thanks is being a rarer thing. Hold here."

He stood a little stiffly, and they were surprised at the man's height. His hair was long and of indeterminate color, as was his beard, just thin enough to show every hollow of his flinty face. He walked backward into the cave with his front toward them, and reaching behind retrieved a crude leather bag, which he carried over and laid delicately between them on the rocks, motioning for them to sit.

The bag was full of an unnatural mixture of water, seeds and grease, all stoppered with a plug of bone. The food was nourishing if rancid, and they thanked him very kindly as one by one they choked a mouthful down. Almost at once, their day caught up with them there in the warmth of the fire, and before they could drag out their blankets, they were asleep on the floor.

Strange and unknowable things flitted through Teidin's slumbers that night, shades of light and dark across his mind. Their chain was brought to an abrupt end by a strangled cry in the utter blackness and a frantic scuffle in the rocks, which began a long, loud journey from one end of the cave to the other and back again. Teidin's dagger was out, but the fire was nearly dead and he could not see to thrust it. He laid hands on a pile of tinder and threw it on the darkening coals, which flared into life again.

When the red light glared against the rocks around them, Elnaan lay against the far wall pinning the old man to his chest, holding his dagger against the creature's throat. Teidin came and held him as Elnaan crawled out and away.

The creature's eyes went quickly from one to the other, but there was nothing in his lean form to suggest fear. "You can be killing me now," he said calmly, and laid his head back down on the floor to wait.

"We carry nothing with us to make a killing worth the trouble, and we meant no harm to you or to your home. Why then did you strike at me?"

It seemed a natural question, but as it was asked, the strange man showed emotion for the first time in the form of surprise. "You must have been expecting it. How could you have been coming here and not have known that I would be trying to murder you?" At their silence, he sat up and addressed himself to the ceiling high above. "Could it be that you were not knowing? That by accident you were coming here?"

"We wanted food and shelter, nothing else."

"All of which I was giving you."

"And nearly ended your hospitality at the end of a dagger. Now why?"

The strange creature pondered for a long time, looking now toward the cave entrance as though planning escape, and now to the far cavern wall. At last he crawled on his hands and knees halfway toward them and crouched there. "I can be showing you if you like!" he whispered with a shy smile, then snatched a flaming stick from the fire and motioned for them to follow him into the farthest corner.

The walls met the floor with a gentle curve, and they saw no variation in its surface until the man disappeared into the floor, and the torch with him. Elnaan followed him through first, his blade out and ready, but before his brother could come through, he called back for him to fetch another light. The hole was only just large enough for Teidin's body, and once through it he fell straight down into a second, lower chamber where he crumpled and came forward on his hands, nearly burning his face on the torch he carried. He straightened up and shone the light all about him.

He could not see the floor for all that was scattered over it, even to the limits of his vision. Wherever the torchlight fell, it came back a lusty yellow, for there was gold here such as 50 men would take a year to count, coins of Old Arlinga and of nations beyond the sea. Scattered throughout the chamber, rearing up as out of a golden ocean, were swords and spears, handled with ivory and gold and studded all over with innumerable precious gems of all colors. Whale figures of the old kind, some small, some the height of a grown man, carved from deep blue lapis, bright marble and glimmering aventurine, breached through the gold never to crash back again, their deep emerald eyes coolly surveying their home of 500 years or more. Out of a great central basket, long powdered with age, had been spilled all manner of uncut precious stones — sapphires, rubies, emeralds, garnets of every color, glimmering shards of opal from the West, Arhamin stones, and others unknown even in the High City. As the torches moved to and fro, Teidin wondered at a large tree growing near the wall of the cave until he saw that it too was of gold, extravagantly festooned with leaves of bright jade, each one a work of intricate genius, fruits of purple and red, and even delicate birds nesting in the branches of twisted wire gold, feeding their gaping young. All around the chamber were more of these, pines, cedars and oaks, all perfect in every detail. At last he realized he was holding his breath, and he gasped.

In the center of the room, Elnaan stood tall, gazing all about him, until at last he looked back and met Teidin's eyes, as wide as his own.

"This is being my treasure." The old man squatted and thrust his hands into the gold. "I am loving it greatly."

As zealously as Hunter trained in the High City, his old friend surpassed him. In the many years of his absence, the knowledge of the Sheewa had weeded over inside him, and there was much unlearning to do before he would be ready to go out into the Island with Hunter. He fought until his old bones cried out for rest, and then he fought longer and harder. The tongues of the West, which had slumbered for so long in his mind, he learned again, step by weary step. And all along the way there were his teachers, young and proud, ready to rejoice at his humiliation. He took their teaching and profited in spite of them, until the old man who watched from the upper shadows of the room laughed to himself.

Finally, at the end of their time, Byorneth and Hunter stood together at the great doors of the city, ready to set off upon their journey. Each carried his long dagger and staff against hostility and the chances of the road, a bag with writing instruments, the necessaries for making ink, and plenty of paper. Slung across their backs were large bags scientifically packed with heavy coats, boots and hats against the harsh air of the Hills. They were as ready as a year's training could make them.

Hunter had said all his goodbyes but one. She watched them from a balcony as they walked with their weighty packs down the long, winding path away from her, losing every feature in turn until at last they were but smudges against the green of the orchards. In less than an hour, they vanished around the first bend, and then there came a familiar ache behind her eyes. Quickly, she turned away from the round ledge and walked back through echoing hallways to her chambers. She sat on the edge of her bed, and absently gathered the covers up into her arms. Why the tears came she did not know, but something within her welcomed them.

She looked forward to nothing as she sat in thought. All the friends she had made in her stay were gone to help with the first summer harvest. Where before the city had been a haven, it seemed to her now a gray, forbidding place of cold stone and dead history, a sullen tomb of morningless night.

There came a knock at the door and she dropped the blankets like hot coals. Wiping her eyes, she opened the door to Algorneth, who stood smiling outside in the hall.

The Keeper of the Slopes began with a low rumble to reassure himself. "My dear, have you been quite comfortable in your time here among us?"

"Very much, thank-you. Has there been any complaint?"

"Oh, no! No, no, no. We have all been happy to have you here, and it pains me exceedingly to address you in this fashion. Pray be thou mindful of my past kindnesses, and suffer me to live in the scrolls of thy remembrance as a dear and most staunch friend." In his discomfort, he had lapsed into formal speech, and Srstri could not help but lay her hand on his.

"It's quite alright," she whispered, hoping to engender confidence. "Go on and tell me. We have been good friends."

He chuckled and sat down on the chair in the corner, his snowy beard covering his chest in an upward curl. "You have learned how important the ancient laws of hospitality are to our people. Have all been honorable in their treatment of you?"

"Yes, very much! For the first time in my life, I am a guest, and not a slave."

"Ah, very good! Yes!" Then he stopped, lingering a while before coming to his real business. "It gives me great sorrow to end all this. You have made a great many friends in your time here, and we all care for you. We will give you all you need for your journey — food and clothing, even an escort, but I wish above all else that you could stay here."

Srstri blinked. "I've long known that I should leave, and now that my friends are gone, there is nothing to hold me. In truth, I desire the cool breath of the Hills, to see my own again."

"It is only that we have so many unmarried men among us, and seeing as you are unattached, and so very — very desirable—" He found himself lost again and stood up as if to leave, but Srstri only laughed and kissed him on both cheeks.

"I will miss you very much, Algorneth."

"And I you. I do not think we will meet again." Then, embracing her as a father would his only daughter, he whispered in her ear with the sudden confidence of wisdom. "Stay with him, Srstri, whatever happens. You are at the crux of his future."

———∧∧———

With urgent steps, the old man Algorneth walked down into the archives. He had rarely gone this way, but he knew it well. There were only two places where guards were necessary down in the depths — this had been the first place. The man was wide awake, and brought his weapon to readiness as he saw the shadow coming out of the subterranean twilight. He relaxed as Algorneth became clear, but true to his training, he remained alert.

"Have you been asleep?" Algorneth's voice was sharp, and the man was taken aback. He had never been doubted before.

"I have not, Keeper. And my brother guard has not. No one has passed me, that much I know, and I will swear to it."

Impatient, the old man took the guards' torch from the wall, went past him and used the huge key that hung around his neck to unlock the secure door with a scraping that set hair on end. Immediately, he shut the door behind him.

All was as it should have been. A table stood in the center of the room, each leg set on its mark to prove there had been no tampering. Each scroll, recently renewed in secret, was scrupulously in its place along the wall. Nothing had been disturbed. Yet still, the old man could not feel satisfied. Only after he had examined all the documents, and two in particular, did he exit the thick-walled chamber and lock the door behind him. The guard stared at the tall old man as he walked away, wondering once again what the little room held.

As Algorneth made his slow, contemplative way back up into the light, he pondered the young Hunter. There was always a doubt there, for him. Hunter was too old. He had not had years of schooling, and he was not of a Sheewan family. There was no way to connect his bloodline to that of the kings.

Yet there had been the debate, and now he doubted his own judgment.

He had supervised the debate himself, for there were young Sheewa there, and he felt it important to maintain a decent order. It had been set to take place in one of the many drawing rooms of the High City, where the light was soft, and all furniture had been removed to make space for seating. The spectators sat beneath the window, foremost being Algorneth, to watch the young and proud argue together.

All debates were on the issue of the kingship.

"The people were under the authority of the Pagrâi, and he was under no authority himself. Thus came all the abuses told of in the scrolls!"

"Abuses were a question of the king, not the kingship. The line of the blood was corrupted, and like a bad thread in tapestry, the monsters appear all through history." This was an unimaginative youth, one who held to what was popularly said, and not by what was written.

His opponent had been chosen carefully to lead the opposition, for he loved nothing better than to oppose. Small, with hair cut short, he looked as if he were exchanging blows on the training ground. "There have been no great men since the days of the kings, and therefore no great abuses. We have been free — why should we not continue? There will be no tapestry, and no evil threads."

The words stopped, for through the door came Hunter, silent and smiling. Algorneth knew that he had been preparing for his journey. Hunter stood against the wall, and the defender continued the debate.

"No civilization can be called such without a king, and there will be no future greatness without present power."

"And why should we need greatness? We are an island, living alone. What will greatness produce but conquest, and what will conquest bring but fear? Let every man live as he will, and be done with talk of trouble!"

There was a movement from Hunter, but no one seemed to notice except for Algorneth.

The opposition went on. He could see his defender quailing. "A high authority will only serve to make our petty jealousies greater, and we will look to a king when we should look to ourselves. We are the only ones that can settle our future, for there is no one so great as ourselves. Therefore, if we are loyal only to ourselves, we are loyal to the highest authority!"

The words were spoken with a great heat, and there was no denying that the lad was an impressive orator.

His argument came to an end, and when it did, his opposite could say nothing in disputation. Algorneth softly asked if there were any from the audience to speak, and there were a few men and women with questions of how such an issue would affect the maintenance of the archives.

Then there was silence, until Hunter spoke from beside the door.

"I am no debater. Argument has never appealed to me. That is why I love the High City, for you are all one, dedicated to the restoration of a just kingship. And I have studied the scrolls, and know that even the highest authority is under a greater one. As long as there is no king there is a constant threat from beyond the sea, from those who will set up a foreign kingship here. This will happen. A headless beast is soon eaten."

What Hunter said interested Algorneth, and he listened with a little smile. But he turned pale with shock, and nearly rose from his chair as Hunter paused, looked at their faces, and said, "The king will come. Who will stand when the king appears?"

The debate ended there, for there was nothing anyone could say in return. Annoyance prevailed in the room as the debaters left, and the audience filed out.

Algorneth found himself troubled at hearing these words from secret scrolls, and therefore he had checked the secret room. No one could have entered without his own key. Now, as he reclined on his bed, he smiled. Byorneth's word was still good, it seemed.

Algorneth was an old man. He knew he would be dead before the truth was proved.

Chapter 11
The Chase

MY BED IS OF GILT, MY SHIRT IS OF PEARLS,
THE STONES OF MY PALACE ARE POLISHED AND FITTED,
THE SLOPES ARE AGLOW.

BUT HOW FAR IS THE SEA AND THE SAILS UNFURLED,
HOW SMELLS THE FOREST WHERE SPARROWS HAVE FLITTED,
HOW LOOKS THE SNOW?

~Unknown king~

So it came that she left the city that very day, carrying the food and gold the Sheewa had given her, along with a parcel of heavy clothing all bundled together in a large leather bag, slung over both her shoulders. She had been given a guide across the passes — young Arneth, elated at this chance, with a company of five men.

At first, she thought they would have to travel once again through the Death Fields, and she quaked inwardly to think of such a journey. But they went instead toward the west, walking along the very edge of the mountains, sometimes with one foot upon the slope and the other on volcanic glass.

As they went, Arneth made the odd passing comment, and Srstri could not help but realize how different from Hunter the young man was. He asked questions Hunter would have avoided, spoke of things best left implicit. The more he talked, the more Srstri thought of Hunter and less of the energetic young man marching beside her.

Days went by, nearly silent after Arneth left off chattering. It was only after they had passed a series of higher and higher ridges, ascended into the mountains and emerged on the upper end of the Great Trail, that she knew they had crossed the Sky Line and passed out of the Lowlands. The mountains enfolded them on all sides, their tops shrouded in cloud. Now they walked on the final and Upper Path to the Great Highlands of Arlinga, passing many more people than journeyed along the lower road — tinkers peddling their wares, stonemasons trudging wearily from work, tea buyers visiting planters, planters visiting buyers, samples of their stock swinging behind them in little boxes. Dozens of people passed every hour up and down the upper roads, chattering back and forth.

They still traveled upward hours later, when the light faded in an instant, as it does in the Highlands, and a heavily laden cart passed them sleepily and came to rest beside a nearly depleted watering trough by the roadside. Beside it was an avenue that led to an *eestranaah*, the first Srstri had ever seen.

A short lane gave suddenly into the broad, sandy clearing obscured from the Trail by a low wall. The small party of Sheewa gathered together and sat across from the second line of troughs, and Srstri watched as they set about preparing the evening meal out of their bags, a rough feast of way bread and meat, setting everything in order with a wonderfully practised skill. Slowly, the clearing filled with three families and a wedding party, who drifted in and laid out their bedding, lighting fires of their own. There is something about the *eestranaah*, an otherworldly strangeness that sets it apart from all the Island's dwellings. Nowhere else in all Arlinga can all kinds and classes of folk blend together with such an easy rhythm. Carters and pickers consort on equal terms with tea barons and planters, secure in their cloak of normalcy. Even the Sheewa, as students of each and every aspect of all customs, found their greatest challenge in the *eestranaah*. Its origins are all but lost to memory, but the Sheewa suspect they once sheltered the king's armies on their long marches. Some of the larger ones could have accommodated entire Lowland villages, even boasting industrious tradesmen selling ready-cut fuel or spiced beef. Marriages have been bound and broken, blood debts made and paid, lives begun and ended in these tide pools of the Trail, dirty, squalid and glorious.

Srstri and her party had not been the first to arrive, for two mule drivers staggered into camp with a bag of water for their beasts. They sat it down in the trough and upended it, and as the animals had cooled, their masters let them drink. Srstri ate in glad quiet, listening to the stillness of drowsy nighttime as it fell, the deep guzzling of mules and the grunting of frogs in the pools nearby.

She had barely lain down in her blankets before sleep began to come, and her eyelids flickered a little and then shut completely. Lips curving into the slightest little smile, she sighed and drifted away as Arneth watched. Everything about her was generous, magnanimous — every proportion of her face, the fullness of her beneath the Sheewan blankets. With a silent groan, Arneth looked away across the *eestranaah*.

The wedding party had settled in as well, but not to sleep. Indeed, none of their fellow travelers had expected an easy night, for the marriage had only that day been completed, and *braaykast* flowed freely. Soon, the younger men began to raise their voices, and joviality took on first a swagger, then an edge of violence. Finally, their sensibilities left them completely, and every other fire in the resting place became theirs. Srstri was awakened as a particularly obnoxious fellow stumbled up to the fire, waving a leather flask that spilled a little high-smelling liquor with each step.

"Hillmen! Brothers! Come join us in a carouse! Our friend has indentured himself to Woman, and we have debased us in drink for him. Come along! No one rests tonight until all have drunk a draught!"

It was tradition, and generally accepted. Each Sheewa drank and wished the marriage well, but when the cup came to Srstri, she passed it along.

The man flushed hot as he took the flask back and flung its contents into the fire, which flared up high at the strange fuel. The challenge was thrown, the insult accepted, and the drunkard walked back to his fire.

One of the elder Sheewa loosened his weapon in its sheath. "You've been long out of the Hills, my lady. To refuse a man's drink is a reflection on him. You should at least have touched your lips to the cup and wished the marriage well."

"I meant no offense. I simply dislike strong drink."

"He cannot know that, and he's drunk." Arneth said. "Whatever happens now, you must keep back and stay silent. We will fulfill our oaths, and I especially will stop at nothing to preserve your life."

"They might do nothing." A smooth-faced young scribe said, hoping more than feeling. "They may drink themselves to sleep. Or we could move camp."

The old one snorted, "Hear him! Barely one journey and he instructs! May our masters give us such wisdom." But the graybeard had already drawn his blade.

The waiting was made worse by a sudden ill-tempered silence on the part of the wedding party. The drinks passed more frequently, and occasionally someone would give a low, dissatisfied growl as he tossed off another burning mouthful. At last the climax came, and of one accord they all stood and advanced toward the Sheewan fire, not swaggering as before, but with careful steps. "You! Longfarers! You think our liquor is bad! Come along, say it out! Tell us the truth, cowards!"

A shriek of steel cut across his words, and the scribes stood in unison, their hooks at the ready. The Hillmen stopped.

"We are scribes, but if you take one step further, you will know how we defend our own!" Arneth's voice rang with authority. "Come and have at it!"

He might have explained. He might have said that the girl had been long out of the Hills. He might have turned the violence aside, but Arneth's words only left the wedding party inflamed. There may have been bloodshed were it not for the elder Sheewa, who stepped into the middle of the conflict, holding his weapon by the blade.

"Gentlemen, consider yourselves. In the cool light of day, when every heartbeat pounds a drum in your skulls, you may once again be reasonable and peaceful men. Whichever emerges victor, this story will not be to your credit. Bloodshed will only cast a pall over the new marriage."

Srstri came beside him and extended her hand to the foremost of the revelers. "I apologize, my friends. I have lived far away for a long time, and what little I ever knew of my people has long been forgotten." As she gently took hold of the weapon, the man's face softened and then melted.

"Can we be friends? Will you teach me a song to bless the union with?"

A smile grew beneath the man's black beard, until at last he put away his weapon and embraced her by the forearms in the age-old familial gesture of his people. The conflict collapsed, and everyone gathered at the same fire to seal their friendship. Srstri drank water, giving no offense. The mantle of the peacemaker suited her eminently well, as she did with humility what others might have done with long negotiation. All had joy but Arneth, who wore his shame like a red mask, and kept it there through the night until they retired to bed.

They were away before daybreak in case of further incident. The Pass between the Arlingan Hills and Lowlands was quite a long affair, and the mountains were very small at the beginning — foothills with little high valleys in-between, where a few sheep and cattle grazed. Though the road was smooth, the upward grade and the long strides of the men around her had Srstri winded within the hour. Traffic was slack, as few men but farmers ever stirred as early as the Sheewa. Each slow kand greeted them with fresh sights, and with each kand she was happier.

A high, rugged outcropping overhung the Trail and seemed to menace their very lives, and just beyond there were rivulets that ran all over the distant rocks like veins in a man's hand, dissolving into white air as they fell to the ground. The Trail was always well maintained and smooth, but at times sheer rock surrounded them so closely that a thin artery of blue sky was all the relief she could see. Soon, the Hills all around were capped with gleaming ice, and behind them towered their higher, dimmer brothers.

The clouds above them were lit as with a purple lantern, and before they could change to pink, the country came alive with chattering women carrying bundles, the first wayfarers of the day. They all flowed down to a stream which Srstri's party soon passed, a modest-sized creek fed by a lake many kaind away, but still ice-cold in the crisp morning. A pall of mist as from a boiling pot loomed over it in the cold dawn, obscuring the country beyond, even to the topmost pillars of the vaulted bridge. "To each woman a stone, to each family a woman." Such is the saying of the Hills, for each family has from ancient times laid claim to its own stone on which to scrub and beat their garments, until they were worn smooth and shiny, even when dry, with the generations of cloth they had seen. Srstri peered over the edge of the damp railing down to the stream, lined with white foam as the women beat the clothing with unrelenting vigor, the same vigor with which they gossiped back and forth across the water.

The Sheewan feet drummed across the stout boards of the bridge, and as Srstri stepped once again onto the beaten earth, she saw that flanking the Trail beyond the river there stood two immense pillars of stone, which at a distance she had taken for trees. They were thrust into the rocky earth about ten paces from the narrowing Trail on each side, and the abuse of the climate had long stripped them of any feature. They now stood uniform, but to what purpose she could not guess. Even had she asked the Sheewa, they could not have told her, for the stones had been standing their stern guard long before the first block for the High City had been laid.

A few children played around the ancient landmarks, and laughed at the Sheewa as they walked past, falling into step along the ditch in an identical flanking pattern, broadly mimicking the strange long-striding lope of the scribes. Arneth kept his head upright as one boy, round as a turnip, boldly sidled up beside him.

"Who are you?"

"We are Sheewa, the scribes of Arlinga."

"What is Arlinga?"

"This land is."

"My mother says this land belongs to the tinkers. She says nothing can happen without the tinkers."

"I suppose she's right. Hadn't you better be going home? Your mother will be missing you."

"Oh, as long as I can hear her whistle at nightfall, she never worries. Why are you walking so fast?"

"We're traveling to the Hills."

"Why?"

"This young lady needs to be there."

"Why?"

But Arneth had run dry, and from behind Srstri reached out and took the little boy by the arm. "Hello, what is your name?"

"Tell me yours first!"

"My name is Srstri. Maybe you should run along home now."

"Very well. Goodbye." And so he was away, yelling after his friends.

Not a tree grew across the low stony ridges but a lone clump of scrub pine, and even the grass, which less than an hour's march behind had thickly lined each side of the path, was now tortured with thick, jumbled stone. For the first time, the air truly smelled of the mountains — crisp, clean, and cold with the tang of evergreens.

Although she had relived the circumstances of her capture hundreds of times in the intervening years, Srstri had never remembered the journey through the Pass being so long, or so full of life. The Chadeyzdeer had taken her mostly over mountains, only descending onto the Trail on the darkest nights when they feared for the safety of their human livestock. Now, in the fullness of womanhood, the wonder of a child was hers once more, the more so with impossible heights on every hand, dead drops when they walked along the knife's edge of nothing, and those very rare and verdant valleys that cut across the Trail without warning, and glare with blue distance before they vanish.

And then Arneth began to talk again.

⁓ʌʌ⁓

The passage of time was all but lost to the brothers as they pored over the infinite treasures of the cave. The one worry they had was the old man, who slunk about the edges of the torchlight and muttered below his breath. As Teidin picked up and admired object after splendid object, he moved imperceptibly toward his brother, and once there he lifted a gilt and ivory goblet and whispered under his breath, "We must go immediately."

"There is too much left to see! Each bauble is more splendid than the last! I think I'll never see such beauties again! Go if you must!"

The tone of Elnaan's voice had changed, as had the color of his face. His brother put his arm around his shoulders and turned him toward the madman who still watched them and his hoard from the walls. "That man has done his best to kill you this day, and with every moment he becomes madder and madder, so that even now we may barely escape alive. Come with me now for the sake of our kin in the Lowlands." They both kept their heads down, but even in the edge of their vision, they could both sense the jealousy in the frantic eyes. Without a word Elnaan nodded, and they smiled at their host as they returned to the hole in the ceiling, where they now saw the handholds cut in the rock, and used them as quickly as possible.

Teidin turned to the man who came up the steps behind them. "Our thanks for showing us your treasure, and for feeding us." Already they had taken up their bags, and Teidin and Elnaan turned quickly and started toward the fresh air, breathless, listening for another attack.

They journeyed for what seemed an hour before they came out to the light, which had only just begun to stretch and yawn, outlining the mouth of the cave in orange against the dark of the rocks. A few paces farther and they were out in the clean air. They had listened intently for the madman's pursuit behind them, and they were surprised there had been none. They hardly dared hope that in his mania he had forgotten them, but they had gained the outside world again, and still no danger came. All the same, they moved out farther into the glow, away from the treasure cave.

It was a clear day's sunrise but for a thin band of cloud above the sun, which glowed pink but would soon change to orange. There was barely light enough to negotiate the confusion of rocks, but soon they found one large enough to hide behind. "I've thought about it," Elnaan hissed. "I went out toward the rock with writing on it, and the sun was in my face. But when we came out of the tunnel, the sun was on the left. That hole in the cleft would have been hidden from the southwest, where we stood to look for it."

There was a narrow opening, nearly as small as the entrance to their Lowland home. The mouth was pointed toward them with a protrusion jutting out between it and the rest of the area, so that it would appear to be nothing more than a shadow in the hours of daylight. Teidin nodded and started out through the rocks toward it, Elnaan following behind, keeping watch for their suspicious host even as Teidin kept his eyes focused on the door.

The moment they entered, they knew it for their tunnel. The smell of good, clean grass blew in their faces, and the air was cooler, nearly cold. They felt safer as they went, so that the first hints of daylight that touched the walls found them smiling.

"The gold I've seen was always worn and dull," Elnaan said suddenly. "Never fresh and bright such as that was. And the stones! All colors, bright and dark, woven in and out of the gold like seedlings in soil. There is nothing so fine at home, nor anywhere else."

The sight of such wonders had impressed Teidin as well, but the way his brother's mind still turned upon it disturbed him. He could not have known of the power of gold, the corruption it spreads through the souls of otherwise worthy men. In the next moment he ceased to care, for a mighty sting bit him in the side, and at the end of the long sword there came a wailing creature out of the shadows, so that only the blind impulse to lunge away saved their lives.

"You've been seeing my treasure! You'll be bringing the men to take it away for yourselves! I must be guarding this place! Stand so I can be killing you!"

Their knives were out and balanced in their hands. Dark though it was, they would not be caught unawares again. Back and forth the old man cut, but the brothers avoided the slow swings easily, parrying occasionally as their attacker stood against the light while they stayed in the shadow.

He had training, though the greater part of his strength had deserted him, and his skill soon told as the sword slipped past Elnaan's blocking blade and glanced across his ribs. The elder brother cried out in pain, but the riposte had taken time and left the man's left side open to Teidin's attack.

Teidin had not precisely meant to deliver a death blow, but his blood was racing, and his own wound as well as his brother's danger lent power to his thrust. It ended in the madman's vitals and crumpled him against the wall so that his blade clattered on the stones.

He lay in a beam of sunshine cast by the mouth of the tunnel, and they could see that the long blade was buried in him up to the hilt, but there was no anger in his face. He strained at his breath until they knelt down beside him and he gave a hard, dry laugh of dust and disrepair. "Oh, you killed me," he chuckled. "You were killing me, you poor young wretch. I am being so glad to be dying in your stead." He laughed again, this time coughing and spitting blood. A red pool was fast growing beneath him, filling the cracks in the rocks.

"The treasure is being yours now. May you be enjoying it as little as I was. But was it not being beautiful? Oh, I am being glad I was showing it to you. To be sharing my greatest treasure was worth all of the years I was being alone, all of my pain." He lifted his head and took a chain from around his neck. With a weakening grasp, he thrust it into Elnaan's hand. "It's all being of you now. You are being the Treasurer and I — I am being free."

With a final spasm, the Treasurer died, and they were left all alone in the tunnel between the lightening clouds.

~

She had walked beside Arneth for hours in comfort, and even after his folly in the *eestranaah*, she had liked and somehow pitied him, with a sense of what was in his mind. At first, he spoke of ordinary things, commenting on the countryside, telling of battles which had happened along the Trail, relating stories remembered from long hours at the scrolls. Presently the talk turned inward, and Srstri's answers became guarded, a sign Arneth failed to read, although by the grunts that came from behind, the elder Sheewa might have translated for him. At last, in the extremity of desperation, he fell to disparaging his elders, and Srstri's thoughts turned more and more to Hunter.

The final break came when they were almost through the Pass, and the Hills stood at their tallest behind them, signaling that their parting was soon, when he took sudden hold of both her hands, all heedless of propriety. "Srstri, do not go away! You can stay as a worker in the fields! I would make you very happy in the city! I have never felt as I do now, and I know that I never will again!" As he spoke, he lost the first flush of confidence he had started with, which only served to deepen his anger and topple the last pillars of caution.

Through her confusion she replied weakly, but with words that cut Arneth's heart. "I cannot, Arneth. Please do not ask me this. Please do not force it. I know not where my home may be, but never in all my time in the High City did I once feel truly at peace. Nor do I feel it here with you, though I know you wish me nothing but happiness. I need to be among the Hills again."

He dropped his hands. "I—I want you. I've wanted you since first I saw you beside the Kaarnaan. Can't you come to be satisfied at our Seng Grandt? You could be kept on as a gardener, a sweeper, anything! And we could be together!"

He said nothing more, but walked by her side until they came to a small holding whose back wall abutted part of the Trail, and she stopped and leaned against the flat-hewn rock. Arneth bent over her, concerned.

"Are you wearied? Would you rest?"

She very nearly shrugged him away. Instead, she bit her lip and nodded, then sat against the wall and closed her eyes. He left her alone.

No sane woman would ever bring such a tempest upon herself, she reflected as Arneth called for a rest. The first rush of washerwomen had ended, and the work of the day had yet to begin in earnest. In this relative void she thought, fought her way past the confusion. When she opened her eyes and once again entered the world, there was steady traffic along the stone-lined road. Perhaps it was her beauty, or her evident pain that drew men's eyes, but the unabashed gaze of these strangers took away what little comfort remained. The only steady face amongst them was that of a little hinai, peeking above the earth by the wall with its large eyes and nearly human face.

With sudden effort she stood, and turning she found that the eldest of her companions stood in her way, the gray beard twisted into a half smile. When she would have sidestepped him, he touched her shoulder and drew her eyes back to meet his. "Forgive me, but I could hardly help overhearing you with our young ambassador back there."

"Yes, I thought you might have. It seemed to amuse you."

"No more than you might expect. The humiliation out-weighed it. We cannot have you leaving our company remembering only Arneth's behavior. The young knight dozes in the shade across the road." He took her other shoulder, pointed her down the Trail, and pushed her away. "You left before any of us awoke, and our young leader will return to the city to solace himself in books. Now go! Hurry!"

It was here that the Hills gave in to the basin of the Caldera, and Srstri used the downhill grade to good advantage in her flight, until it became so steep that she slowed to a walk. At last, with a breathtaking suddenness, the entire wide majesty of the great and fertile Caldera opened before her. At the sight of her homeland she began to weep, until at last she stopped to stare by the roadside as the lifeblood of the Hills walked by along the road.

—⁀ʌ ʌ⁀—

Have you never strolled through the high Arlingan tea districts? It is an immense green basin surrounded by small dwellings on all sides, and beyond those lie the sweeping, terraced hills covered in row upon row of those famed tea bushes, where singing pickers move and pluck delicate leaf sets with careful, expert fingers. Whether the sun shines or the rain falls, each distant mountain beckons you nearer, and every face you meet, like the sun, makes you feel it shines just for you. When the day is hot, there is always a fresh lake breeze or sudden rain to revive you, a hospitable householder ready to offer a cup of cool water, or even his own bed if you ask him.

The sun warmed Srstri's back as she went along, and the song the pickers sang lifted the cares of the past days from her shoulders. It was a picking song, swaying with a thrumming rhythm. She had been very young when last she had heard it, and it raised sweet half-forgotten memories of her earliest days. The smells of mountain air and tea harvesting dissolved her Lowland existence into tears, and with each drop that flowed down and fell into the dust, another year slipped away.

The song the pickers sang was of love, as is much Hill music, and not meant to make any particular sense, but rather crafted to evoke a far away feeling, or *prashkah*, as they are sung.

A high, clear voice would sing the rhyming couplet:

Many times has the sun gone over the
mountains,
Since the first lovers have loved.

Then all the voices within earshot would chime in a long-
drawn third line of vocables, weaving voices in and out, and
finally flowing back together again.

It was simply learned, and as Srstri hurried along, she
found herself adding her voice to the general melody, the
pickers smiling up at her as she walked by. She was now well
clear of the Pass, and once again the old familiar mountains
encompassed her in a familiar embrace. Shaped like the first
three letters of the Mountain Script, there was the Kyargh
itself, extending across its two connecting peaks, and old
Garchnyamp the limping man, whose right leg was hewn off
by his brother Ghrtsk, grumbling faintly day and night over his
loss. These and scores of others stood guard, dim and blue, all
around her.

As she went, Srstri asked all she met how far ahead the
Sheewa were, delighted at last to use her language with her
own people. They all returned the same answer — two Sheewa
had passed that way a day ago. She hurried on, and the answer
changed to half a day, and then two hours, until at last she had
cut their advantage down to a half hour. She had been running
for some time, but winded though she was, she kept on, past
pickers and workers withering leaves in their yards, heating
and scooping them in large curved pans.

She had never been allowed much exercise while in the
village, and in the High City her work had been similar. She
found herself easily winded, gasping the thin air, until at last
she had to stop and sit on a large stone placed beside the
Trail for just such a purpose, and polished by generations of
breeches over the years.

"Are you running toward or away from something?" The voice was that of a little man who knelt and rolled a bag of leaves beside his house on the other side of a wall. He never looked up, intent on his work, putting equal care into each rolling stroke. Short and stalwart, he was well suited to his calling.

Many who drink tea think nothing of the well-shaped curl of it, the spirals that unfold into such delicious infusions, much less of the skill and labor that produced them. And no two varieties of tea are prepared the same, or with the same twist. Some broad and flat like chips of green wood, others coiled all about like black and gold wire, each restricts and controls the release of the tea's essential character. This man's tea was to be in the shape of snail's shells, and it was this shape he was now creating.

Srstri took a few moments to recover herself. "I run home. I've been in the Lowlands for many years."

The constant roll and push on the bag of leaves ceased, and the man appraised her more carefully, sitting back on his heels. "Where have you been? The Lowlands? Why for all the tea of the Prrndaai would a Hillwoman go there?"

"It was not by choice. I was a captive among them from childhood, and I have not been in the Hills for many years."

There had long been disappearances from homes along the northern slopes, but never any certainty as to their fate. He himself had lost several friends to these raids, even distant relations, a class of person highly prized in the tightly knit Caldera. The woman was young, and besides being out of breath she seemed healthy, even thriving. However badly she may have been treated, however great the disgrace of her captivity, she herself was healthy, and for this the man was grateful. There was yet hope for the others.

"Have you seen two men, two — Longfarers pass by here in the past hours? One old with a gray beard, another young and tall?"

"Yes, they are not so many that I would forget. They stopped to rest here. The old one sat on that rock where you sit, and I offered them tea. He refused, saying they had to be away quickly."

Suddenly, the stone was less comfortable. She stood and stretched. ""Thank-you for your kindness. I must be away now."

"Farewell." With a shake of his head, the man returned to his work.

She went at a more rapid pace, looking neither right nor left, but aiming her steps far ahead. She berated herself for the time she had lost, and lost no time in making it up. Her path took her around the outer rim of the Caldera, and though she was near to the Highest Hills, their aspects changed but slowly as she ran. This made her journey seem even slower, and pressed her on to greater speed, mocking her stiffness.

At last, two figures became visible in the distance, with broad hats and dark cloaks. They were yet a long way off, floating against the rippling mountains, but she took three long, gasping breaths and called out.

Mountain air carries sound as though through a tunnel, and Hunter, Byorneth, and half the mountainside turned at the long cry. The taller held still for a moment, then broke into a long run back along the Trail toward her while Byorneth watched, leaning on his staff.

Chapter 12
The Oath

YE LORDS AND LADIES, SWELLED WITH GOLD,
YE GREAT AND HIGH, YE KING AND QUEEN,
DOFF THE CROWN, FORSAKE YOUR FEASTS AND PLEASURE.

KNEEL, PROSTRATE YOUR PRIDE, BEHOLD
THE JUNCTURE OF THE PASSING STREAM,
THE ORE AND FOUNT OF WORLDLY TREASURE!

~The Wedding Song~

The road was long and seemed longer, but their pace never slackened. Hunter's staff clattered on the road, and his hat would have joined it but for the strap which kept it in place. When they came together with a jolt, her tears dampened his cloak and she pressed him as close as she could, crushing into him. "I can give you an answer now! I love you, and I care not if you travel for ten years! I will wait!"

There were no pickers, no breezes in the grass, no Hills towering over them. All things outside this moment were forgotten. He had no words to say, but simply gave the *ngyaarban* — the caress of dearest lovers which runs from mouth to hair. She delighted all his senses at once, but most of all it was herself, her presence and the gray eyes which held his. He thought he had never felt so deliriously happy, and she certainly had never been so content. It was only now that the inevitability of this moment occurred to him. Now he could see how that even in their first days in the Lowlands, their paths had converged on this small square of ground.

The pickers who had stopped to watch smiled down on them with the Hillman's typical lack of reserve. A woman working almost at their elbow started another song, made up on the spot, as many picking songs are. She was especially skillful, and the song was especially lovely. Once again, the burden was taken up by the other pickers as it reached them, and although most were ignorant of its significance, it was to become an anthem for Hunter and Srstri:

> Two lovers stood in the morning air,
> The moon was full, and the stars were fair.
>> On the Hills that whisper their pain,
>> Turning to gladness again.
> The wolf was slinking to his lair,
> His hands were lost in her shining hair.
>> I would that I were there again!
>> Were there again.

The high notes echoed down the Trail in resonating waves of melody, interlocking like lovers' fingers. Hunter lifted Srstri's chin to meet her eyes, and he heard himself speak. "You are very dear to me, my love, and I must marry you."

His joy, which he had thought at its zenith, attained even greater heights when she smiled into his eyes and came up to kiss him. Her lips clung to his as they pulled away, and so he kissed her again and felt her breath on his cheek. When they parted again, she clasped him all around with a surprising grip and looked up into his eyes. "And I must marry you, Hunter. My Hunter." She laid her head against his shoulder and they walked together down the road to where Byorneth stood waiting. Hunter's cape was around her shoulders, as is the way of a Sheewa when he has taken a wife, and Byorneth bit his lip as he saw it.

He inclined his head and gave the formal congratulations of the Sheewa, an ornate and resonant invocation of blessing and love. They went down the road together, the two younger walking as one person, the elder smiling on the far side of his face. Hunter and his love never touched the rough ground, but bobbed on the air like seeds blown from the same plant.

⌒ʌ ʌ⌒

The day was bright and glaring above them, and they had still not come to any agreement, so Teidin and Elnaan sat in the shadow of a ledge together in thought. The latter held a medallion, turning it over and over in his fingers. On one side there was inscribed a stylized whale, and on the other the likeness of a crowned head with a royal name below it. It had seen considerable wear, but the patterns had recently been renewed with a stylus.

Teidin was tossing pebbles out among the rocks, holding a pad of cloth to the wound beneath his arm. It was not deep, but had taken a long time to stop bleeding. "He was a madman, squatting all alone by his miserable pile of gold. Nothing he said signified anything. Come away with me!"

"He gave me a charge. The gold must be guarded."

"Do you know that the smallest of those stones could buy us a share of the largest plantation in the Hills? With the entire hoard, we could buy mastery of all lands! If you will not take the gold, then by all means forget it, only I will not return to Allend's End all alone!"

"I am afraid you must." They sat for a time in silence. Teidin felt almost at the edge of tears. When Elnaan spoke again, it was with a great sorrow behind his words. "I am sorry I ever saw the treasure, or walked into the mountains. But that is all done, and there is no other way for me than to abide here. If I leave the gold, within the space of a year it will be picked clean, scattered abroad throughout the land, melted down — the gems removed to be traded."

"But who besides us knows about it? It is buried in the back of a cave."

"There are legends of treasure hidden in the mountains. It is no secret. I feel there is something great behind it all, and I cannot bear the thought of the gold dissipating."

"That is none of our concern."

Elnaan stood and sighed. "It would seem to be my concern now." He pulled his brother up to his feet. "When you see home again, be giving them all my love. Perhaps we'll be hunting together again."

Tears filled Teidin's eyes, and as he took Elnaan's hands in both of his, there was an oppressive finality in the act that made him doubt for the future. "If I pass this way again, I will stop and see you. Listen for the long call." Sorrowfully, they embraced as brothers and fastest friends, and Teidin was about to make a clean break and walk away when his brother caught his arm and thrust something into his palm.

It was the steel and darkwood knife of their father. "I will use the Treasurer's," Elnaan said. "This belongs with one of our kin."

Elnaan stood and waved to his brother until he was out of sight. It was not until Teidin reached the daylight of the outside world that he sat down to wipe his eyes and drink out of his water bag. The lone journey eastward through the mountain had felt distinctly wrong. He should have stayed, should have insisted, should have persuaded his brother to leave the treasure alone. An errant trickle of the water choked him, and he coughed.

Of their own accord, his footsteps inclined not to the north and home as they should have, but rather off to the east among the kindly Hillfolk, seeking comfort in the strangeness of that place. To most Lowlanders, the Hillmen are not to be trusted, for everyone knew their hearts were as dark as their skins, and there could be no fellowship between them and men of normal desires. But since the brothers first crossed the Sky Line into the Hills, that image had faded in the smiling faces around them. It seemed that laughter was only another vowel in their rolling language, and with few exceptions he and Elnaan had been well treated by everyone they met. Far from condemning these pale strangers in their midst, there was instead a rare curiosity, which rarely overflowed into presumption.

The runaway slave, the very thing which had led them to leave their home at the beginning, was all but gone from his mind, so consumed had they been with the excitement of exploration, so low were his spirits now. The roads were full but not crowded, rippling up and down in the bright dust, the heat of the scene freshened by the cool colors of distant tea.

He was hungry, and the stuff he carried was too little to satisfy him, but he regretted taking of these people's food without payment. At last, his belly cried out and he halted in his way. His path had been a little-used local avenue which intersected with one of the main arteries of the Great Trail, visible across a wide hedge. Upon the right hand there was a small landholding which extended up the hillside behind him, and he watched the workings of the plantation for a while as the laborers went back and forth. He drew three long breaths and walked forward into the bright yard.

A woman, youthful though her hair was gray, looked up from a pan where she was heating several handfuls of leaves over coals, and then looked down to her work again as she gave a friendly salutation. Such work is best uninterrupted, and so she stayed by her pan, scooping the leaves with a repetitive swish.

Teidin's Kyarrghnaal was limited to only a few words, but he used them with careful diction and a humble smile. She smiled kindly back, and looked him up and down expectantly. A few men came around and stood, for even in the Hills a stranger may mean harm.

It was to the men that Teidin looked, regretting that the language had come so much more easily to his brother than to him. It was too full of consonants, all standing shoulder to shoulder on his tongue, bearing it down. "Food," he said, and made the motion of cutting wood, a universal sign for any sort of work. The Hillmen conversed, and soon a man brought a shovel, and another showed him where to dig in a long line beside the hedge. The man clapped him on his shoulder and he began to work.

The labor pleasantly reminded him of home, except that the soil here was darker and more rocky. He had labored hard every day of his life, and it was evident in the way he dug, the vigor with which he tortured the dirt and worried stones from their deep sockets.

He had not cut two shovelfuls before the workers around him began to sing as if on cue. The melody, strange at first, began to please him, and the words came more easily than speech. He began to hum as he dug, and soon he found himself forming the words. There was no effort, simply a blissful division of attention between the dirt beneath and the song above.

Suddenly, he stopped digging. He did not know how long he had been singing alone, but all the eyes in the yard were on him, smiling broadly. The blood hot in his face, he turned to his work again in silence with twice his former vigor.

Soon the sweat came, stinging the superficial gash the old Treasurer had given him, but he did not stop until a hand touched his shoulder and the woman of the place stood there, holding out a bag of water for him. She said something beyond his knowledge, but her meaning was clear nonetheless. Taking it in both hands he gave his thanks, first in Harniyen by mistake and then in an approximation of her language. Then he tipped the water back and took a long drink. He tried to return it, but she refused and urged him to take more. When at last he had finished, she told him to keep it, and gave him a motherly slap across the cheek which shocked him. Then she was away and he turned once more to his work.

People went by on the Trail in a sporadic stream, heads and shoulders behind the hedge. They occupied his mind as he worked, for the trench required only bodily effort, but thoughts are restless, whirling in ever-hastening circles between the ears of the young. He invented a game for himself, trying to guess the object of each person's journey. A more universally attractive people he could not remember seeing. It was no wonder the Lowland farmers would pay such a high price for such beautiful labor.

All of a sudden his shovel fell to the earth and he was running along the hedge, jumping to see over it until he came to the edge of the landholding. He dropped his water bag and picked it up, said an unintelligible thanks to his hostess and everyone else in sight, and then cleared the hedge and started off down the road. The woman shouted to one of her laborers and he ran after Teidin, carrying the bag of food she had prepared for him.

But Teidin could not be stopped, for there had passed upon the road three passengers, and they had forged a long way ahead before their significance occurred to him.

⁓⁓

At last, they found what they wanted — the wooden archway and canopy, and beneath it the broad hearth of the blacksmith. Those of the Lowlands may find it strange that Hill marriages are made at the ironmonger's forge. But he is the man who joins metal, makes tools and melts them down. He casts rings, and his words braze the mystical union of husband and wife.

As they approached the hot stone under its iconic canopy, the blacksmith, an affable fellow of about 50 years, was deep in conversation with a tiny, tightly strung woman. She was not affable.

"You promised me my tools fully one week ago, Arron! How long will it be until they are ready? I have a good many flowers to get into the ground!"

Arron shrugged helplessly. "Well, you can see that pile of tools over there on the other side of my forge. Most of them are for the planting of tea or vegetable gardens, which people need."

"I only want an estimate."

He ran his hands through his curly hair and sighed. An estimate was the least of what she wanted. "I will try to get it done soon. My son will be around with the message when they are finished." All this he had told her one week before, but she was a notoriously impatient woman. That she was anxious about her flowers he did not for one moment believe.

Her chief concern could only be the laborers which she had accumulated at home, chief of which was her long-suffering husband. She hated to see anyone but herself lying idle.

She pursed her lips. "Good day to you, then."

"Good day."

She walked away briskly, and her short hair shivered with every step. The blacksmith returned to his hammer and tongs, not seeing the woman and the Sheewa, who had hung back to watch.

Hunter and Srstri came forward, but Arron the Blacksmith continued working, the ringing of his hammer loud to the point of pain, shooting sparks across the bare earth. One would not have taken him for a blacksmith, for his strength was all inward, not bulging in his sleeves, but more than sufficient as it was needed. Finally, he saw them standing there, and ceased hammering, smiling in the strained manner of one who has often been interrupted in pressing work, but whose nature constrains him to be charitable.

Then with a closer look at Hunter and Srstri, standing almost in one another's footsteps, he realized their business, and a wholehearted, beaming grin enveloped his face. Now they saw that it was quite a nice face, wrinkled around the eyes with good humor, with a whitening, short beard that magnified his smile. He was by no means a tall man, but he grew at least six inches as he asked, "And what might be your business?"

"We wish to be united."

A sudden solemnity overtook him as he inclined his head and looked at Srstri. "And you, my dear? Is it your wish to marry this man?"

"It is."

"Who stands for this alliance?"

"I do." Byorneth stood forth, removing his hat. "These are Hunter and Srstri, come from far away."

Every movement careful, every action slow, the blacksmith bent down in a special corner of his workshop and rose with a massive book in his hands. When he opened and held it out in front of him, they could see that it was full of handwritten characters, the Mountain Script, which one of his forefathers had set down when the marriage service had first been made. The man's attitude impressed Hunter greatly, for it showed a deep respect for his sacred Trust, a reverence such as he had only seen in one other place — before the throne in Seng Grandt, where every returning Sheewa, be he straight from the remotest corners of the Island, hot and thirsty, will nevertheless prostrate himself before the memory of the king.

He stood them apart in their required places, and following a long pause, he began to recite in elegant, archaic speech:

> "All ye people in every place, hail to the name
> of the king, lord of all our lands beneath
> the heavens, this being his great Binding of
> Hearts, the Great Tie, the Stalk and Marrow
> of all things."

It is forbidden to relate the words with which Srstri and her husband were joined. Those of Arlinga who have wed have heard them, and understand their strange power. They know the solemnity which they evoke, and may have an inkling of Hunter's mind as he listened. These are the words that, once uttered, forever alter the complexion of life. It is this Pledge and no other upon which every nation is founded.

The ritual was not unobserved, and the placement of the players was enough to inform Teidin of the nature of their oath. He leaned against the fence at the side of the road, looking on across the little distance. Who else could these be but the two mule drivers and the slave they had stolen? They were in different garments, but they were not of the Highlands any more than the woman would pass for a Lowlander. The hopes he had built as he followed them were shattered, for marriage was still a sacred thing, and he had not such a love of gold that he would suffer one to be broken for the sake of it.

Calmer now, he began to walk back the way he came, toward what, he did not know.

Unto every blacksmith there is given the right to make a bond of his own, as only those who have married and remained so may bear the Book. The blacksmith now shut the volume and addressed Srstri and Hunter earnestly, eye to eye.

"I need not remind any present of the burden which this oath implies, its responsibilities of love and labor. But in heartache, there may also be found supreme comfort. It is in consideration, plain and simple good manners (which are a direct product of love) that a union for life is tempered, and in careful affection in the heat of anger. That which you do, do together, each protecting the welfare of the other." His eyes burned with the fury of a rebuking father, and as they addressed each face, everyone present felt their power, the very authority of bygone kingdoms, reaching palpably down through the ages. For these few moments, the man was a blacksmith no longer, but a herald of the king.

"Hunter, swearest thou to these things?"

Hunter did, in a husky, quiet voice, which echoed strangely as in a dream. Each moment, he thought with dread that he would awake suddenly and be unable to return. At the prompting of the blacksmith, he stepped halfway toward the woman who was his and only his.

"Srstri, swearest thou to these things?"

She gave her word calmly and measuredly, as a woman does when her most cherished hope is made real. She stepped forward beside Hunter, and they held hands in the prescribed manner. It was as iron and lodestone.

"As it is sworn, so be it from this day." They embraced again, and the blacksmith stepped back to his hearth, taking up a small box full of silver scraps. There followed a flurried fanning of the fire, arranging of the metal in circles, and melting them into rings, which he quenched and fitted around a tapered cylinder, beating them with a hammer. Hunter and Srstri put them on, and several times the smith took them again, firing, quenching and beating them until they fit, two silver bands — dull, white and binding.

Everyone had watched the rings made. None could turn their eyes from the hearth, and none dared to speak or otherwise break the spell which the blacksmith's words had cast. When at last the work was finished and on their fingers, none could ever dispute their state.

The smith smiled broadly all around him. The Hills felt right again.

⌒⌒ʌ⌒⌒

Byorneth stood as witness, never objecting in word or thought. Perhaps over the past months he might have resented Srstri's presence, but as his best friend's wife, she assumed stature in his eyes, and her acceptance of the terms of the oath set the seal on his acceptance of her. He reasoned that a married Hunter would be truly a man, perhaps free from the hazards of youth. Today, he smiled nearly as broadly as the smith, and Srstri hardly knew him.

The sun was yet high in the sky, and there were many weary kaind to go, but much to their surprise the stern Byorneth called for a halt until the next day. As it happened, the first place they came to was owned by a hospitable man who willingly opened his home when he heard the couple was newly married, and his fat, beaming wife agreed wholeheartedly while her many bright-eyed children stared shyly at these new people from behind their mother's skirts. Outlanders without mules were unusual, and strangers in cloaks and broad hats were of the greatest interest to them.

The man and his wife, given to hospitality, kept a separate dwelling for guests, and this was assigned to Srstri and her new husband. They had not stopped for a moment before the woman set to garnishing it, and as soon as Hunter and Srstri had eaten, they were ushered into the opulent hut. The flap closed behind them, and the man and his wife foretold dreadful retribution against any child who so much as ventured near that place.

But the young of any tribe are curious, and few are perfect in obedience. The very fact they had been warned away drew their eyes irresistibly toward the forbidden house, even in their play, until the boldest of them began to test their parents' orders, venturing nearer and nearer.

Not a man to fall behind in his duty, Byorneth proved equal to his role. His deep voice rang clear. "Who would hear a story?"

Each tousled head shot up, and a score of wide little eyes fastened themselves on him. Removing himself to a high spot on the other side of the main house, he stood tall under his strange hat, while the children, old and young, flocked about him until fully ten families were represented. The eldest stood in back, feigning indifference, but you may be sure that no one, young or old, would have been satisfied elsewhere. As he stood apart, it was as if the wind that blew his cape came from another time, and they could see in his eyes a monumental connection to the half-forgotten age of legend, of heroism. Even before he spoke in his compelling, work-hardened voice, every listener had been transported with him, drawn away into the remotest past.

"I tell you of the island of Ashtranaag, its people, and the adventure which I had in that strange place."

A child, nine years old, nearly shattered the moment when he interrupted. "But there is no such island. There are a few smaller ones, but none with any people on them."

Then the old man fixed the child with a glare that seemed to reach through him and grasp his backbone. He drew himself to his full height and rumbled dangerously through his beard. "Ah. I perceive that we have a scholar among us. Do you, young one, know as much as I? I who have traveled over this whole land and speak in seven tongues? I who have seen a land as wide across as your little Caldera awash with the blood of valiant men? If at any time you are so full of wit, then speak and I will hear you. Otherwise, keep silent and let the story be told by one who knows."

The offending child sank back into himself, and the people around him smiled. He had caused trouble before.

Byorneth resumed as though he had never stopped. "One day long ago, when fire was in my blood and strength in my arms, I signed aboard a ship, a great wooden boat with two long masts and great sails to catch the wind and push us across the ocean. We sailed far, far to the west for to trade in spice and bone. About our fifth day on those strange waters, a wind came up that grew into a gale, finally blossoming into a storm, and with a violent surge the vessel was thrown against a great wolf-toothed reef. The timbers cracked and tore asunder. A great wave like a mountain washed me from the ship, and

I was thrown onto the jagged shores of that rock-bound crag called Ashtranaag. Many ships have met their end in that surf, and the scene was dotted with their miserable hulks, ever ready to pull others down with them. Foremost of these was mine, and a few dead men and shreds of ruined sail were all that remained of its glory.

"I lay for a long time on the salt-whitened rocks, freezing and nearly dead. The wind whipped an inch of life out of me with each chilly gust, and at last I lapsed into a sleep as of death. Awaking, I found I was no longer on that shore, with the cold brine licking my feet, but curled up next to a warm, smoky fire. I was still wet, but not with sea water, for that had all long since dried, but from blood. Someone had dragged me across the sharp rocks, and my legs were all covered over with blackening life."

Some of the younger children looked pale, and he continued, satisfied. "When I sat up, I found that I was surrounded by men and women, sitting on their haunches, eating fish all nearly raw. When they saw that I was awake, several of them seized me beneath the arms and dragged me again over the black rocks to where an older man squatted by his own fire. They left me facedown in a pool of gritty water, and turning over on my side I saw that I was on a hill, affording a view that stretched across the whole width of that barren place.

"The man did not speak, but stood and wrapped his gray furs around his shoulders, then kicked me viciously in the side. Reaching down, he pinched me hard on my shoulder, and still I did not understand, but as I saw the others gather around, licking their lips, I remembered a pile of familiar clothing, and I saw meat that was not fish cooking in the fire beside me." The meaning escaped most of the younger children, but the elder ones clarified in quick, whispered sentences that widened already wide eyes.

"They clustered about me, obsidian knives in their hands, but a voice rang out, and a young woman sprang in front of me, facing the people with hands upraised. I knew not what she said in that strange tongue, but it stayed them, and I was brought to a cave among the rocks, and a few of the young men brought armfuls of fish for me to eat.

"My life hung by a thread as it was. I knew that to prolong my life, I would have to eat what they gave me, and so I began, trying not to be sick. Finally night fell, and I was left alone to toss and turn in the dark, the fish I had eaten and the rocks upon which I lay driving sleep from my eyes.

"In that black night she came, and disheveled though she was, I had never seen a fairer sight, for there was hidden in her arms a blade such as has not been wielded since the days of the last kings, a two-handed sword of the White Metal, intricately inscribed. Even bent and old, it was still as fierce a weapon as I had ever seen. Trembling and fearful, she gave it to me and slipped away into the darkness.

"This could only be the chief's sword. It was carved with ancient letters, each of which was inlaid with black jade, with knobs of the same surmounting the points of the hilt. It was a great sword, with a great name, and it had been wielded in celebrated battles against renowned foes. How it had come to this sterile rock, I could not but guess.

"Looking around, I saw that all were making ready for bed, each family at its own fire. Two men came up to the mouth of the cave to guard me, and soon all the island but them was sleeping. An hour passed, and my guards began to nod and yawn. If ever I was to have a chance, it was now.

"With the sword, I slew my jailers, and their souls passed undisturbed in silent slumber. I began to make my way through the fires and sleeping bodies, the bright sword hidden beneath my tattered clothes. Around me people snored and stirred in their sleep, and although some were still awake, in the faint light of dying embers they could not discern my features, and assumed me to be one of them. I was almost through them, and I thought I would get away free, but a sudden cry went up far behind me. I began to run.

"They must have found the guards dead. Their shouts were still a long way off, but soon these sleepers would awaken and overwhelm me. In moments, hand after hand snatched at what was left of my clothing, but my speed and momentum were too great to be stopped. A man stepped out with a big rock and tried to lay me out, but I slashed him with the sword as I flew past. Scores of bodies surged behind me, swarming out of the rocks like ants from their nest, but nothing stayed my headlong flight.

"All at once, the ground dropped before me in the great cliffs and straights that separate Ashtranaag from Arlinga, booming with surf far below. I hesitated, and the people gave a great shout when they saw that I was trapped. Fully expecting to be torn to pieces on the spot, I judged the drop to be a kinder end, so I took three long steps and leaped out as far as I could over the water, the sword still clutched in my hands. At least they would never feast themselves on me.

"I fell forever, bursting through a flock of seabirds before I hit the water. I held the blade before me in both hands as I landed, and it struck me a vicious blow to the head with the surge of water. For many moments I could not move, but only watch the shimmering surface float farther and farther upward as I sank, by some miracle still clutching the blade in both hands. At last, I called on all my strength, slipped the weapon into my waistband, and began to swim to the air again.

"How I gained the surface, or how I gained the shore, I do not know, nor yet how I kept my prize, but at last I reached the other side and dragged myself upon a ledge that overlooked the channel. Far above, the savages began to drift away from the gorge, and I saw no living man until, out of the sickening distance of the sea, there came a small trading vessel, which brought me to the green shore again. Never more did I venture out upon the waters."

There was a hush as he concluded his tale. Mouths hung open. Here was a new story of warfare and legend, and actually told by the hero himself, a thing unheard of. Even the adults had fallen under its spell, borne along with the young far out over the reaches of years and distance. Byorneth's skill was such that each listener had felt the chill of that water, the rush and panic of that headlong flight toward the sea.

It was time to retire, and the children complained as children do, for however their bodies craved rest, their minds tingled with the magic of the story, and the hazy waves still dashed upon the rock-bound islands within them. In the days after Byorneth would leave, each child would beg his parents to recite the tale, so that it changed with each telling, passing into legend. Byorneth would be set up among the ancient heroes of the Hillstories — Teerntst the Crooked who dug a new riverbed for the Rrakhana to win the love of his neighbor's daughter, and Hingaasht of the South who hunted down and slew the Great Boar of the Prrndaai Hills. In the years to come, those of the Sheewa who traveled the Caldera would find one of the tales from their own scrolls in the mouths of the Hillmen.

None of the children had volunteered for bed, yet within ten minutes each pillowed head dreamed happily of adventure and danger. Byorneth was about to retire as well when a woman approached him in the gathering dark, a tightly strung, nervous woman, probably still upset about her tools. Few things Byorneth had ever seen could make him back up, but he very nearly did so now.

"Your story tonight was beneath notice! I have never heard such a violent fabrication in all my life!"

What she had hoped to accomplish by this thrust, who can say? A frustrated mind turning to the trivial. For a moment, Byorneth was at a loss for words, but he felt he must strike before the enemy retreated. "I could have told them the exciting tale of how a reed pen works, or the Sheewan method of bathing, but I doubt it would have kept your young quiet. My closest friend has a special need for privacy tonight, and my sole concern was ensuring that he have it. Perhaps you might have preferred some of the gentle little stories of monsters and dismemberment they are more used to."

This was entirely true. Many Hillfamilies would educate their young in the horrors committed by passing strangers upon disobedient children. The woman would have denied this if asked directly, but the shot told.

"Well, know that I'll keep my children far away from you in future!"

Byorneth shrugged, but she had already turned and walked away. After the manner of all angry women, she had the last word and would keep it. The old man had already forgotten the exchange as he retired for the night.

Chapter 13
The Stones

HOLD MY LAST KISS FULL UPON THY HONEY HEART,
THAT ALL THE SWEETNESS OF HOURS LOST
MAY FIND IT THERE.

*~Speculations Upon the Tribute
of the Returning King~*

The morning came too early for Hunter. The sun cut through the darkness of the tiny building, shining on the skin of the wife asleep beside him, her long hair spread across his chest and mingling with his beard. She stirred a little as the creeping rays pierced her eyelids, and soon they opened and she saw him watching. With a little smile, she held him closer and laid her head on his shoulder.

Hunter leaned across and kissed her head. "You know, you have very lovely hair."

With a little groan, she stretched and yawned. "It's just the same as every Hillwoman's. Add a little white and it will get ugly."

"Never." He gathered a handful and let it fall. "White or black, I will always love it. Did you sleep well?"

"Mmm. Yes. I thought I would get too cold, but I never did. And you?"

"Very well."

She sat up and rubbed her eyes, looking across as someone knocked at the door, so softly that at first they took it for the wind rattling the door against the frame. There was no answer to her hail, so Srstri opened the door a little and dragged in a platter loaded down with breakfast. Strips of tender meat cooked in wild onions and garlic adorned two little wooden plates in crisp rosettes, and all around were arranged dainty portions of fresh peas encrusted with mountain seeds and roasted over a slow fire. These and many more dainties lay before them, sometimes in spiral wheels, others piled high and topped with dollops of thick cream. A rich meal, it would have been worth many days' wages had they been ordinary travelers. They made tea also, in a quaint little clay pot the woman had provided. It was a dark, lively tea, good for the morning.

Srstri began to eat with a good appetite, but her husband touched nothing until he had read the slip of paper which had been stuck to the side of the platter with wax. The hand was Byorneth's, and the writing was that of the Black Lands far to the south, which Srstri had never learned. "Eat and come out quickly. We've lost enough time." Byorneth had surprised Hunter by allowing them to stay the night. This was more like him.

"Try this!" Srstri offered Hunter a morsel, which he ate out of her fingers.

Between laughter, they ate their fill and talked of the future, until with perverse quickness their time ran out, and in the stillness of the morning, he told her that he had to leave, banishing all joy from their house.

⁓ʌʌ⁓

There were very few years left to Byorneth, he reflected as he watched the sun rise with some impatience. The early work of the tea pickers had begun a full hour before, and he had to summon all his restraint to refrain from awakening Hunter as soon as the light appeared. At last he could wait no longer, and he tore a tidy strip from one of his precious scrolls, wrote the note, and stuck it on the tray of breakfast as it went by in the woman's arms. And still he waited.

The man of the house sat down under his oldest tea trees, waiting for the pickers to come in. All his life, he had worked from dawn to dusk, and even now that much of the labor had gone to hired men and women, he still rose early to see the new sun. The old Sheewa joined him in the slanting shade.

"Good morning, Longfarer. Was your sleep pleasant?" the man asked, concerned. Had Byorneth thought the bed hard, or said aught against the morning meal, he would have been given anything, even unto the house itself to redeem the fault. But all had been well, and he said so very prettily, as the Sheewa are taught to do.

"You might even consider the barter of hospitality for your living should the tea fail you."

The Hillman shuddered, half at the thought of the ruin of his precious leaf, and half at the idea of selling anything as priceless as kindness. One might as well take gold in exchange for water. Turning away from such thoughts, he gestured toward the little house out across the lawn. "Is he your son?"

"I am the nearest thing to a father to him. This is the first time he's ever made me wait."

"There could not have been a better time. Why do you hurry? And where do you go?"

"We have business on the other side, in the Desert over the Kyargh. I believe it is still the easiest route?"

The man took a moment to think. Few Hillmen ever forsake their fertile Caldera for the inhospitable West, but who knew why a Longfarer did anything? "I suppose the Pass is still open. But I would hesitate to take the woman there. Word has it that the scum of the Highlands has gathered itself at the mouth of the Pass."

"We go another route to the Kyargh, and the girl will stay in the Caldera, anyhow. We want no wives with us."

The Highlander stared. "And why not? She seems a capable girl, strong and hardy. If you avoid the mouth of the Pass, there will be few dangers that will not affect you all equally. Besides, she will want to go with her husband!"

"I dare say she will, and I have never worried for her safety. We have much to do in the West, even without a young husband and wife bringing seven kinds of nonsense into the work. She stays here. She's a Hillwoman by birth. There must be something to keep her busy."

The fat woman walked across the yard, a squalling child balanced on each hip. Her husband watched her until she sat the children down and bent over her garden, vanishing behind the intervening hedge. "The woman will stay here with us," he said suddenly. "My wife could use the help, and another woman to talk to. Tell her husband she will be here when he comes back."

At the jingle of Byorneth's gold, the quiet little man snapped a hand out, flinging the coins across the yard, and came near enough to Byorneth for him to smell the tea on his breath. "Kiss your money, man! We of the Highlands value our honor more! Until now, I had thought the Sheewa were the same sort, but now I can see more clearly! Yes, she will be here when you need her, but while she is here she will be an honored guest, working for her own and better out of your reach!"

It was a strange breach of manners for a Highlander, and the man looked a little red as he turned and walked away, but Byorneth thought it was more out of shame than regret. He sat down on the flattened grass where the man had sat and watched the hut again. It was getting very late.

— ᴧ ᴧ —

Srstri could not remember having cried in all her young life. Even on that sorrowful first journey through the mountains, away from all that she loved, when the boys had sobbed as the Stinking Men drove them like cattle, there had only been an echoing void within her, which in the days ahead was never given the time to spring up into tears. But she had wept when she entered the Caldera, and she wept now.

He said things, soft and quick, foolish things which are said through tears by lovers, and they clung to one another as though in a shipwreck.

With her at his elbow, he reached into his bag and produced a small sheet of paper. It was a poem he had written, when once in solitude he had thought of her far away in Seng Grandt. Such a poem is called the Tribute of the Sheewa, the first such writing a man ever dedicates to the woman he will marry. He had broken tradition by writing in Kyarrghnaal as well as Sheewan, but Kyarrghnaal was the tongue of their earliest days together, and no one else would ever see it. He read it to her by the morning's half light, clasping her around her waist, kissing her between each line. It was sufficient as a reminder of their love, if not of their passion, and it was all she would have of him until he returned. Hunter put it in a Sheewan leather case and hung it around her neck, and she kissed him again for the hundredth time that morning. It would be for her eyes alone.

Wives take their husbands' minds from their work, occupying them with thoughts of comfort, and so ought to be left behind, or so said the Sheewa. A year ago, he thought the rule sensible. Now, the young husband inwardly cursed the Sheewa and all their forebears as they exited the dwelling together.

They had said their final goodbye in the warm sunshine beside their house, kissing once more, long and lingering. She presented him with a memento of her own — a long lock of her hair, bright and black, which she braided skillfully there where they stood. Byorneth rumbled, and they kissed yet again before Hunter dragged himself away, hefting his bulging pack and falling in beside Byorneth with the long, road-eating Sheewan stride. Then he walked backward to keep Srstri's waving figure in sight as long as he could until she was gone, hidden by a stand of pine trees. Hunter's heart left him.

It takes a good many days to cross the broad, fertile Crater of Arlinga, but they had an easy time of it whenever they stopped. It had been a long time since any of the scribes passed that way, but the traditions of the Hillfolk live long, and in a district where some could barely read their own language, a deep respect was accorded to those who could speak, read and write as many as ten.

Soon, the Kyarrghnaal around them became softer, with the hard gutturals losing their edge, but the people remained the same — friendly and easygoing, always ready to offer what poor entertainment they could. Hunter found himself wondering how the austerity of the High City could possibly be preferable to this calm life.

Soon, they made ready to begin their ascent into the snowy peaks, among the older tea bushes that lined the valley. But it seemed that they had hardly started when the ancient plants were past and there were no more workers, no more songs. They dipped down again into a shallow depression behind a vast crest of rock which curtained them off from the Caldera completely, and gray stone and stunted bushes surrounded their path. Here, they were beyond the observation of all but the soaring watchers in the clouds. The wind whistled through Hunter's beard and the air tasted bitterly of snow. It bent the brim of his hat down in front of his eyes, so he turned it upward in the front, exposing all of his upper face to the chilly blast. Gradually, the stones that emerged from the gray distance became taller until they stood as high as men, and then they grew larger still, becoming the giant guardians of the Pass.

Any path there may have been had long since passed out of remembrance, so Byorneth led the way by landmarks, learned by heart long ago and studied before they left. The mountains were much closer now, frowning down with stern propriety, but strangely Hunter was glad to be out of the Caldera, happy for the utter solitude. They walked through a break in the foothills, a bare 15 paces wide, and on each side the land mounted in a plateau. At last, his footsteps surpassed those of his friend, and Byorneth muttered below his breath to the effect that those who both lead and follow hasten to their deaths. So Hunter followed circumspectly, for with Byorneth, one never knew.

They mounted upward again with the aid of their staffs, and the way behind them was very clear, even past the ridge down into the inner farmlands of the fertile Hills, progressively shaded by thin mists. Then all was lost to their sight once again as the notch through which they had come closed off, this time completely. They were left all to themselves, two strong men on a lonely path. Then the notch ahead of them opened, and they stepped down into a broad plain, bounded on all sides by great banks of fog which spread in damp fingers down through the valley, intertwining through the columns of stone that littered their way.

As they traveled along, the tapered monoliths sprang up larger and larger, occasionally clustering together in a close group, the tops obscured by thick mist. These surrounded them, and only these, and they drew closer until even Hunter's lifelong love for the thickest forests could not reassure him in the absence of easy vision. These may have been brothers to the stones which stood as sentries on either side of the southern end of the Great Trail, but he did not feel it appropriate to ask Byorneth, and lightly break the silence of that place. Beyond it all, Hunter heard the shrill cry of unseen eagles, even the piercing beat of their wings, for this was the domain of the Killers of the Wind. There were stories of them in Seng Grandt, of scribes who had been snatched off cliffs and carried away to be devoured. He asked Byorneth about them.

"The eagles are not generally troublesome," said Byorneth, turning a thoughtful eye upward, "but there are some large ones nearer the mountains. Keep close to the rocks whenever you can."

Hunter nodded and swallowed hard against the lump in his throat. The fog shrouded them, and that, he supposed, gave them safety, but still his eyes wandered out amongst the gloomy pillars, seeking danger from the hidden sky.

A filthy man stepped out in front of them.

Their weapons were nearly put to use, only held back by an instant. Byorneth spoke loudly out of surprise and annoyance. "What mean you here? Why would you block our path?"

The creature hunched low and leered up from under its black brows. "My apologies, good masters, but I had only just heard you approach, and I desired an audience with your graces."

"We are not noblemen, but simple travelers. You must know that the Time of Eminence has long passed, though we all hope it may come again. State your business, fellow, or let us go by."

The wretch drew himself upright with an amusing dignity. "You may not think so, but I am the king of this mountain, having authority over all the Island. I must be, because I am the only king on the Island, and in the absence of any other, I rule all of you absolutely. I rule this district especially with an iron hand, and none may pass without paying homage, my masters." The man puzzled Hunter, for he spoke with a strangely fawning arrogance. He was clearly mad, and Hunter was about to humor him and be on his way, but Byorneth spoke first.

"We will not, sir. You are not ruler over these Hills, nor yet over the Island. There is but one king in Arlinga, and he will earn your homage soon enough, but now we have urgent business in the country beyond. Let us pass, or suffer for it."

Before Byorneth had finished, the strange man disappeared into the curtain of mist, as if the fog itself had risen up and devoured him. A high voice by Hunter's elbow uttered the filthiest of curses, but his reflexive backhand stroke met naught but air.

All was again silent.

"I know of this man," Byorneth said in a changed voice. "Khornang. He was banished from the Hilltribes because of his madness, which threatened even his nearest kin. When last I heard, he was marauding down South in the Fire Pass." Then, more quietly, "He was very dangerous to begin with, and this solitude could not have steadied his mind. He will probably try to kill us, or at least stop us. But one never knows with such as him."

And so they went, now avoiding the rocks and the danger of surprise by Khornang, choosing instead to risk the snatching death from the air. Hunter's hand rested gently on his belt beside his hook, and twice he very nearly drew it.

Partly to relieve his straining senses, he spoke, still keeping a steady watch all around. "You spoke of a king. If there has not been one for five centuries, how can you be certain that one will arise now? I have been with you constantly these many marches, and I know naught of such a thing."

"He is being prepared in secret, and will take the throne when the time is right. All else is best kept dark even from you, my son."

Hunter had many more questions, but he knew that for the moment, it would be useless to ask them. He would have to be satisfied with keeping watch for their hidden companion as they walked along, waiting for the end of the field.

Still, the formless gray of the far distance was a long time in coming. The constant watching dulled his perceptions, and he caught himself losing touch with the world, watching the dank grass as it went by instead of the passing distance.

His eyes were down when an arrow pierced the ground at their feet, and Hunter and Byorneth broke apart and made for the cover of two great stones, some distance apart, hardly visible from one another through the fog. Byorneth's voice reached Hunter from out of the void in the pure language of the Sheewa. "Our adversary must be on the top of yonder stone."

Hunter could just barely see the stone he spoke of. "We can circle around through the fog and take him from behind."

"Good. You take the right. If he sees you, fade back into the mist."

They moved as quickly as they dared, crouching. There was little danger of noise, the ground being soft and spongy with the fog, and both men were experienced hunters who knew how to tread lightly.

The madman on top of the rock was confused, and the feeling angered him. He scowled down from his perch and nocked another arrow.

The height of the stone amazed Hunter as it appeared out of the mist. It was nearly half again as high and as wide as the others, and curiously streaked with clusters of red spots which spiraled all up and down its entire body. He nearly struck at Byorneth when the old man suddenly appeared beside him. Then, without a word, they moved apart for fighting space and advanced upon the stone.

This time they were ready, and at the note of a bowstring, each leapt far to the side. An arrow whistled into the ground just behind where Byorneth had stood. "Now! Go!" the old man cried, and they ran together into the covert of the stone, standing silent together for a time, their backs against the rock.

Between them, there was a set of crude stairs carved into the sheer stone, leading upwards to the pinnacle. It was only just wide enough for one man to ascend at a time, with little chance for self-defense. Byorneth reached out and laid his hand on Hunter's shoulder. "You start up the steps when I give the call. Careful, now." The words were scarcely out before he vanished into the mist.

Each step was barely a hand's breadth wide, and he would have to ascend using only his toes. He laid his quiver on the ground along with his bow, hat, staff, cape and pack, and drew the hook from his belt. Training can only prepare a man for so much, and it was this thought that occupied Hunter as he waited. Well used to hunting, there was something different in this breathless waiting, the perverse slowness of time, the pounding in his ears.

A long call came up from the other side, and Hunter took his courage in his hands and began to run up the steps toward the sky. He was a strong man, well suited to walking, but this balancing on his toes with hardly any purchase, climbing into thick cloud, unsettled him. The shroud around him became thicker until at last the steps before him were completely hidden, and with the lost momentum he almost pitched backward. The walls on either side grew taller the higher he climbed.

Soon voices reached him, the fawning sounds of the madman of the rocks and fainter, the reasonable tones of Byorneth down below. Now he began to see two towers which crowned the pillar, and a succession of ramparts all around. In the former ages, it had been a watchtower, and though it seemed like any other stone from down below, the top was carved into a little castle, with loops in the walls for archers.

But he gave these no more than a glance, for a shadowy man paced back and forth along the wall, very straight with a bow ready at his side. Now he heard the words clearly, even those of his friend down below. Step by silent step, Hunter kept on with his advance, hardly breathing, especially when he came into the atmosphere of the pinnacle, thick with the essence of that filthy man.

"But you will concede, will you not, that the only man in the valley owns the valley?"

"Perhaps he has certain rights upon it, but the ultimate authority is that of the rightful king." Byorneth's voice was such that he could speak conversationally over great distances, and though he must have been hidden away in the fog, every word reached the pinnacle clearly. "You have no right to levy allegiance from any traveler."

"But I am the king — the only king."

"As I said, there is another who will rise and seize what is his, and it is he who will bring you to account. It is to him that we bow, and none other." Hunter now stood on the wide platform, and his steps were solid again. A sure grip around the fellow's windpipe and he would be at his mercy.

"Sir, the choice is so simple. One little humbling and it will be all over—" The madman pivoted on his heel and brought the bow to its fullest extension with one movement, and the shaft broke against the wall behind Hunter as he threw himself backward onto the hard floor. Without hesitation, his enemy nocked another bolt and leapt to Hunter's side before he could regain his feet. Hunter knocked the rough-knapped arrowhead aside with the dagger, and brought the blade across again in a wild swipe at the man's midsection. It missed, but it forced him to step back. Hunter used the moment he had gained to get his feet under him.

In the confusion, his adversary had kept hold of the arrow and drew it back again, but this time Hunter was ready. With one long stride, he was beside him, and in an instant the tightened bowstring was cut with an angry buzzing note, and the archer cried out in pain as his arms extended with the released pressure and his elbow smashed backward against the parapet.

But the pain never gave the man pause. With a renewed vigor, he twisted and began smashing Hunter backward into the stone, holding the hooked dagger at arm's length with his injured arm. "Kneel!" he growled with each blow. "Kneel, my master!"

Hunter's training acted through him when the man came forward to strike again. He kicked Khornang's legs out from under him, and the Man of the Mountains fell down on his face before Hunter. Instantly, the young Sheewa knelt between the writhing shoulder blades with both knees and cut away the belt that held the rest of Khornang's weapons. Then Byorneth's rough shoe was across his enemy's neck.

"Those are awkward stairs, or I would have come sooner. I see now there was no need."

"No need." Hunter put his hook away and stood to collect his wind. "Now, what to do with him?"

Khornang seemed almost to have fallen asleep, but at the sound of Byorneth's blade sliding out of its leather he came alive, and with a supreme effort overthrew the elder Sheewa. Before Hunter could stay him, the madman had run to the wall, snatched a bow and quiver out of a corner, and was gone over the side. They arrived not a second after, but Khornang had already slid down the impossible slope of the west side of the tower, rolled to his feet, and dashed away.

—∧∧—

Why should Srstri not have run after them? Who had a better right than she? As a wife, according to the customs of the Hills, her duty was to remain with her husband, and he with her. She had only just begun to be accustomed to Hunter, his smile, the warmth of his body. When at last he vanished, she cried out in sudden pain and bowed her head as the tears flowed. All who saw her stood aloof out of respect for her grief. She remained immobile but for her hair, stirred by the breath of the wind.

The woman of that house was as practical as she was large, and she had a great heart in these matters. When at last Srstri wiped the tears away with her sleeve, the woman wrapped a heavy arm around her shoulders and ushered her into the kitchen, a small, warm hovel full of good, strange smells.

What a woman she was! Even if Hunter had not taken her aside in the early hours to arrange for Srstri's stay, even had the man of the house not sworn to take the girl in, she could not have kept herself from helping. Indeed, being a young wife with no example, Srstri had feared for her skills as a home-maker, and in that close, cozy house, pine lined and warm, she received her first lessons. The woman was frank and earthy, preparing the girl in her own rough way for a marriage post-poned. As she listened, Srstri began to smile and laugh, and soon pretense became truth as she was put at her ease. It was a good place, and now that she really saw it, there were many connections, many sights and smells which put her in mind of a life long forgotten.

After all, Hunter was not dead, and she was not the first wife who had ever waited for a husband from far away. Soon, the big woman stood and opened a little door that led out into the bright sunshine. "Come along, and I'll serve you tea. We both need a change of air."

Srstri's heart leapt at the thought of the drink. She could remember that as a little girl, her parents would allow her one little cupful in the morning, out of her special little cup with her name lovingly carved by her father. Even this small amount would give her such zest throughout the day that her mother must have regretted the concession, but her father laughed and said that it was good for her to experience the joy their profession as tea planters gave to the Hills. She never had any tea again until the cup she drank with Hunter, and so it had an even greater significance to her.

The little house was low and covered with sod, its floor being about a rophoil[3] below ground level, and it had been built next to a grove of very old tea trees. Centuries had passed since their planting, and their branches were gnarled and twisted, but still they bore good leaves. Better leaves, if you believed their owners, than the more plentiful output of the newer plants elsewhere on the hillsides. The family kept the best for themselves. Insects were allowed to eat holes in the leaves before picking, so they developed unexpected flavors of mountain fruit and spring flowers.

The woman produced a quantity of this precious, wiry stuff, strangely brown, white, gold and red, and it was infused lovingly, as it deserved. Cold spring water was heated quickly and poured over the leaves in the heated pot before boiling. Inside the pot, Srstri knew each miserly leaf was slowly opening its tight little fist, giving up its essential treasure to the water.

It is the custom of the Hills to brew tea no less than three infusions at a time so as to completely exhaust the leaves, and Srstri loved them all — the high, strong flowery notes of the first infusion, the leveling effect of the second with the base honey and spice notes rising, then top and bottom meeting sublimely on the third brewing, blending into a rich, full symphony. She felt the honor that was being done her, for this tea was far too choice to waste on foreign merchants. As they finished the third infusion, she told her hostess so.

"Nonsense," returned the woman. "We have to talk over a cup of something. This poor stuff is all I have to hand." But she was pleased, and smiled proudly. "Do you feel better now?"

"Yes, a little. I am very refreshed, and thank-you so much for the talk! I appreciate your concern."

---

3   The length of a long Sheewan stride, or 3.25 feet/1 meter.

"What are you going to do now?"

"I'd not made any plans."

"How about your family?"

"I have no clear memory of where my home was. Even if I were to find it, wouldn't my arrival bring greater pain upon my parents?"

"How absurd! Why would they be anything but joyful to get you back? They would have no hope of seeing you again, no thought for you but sorrow. It is as if you had died, and your return is a renewal!"

Srstri thought for a while. "I remember from our doorway I could see a mountain that looked like a great snail. There was a little river I used to play in higher up on the ridge. My mother found me there once, and I was forbidden from ever going again. They used to take me with them to a great sea when they went on business, and sometimes I played in the water, or my father taught me to fish."

"How long did you travel to get there?"

She thought again for a moment. Time is a hard thing for a child, subject to the feeling of the moment. "I think perhaps we used to sleep in the house of friends on the way back home. They let me feed a calf once."

The woman stood up and set to clearing away the tea. Srstri could not guess the effect of her words on the mind behind that stolid face. When the woman returned, it seemed the subject had been forgotten. "When your man comes back, you should have something to show for your time away from him. It will impress him, and remind him not to take you for granted. Have you any gold?"

The girl shook her head. "I was lately brought out of the villages, and afterward I spent a year — elsewhere. I've not had time."

"You have time now. You must earn some." She looked away for a moment. When her eyes met her young friend's again, it was obvious she had come to a decision, but it was needful in all such things that the spouse be consulted first. Calling him from where he worked, silent and agreeable, she took him to confer among the trees before returning to the benches and tea table where Srstri sat.

The husband spoke first. "Srstri, my wife and I own a great deal of land hereabouts. Our workers come from local families who need the work, but we have always needed more. We would appreciate it if you would work on our upper section until we can get someone else—"

His wife cut in. "Until your husband returns for you."

"Until your husband returns for you," the man continued. "By then, you will have enough gold to invest—"

"To buy a place of your own."

"To buy a place — and, ah—" He looked to his wife, now completely perplexed.

"And be ready to start your family."

Smiling, he walked back to work, glad to be safely out of it. The woman looked impressively down at Srstri and smiled.

Up above, an eagle screamed. It was headed westward, toward the Desert.

Chapter 14
The Madman

IT IS AGAINST CRUELTY WE STAND, NOT ROYALTY.
AGAINST DISHONOR, NOT OBEDIENCE.
SO COME ALL WHO WILL,
AGAINST THE FORTRESS IN THE WILDERNESS.

~The Ranger's Challenge~

He knew the heavy figure through the rippling air even before he saw any feature. Teidin knew of no one else who would walk abroad on such a genial day wrapped in so many uncongenial coats of wool. There should have been no reason to fear, for the brothers had sworn no oath to remain, yet he shifted his belt around so his long knife was ready to hand.

There were still men with Banat, jackals walking several paces behind their lion. The brothers had been sure Banat would soon be alone in his quest, but the men were still there. As they saw Teidin, two of them nudged Banat, who brushed them away and nodded.

"So, the digger has come back to its master!" one of the men said loudly enough for Teidin to hear, using the name Lowland farmers least like to be called, but Teidin said nothing in return. The man would have been lower than a digger himself were it not for his patron.

They met in the middle of the quiet hill road and stood to look at one another. Banat and his followers had come through hard times, every step of which was written in the dirt on their garments and the ill-humor in their faces. "Well, give account! For what great and compelling reason did you desert me?"

"We are our own men." Teidin shifted his belt around further. "Our goings were none of your concern. We thought we could find some trace of the slave here in the Hills, but we found none. Now I go back home, and leave you to your obsession. Let me by."

No one moved. A tight suspicion formed between Banat's eyes, over and above their naturally skeptical cast. "And what, if anything, did you and the other whelp find in this land? And where has that traitor gone? Did he desert you as you forsook me?"

"He was lost. Any who doubt his character will see otherwise in blood. Let me by."

Banat's hand raised and his minions moved across the road, drawing their weapons. They were men without conscience, motivated by gold, it is true, but the very zest of their life lay in pain and disorder. A fistful of cold fingers took Teidin by the throat, and he brought out his knife, edge upward and ready.

"Hold!" the man in wool ordered, and his men relaxed. "Tell me, digger. If my men and I were to walk on down this road, what would we find? A filthy swarm of Hill carrion as we have seen so far? Or perhaps one filthy slave and a couple of muleteers along with her?" The men laughed, though Banat never intended any humor. The source was everything.

Teidin laughed with them. "Oh, you'd waste your time going on this way! Squalid tea farms, nothing more. We've seen nothing like mule drivers anywhere!" That much was true.

At a signal from Banat, his men came forward down the road, weapons raised against Teidin's knife. He hesitated, and then stepped aside and let them by. Who was the slave to him? Who were the mule drivers? A marriage between a thief and stolen property was absurd on the face of it. One by one, each missile of logic was hurled against the pillar of his mind, but the single unassailable image remained — that of a black-smith's hearth and two people who stood before a man with a book.

The shrinking backs of the men who walked past changed his mind for good. He put his knife away, but turned his steps back where he came from, following the little troop at a safe distance through the farms and tea bushes. He was sure his manner had told them everything, and soon the new marriage would be imperiled before it had begun.

They passed by the smithy, but as there was no one there, Banat went by without a glance. All who met them gave them a clear path, passing by on either side.

It was only when the sudden nighttime set the men yawning that Banat acknowledged the necessity to make camp. Impatience was no longer a transient emotion in his character, but rather it dominated him altogether, and that gave Banat a perverse sort of patience. It was a joyless camp that night, and the men ate silently, each little sound glared down by their leader almost before it was out.

They had barely started eating when a noise like that of an advancing flood came slowly out of the gathering night, and the Lowlanders pricked up their ears like so many dogs. The camp had been made at the side of the Trail, and many still traveled that way back to their homes or out on visits, anxious to go to bed themselves. But this was a noise of many people, chattering like birds as they walked in a long, lingering group. At its outer edges were a great many silent fellows, their weapons ready to hand. Leaping and dancing, singing loudly, the travelers seemed guided only by these few guards around the borders, and even they moved in a sort of half dance that rattled their swords with each step.

A young woman leapt out of the little throng and danced off ahead of the rest, singing a lively cadence in which the rest of the company joined. The burden of her song was a mystery to the men who lay listening as she danced by, but the joy it expressed was evident. The folk of that company were engaged in *tsalokh*, an exuberant expression of joy at some great success. The *tsalokh* was customary when a plantation had made a great sale, as this one had, and at such times workers and owners would range far together, dancing and singing into the night, inviting all to share in their windfall and spreading gifts in their wake.

The *tsalokh* passed by, and with its passing a sudden change occurred in the Lowland camp. Teidin had never seen such a quick packing away of bedding, a stomping out of fire. All was put away in the barest instant, and the old camp was deserted as Banat and his servants slipped into the darkness.

Teidin had not yet settled, and so he followed quickly, this time in the open, for the darkness would hide him well enough on the road, and could only hurt him among the close trees. But even had it been broadest day, they would never have seen him, such was their rabid haste. They practically foamed in excitement. Nearer and nearer came they to the *tsalokh*, and the sound of their frolicking grew.

He could not see very well in the gathering twilight, and so he completely lost track of Banat and his lackeys in the storm of celebration that trailed in the *tsalokh*'s wake. Still, he followed, and the distance and time of night made no difference in the revelers' pitch or their pace, for the *tsalokh* happens but infrequently, and five participants more or less would pass without comment.

At last, as the wind began to carry a hint of lake water, the party lit torches to guide them. At the rear of the procession, a tiny knot of people broke away with such furtiveness that Teidin stopped. The light passed quickly away down the road, but he had seen enough. Two of the men carried a burden between them, and Banat led the whole group off into the utter night. He followed them easily, a ghost in the shadows, to a covert among the high grass in which he lay and watched.

"Set it down there by the stream," Banat ordered as he lit another fire. The men set their load down roughly by the side of a babbling rill that flowed downcountry toward one of the great inland seas, and sat all around it, some stooping to drink. The burden was a girl, young and wide of eyes. Her mouth was gagged heavily, and her muffled screams must have been drowned in the din of the *tsalokh*, but now she lay silent, speaking only with her eyes, which darted back and forth like those of a stricken deer. From where Teidin lay in the outer darkness, he could see her perfectly, and the villains that framed her, all ruddy in the firelight. Some began to cook their supper.

"The whetstone!" Banat ordered, and one of his men tossed it across the stream. Smoothly, he began to rasp a knife across its surface.

One of his men stared for a moment, and then asked, "Why are you dulling that knife? You're taking the edge off."

"I know." He kept working the blade.

"But why?"

Banat growled, and before any could react, he had seized the man's arm and jerked it near him as he took a longer dagger out of his clothes. "Now tell me, Hornaal, which hurts most? This?" He drew the long blade quickly across the man's skin, bringing a gasp at the sight of the red line. The unfortunate man tried to pull away, but Banat held to him like a leech.

"Or this?" This time he used the dull blade, pushing the rounded edge through the skin in an even longer line down the length of the man's arm all the way down and into his palm. They must have been away from any settlements, for the wild screams through the night brought no response from any neighbor.

Dissatisfied, Banat set to dulling his blade once again. The girl had been still during the display, but now she thrashed like a landed fish, straining against every knot that held her down. At last, Banat felt the knife's edge and, finding naught but ragged metal, he stepped over the man who lay whimpering and holding the hem of his cloak against his arm. The eyes of the Highland girl were wide as he knelt beside her.

"Now, you. You stole from me a very great treasure. You will tell me the secret you are keeping. The stone that you took away for yourself. Where is it?" Very lightly, he touched the dulled point to the flesh of her upper arm. She recoiled at the chill of the metal. "Now, if I were to remove the cloth, you'd not scream, would you? No, I thought not. The screaming comes later." He reached up and pulled the gag down over her jaw around her neck. She did not comprehend his words, Teidin could see that, but the point of the blade gave her the essence of Banat's meaning, and she never offered to scream.

Instead, she talked, informing him of her innocence, begging for release, and at the last, threatening him with the wrath of her kinsmen. He stopped the flow of words with a resounding backhanded blow across her face that started the blood from the corner of her mouth. Strangely, the pain seemed only to dry her tears, and the fear in her eyes turned icily to quiet hatred.

"Cease your gibbering, and speak properly! Next time, I use the blade!" He understood her every word, but loved the helpless fear he inspired by pretending not to. It enraged him that there was no terror here.

All night, it had not occurred to Teidin that he should act. He had not followed the men out of any sense of duty or personal vendetta. Indeed, he could divine nothing but curiosity in his own motives until he heard the sound of the slap. One sight of the Hillwoman's reddened cheek settled him. He jerked his knife and came forward into the firelight, and at the sound the men stood in disorder, fumbling for their blades.

Banat turned, but remained crouching. "Well, the field rat shows himself at last! Come join us and see the *deesard* talk!"

Teidin came across the water, brought the handle of his knife around in a swing that stunned Banat, and pulled the blade through the knots that held the girl's hands and feet. With barely a sound she disappeared into the night. When Teidin faced Banat and his henchmen, the woolly man still kneeled where the girl had lain. It had been in the young Lowlander's mind to vanish into the darkness along with her, but the men would surely have followed him, and perhaps put the child in danger again. Here, at least, he could delay them.

"Kill him." Banat may have been ordering a field plowed or fowl plucked for all the rage he showed. He only smiled, a dearly held suspicion at last confirmed, and sat back to watch as his men moved to fulfill their orders.

"She was not the one!" he cried as they came at him. "She was passing by, that was all! Your *deesard* was marriageable, but this was still a child!"

"Hold," Banat told his men, and they stopped. "You. You have seen her. You have seen the *deesard*, and you lied to me. Would you care to purchase your life and tell us where this vision appeared to you?"

Teidin was not fooled. He had seen Banat's honor at work, and knew he loved murder more than truth. The danger was in no way lessened, for he could never lead these men to that for which they sought. "She was down at the lake. There was a little farm, and I saw her tending the cattle in a green field. Maybe she's still there, I know not."

"Why did you fail to tell us this?" one of the men asked in anger. "How many days were you going to let us wander all over the Caldera with no hope of success?" He raised his broad bush knife for a killing swipe, but Banat had already stood and now he stayed the fellow's hand. When the minion sought to free himself, Banat stepped in again and threw him to the ground with an easy sweep.

The man in wool stood for a while and looked once again at Teidin, his head cocked like a mongrel dog's. Then approximating a warm smile, he gestured regally. "My boy, would you care to lead us to this farm in exchange for a fair wage, equal to that of these others? It will be a pretty penny, I can tell you!"

Without hesitation, Teidin agreed. "But we should sleep first." Another deception. He needed rest, but he doubted he could really sleep. "She can't know we are after her, and travel is better in daylight. You've all waited this long, and only slaves can work without rest." He never waited for consent as he unslung the pack from around his shoulders and spread himself out for the night. From where he lay, he calmly stole a morsel from the flames, ate it, and cleaned his teeth as though he were in his own house. Elnaan could have done no better.

The girl ran to and fro, searching for a familiar path until at last she came to her home in the bright moonlight. The *tsalokh* had only just ended on its meandering road, and her mother and father had only just missed her. The family's hired labor, who had joined in the frantic preparations for a search, loudly proclaimed the good news as they saw her. Soon the master and mistress of the house, all set to lead the expedition, parted their number and descended upon their youngest child in an exuberance of relief. Then, in the broad front room of the finest home in all the Western Caldera, she told her father a tale.

The man turned darker with every word, until at last his daughter's story concluded, and silently he went and took a long object off the wall, calmly summoning his men.

—◠◠◠—

Khornang had not reappeared.

Byorneth and Hunter pushed on through the mist, maintaining perfect silence until finally the light was lost, and the world around them began to fade. The old man pointed off to the north where Hunter could only just make out a stand of timber, and soon they were setting up a cold camp among the pines. Hunter knew better than to feel safe in this place, but he hoped the madman's injury would silence him for tonight. The Sheewa kept a strict watch, one or the other on constant guard with bow and hook ready to hand.

When they broke camp in the early light, the mist was already drifting away. Soon, the air was entirely clear, so that the high spires sparkled in the slanting sun, and they saw the walls of the Kyargh stretching out far in front of them. Beyond the trees and the few remaining pillars, there was the head of a ravine, the gate that would lead them into the country beyond. After a pause to stretch the stiffness from their legs, they started out once again on their journey, glad to be out in the open at last.

Byorneth halted before a certain tall tapered stone, broad and flat and carved into a platform at the base where Byorneth went and stood, Hunter joining him. Looking closer, Hunter saw the stone bore marks, put there years past by the hand of man, weather worn and rounded, but still clearly a map which covered about half the stone's face. The skill of the carver and the many languages represented proclaimed it a Sheewan chart, and Hunter could clearly distinguish the terracing that represented the tea plantations of the Hills and the convoluted path that led across the Kyargh into the Desert. At certain points along the stone, far predating the rest of the work, there were notes rendered in the Old Monumental Script, now largely illegible. The map stone stood at the mouth of the broken trail which began the tortuous path up the slope of the High Hills. Though he had made the minutest study of every map available in Seng Grandt, even as Hunter had, Byorneth studied the stone carefully for a long time, tipping his hat onto the back of his head. Finally, he laid a hand on the map and spoke. "This is the head of the gully, where we are. Up here," he pointed to a section where the trail swept across a wavering line that meandered across the map, "our path crosses this river. It is swollen this time of year with the melting snow in the mountains. We follow through the long gully until then. There will be no lack of places on the way for our new friend to lie in wait to waylay us." Byorneth stayed looking up at the stone until finally he sighed and said, "Come along, then," and they entered the mouth of the ravine.

The level grass continued for a time as they walked along the narrow way, but it soon gave way to bare gravel and rough bushes, and their pace became slower and more labored. Byorneth, much to Hunter's surprise, began to show his age, wheezing softly as he went, stopping occasionally and unashamedly leaning against Hunter or a convenient wall. The ground grew more uneven still along its slow upward way, and at times they would slide, sending little showers of pebbles down around them. The gravel became small boulders, and soon they had to contend with the very real danger of broken limbs. The high walls which reared on either side proved at least as treacherous, for one could not lay a hand to them without bringing pieces of them down.

Finally, they stopped to rest, having gone about a kand from the valley of stones. Byorneth sat down between two little bushes and put his head between his knees. Hunter worried, for while he was young, and his youthful frame rejoiced in the fresh challenge, even he had nearly turned his ankles on the sharp stones.

"Byorneth, is there not a better way off to the west?

Byorneth slowly raised his head and fixed Hunter with a blank stare. "Do you desire a safer road for yourself, or to spare my old bones?"

There could be no safe answer. "There are many places of ambush along here. You said so yourself. Besides, the straighter path would take us across that hummock yonder, and point us across to the Desert." He motioned toward the west, where the gorge's wall had broken down, affording a clear view of the mountains and the low hill between. The breeze that moaned faintly across smelled more of dust than of the clean heights beyond.

Byorneth's hackles were still up, and he answered, coldly amused. "You may go that way if you wish, Hunter, and if you get across, you must tell me how you managed to cross that stretch of gorge just beyond the hummock. It spans the entire distance from the River Garracheer to the mountains, and it is deep and sheer. Or, you could go on with me." Hunter's face burned, and he might have protested, but there was nothing his friend despised more than a man first in his own defense. He swallowed the disgrace and kept silent.

So they traveled on, their attention entirely occupied with the simple task of walking. Soon, even their staffs were no help, and they threaded them through the straps of their bags across their shoulders. If they had had extra eyes to watch for Khornang, they would have, but as it was, they were once again taken entirely by surprise when suddenly hailed from above by the filthy wretch who had assailed them before.

He smiled down at them regally from his perch on the edge of the rock wall. His bow was at the ready, and Hunter and Byorneth knew from experience that the dirty little man was, if nothing else, a clean shot. They stood without moving, entirely in the open and exposed as he spoke.

"My honored masters, you seem to have chosen a singularly slow and dangerous path. There is no telling what manner of highwayman might hinder your march! You are tired, and must rest. Please, stand for a moment and catch your breath. But while you do so, there is no impediment to your kneeling and bowing before me, the native ruler of this realm."

"Byorneth!" Hunter hissed furiously. "That bow is very real, and he will surely kill us if we again refuse. For our lives' sake, I am going to kneel and be rid of him!"

Byorneth's reply came upon the instant. "If you do, Hunter, then you may claim this breath as your last. I will kill you if you so much as bow your head. You just stand there and keep still."

Khornang's domineering expression gradually shifted to that of annoyance, and finally, complete rage. He screamed and drew back his arrow, and his first shot barely missed impaling Hunter through his chest as they dashed beneath the ledge overhanging the ravine's wall.

Despite his unreasoning burst of passion, Khornang used only that one shot. He could see nothing from his position on the same side of the ravine as the travelers, but his ears picked out what few others could have — soft breathing, scuffling shoes. He dared not descend into the ravine and expose himself to their wrath. From where he sat, he could command both sides of the overhang under which his quarry sheltered. He would show them how patient he could be.

Presently, the sun tilted and shone on them as they reclined against the wall. They began to sweat, the brine dripping from their noses, and then their skin dried and their limbs waxed heavy. Where Hunter's mouth had been wet it turned to glue, and then it dried entirely so that his tongue was leather against his teeth. He sipped at his water, but there was little enough left, and it merely prolonged his thirst, never satisfying it.

Profound though the sun's effects may be upon human flesh, they are even greater upon ice and snow. Far above their heads, high up on the eastern slopes of the Kyargh, accumulated winter seeped into little trickles of water, which joined together into rivulets, the rivulets into furious little streams. And then the rain began to fall, and with a great, gurgling growl, the floodgates of the mountains were breached. Its fury gathered together in ditches, filling them to their brims, and then rushed down the larger ravines, and then the narrowing gorges, the most violent of which led all the way down to where two men sat beneath a ledge.

So they sat for a long time, their throats crying out for water. A small horned beetle, striped across its folded wings with red and black, scuttled unhurriedly across the rocky floor, tumbling over the rubble with a clicking noise that echoed in the silent air. It flew off on the breast of a cool breeze, and Byorneth's eyes widened in horror.

He sprang to his feet and took Hunter by the arm as a low rumble shook the ground. "Come! Climb the wall! Quickly!" Hunter hung back, fearing arrows from above, for he knew not his danger until the vast wall of branches and water rushed into sight. It pushed several great uprooted trees upon its crest, gathering up great stones and kicking them into the walls with a great lethal clatter. It was the Devil of the Hills, awakened to its fury.

All weakness forgotten, they bounded across and up the massive wall easily. The greedy water snatched at Hunter's foot as he climbed up, nearly peeling his shoe away into the current. Their enemy was ready for them, and had only just taken deadly aim at the small of Hunter's back when the roaring torrent undercut the ledge where he stood.

Hunter and Byorneth never heard the scream.

The ravine was instantly impassable. Even long after the first rush of the flood had died, its brown water ran deep and showed no signs of receding, gradually overflowing the bank and lapping in a large, shallow pool around their feet. Khornang was not to be seen. He must have known the danger before they had and gotten far away, or he may have been on the point of releasing an arrow when the water came. They had best be away quickly.

Wary of their enemy and the busy water, they walked around in a wide circle away from the ravine, toward the Garracheer and their intended path. The going was much smoother, and Hunter wondered again why they had not abandoned the ravine before. The flood steamed like a kettle, and the solid gray swells shook the ground all around the channel. Soon, the land was wet for a kual around the ravine, and still it rose, murmuring unhappily to itself at the waning of its power.

"Be more careful with your water from now on," Byorneth said as they walked on upstream together. "This flood will cloud every pool on this side of the mountain. After a wash like this, you do not drink water. You eat dirt."

Suddenly, the water bag under Hunter's arm felt perversely light, and his thirst, which he had forgotten, came upon him at once.

Chapter 15

The Bird

They reached the confluence of the river and newly made waterway just as the sunlight faded. The icy channel still ran brimful and swift, and so Hunter and Byorneth made their beds and lay down on a hillock far out of its path. A snow-scented zephyr played about their faces and among the folds of their clothing. As there was wood nearby, and in spite of the possible continued danger from Khornang, they built a fire and cooked some of the salted meat they had in their packs. This along with two pieces of nourishing Sheewan journey bread made their meal, and they lay back, satisfied. There was little need for talking — both were acquainted and friendly with silence.

Gray turned to black, and black to deep speckled blue as one by one the stars appeared all around them, mapping their way for tomorrow. The moon was waxing, almost full. Hunter thought of Srstri, wondering if she was looking up at the moon, their only contact across the mountains. He felt a gnawing longing to see her again, almost fancying he could feel her, pressed close and warm. He shook himself and put such thoughts from his mind, until at last he surrendered to the beckoning force of sleep.

Morning, when it came, came quickly. It rose among the dim slopes of the east, and illuminated the Hills across the Caldera with a rim of golden light. Hunter and Byorneth broke camp, jumped the narrow part of the receding stream, and moved on, a little sore, but otherwise well. With each successive step up the long hills to the Kyargh, Hunter's breath came faster, his limbs hung heavier. He had been given to expect this with the higher ground, but nothing can prepare any man for the waning of his youth, be it at his 20th or 81st year.

Their target was the broad gap between the twin summits of the Kyargh, which stood like a near thing in the crystal air. Besides themselves and a distant wolf pack which vanished almost immediately, the land was devoid of movement.

Mountains are maddening things. They become visible long before they are near, and remain aloof far longer. Their ancient, knowing faces went on forever all around, but it was not until the fifth day that at last they showed the least change, and by then the land had begun to rear up in a low mound before the High Hills. Vegetation suddenly appeared in greater profusion, and low gray bushes filled their path, encumbering their steps and slowing their pace.

There had been no sign of Khornang for these many kaind, but madness is a curious thing. A lunatic may pursue the same object for a lifetime, or he may abandon it suddenly for a swim in a river, or a run through the tall grass. Hunter did not think it strange, but Byorneth, a careful man, swiveled to look around every few steps.

At last, they arrived at the base of the slope that leads to the snowy tops of the Kyargh, and Byorneth led the way upward. If they were to keep to their determined pace, they could not afford to stop in awe of the climb ahead, as Hunter was tempted to do. Rest would come later. Now was the time for climbing.

Men seldom ventured across the Kyargh to the land beyond, for they seldom had reason to, and so the Trail was ill-worn. The vegetation changed again, and low evergreens lined and many times blocked their path, while the heavy scent of pine filled their nostrils. The Trail widened, narrowed and widened again, passing from pine to ever smaller pine. They went up grades and through dense thickets of briers, inching over ledges that flanked gorges, leaping broad chasms. Many times the Trail simply disappeared, and only by Byorneth's experience could they divine its recurrence. As they mounted the first tier of the mountain, they could overlook the whole valley, from the gap where they had come from the vale of stones through to the gorge, still flowing with water, and the river of its origin.

Hunter rejoiced in this newfound country, bleak though it seemed. Soon the scrub pine was gone, and the nights were numbingly cold, the frigid wind howling down the canyons and cutting keenly through every layer of their clothing. Still, the rugged grandeur of the mountains that surrounded them, the elevation, the very coloration of the stones, aroused a boyish delight in him, the feeling he had pierced the highest sky. It was no wonder Khornang conceived himself to be a king, for who could scale such heights, stand upon such peaks, surmount the very spine of the upper earth, and not feel a little grander than his fellows?

They bundled on layer after layer of clothing as they went. Before they were halfway up the mountain, they had changed trousers and cloak for heavy woollen leggings and bearskin coats, thick woollen hats in place of the Sheewan broad brim. Their breath began to freeze into white blades in their beards, and frost formed on their lashes and chilled their lids when they squinted it away.

They stopped as they passed a certain icy rivulet and had tea out of their stores. It was one of the best of the green teas, and as they drank, a portion of their weariness seemed to leave them. Hunter leaned back on the lichen-covered stone and gathered his clothing around him, sheltering his steaming cup from the sharp current. Cold air always makes tea taste better, but it would be a shame to allow it to cool too soon. They dangled their feet off the ledge over kaind of empty winds. He looked up at the peaks above and sighed.

"When were you last over this path, Byorneth? It seems easy enough to you."

"My training was only just completed, so it was very long ago."

"But how can you remember it so perfectly?"

"I was cut off from my fellow Sheewa, and I spent some time finding my way through the mountains. I vowed I would never be ignorant again, and so I learned the Trail far better than any Lowland farmer knows his fields."

The old man was in one of his rare forthcoming moods, and Hunter knew enough to take full advantage of it.

"What manner of country is the West?" He had read of it at Seng Grandt, but being told of it by one who had breathed its air was a different thing, and with the rigors of training there had never been time. It was all too easy for the royal scholars to forget that written records are but one small part of any history. There are always details which escape the scribe's pen.

Byorneth leaned back on the rocks and smiled to himself, not the teacher now, but rather a fellow traveler beguiling a little time for warmth. "A people have never been born better suited to their land. Stout, proud warriors all, even their women, and expert upon the backs of their magnificent horses. You have never seen such beasts! It is as if they were gathered up out of the sand and filled with life from the sea wind, blown across the Desert on the breast of the clouds. To look in their eyes is to feel small. To sit astride is to be more than a man.

"When you talk with the folk of that country, learn to scent the wind carefully, for it may shift without warning and leave you alone in the Desert with a blade in your belly. They are a people ruthless in honor, quick to take affront." He stood and adjusted the straps on his pack. "Let us be off. The Trail is hard, and the day grows short."

The shoes they had put on were of bearskin with the fur turned inward, and the Sheewan craftsmen had made the sole with thick stitching and a double layer of tough hinai skin. The tops could be laced shut with rawhide thongs, and the lush fur curled up to cover the ankles, meeting the leggings above. They were very good shoes, yet still their toes lost feeling as they came suddenly onto the snowy flats and the ice caked their soles. Soon, it reached to their waists, slowing their pace to a crawl. The rest of nature was dormant, all asleep except for a high, lone eagle probing the earth for the least movement.

At last, they could go no longer. Hunter's thighs burned and his thoughts blew like smoke, wafting to his pushing footsteps as the light faded and the cold world turned ever colder. They were in the middle of a mountain valley, full of drifts and protruding fingers of rock, and Byorneth knelt at one of the larger drifts, hardened with the wind, and began to scoop snow away with his gloved hands. Hunter had heard mention of snow caves, but had never seen one built, or had the procedure explained to him. He knelt beside Byorneth to help him, and soon most of the snow inside the cocoon was scooped away, leaving a low space, just large enough for both to lie down in. Their combined vital heat would keep them alive, harden the snow and banish the killing cold.

The skin around his eyes that his coat and hat did not cover felt as though it were crisp, and might crack if jostled. This he warmed with his hands as they lay down where they stopped digging, close together. They kicked snow up around the opening until they were completely closed in and the wind sealed out.

Srstri came to him that night, just as she had been on their last day, fresh and lovely, but wearing a red ribbon in her hair, and there was no pall on her happiness. With her old smile she came near him, soft and warm, and he was about to kiss her when suddenly she moved away into his thoughts, and he sorted through them to no avail. All at once, he was running, but he knew not why until he saw her, glinting in the darkness of the Lowland forest. Twice he thought he had her, but each time she forged ahead farther than before, until at last he toppled from the heights by the water and plunged headfirst into the frigid sea. They swam spluttering out of the mess, gasping as the ice fell down their coats, nestling in up underneath and invading their breeches. The early morning was only just turning the sky pink, and that indefinable air of awakening had begun to color the breeze. Byorneth stared across the broken snow at Hunter, and the young man, when he could open his eyes again, kept them low.

Very soon, they were fed (the food inside their coats was still unfrozen), packed, bundled and on their way again. The land had frozen hard the night before, and the cold did things to the country Hunter had never expected. The wind had covered the snow with a hard crust so they could walk on the surface as though they trod upon solid stone, and ice crystals like tiny swords protruded above it, tinkling under their feet.

Hunter enjoyed the easy path while it lasted, for at the end of the mountain valley and directly in their path stood a stone, a creditable obstacle even among these High Hills, doubtless some daughter of the Upper Peaks, tumbled down ages ago into their path. It stood as straight and high as the sea cliffs of the west, so that they could hardly see the top, and it sprawled out to the north a full hual.[4] At last it reared near, and they began to break through the snow even up to their waists as the drifts sloped up against the wall.

It was smooth across its dark face, with no more feature than a hen's egg, and the few lines of snow which clung to it hung there more by chance than by purchase. Byorneth seemed puzzled for the barest moment. Then, pulling the cap down further over his ears, he paced back and forth for a time, eyeing the structure up and down, and soon his steps quickened to a trot, and he disappeared around to the south. Immediately, he shouted for Hunter, who had followed a little behind him and found the old man standing with a slight smile. On that side of the rock, hidden from their path by its jutting edge there were footholds cut, worn smooth at the edges, but deep enough.

"I knew they were here," Byorneth said and started to climb. "Start with your left foot or you'll certainly die before the top."

---

4   Half of a kand (1.3 miles/2.09 kilometers).

Byorneth began climbing and Hunter followed a moment after, taking care not to look downward or even think of the distance that stretched longer and longer toward the hard ground as he climbed up that neverending ladder. At last, he thought he would look, judging himself to be halfway to the top, but the crest was yet far out of sight, and the ground was only far enough to kill him should he fall. His fingers and toes, by which his life hung from the stone, felt suddenly weaker.

With a final effort, he threw his leg over the top and rolled to safety. Byorneth sat on a high place across the rocks, calm and still. It always unsettled Hunter that a man more than three times his age could do such things and show no effort. Hunter's body suffered more today than it had yesterday, and the extreme cold tightened every muscle, helped by the high wind that made the weather seem even colder, and the wearying effect of the ever-thinning air.

From this high place, one could see everything, even the higher ledges of the peaks nearby and the few wild goats that walked over them. The world gleamed like the sun, and it stung their eyes. Hunter's had long since made their adjustments, and hawklike they flew suddenly to a speck moving out of the rocks bordering the valley on the other side. Byorneth pointed it out even as Hunter saw it, for it was the one thing that moved in that world of white below them.

"Our companion has come at last," Byorneth said.

Hunter strained his eyes. "How could he have traveled so quickly?"

The old man stood and started once again up the winding slope that would take them up to the Kyargh, where the Mountain Twins join in a broad bowl, slanting down toward the shallow cleft running down its center. "There are trails that even the Sheewa do not know. If we would not lose more time on him, then let us be away quickly."

The climb was not particularly difficult in contrast with the height they had just scaled, and after several flat kaind Hunter got his first sight of the shallow cleft itself. It ran as straight as an arrow, bright, unbroken, and to all appearances safe across the snowy col, but Hunter knew the smooth snow layer in the cleft concealed a pattern of jumbled stones beneath the surface. "Mind your step on the sides," Byorneth told him, even as he spoke leading off across one of the two gradual slopes that met in the cleft. "One slip, and the whole hillside of snow will come sliding down on top of you."

All at once, the snow gave out under Byorneth's feet, and he slid down to the center on his belly, at last rolling like a ball down the incline until he came to rest in the lap of the cleft with a jarring crunch that rang clearly across the heights, even reflecting from the walls off to the west.

All was a dream as Hunter watched Byorneth fall, and without thought the younger Sheewa threw himself forward, sliding down to where his friend lay in a prone heap. Having dived out of blind instinct, his action had no plan or even hope, and he hit the uneven rocks beside his friend with an impact that shook his breath loose. The pain might have slowed him had his blood not thundered so, had his friend not lain so still. He was up in an instant and crouched in the thicker snow beside Byorneth. The old man's right leg, broken by the stones, splayed out unnaturally to the side, and try though he might, Hunter could not bring him to.

At the rumbling sound, like that of the flood down below, he looked up the slope and saw a long feather against the gray peak. The snow was coming down. On impulse, he threw himself on top of his fallen friend, and the snow covered them.

The pressure of the slide shocked him, and dully he felt the beginnings of bruises across his ribs where he hit the rocks. The snow had fallen far less on the Kyargh than in the glen below, and as Hunter cleared the snow from his face, he found it was mere sluff. Only a few feet of the slope had moved, and the rest lay on a thread, ready to follow.

He looked down at his friend, and stooping quickly he brushed the ice from his face, hung the bag around his neck and hoisted him up. The weight surprised him, and his first few steps toward the west rocked him back and forth unsteadily. He would have to travel along the cleft, braving the danger to his legs from the hidden stones. But in such a place, it is never wise to think far ahead, except to keep the goal in mind.

He was a long time crossing the col, and many times he felt he might collapse unless he stopped to rest, but if he did, he might never get Byorneth's bulk up into his arms again. The constant effort he expended in pushing through the snow reduced his consciousness to a thin stream, his complaining muscles began to harmonize with the moaning wind, and Byorneth's dead weight doubled and redoubled before he reached the other side of the cleft. But reach it he did, and that with a dull surprise.

For a time, he let Byorneth lie on his back in the snow among the higher rocks, and he lay down beside him, taking the rest he had promised himself with every step of the weary way. He sucked great, gasping breaths of frozen air, and stared up at a lone cloud blowing slowly across the blue until his mind returned to itself and he sat up, suddenly remembering Khornang.

The familiar dot still moved in the distance. It was just entering the cleft, walking in Hunter's footprints, and making better time than the young Sheewa could ever hope to.

Whipping off his scarf, Hunter bound Byorneth's legs together, then groaned, heaved himself upright onto his feet and hoisted his burden once more.

He paid his body no mind throughout that journey, though at every step it cried out for sympathy, until at last his mind left him, and he walked alone. What little remained thought only on the madman behind them. If he were to stumble or even falter, their enemy would as suddenly gain and slay them.

Then suddenly, the weight lifted. The 200 pounds of limp Byorneth remained as they were, the pain in his ribs and the aching in his back remained, yet all at once he was a young man again, and he laughed as he saw the road before him, winding crazily across the cliffs. There was room enough, the way was clear, and he had carried weights before. Pain was an old and trusted friend, and he was almost glad to have it as the unforgiving rock and snow stretched endlessly before him. He remembered the way, and all that remained was to tread it.

He hefted his friend higher onto his shoulders as they mounted a thin ledge that bore them higher and higher above the earth, and he thought he heard the old man groan. They passed above the thin clouds, through which he caught a fearful glimpse of the succession of gorges which the path across the cliffs avoided. Finally, he laid Byorneth down once again, stretching and flexing his back and arms.

Here the ledge was wide enough for a man to lie comfortably, beyond which the path narrowed to a rophoil wide. Hunter kept his eyes from this, instead looking at the distance out across the sky. It sparkled with innumerable frost crystals, and he could see a pine forest off toward the north on a perfect level with the ledge, although several kual of void intervened. In this empty space, a lone eagle flew, sliding easily across the air, barely exerting itself. It was all very lovely, and he began to think that perhaps the ledge would accommodate two sleepers, if only for an hour before risking their lives again.

The eagle swooped around, playing upon the wind as a child plays on a fence, now flirting with the rocks across the gorge, now hanging perfectly still, shining in gold against the peaks. It was as if the great creature were on display, for to Hunter's wondering eyes, all manner of hidden colors were revealed in the bird's tail and wings, little flecks of crimson in the lustrous beak, and a ring of vibrant yellow around each eye.

A shrill scream rang in the air, and with the suddenness of death, the huge eagle was on them, beating the stones with its great wings, and the black claws nearly seized Byorneth, but Hunter reached for his blade with such violence that he lost his footing and his feet shot out over the ledge, obstructing the bird's grasp.

He did not fall straight to the bottom of the mountains as he feared, but rather came to a violent rest on the point of his left shoulder just below the ledge. He barely felt it, his blood was so high, and he climbed back up to the ledge at once, but the eagle had already gone and left Byorneth. The bird was longer than three men across each wing, and having missed once would have to tack around again.

Hunter's mind still echoed with amazement at the eagle's great size, and shock at the speed of the attack. The bird soared around in a great circle, and would presently try again to take its prey. Hunter's blade was out, for his bow was unstrung across his back, and he doubted he could have made a straight shot with a hurt shoulder from the narrow ledge. The beating of the gigantic wings grew louder and louder until he thought they would suck him out into empty distance. Then it was on him again, and this time its claws encircled his waist with a ferocious grip, and all at once he was in the air below those beating wings. The ground was yet near, and the dagger was ready, so its point soon found a feathered home.

The cry the creature gave at that insult must have been heard in the Caldera, for it nearly split Hunter's ears, but the grip was released and he fell free. This time, Hunter landed painfully upon the sloping cliff face, rolling over and over until with a loud grunt he was brought to a rest against a ledge, and he pulled himself upright with a great groan for his shoulder. But even now the bird reeled slowly on the wind, making its long way back to his friend. A fire lit under his heels, and he climbed like a goat, heedless of the pain.

The immense rush of wings turned and came nearer, but he was still too far below the ledge to help Byorneth when the eagle perched and set itself to carry off his fallen friend. Hunter's blade had clattered farther up the mountain upon the last assault, and so unarmed, and with a quickness that amazed him, he mounted the steep slope again.

As he climbed onto the upper face, he gave a loud cry, and the bird turned and reared back, balancing itself on the stones and beating its huge wings. It swept a wing backward, thinking to toss this strange being into the empty air, but the man dropped and rolled partway down the incline, and once more the bird shifted downhill. Hunter gathered himself and bolted underneath the eagle, snatched up his hooked dagger, and landed a vicious cut on the upper leg as the monster lunged backward for a swipe at its tormentor with the keen edge of its beak.

The bird's movements bowled Hunter over and he fell back again. Now, there was time enough for the eagle to take hold of Byorneth, and this it did with a triumphant shriek. But Hunter was quick as well, and it had not achieved flight before he had fetched it such a cut that it dropped its prize back on the ledge with its loudest scream yet, and Hunter just barely avoided the frantic wings.

The eagle recovered from its first qualm of pain and renewed the struggle. How Hunter escaped its furious blows, he would never know, but at last it missed its aim by just enough, and Hunter, having climbed as the eagle descended, thrust his fallen blade into the great eye up to the hilt. The tip must have touched the eagle's brain, for after a few feeble struggles it pitched backward away from the mountain, tumbling over and over on the sliding shale until it settled, lifeless, in a gully far below.

Hunter stood for a moment, then replaced his blade in the scabbard, picked up his friend, and walked on through the mountains.

⸻

The day had dawned widely through a thick, transient fog, risen up from the nearby sea in the early hours. It awakened Teidin with its glare before the others arose, but his first stirrings opened their eyes. There would be no easy escape today. He avoided their stares, keeping his eyes on his bedding as he rolled it up into a tight bundle and stowed it away with the quick skill of a practised traveler.

Where last night the abounding fresh water could only be scented upon the east wind, today they saw it clearly from where they stood. Standing water is scarce in the district of Allend's End, and to Teidin's Plain-bred mind, such a large lake seemed a singular waste of arable land. It was a strange smell, suggesting fresh-caught fish and rain-pregnant clouds. Teidin led as they set off together, doing his best to walk as though he had come that way before, and as the mist thinned and lifted, the glimmering blue of the lake began to hurt his eyes.

Teidin could only hope there was a farm near at hand, with a green field as he had said, though in finding it, he would bring great harm upon the owners, and especially any young women nearby. To a Lowlander, all Hillfolk tended to look alike, even to their owners, and by now hatred had displaced reason in Banat's mind, so that he held the entirety of the Highlands to account for his stolen treasure.

The land became softer as they went, and the grass began to split into islands which grew farther and farther apart until they ceased jumping from lump to lump and walked in-between. At last, their feet were wetted in a series of shallow pools which fed one into another, flowing among the mounds of dank earth, hairy with grass, and so into the great inland sea. All manner of creeping things dwelled there, nesting in the slime and sunning themselves among the dark rocks. Their feet crunched over curled shells, squishing among the bright green polyps. On all sides, the patches of grass began to rise up like walls.

It was with a relieved sorrow that Teidin saw the green fields across the earth which bounded the pools. As they drew nearer, it amazed him that the entire landholding far outstripped his own home, even his entire village, in size and population. Ten families could have prospered in the least of the fields. He was half minded to stop and lead them elsewhere, to find some convenient covert where he could forestall them somehow, for these barbarians would pillage the whole farm before they had done with it, slaying all they found. It would profit no one to ruin a farm.

"Banat! Everyone! Look back!" One of the men who trailed the party pointed toward the hollow where they had slept, which now spouted black smoke like a chimney. "If we had stayed, we would be burned! Who could have done this?"

The question meant little, for men such as Banat attract violence as blood draws wolves. "Keep your eyes forward, if it frightens you." The man in wool was unimpressed. "We are away, and what may have happened hardly matters." But he quickened his pace. Fear of being overtaken had overtaken them.

And well they should have feared.

Banat and his men stopped suddenly, for their path was blocked by a black shape that stood up from behind the grass. Man after man sprang into view, until the Lowlanders were entirely closed in. All around, there was the acrid scent of tar, such as might cling to men if they flooded a covert with it and set it ablaze. The dark men looked to one man in particular, dressed in costlier clothes than they, a grim, thin pillar, his hands smeared black. Beside him stood a young girl wide of eyes and tight of lips. One lip was swollen and red, and all at once Teidin understood.

Before he could recover his mind, he was seized roughly from behind and relieved of his blade. The leader of the Hillmen held a weapon, not a sword as did his men, but rather a long scythe. He walked among the kneeling men as one might browse through a fair, and the girl walked beside him until they stopped before one in particular, who had begun to tremble and sob, pleading for his life in Harniyen, but his words would have been worthless even had the man understood.

Chapter 16
The Strangers

AND WHEN YOU COME INTO A STRANGER'S HOUSE, SPEAK SOFTLY,
FOR YOUR FAR-REMOVED FATHER MAY HAVE DIED THERE.

-The Bôlairrun of Tagrri-

Ten Lowland men knelt before a Highlander, a strange sight in Arlinga. But then the land was changing, as the Sheewa had often said. Or hoped. Yet even they would have stood aback at this sight.

The girl spoke softly to her father, and with a singing swipe, a man's head rolled across the turf, resting at the feet of a farmhand who kicked it contemptuously out across the rocks.

The next man did not seem to have comprehended his fate, and he still looked confused when at the girl's word, his fate overtook him. This time, the head flew through the air, touching the earth only once before it splashed into a pool near one of Banat's men, who very nearly fainted. Along with it jingled an amulet, stamped with a black star, which had hung around the man's neck.

Next came Teidin, and his eyes raced back and forth between the gory blade of the scythe and its wielder's face. The arm was cocked for a blow, but at his daughter's word the weapon lowered, and he reached out and tousled Teidin's hair before moving on.

Finally, only Banat was left, kneeling impassively and without concern for the fate of his men. The few words the girl spoke brought a grim smile to her father's face, and slowly, rapturously, he drew his weapon back. Before he could follow it through, the man in wool revealed a knife he had kept hidden in his innermost clothing, and used it to draw blood in a vital place upon the man's arm. Banat was quick in spite of his size and the bulk of his clothing, and he lunged to his feet at once, wrenched the girl from beside her father, and disappeared with her into the outer wilderness.

The father had to be restrained from giving pursuit, for the wound pulsed out a red stream, and so his men sat upon him and stemmed the flow as he cursed them and the man in wool most thoroughly to the third generation. All who were not busied with their master were already out after the quarry, and Teidin went after them, wanting to prove helpful before the man thought better of his mercy.

For a time, the man's trail was easily seen in the soft earth, weaving through the hillocks, with the girl's set of tracks dragging and scuffling along after. The Hillmen knew their country well, and were as skilled as Teidin in tracking. It gave him a kinship with them as they called back and forth, scattering and regrouping over the rocks with the ruthless skill of a pack of maned wolves. At last, the man farthest toward the sea gave a cry that could mean but one thing, and held a familiar woollen surcoat up for them to see.

And so went the hunt, cry after shrill cry going up along the man's trail. The Highlanders followed Banat as quickly as he could run himself, and judging by the growing blood trail, the girl was no help to him on that score. Soon, they could follow along the spotted earth with no more than a glance at the ground, and all at once they rounded a corner of raised earth, across from which the man in wool lay, a sharp blade laid against the young girl's throat.

She was stunned, and hung against the man in wool limply, a cut over her eye bleeding into his shirt. His face was criss-crossed with bleeding scratches and tooth marks, and one eye had already begun to swell shut. The air was cool coming off the inland sea, and he shivered with the lack of his coat. Only the hand that held the knife was steady.

Teidin motioned for the Hillmen to hold back, and this they did willingly. Even he dared not step forward more than a single pace. "Banat, hear me! Release the girl and flee! I will keep these men back!"

"Bid it return the treasure it stole! For nothing else will its life be safe!"

"Banat, you fool! This is not the woman! Can you imagine that your *deesard* would have had such a thing all this way, keeping it a secret all the time? The woman is lost! Go back to the Lowlands where you have lands and servants! The Highlands will kill you!"

The man in wool drew the girl nearer to him. She never struggled against the cool blade, and her eyes were calm. If anyone provoked the man, it would not be her.

"I have nothing in the Lowlands," Banat spoke as a dead man. "All that I ever had, I gave up to retrieve my jewel. So you see, I have nothing at all to lose by anything I do here."

"Nothing but for your life."

At this, Banat laughed and cursed them all in a voice of doomed thunder. He threw the girl hard across to her kinsmen and scuttled like a beetle into the outer Caldera.

They gave pursuit, but all in vain, for with no baggage he was a ghost in the wet land, his blood trail vanishing with the rest of him. In the end, they could do nothing but bring the girl back to her father. He lay where he had fallen, held there by his men, and at the sight of his daughter in Teidin's company, he lay quieter. Banat was lost, but such men carry vengeance with them, ever turned against themselves. At the father's silent bidding, Teidin drew near and took his hand as one of his servants bound the wound tightly with an ever-larger mass of dressings.

He said something in his own tongue, and Teidin said something in his. At a few words from his master, one of the men returned Teidin's long knife. Another servant removed the belt the wounded man wore over his shoulder and gave it to Teidin.

It was a work of careful craftsmanship, eminently durable. There was a buckle upon the front of it which bore a curious badge, bearing the likeness of a fish run through with a spear, and below this was affixed a very long, thin dagger, which Teidin had assumed was more a matter of show than function. A closer look revealed it was an excellent work of immaculately forged steel, with a handle of exotic gold-swirled wood. The tang extended all the way through the handle and ended in a knob, worked into the same fish and spear symbol, giving the whole work perfect balance. It was more than a weapon — it was an heirloom.

Teidin tried to return it, but was rebuffed, and so he put it on with the few words of thanks he had learned. It fit well.

The master of the house was carried home by his servants, the girl walking beside the makeshift litter, and now Teidin saw she could not have seen 13 years. With the resilience of youth, she had already recovered from her fright, even walking proudly, perhaps for all the wounds she had given her captor, the blood under her victorious fingernails. A pretty girl, she bore no other resemblance to the woman Banat sought.

The house was grand indeed. A great mansion, it had been cut into a tall knoll so that upon three sides it looked nothing more than a seaside hill. Upon the side facing them, there was a door, built out of the tallest timber dragged from far away among the peaks and rivers. Grass grew on the top of the house and even a formidable garden, and one could see that below the sod had been set layer after layer of hard-baked bricks and tiles, overlapped against the seeping rain. It boasted four chimneys, each set at a corner of the house.

Behind this was the sea, the far shore of which could barely be made out against the far-off green. It was much like the ocean his father spoke of, with its booming breakers and the high screams of the gulls which bounded and wheeled on the wind. About a kand offshore there was an island of wave-polished obsidian glass, which had begun to reflect the sun into their eyes.

They drew near to the door, and he saw the posts and lintel were of great hardwoods, carved and inlaid with beautiful Hill characters, woven together in an unbroken fabric of writing. Before they stopped, three women rushed out and walked beside the servants as they bore the man into the house. One woman in particular took the girl in a tight embrace and walked her inside.

Teidin had been forgotten. He was about to move on again before a voice from the house stopped him.

At the end of a thousand years, Hunter, with his friend across his shoulders, marched out of the mountains. He had no way of knowing when this occurred, for he simply looked up from the joggling ground and saw the foothills all around him, overlooking a broad expanse of sparse grass and dust, yellow and brown that bled up into the sky. Bred in the forests and well acquainted with the Caldera, he had never before seen such a land, never heard of it outside the Sheewan scrolls. It was the heat of the summer, and the land seemed dead, from the hot sky down to the dry plants that littered the surface of the Desert.

He saw not a soul, and he cared not. Even Khornang was no longer important. As he dropped Byorneth, he was only vaguely aware he should have been more gentle. And that was the end of Hunter's consciousness. There was no memory of his sudden fall to the ground, no brushing away of the pin-footed insects which crawled over his prone form. There was simple oblivion, a hovering between light and dark, a freezing hot, motionless hurtling from the earth to the heavens and back again.

His long journey ended on a bed of skins in a hut, and Hunter thought for a few moments that he was among the Plainsmen, and that Srstri would soon come with a cup of water to revive him. He turned and looked across the warm little room, and saw a cooking fire with a spitted chunk of meat revolving above it. A woman bent and tended the meal, rather slim but well-looking. She glanced over her shoulder at some noise outside the hut, and he saw a suggestion of her face. Shreds of his wedding came back to him as he watched her, then he remembered himself and averted his eyes, blushing all the way up into his hair.

His head throbbed with every heartbeat, and every muscle spoke with an insistent eloquence, which broke into so many screams as he stretched out, and at his gasp the woman turned. She was beautiful indeed, even as he half hoped, half dreaded she would be. Her hair, like burnished gold even in the dark of the tent, stilled his breast, for dark features are the rule in the Hills, and brown hair in the villages. The rumors he had heard in no way prepared him for his first sight of a Tribeswoman's hair.

The clothing could have been copied from a scroll, down to the very pattern of the woven shoulder covering, which flowed down to the edge of her green shawl. All of her garments were very light, moved by the slightest breath of air, yet at no time did they transgress the rules of tribal modesty, which strictly forbid the revealing of the female upper arms and thighs.

She smiled down calmly, and spoke in the language which Hunter had learned in the High City. "You must have really been tired! The Persuader is awake and we've set his leg, but he's often asleep. He told us what you did for him."

Hunter replied drowsily. "What is your name?"

"I'm called Tierna, epithet Doe. I've been watching you as you slept, almost two days and nights. I think you made yourself sick up there. You're at Tyeeymił Spring." Dully, he wondered just how long he had been carrying Byorneth, but he could not seem to mark the days in his memory. Even his encounter with the great eagle only occurred to him as a dream of deepest night, not so much remembered in precise detail, but felt.

"How long a walk would you say it is from the beginning of the cleft to the edge of the foothills?"

"The Persuader says it must have taken you three days." She motioned to the fire. "Would you like to eat?"

He nodded and smiled. She removed the meat from the skewer and laid it on a wooden serving dish, curiously carved out of the roots of a tree, brown and yellow. This was laid on a low table in the middle of the tent on which were already set two cups, fashioned out of the same stuff as the platter. She laid a dollop of bean paste on each side of the meat, and so they ate, cross-legged as was the custom, Hunter barely suppressing a groan as he bent his legs to the position.

He thanked her and used the table knife to slice an edge of meat, smearing a dab of bean paste on the end of it. These two delicacies are meant to be eaten with one bite, the paste spread over the meat and washed down with water, which he found necessary to quell the heat of the spices. He had never eaten such food before and it nearly choked him, even as it intrigued his palate. The surface of the meat was encrusted with dry spices, and the heat had cooked their essences into it, rendering it tender and strangely nutty. He even enjoyed the beans, an acquired taste for some, but these were not like the ones he had eaten in the Lowlands, where all forms of pulse were merely sustenance. Here it was art, and executed by an artist of exceptional feeling.

"Is it to your liking?"

"Oh, yes!" he said, smiling. He could not look directly at her. "What — what kinds of spices do you use?"

"Many. I use *tusaia* flour and ground *leedh* blossoms mostly, but I like to use about 12 other seasonings to help complete the flavor. Please, have some more!"

Silence again, and Hunter chewed frantically, searching for another topic. "This person you called 'The Persuader.' Who is that?"

"You know him! The old man, the one you carried in your arms for three days. Being a Sheewa, you would know about our epithets, how each person is given both the name of an ancestor as well as a descriptive. My epithet is 'Doe,' because my father celebrated my birth feast with a deer he shot from the door of his tent. I've always been glad he didn't kill a goat instead!" She laughed, a bright, tinkling laugh that did strange things to him inside. It has been said by a very wise Lowlander that a woman's house is at once a place of execution and haven of refuge, and Hunter thought of that as he sat struggling with his own mind.

"This food reminds me of my wife's cooking," he said, digging into his meal once more. "Her meat is spiced differently because she learned her art in the North and East, but this is quite as good." And he continued, telling her of how he met Srstri, showing her the scar on his forehead as he mentioned his fight against the bear. He told her of waist-length raven-black hair, bright and shining, and lastly of their sudden parting. As he talked, he could now look at Tierna comfortably, and he saw that something had confused her. This was not the manner of conversation one normally employed in a stranger's tent.

Their eyes met and she said with a crooked little smile, "You were only married one day when you left?"

"Yes. A day and a night."

"Well, that could hardly have been fair to her. Or you. Why not bring her here with you? It would have been nice to have her to talk to."

"Sheewan custom demands that their scribes go traveling only with other scribes. Byorneth sidestepped tradition as it was by letting me marry at all. To this day, I am not sure why he did." He looked in her eyes again and half smiled. The position was now clear, and he felt he could safely open up to her. "Have you a husband?"

Married women wore their husband's colors, but they were indoors and she wore no cloak. "No, I live in my father's tent." She took another bite, and smiled again. "You must be very sure of yourself."

Hunter put another morsel in his slack-jawed mouth. He did not speak, and she finally filled the silence herself. "Have I offended you?"

"No, you have confused me."

"Well, you were so sure I'd be seducing you that you had to tell me so much about a wife a dozen marches away. Have you had so very much trouble with other women?" Her eyes were full of mirth, but there was a little danger in them as well.

It could do no harm to tell the truth. "I only guarded against myself, being young and but newly married. I am sorry — I ought to leave. You've been hospitable, and I've dishonored that."

At this, she laughed. "Take no thought for it, please! I hope I have such a faithful husband one day!" She began to clear the table.

Now, one of humankind's most dangerous facets is its egotism, and like most attractive people, Tierna had more than her share. Hunter's implied compliment pleased her, and she hummed a little to herself as she tidied up. Perhaps sensing this, Hunter suddenly wanted out, and he got to his feet, stopping only once to smile back at her. "I hope you will excuse me, but I must see how my friend is. I enjoyed your cooking very much."

He stood still for a moment in the rough little camp, taking it all in. All the houses were made of skins sewn together, and each with its own wagon beside it. Men and women sat or stood all around as they mended blankets, clothing and saddles. Little children, light skinned and laughing, rushed past in a group, yelling for no particular reason.

He had overstepped himself, and was now outside with no idea where Byorneth was convalescing, but he shied from going back to ask. Craning his neck, he took in the entire camp, seeking out a friendly face. A sour old man berating a child, a sullen young lover fresh from the tent of his sweetheart, even a sleepy camp dog, all these he glanced over until he saw a little old woman sitting next to her tent, mending a hole in a very familiar pair of pants.

She sat singing to herself, beating time with her heel and rocking a little in her seat. She was framed by a crown of short, curly blond hair, and her robes were of a better kind than those around her, as Tierna's were. Hunter approached her across the courtyard with the formal Huaynił greeting. "Is all well in thy house?"`

Looking up with bright, eager eyes, she gave the customary, "All is well and well fed," and went genially back to her work. Her fingers, twisted as they were with age, worked the needle in and out with such skill that the garment might have been repairing itself before Hunter's eyes.

"I have a friend who has been hurt. Know you where he lies?"

"Yes, I do!" She put her work down beside her chair and pulled herself to her feet with a short stick. The tops of her curls did not even come up to Hunter's shoulders, and her gait was short and henlike as she stepped over to the door of the tent behind her, and pulled it back so that Hunter could go in. Byorneth lay like a dead man against the patchwork wall of the tent, and Hunter feared for a moment until he saw the subtle rise and fall of the old man's chest.

The old woman flapped the tent door a little to cool the room as Hunter moved over to the bed. It hurt him to see Byorneth brought so low, to see his true age for the first time. The leg had been treated with unusual skill, the splint precisely assembled. "Will he recover?"

"Oh, yes. He's an old man, but not much older than me, and I might be around for a while yet."

Byorneth groaned at the sound of their voices and looked up. "My son." Looking around, he saw the style of the tent, the curly fair hair of the old woman, and smiled up at Hunter before his eyes pulled themselves shut and he fell asleep again. But the change had happened, the death pall had been lifted, and the man was a man once more.

The old woman sat by the bed and continued to mend Byorneth's pants, and, satisfied at his friend's care, Hunter faded back out and into the street. The sun had commenced its work in earnest, and the distance was obscured in waving veils of heat.

He had read what the scrolls told of this people. They had landed on the western coast years before the last war, astonishing the kings who had seen the land empty the previous year. Once arrived, their union shattered into pieces, and each shard became a tribe, traveling from grass to grass, developing their own tongues and traditions, to the delight of the people of Seng Grandt, who rejoiced over the change like small children. He and Byorneth were to record what had happened in this tribe that may have been left out of previous accounts — tribal politics, history, leadership, and any other thing that might prove fruitful.

With Byorneth infirm, Hunter determined to set to business and introduce himself to the chief. He looked around the huts, and at last found what he searched for — a dwelling much like the others, off by itself on the highest place in the camp. It bore the chief's emblem, two stags locking antlers, woven into the fabric with leather cords, and surmounted by *feeleueenakh* — a horse and rider at full gallop. Hunter approached and, as custom dictates, called out at the door to beg an audience.

A hand was laid on his shoulder, and turning he faced a clean-shaven man, who smiled and lifted the tent flap for him. Nothing distinguished the chief but the sword at his side, which was not curved like the others but straight, with a longer, ornate handle that curled around and joined the hilt in a silver plume. It was quite unlike the weapons hanging in Seng Grandt's treasure room, yet in its own way it was quite as beautiful.

They went through a door flap, dampened so as to cool the interior. One side of the room was dominated by a stool of thick-layered red cloth stretched between two spindles carved with wolf's paws, and the floor all around was adorned with ornate rugs. Hunter sat cross-legged on the ground and laid out his scribal tools, while the chief took his place on the stool. He waited for the chief to speak.

"It's been many years since one of your tribe has come here, but you're as welcome as my father was wont to make your brethren. Ask, and I'll answer your questions."

Hunter took up his pen and began a new heading — "Waileng Tribe."

"Great Chief, my thanks unto thee for this audience, and for consenting to unfold the history of thy great tribe unto one so young. My skills, though adequate, are unrefined. Overlook thou my youth, I implore, for my betters shall put my labors right."

The chief smiled, and his smile wrinkled the skin around his eyes. "My people address me in plain language. Please do so as well. I would like this to be a meeting between friends."

Hunter inclined his head. "Thank-you." He was glad to abandon such florid address, but his training was too strong to permit him to be entirely familiar with tribal royalty. The chief removed his outer robe and sat back in his chair.

"Well now, where should we start?"

"If it pleases you, let's begin with what happened just after the last of my kind left this Desert."

The chief cleared his throat and leaned back, his throat working up and down as he thought. "Well now, I'll have to go back to my grandfather, in the year after the last of your people left us to return across the mountains. He was an honorable gentleman, my grandfather, with many horses and goats, and the tents of his people were many and rich. We were at peace with our neighbors, even giving our young in marriage by arrangement, as one tribe. Our riders were far famed, and acquitted themselves in many races, winning honors as well as the greatest breeding stock in the land.

"As it happened, our success was noticed from far, and engendered a great jealousy. It made friends into enemies, who never showed their intentions until opportunity came of plundering us. Young bloods from other tribes raided us for sport, and it became a mark of status for those to bring Waileng horses home to their tribes. For a long time my father, advised by his father, fought against this, but finally a larger raiding party slipped through our defenses and made off with five of our girls all at once, one of whom was my father's sister, as well as several of our most valuable breeding stallions.

"By this time, we had precious few women left, and our equine stock was seriously endangered. My father sent a raiding party of his own to recover what had once been ours.

"All went well for that party. They crept into the camp (ill-defended on account of our inaction), and once they reached the horses, they stormed through the camp and routed it. Some of our women were retaken, many of theirs captured, and the men returned in high spirits. Finally we had struck for our own and won.

"And so it went. We raided them, they raided us. And then one night it all ended when two raiding parties met between camps, and there followed a running battle. It began with bad language, then outright challenges, maturing into a bloody conflict that grew as it raged near one camp or the other, young and old coming out to the defense of their own. We fought on foot and horseback, each side barely recognizing their foes, until the earth was scarred with hooves, and many had fallen. I was in that battle, just 14 but strong of arm. One particular man had latched onto me and we fought for a long time, matching one another's blows, he with experience, I with my greater strength. Finally, I lost my grip on my sword and he thrust me through the shoulder. Falling, I struck a stone and lay senseless.

"They left me for dead, and when I awoke they all lay where they had fallen in heaps, the fury of combat still on their pale faces. My wound pained me greatly, and I was sickened by the sight of that field. So in poor condition, I walked out and back to our camp, fully expecting to find all that I knew and loved slaughtered by our rival tribe.

"But they had known what might befall them, vacating camp and finding refuge in the nearby Hills, along with our precious writings. We wandered a while, and then I became chief with my father's death. Since then, we of the Waileng have been against all tribes, even as they are against one another. Our stock of mounts has not recovered even yet, and because of our former wealth, all those around loathe and plunder us. Soon we shall move farther south, now that you are well and your friend mending. Perhaps then we'll have peace for a while to replenish our strength."

The words dried up all of a sudden, and the young Sheewa looked up from his work, but Waileng simply sat, looking at nothing at all. He thanked the chief politely but informally, and ventured to ask a few questions, probing, sensitive questions concerning culture, etiquette and their more intimate history. More than an adjunct to the scrolls, this information would ease their stay, ensuring against offense. Realizing this, the chief gave answer patiently and, Hunter felt, completely.

Finally, the meeting drew to a close, and Hunter smiled widely at his host in a sudden swell of goodwill toward the quiet man and his simple story. All the training the Sheewa could offer would be less than useless without acquaintance with the people themselves, and it was good fortune for the Sheewa to encounter one so open. He put his tools away, each in its proper place in the bag. He was about to take his leave when he turned to address the man once more. "Excuse me, but the girl who was looking after me called Byorneth 'the Persuader.' Why did she do that?"

The Waileng chief chuckled, the first time he had smiled in all their discourse together. "When your friend was last with us, young scribe, it was not as a Sheewa, but a — traveler. He said that he searched for a king, but I suspect that his true aim was to turn back the tide, to restore days that have long been dead and may never be again. He spent his time among us persuading anyone who would listen that an ancient kingdom would soon be restored." He tapped his knee and looked contemplatively through the door of the tent. "He was very young."

Then he smiled again, and bowed his head slightly as one does when dismissing a guest. "Pray, tell us, Sheewa, if there is anything further you require."

Then he looked away, and his hand rested on the hilt of his sword.

Chapter 17
The Vengeance

At least 30 years before, a man of vision left a high city in the uplands of Arlinga. In youth and age, he carved a path through every quarter of the land, a wandering zephyr that brought rain and withering heat, harming and profiting, until at last, wearied of the fight, he drifted onto the Great Trail. To reconcile this Byorneth with his friend, who had emerged years later with his mules in a haze of dust, halting on his way to speak with a poor fisherboy, strained Hunter's imagination.

When Hunter returned to his friend's sickbed, he found the little woman still in her place by his side, busy with her mending. She gave her quick smile as he entered and said, quietly, "He's sleeping now, and I think I should let him rest all he can, don't you?"

Hunter nodded. "How is he?"

"Oh, he's well. I think he's a little put out with me. Can't really blame him. I don't know how my husband ever put up with a silly thing like me all those years!" She tried to get up, but collapsed back into the chair with a wheeze. Once more, she bore down on her cane and struggled to her feet. "I'm baking some bread in my tent. Why don't you come and reach things down for me?"

"Thank-you, I would like that." He was at a loss for what do with Byorneth asleep, and old women are full of amusing stories and useful information. The proportion of these elements varies with age, intelligence, and wealth of experience, but this woman impressed him as being both amiable and astute.

He followed slowly to her tent, holding back with her short gait. She lived beside the chief on the southern side, indicating a close bond, likely that of a mother. She lifted the flap and he followed her in to be met with an aroma that brought the water to his mouth and tears to his eyes. His home had smelled so when he was a young boy. Perhaps Srstri would bake such bread for their children. Srstri, now many marches away across his world, had once cooked for him. If the old woman saw his emotion, she said nothing.

The tent was larger than many of the others, but otherwise no different or richer than the common man's dwelling. The bed was small, and had been put away in a corner to make room for the bustle of cooking, and mostly for the great oven. It was an ancient affair, entirely of iron, but constructed in sections for ease of moving. The front of it was plain except for two spiraled trees which formed the corners, and it was very wide. Opposite this, and in the center of the tent, stood a large table covered in strange flour on which lay four large lumps of dough, swollen and fat.

"Open the stove, will you?" She had turned to the table and lifted a soft double handful, placing it in a steel baking pan, about a lîoš[5] in length with a chain at each of its four corners. The door was very hot, and he was at a loss until he saw the iron hooks hanging from a post at a corner of the table, and with them he lifted the door from its pins, unleashing a withering blast that burned like hot coals and smelled royally.

There was a long pole leaning on the table, and the old woman hooked two of the cupped pans onto it, walked across and thrust them into the heart of the heat, running the hooks through a ring in the interior to dangle and brown. Twice more, she braved the flames, and then Hunter replaced the door after her. The heat and effort had started him sweating, but she seemed unperturbed as she opened a little flap in the roof of the tent with the same pole.

It was a small flap, too small to do much in the way of cooling, but then he saw the notches in the dirt of the floor, and he understood. As the patch of sunlight moved across them, it would measure the time. He made note of this as one of the many items absent from the Sheewa's knowledge of the West.

She saw him looking. "I don't use that method much anymore. It's hard for me to remember the placement of the notches in any season but midsummer." She smiled around her little kitchen in thought, tapping the ground with her cane. "I don't think that will be nearly enough bread, do you?"

---

5   9.75 inches (25 centimeters), or the width of a column of writing on a Sheewan scroll.

He had no way of knowing, having only eaten bread and never made it. But he trusted her as an experienced baker and agreed. More bread would not be regretted. "Well then, we have just enough for another batch. This bread keeps pretty well, anyway. Come on over here and help me."

It was not so much an order as an invitation, and he accepted gladly, joining her at the long central table.

"Now, if you could just reach that bowl down for me, will you?" She pointed up at a bowl hanging from a hook on one of the corner posts, well out of the way, but within easy reach for a tall young man. It was beyond him how she reached anything on her own. He brought the heavy bowl down and set it in front of her.

And so they set to making bread. He fetched things for her and watched as her gnarled fingers kneaded and prodded, mixed and sifted. She was very good, he decided. There was no recipe, but her instincts were always right, her movements ever deft, and although she showed no sign of any particular pride in her skill, there was a supreme confidence that made the job seem easy for her.

There was even time to talk, as Hunter had hoped. She did not object to visiting in the kitchen, and since most of the process had become automatic with long experience, she was not distracted by it. As Hunter suspected, she soon proved herself a very interesting woman.

"What relation are you to the chief?" he asked, and as she answered, she took a half handful of flour from the rough sack that hung from a peg and threw it into the dough.

"I'm his mother. My husband used to be the chief."

"Have you a large family?"

"No. There was only him. He has a daughter, Tierna. You might have seen her around here someplace. Her brother died in childbirth, and my daughter-in-law died with him." She pounded the sticky dough several times, sending a jet of flour into the air. "Tierna and I get together and cook sometimes. That's her gift, cookery. I'm more of an everyday sort of a cook."

Hunter would never have said so, for even the raw dough delighted his nose. With a final vigorous poke, she stepped back from the table, dusted off her hands on a rag and nodded. "Well, that's about done it, I'd say. Wouldn't you? How would you like to get you some flour and start kneading while I get the bread out of the oven?"

He never noticed the sunlight move, but now he saw it had traversed two notches on the ground. Though at first he doubted he could do it, the motions and theory of kneading came back to him through the years, helped by the smell and atmosphere, until he had a solid mass, smooth as a deer's flank. The little woman shook the loaves, now brown, out of the pans onto the table. They were square, and patterned at their four corners by the links of the chains against which they had risen, so that they resembled the stove itself with its ornate steel corners. She reached over and thrust two fingers into the lump in front of Hunter, which sprang out again almost as if it breathed.

"That's fine! Well, should we go get some fresh air while this rises? Come on, you can pull the grass out from around the tent for me."

Why a few strands of dry grass around the tent should matter he did not know, but did not protest. Certain things are a woman's province, he reasoned, and men had simply to obey, not to question. While he worked, she collapsed back into her chair, breathing quickly.

"What's your name, mother? As a scribe, it would be a shame to leave without knowing the chief's mother's name."

The strands of grass roots were intertwined almost inextricably. Each had to be pulled at least twice before it came out.

"Jooenin Gueykikh, but the whole tribe calls me 'Grandmother.'"

"Gueykikh. Old hen. How came you to be called that?" He was nearly behind the tent now, and paused to hear her reply.

"Well, it was before my husband died. He told me so many times to keep my hands out of the way while the young men loaded my oven into the cart, and I don't know why I didn't listen. So one day, I had my fingers resting on the wagon and down the stove came right on top of them! Well, I let out the loudest squawk you can imagine, and I've been called Gueykikh ever since!"

The grass seemed to come out easier after that.

—⋏⋏—

Teidin turned as the woman came out of the house and called to him. She smiled and motioned to him, matronly although she seemed just barely older than her daughter, and he followed her in through the vast doorway and stood still in the sudden darkness. Little by little, the walls emerged out of the black depths, and a cedar-ribbed chamber was revealed to him, stout timbers extending further and further into the hillside, until he thought the far walls must have protruded into the daylight. He smelled clean earth and cedar as he followed her, mixed with the old familiar smell of living and growing up. The wall was in two sections with a ledge in-between, and he wondered at that until he saw that above one of the ledges was a second ceiling, secured with ropes. In the winter months, one could pull it down and shorten the house, so that these ingenious Hillfolk could more easily heat it. The hall could have comfortably seated all the people of Allend's End, and from what he had seen of the richness of the farm, the family could have dined them as well.

They walked together to the far end of the hall, and Teidin stooped to follow her into a smaller room, although still bigger than any other he had ever seen, carefully crafted out of fitted stones, patterned with depictions of kings and knights of old. The man of the house lay there in the light of a broad window that faced the shining glass island, and he smiled when he saw Teidin. He was perhaps a little less dark than the other Hillmen, clean-shaven.

One of the other women, evidently another daughter, brought Teidin a steaming bowl with a spoon, and with one sniff he understood the true measure of their fortune. A pauper may become wealthy, occupy a mansion and hire servants, but to craft a truly great soup needs a special art and the richness of practise. He accepted it with a smile and thank-you, held it up to his host, and took a tentative sip, and then another. It was more of a stew, he found, with crusts of savory bread floating just below the surface, which along with the flower petals and strips of fried beef gave a mellow effect that deepened with each sip. A little girl followed with a little platter of rolls, dotted all over their swelling tops with spices such as must have been brought at great expense from far away. He sat in the chair they offered him and listened as each girl introduced herself. Smiling, he told them his name as well.

The whole family was sitting on the floor in a wide half circle, their backs to the light. The hair of the children was not purely black as he had first thought, but thoroughly tinged with red, brought out by the reflected sun. He finished his meal and handed the dishes with a smile back to the girl who still stood there.

He had not yet swallowed his last mouthful before the children, all girls, began to sway a little where they sat. The one nearest the window began to hum lowly, and then the youngest, whom Banat had nearly taken, sang out softly in a voice that twinkled like a distant star. The song continued thus for some time before the rest of the girls joined in the melody. In the Lowlands, music was a simple thing to be gotten through all at the same time, but here each girl had a part, trilling, rising and falling, never meeting until the end of the verse, but at all times harmonizing. Suddenly, the melody changed, and they lapsed into a fresh song without stopping. He found that the music itself was a language, speaking to the largest, most personal part of his understanding, expressive of the utmost gratitude and friendship.

With the songs' ending, he shut his mouth, which had begun to hang open, and he smiled and thanked them once again because he knew no other words. In all his life, there had been no songs like this, and no eloquence which could hope to answer theirs. His expression must have been enough, and the girls beamed across brighter than the light of the settling sun from the island of glass behind them.

That was a strange night, and the span of time could not be felt until the wife closed the window and lit the fire. Still the singing continued, and soon Teidin indicated that he wished to learn a Hillsong. The children were delighted, and barely tittered at his pronunciation, although the Kyarrghnaal phrases were easier learned within the structure of melody. It was a children's song, evoking carefree hours and woodland streams, and it brought him back to his earliest years, to the few times he used to wander on his own through the forest, smelling, seeing and feeling new things. The family all gave him applause as the song ended.

Finally, the man of the house saw him suppress a yawn, and with a few weak words to his family they went off to bed. Before they left, each girl kissed Teidin on the cheek as they would have a respected family friend, although one daughter was fully as old as he. The wife showed him out and they crossed into yet another room, larger than the sitting room and constructed of hardwood paneling. The bed was wide and luxuriant, and along one side of the room there was a long mantelpiece lined from end to end with rows of books, objects as strange to him as the songs they had sung.

He turned to thank his hostess once again, but thankfully she had vanished, and there was no need to use the phrase again. All at once the thoughts of day became unbearable to him, and he collapsed across the bed, sleeping as he had not in many days.

The mother and her eldest daughter entered a moment after, but still he slept like a dead man, never hearing them. "We should undress him. We can't have him sleeping in all his clothes like this." The woman started across to him, but the daughter held her back.

"No, let him sleep. It is hardly worth disturbing him. He seems to be in great need of rest, and he can bathe in the morning." She sat down in a reading chair, and her mother sat beside her. The woman had long since learned to treat her daughter as a grown woman, depending on her. She was not yet married, and she had proved herself wise in the management of the farm. Both parents valued her, and her mother especially was grateful for her presence now.

For a time they sat considering the stranger as he slept, his head pillowed on his arm. The hair that hung across his brow was dark, but with lighter tinges through it, and his skin was far fairer than that of a Hillman, his garments rougher. "It is a good face," the mother decided. "Your father says he is like the others, the ones who took your sister, except that he set her free. Whence did they come, I wonder?"

"The Lowlands, I should say."

"Without doubt, but why would such as they come into the Caldera? Did they come all this way only to threaten my little girl? I wish we could speak with this one. But his Kyarrghnaal is very bad." Slowly, she crept to his side and gently pulled his legs up onto the bed. Her daughter came to help, and together they shifted his insensible body around until his head lay on the pillow.

"I wish I could speak his tongue," the young woman said as she removed his belted weapons and propped them up beside him. "We owe him thanks." It had turned colder, so the daughter pulled a quilt over him and tucked him in as her parents used to do for her.

In his mind, he awoke only a moment after drifting away, but the morning sun was full in his face. One of the daughters was there, and as she breezed out of the room with a quick smile, he heaved himself upright on the mattress. A fresh set of clothes had been laid out for him, and he was grateful to peel out of his old ones. A bath would have helped, but he had come to stop expecting the opportunity in his travels. His smell had begun to feel like a natural part of him, like the hair on his arms, but even he recoiled from it in the close, still room.

He had wondered about the objects on the shelf, and now he very gingerly took one up and looked through it. Books were a thing entirely unknown through most of the Island, but he had seen writing before, and admired the skill this script demonstrated. The pictures too were excellent, and it was these he focused on — men walking back and forth with farming instruments or weapons, bears and wild boar among close trees, a great man and his train marching through marshlands up to their horses' bellies. Then there came another hand, equally skilled, which told of pitched battles of men and beasts, one scene separated from the other by brightly flowering trees. Something within him responded to such things, and soon he lost himself between the pages.

There came a clanging behind him as two of the women carried a very large tub into the room, and then steaming stump buckets full of water. Soon, the bath was ready, and they went about tidying things in the room. The elder sister smiled up at him and motioned toward the water, but his wide, shifting eyes told her his mind, and she laughed, shooing her sisters out. With another smile, she tossed him a big brush and shut the door behind her.

These people are something akin to the ancient lords of the land, Teidin thought. He had been told stories of those times, as had all children, but he had never before imagined such wealth. It was said that in the distant past, these people had answered only to the king himself, and otherwise ruled absolutely. He would gladly be ruled if they were truly such folk as these.

The water was very warm, and he gasped loudly as he lowered himself down. He scrubbed himself all over with the brush and finally emerged, raw and glowing pink all over, every inch of skin touching the air anew. When he stepped outside in his fresh clothing, it was into an entirely different hall, for it had filled with people since his arrival, and a central fireplace and been lit, with a great beast cooking in sections on stakes all around it, releasing its tempting fragrance all through the house and skyward through a large window in the ceiling.

No one noticed him, one among many in the teeming hall, and he would have gathered his belongings and fled except the garments on his back were not his. He made it to the door before anyone saw him, and he opened it to a wash of noise. There was another animal dripping over flames, and all around it such a loud thrum of voices that he found it painful. The people of the house stood as he appeared, all but the husband, who in view of his wound was compelled to recline by his wife. The girls tittered together, remembering his modesty.

The big yard was entirely full of neighbors, drawn to the rumor of a great feast, and at their host's loud cry, they all took up a cheer, raising their cups in Teidin's direction. The women, all clustered in a chattering knot with their babies on their hips, cried out their own greetings, greetings that would have made him blush had he understood. The reveling of the *tsalokh* was over, but there was still fresh wealth to be shared, and now the safety of the youngest daughter and the presence of an honored stranger lent still more joy. Had the girl been lost, the house would have stayed a meager appetite on bread and milk.

At last, he could stand no more, and somehow among the revelers he slipped out unnoticed, wandering through the pasture, away from the sea. It was a grazing ground, left alone to recover a while before the cattle were let loose on it again, and he weaved his way among the flats of dung, enjoying the quiet and familiar smells. But he turned back at a run as a loud scream rang above the wind.

As he drew nearer, other cries could be heard, a general voice of wailing and of anger. Out of the yard a man came running, and with a sinking in his heart Teidin stopped and waited. He knew how the man in wool thought, had seen with what swiftness he moved. He should have known they would meet again, that no one would be safe. Banat stopped short, and he and Teidin faced one another across the grass.

The eyes of the man in wool were brightly ringed with white. There was something dead in them, like the corpse of a soul far off in the back of his mind, and the decay imparted its native chill into Teidin's bones. Where before Banat had been cold and unfriendly, he now seemed affable, and it was this above all that disturbed the young man.

Teidin spoke calmly through his anger. "Who is dead?"

"The sow, the mate of the swine with the scythe. Also three or four other beasts. You were correct. She left the jewel elsewhere."

The casual tone changed Teidin, awoke in him a fury he had never known before. The family could not be far behind, but in that moment, it became important to Teidin that he deal with Banat himself, that as a fellow Lowlander it should be his hand that laid this beast low. When he spoke, he screamed, pulling out his two daggers, that of his family and that of the Highland nobleman. "See me, Banat! See me, ready to stop you! Whatever happens, your death will be settled right here!"

Here, Banat laughed long and loud. "I slaughter my beasts at home as I please, and I slaughter them here. Why should I hold off, I ask you? Any Harniyen man is worth twice any Hillswine." He spoke as a man reasoning with an equal.

"Maybe at the Great Trail that is true, but in Allend's End, men still have honor! I will not let you by! Better for you to die upon my blade than by those of the people behind you!"

When he looked over his shoulder, Banat showed fear for the first time. Despise the Hillfolk as he might, the sight of their grim faces, especially those of the women, and the glint on the blade of the old familiar scythe, sobered him suddenly.

Banat, the master of his village at home, killer of Highlanders, scurried like a field rat away from Teidin toward the north. Though he had proved himself quick and deadly in close combat, and nearly invisible in a throng, the open ground ate up what little speed he had. Teidin flew across the ground like a bird of prey.

He gained easily on Banat, and the woolly man turned to face the threat. He was thrown backward upon a hillside that divided the fields from the yard, parrying swiftly left and right against each furious thrust of Teidin's daggers. Banat booted Teidin in the belly and gained his feet again, with his enemy on the defensive. The husband had dropped his scythe and now ran forward brandishing a sword of impressive size. With a relentless momentum he attacked Banat from the left, driving him backward again.

Yet somehow he survived, avoiding being hurt by the blows that rained down upon him from every direction. His balance was perfectly maintained under the attack, and he even managed to return several blows of his own. Through all the thrusting and hacking, by the smallest of chances, Banat's blade came through like a darting serpent and stung Teidin very deeply through his belly.

All at once, there was no strength left anywhere in Teidin, no power to remain standing, much less to keep up the attack. Through fading eyes he saw the Hillman's long sword cut through a wool-covered shoulder, sending an arm flying off onto the close-clipped lawn.

That was the last thing he saw.

Chapter 18
The Tribesmen

THE LOT OF A SERVANT IS BETTER THAN THAT OF HIS
KING, FOR THE SERVANT SEETH HIS MASTER.

*~Hinas Bòrainu, to the Noblemen of the
West Who Came to Ask Hard Questions~*

Some time passed before Hunter paid another visit to the tent. When he did, he found Byorneth awake, staring at the ceiling, counting stitches with eyes half closed and absently braiding his beard. When he saw Hunter standing in the doorway, he shook it out and scowled as his young friend came and sat by the bed. They must have stayed silent for fully five minutes before Byorneth spoke, hardly moving his lips. "I loath this more than anything else in this world."

Hunter nodded, but he knew better than to express pity.

"I am powerless," the old man continued. His voice was small and feeble, but it still bore a hint of the man underneath. "Cut off from the good clean air, the sun. What does the day look like out there?"

"Oh. Well, the sky is clear and blue, with just a haze of white cloud all around the horizon. The world is still and yellow with the sun, rippling like the faint floes of clouds above. All the village is silent, and those who come and go seem loath to make a sound." Hunter would have found it all too easy to slip into florid speech as he described all he had but lately seen for the first time. He had read of this land many times in the past year, but now he felt he had slipped through a curtain and lost the intervening passage of time.

Byorneth would have stopped him if at all possible, but he had seen this before, and had even sought the same escape himself. Hunter finished and was silent again for a moment. "What have you been busy with today, Hunter?"

This time, Byorneth spoke in Harniyen, and it brought Hunter back to earth. "When I awoke, I had a very confusing conversation with the first yellow-haired girl I have ever seen. I broke my fast with her, then I had an interview with the chief. Now I've only just finished baking bread with Grandmother."

Byorneth snorted. "My, she is a one. Wonderful cooking, though. What did you discuss with the chief?"

Hunter detailed his work with the Waileng chief and showed Byorneth the manuscript. It was a good work for his first, and Byorneth nearly said so. Instead, he pointed out the mistakes — a few errors in dynamics, the occasional awkward phrase or imprecise construction. "It will do," he concluded, and Hunter felt the swell of pride that comes with highest praise.

He put his scrolls away, his pens and ink, and steeled himself for the question that had been most on his mind. But Byorneth spoke first.

"You've been told of the Persuader, have you not?"

"Yes," Hunter chuckled. It was just like Byorneth to antici-pate him.

"My son, this was long ago, and I am not one to tell of youthful errors easily."

"I've never held them against you before."

With a long sigh that ended in a grunt, Byorneth began. "You've already heard of the time when I took my leave of Seng Grandt. I had been traveling with an older Sheewa, and we were about to cross the Kyargh when we got word that the Western lands were entering a state of turmoil, and my com-panion decided to take me through the Caldera instead, as we had so many times before. Like a young fool, I rebelled and set off through the passes myself. I cannot tell you how I ever saw the flats again, only that fortune favors the fool.

"When at last I emerged, more dead than alive as you did, I came upon this very tribe. They welcomed me, being a stranger to the Desert. Years before that, I had become con-vinced that the kingship must be restored through me, and so soon they gave me an epithet. An epithet is—"

"Yes, I've heard."

"The chief at that time could allow no rival for the affec-tions of his tribe, so after having fought, traveled, worked, lived and ridden with them, they forced me out. All I had persuaded were threatened with expulsion should there be any further talk of a king.

"That chief was this chief's father, and his anger against me was doubly kindled because most importantly among those I persuaded was the chief's son himself — he who today is called Waileng. He was very young, but I have matured greatly, and I hope that he has as well. There's no thought in my mind of spreading trouble again. The king will come, one way or another. It is a thing to be depended upon, like the tides."

They were silent for a while, and at first Hunter thought Byorneth had fallen asleep again. "Hunter, you have heard very little from the chief, and as you know, there are a great many things no one has ever written in scrolls. Go out among them, talk with them. You must learn to live as a Tribesman before you can be a Sheewa. I would sleep now. Leave me."

So Hunter went out through the wet flap, and found the day was so far advanced that the heat took his very breath away. There was a sweet smell on the fiery blast, and grasping at the familiar scent, Hunter turned his steps toward the stables. All the tribe had heard of him. The Sheewa were the stuff of the past, a real living piece of their history walking among them. To see one in person, such as they had heard of from the cradle, was a great curiosity, so there were many eyes on him as he walked through the camp. And then he saw the horses.

Very few Plainsmen at that time had seen any truly great horses, most of their stock being intended for the breeding of mules, and good for little else. Small horses were all he had seen, never any stately, regal beasts such as these. Six were there at present, standing three-legged and chomping grass, but there were pickets for a good many more, out grazing or being ridden. The stables were in the center of camp away from night raiders, white and shimmering in the day's heat. There was a space reserved for each horse, with a stout rope framework running through the center of the area within which was suspended a leather trough, the seams straining with a fresh load of water.

The wind shifted slightly, and the horses caught his scent and whinnied, clashing their ground hitches together and shifting their feet back and forth. "Ho, there! What are you up to around our horses?" It was a young girl who challenged him with shrill authority as she came out of a nearby tent, a bundle of clothing under her arm. There was a covering over her head, for it was an all-but-vanished tradition that only a woman's husband should enjoy the beauty of her hair, and some conservative parents still required it of their daughters. "I've never seen you before! Are you Laiopej? Haven't you got horses enough of your own?" Drawing her sword, she advanced.

"Maiden! I'm peaceful!" He raised his hands. "I'm a Sheewa of Seng Grandt, here to learn about your tribe so that I may teach others in the High City. Knowledge is all I seek."

The young woman shifted her load and moved alongside him. "I should have known. They said there were two strangers in camp, dressed very strangely, and you're a little dark for a Tribesman. Do you like horses? The really fine ones are out in the field. You should go and see them. We're all excellent riders! I was afraid you were one of the Laiopej, looking to steal more of our stock. Just let me put this laundry down and I'll show you where the rest of the herd is. There's nothing we love more than our horses!"

She set her load down by the tent she had come from, and led him out beyond the last dwellings into a wasteland of dry sand and ruffs of dead grass. As if in welcome, the wind blew a shower of grit into his eyes as he passed the perimeter. It did not seem to matter to the girl. She wrapped the edge of her long garment around her face and fastened it. There was nothing whatever to see off to the west except distance.

As they approached a little hummock not 20 paces from camp, he began to hear voices and hoofbeats, and the ground began to dip into a tiny valley that slowly unfolded with grass such as he had not seen since he had left the Lowlands, bright and lush, spanning both sides of a tiny stream. Evidently at its lowest ebb, there was still a song in the rill's flow, over and above the sounds of riders passing on their fleet mounts, wheeling without effort, putting the horses through their complex paces.

It would have been chaos to the ordinary Lowlander, but somehow Hunter could see the beauty in the galloping back and forth, the snortings and scrapings. A few of the horses must have been in training, young colts taken out to get a feeling for noise, as well as older stock that children could ride safely and would lend their calm to the volatile members.

"Lovely, are they not?" The girl, he suspected, had come as much to get away from her chores as to show him the horses. "We put a child on a horse's back before he takes his first steps. They say I made a perfect ride my first time, and then fell down, and climbed back up again by myself, but that sounds like a big story to me. Even the girls ride, and can handle arms, though they always make us stay in the tents when the raids come. Of course, we naturally want to guard the—"

There was an angry call from behind them, and with a deep sigh, the girl turned. "I'll have to go now. Just ask any of the Tribesmen. They may not know you, but your people have always been welcome here." And with that, she started back to where a stern-faced woman stood waiting, holding the bundle the girl had set down.

By now, the riders in the meadow had seen him, and several were walking their horses up the little slope. He raised his hand and started down toward them, greeting them when they came near with the formal dialect. They reined back and returned the greeting with the Horseman's salute, a bow and slap of the chest. "Well met, sir!" the eldest spoke first, as it should be in the West when greeting a stranger. "We bid you welcome! We were the ones who found you and your friend at the edge of the Desert. I hope you're both well again."

"Thank-you, sir! Yes, we are all the better for the care of the women. The Persuader will be a while in recovering."

The horse under the speaker, a young one, sidestepped. The rider soon got him under control and patted the dappled shoulder. "Come and ride with us, if you wish. Our finest horse is yours as long as you'd like!"

"Thank-you, no, Rider," Hunter replied. "I know not the way of riding as you do. I only know horses as breeding stock for mules. It would be a great honor, however, if you would teach me the way of it." They were indeed different animals. Bright and flickering, they pranced in place, dancing like flame, and slim as they were, their chests were all broad and their flanks quivered and rippled with each movement. If this was poor stock as the chief had insisted, it would be a great thing to see their more impressive brothers.

The eldest rider was a merry fellow, and chuckled through his yellow whiskers. They curved and drooped all the way to his chin, completing his resemblance to the wild Tribesmen of old so skillfully rendered in the scrolls of Seng Grandt. "Mules? Those flap-eared pests that never breed? Why would you work with them when you have horses?"

"They are very strong, tough, and fast if it comes to that, though it rarely does. But their bloodlines were never like this. It's said these were formed of wind and water, coming to land with the tide."

The man laughed and stepped down. His long tunic was bound at his waist with a broad belt on which hung his sword, an immense, curving instrument that dragged on the horse's rump as he dismounted. On the heel of each high boot was a rowelled spur that rattled with his movement. His trousers were baggy and tucked into his boots, but when he was on the ground they were all but concealed by the ends of his long coat. "That's what we're told in the cradle, yes. Come, use my saddle and horse. Take a ride yourself."

⌇

The leaf set was perfect, the bud young and tender, the two leaves whole and healthy. She pinched it between thumb and finger, twisted it loose from the branch as she had been carefully taught to do, and tossed it into the large basket on her back. And she sang. Over the centuries, songs had become one with the work, with the identity of the people. It was a good rhythm, and made the repeated motion seem lighter and more satisfying, and she rejoiced inwardly as she felt the weight on her back increase, knowing what the leaves would become. More than that, she rejoiced that at long last, she was able to labor of her own account.

Their parting grief had eased somewhat, leaving nothing more than a gnawing, bitter yearning deep in her soul for her husband's return. Little as she knew of his work, she could hazard no guess as to how long he would be away. There was nothing to do but work, count the days and reacquaint herself with her people.

Much to her delight, Srstri had become a favorite among the local children. Ever since they had heard Byorneth's story, the little plantation hummed every night with the young of the Hills from farther and farther away, and every night she was made to tell the story of her captivity and rescue. When at last this grew stale, she turned to the few stories she had learned in her time in the High City, which told of great adventure to please the young children, and famous passions, which captured the young men and women. Several of the young boys even developed what they conceived to be a great love for her. The language completely returned, and she no longer stumbled over the rolling sounds as she had before, hardly ever had to reach for just the right words. At last, her stock of stories ran dry, and the woman of the house insisted they allow Srstri to rest a while, as much for the sake of the trodden grass as for the girl.

At last, the day's picking was done and she walked down the hill back to the farm. Her basket was emptied for the last time and put away, and she stood and watched a while as the work of bruising, withering and airing of the leaves was done. Daylight still remained for this work, but she had begun her day in the second hour of the sixth watch, before any of the others, and there would be work to do inside.

The fat woman was shelling peas into a large pot with a constant popping rhythm. She worked by the dying sun in the window and a lamp behind her, lit against the coming dark. Srstri slipped her shoes off by the low door and smiled at her hostess. "Peas for supper?" she asked. "Will it be the same recipe?"

"More or less." The woman kept on shelling, and Srstri wondered how the pot remained upright, propped as it was half on her lap. "I've put wild garlic in the pot, along with a little milk and cheese."

"Oh, it sounds lovely." Indeed, it sounded far lovelier than plainly boiled, as they had eaten the past few nights. The woman had planted the same number of peas as every other year, but the season had been unexpectedly fruitful, and they had passed the last few mealtimes in an epic struggle to consume all the ones that were not to be dried for the winter. Why they could not be eaten raw, she did not know, but she supposed that among the Highlands, cooking them must be the fashion, and fashion is the toughest pod of all to crack.

Srstri sat to help her. Ever since she had begun to work, her quiet hours had been haunted by images of leaf sets sometimes inverted, sometimes curled in the fresh bloom of youth. It was called *barraakang*, or "leaf vision," and it affected all those who pick tea. But other thoughts overlaid the *barraakang*, and above a downy young bud there came the sudden image of the boy — no, the man who had left her a bride. She feared his face would fade in her memory, and she struggled violently to retain it, to remember how his hair was wavy and curly, and that it would form ringlets as it fell across his clear brow. His eyes had been brown, brown and hazel, the latter framing the dark walnut around the pupils. But most of all it was the way he spoke, his frank tone, his honest smile that had wooed her long before he had. Soon her eyes were clouded with tears. The woman was still bent to her work, one bare foot propped up on another chair.

The children, whom Srstri had never counted, were suddenly freed from their work, and crowded into the small dwelling, milling about like a river suddenly dammed. The woman never moved but to reach across and slap some evildoer across the wrist. When the husband came in, she could not tell, but suddenly he was there, smiling his quiet little smile, watching them work.

The woman rose to tend to the night's supper, and soon the table was all set, the meal steaming. Srstri found it good, and added her compliments to the general consensus, but ere her plate was empty, she found herself nodding. At last one of the smaller children laughed and shook her by the shoulder, a shocking familiarity that earned his hand an immediate slap.

Bed was welcome, and she sank ever further into the blankets as she gave up the battle that all sleepers fight against the rest they crave. There was no awakening all night, not even when a little body crawled into bed and snuggled into her arms. Even in dumb sleep, she who had cared for the ancient treasure of a dead kingdom for more than 15 years was now the instinctive protector of a far dearer jewel. The child had vanished by morning, with only his warm trust remaining.

Her room was small by Lowland standards, as indeed was the entire house, so as to be easily heated. It was dominated on one side by a large window, open now, which spread warm sunshine and living air through her mind, melting the webs of night into a stiff yawn.

The wind was cooler across the slopes, and she worked with a scarf around her neck. Yet somehow, the buoyant high spirits of yesterday returned as she picked, the plucking rhythm coming easily to her. There had been much more to the work than she ever thought, and the woman had invested many hours into her schooling. Now it was a natural feeling, like the weight of the ring she still wore. And she could afford the occasional moment to watch the folk who passed below her.

Every cloud edged itself with bronze and then gold as the day around her brightened. The road was empty as it was every morning, the sole exception being a single lonely figure, a mere speck against roads from the lower farms. Her heart leapt, even though her husband had been gone but a few weeks, and would not be back through the Pass for a long time. It was not him. But it could have been.

Soon the road became busy, and a gay chatter grew in the air as the swaying, steady rhythm of daily life resumed. She was now acquainted with every type that might be expected to travel the roads across the wide Crater — farmers, blacksmiths, families. She had no friends left from her days as *deesard*, none that would ever pass the Sky Line, though through the efforts of her hosts, she had begun to make a few new ones.

Some minutes passed before she looked down the Trail again. The day had turned sweltering, but in spite of this, a chill shook her spine and she dropped a valuable leaf set in the dirt when the distant figure resolved itself into a large man swathed in layer upon layer of wool and skins. A strangeness upon his right side told her that he lacked an arm, but it could only have been one man. He was death, and something in his manner told her how very deathly he had become. Though she was too far away for him to recognize, she hid herself behind a bush until he passed out of sight.

The woman knelt in her garden, fending off flies and small children as she tortured weeds out of their dirt. She looked up as the man approached, fur hat in hand, and saluted her in fair Kyarrghnaal. "Lady, I have need of help. A very close friend passed by here some weeks ago. We expected her back, but it has been a long time with no word. Have you seen her? She has long black hair, wears the clothing of the Lowlanders, and travels in the company of two muleteers."

She considered a while, plucking two tiny weeds as she did so. Srstri had left no friends behind, as well she knew. Finally, she replied with a vacant shrug, "I'm sorry, but I've been at home all day, and no such girl has passed by."

"She would have passed before today, perhaps within the last two weeks."

She bent to her garden again. "I could not answer for that. My memory is short." It was the first lie she told that day, and she was grateful none of her brood was present to hear. The stranger pulled his hat far down over his ears and continued on his way.

As he disappeared, the woman scowled down into the dirt. Strangers who spoke awkward Kyarrghnaal were scarce in the Hills, but those who spoke awkwardly and sought young women who had recently escaped captivity in the villages were rarer still.

The man in wool stopped and scowled as he passed beyond the outskirts of the plantation. The very moment the land-holding had come into sight, he fancied he could feel the nearness of his goal. A devious man as well as cruel, the woman's manner told him far more than she had intended. He nearly brought his knife out, but then another thought struck him.

He was bored with knives anyhow. There were other methods.

~^^~

Hunter rode a great deal over the next few days. The soreness in his knees soon left him, and the horses were nearly always gentle, but still he slouched and took every bump and bounce in the bend of his spine. The men laughed, but each day he rode straighter, stronger. One man in particular took charge of his riding, and soon he began taking the young Sheewa away across country, making sure he always had a particular gray horse, a knot-headed creature with a muscular rump and a short, choppy gait that had Hunter urging him constantly to keep up with the long strides of his teacher's brown steed.

Twice a day, as he gained stamina and confidence, Hunter and the horse would go through their paces together. The days flew sweetly, and there were nights when he fell into bed in his tent without stopping to see Byorneth. He had heard tales of the old man's prowess, and he was determined to be a proficient rider by the time the leg mended. At last, his riding master let him go near the other horses, and a new world of delight opened up.

He rejoiced in the smell, the thrill of a horse who loves to be ridden. They were all different in every way, so that soon he could have named each steed by simply sitting in the saddle. But out of all these creatures, one particular young stallion caught his eye the first time he saw him. The man who rode him was skillful, but Hunter only saw the horse. It was being ridden for agility, weaving at a dead run between wooden obstacles. He had never seen such perfection of form, such flow of movement as he found in the shining black horse, for he moved in and out like quicksilver, the charcoal mane echoing each ripple of the swelling shoulders, scarcely needing the control of his rider. The first time Hunter faced the horse, it was picketed, calmly cropping grass, but as Hunter approached, the black creature's eyes grew wide and he reared up on his hind legs.

Hunter was not afraid, as he had been. He came nearer, and as he did the stallion became still, though it still viewed him through wide-straining eyes. Very slowly, he approached, speaking softly under his breath, until at last he held his hand out under the velvet muzzle and the horse smelled him, grunting. Touching the horse as he had been taught to do, he made a motion toward the glossy legs and immediately one came up and into his hand. "The pride of our stock, that," a man said, brushing a dappled roan at the next picket. "He's called Olonj."

Hunter had studied the Huaynił tongue extensively, yet this word was new to him. Nor did it sound like any other word of the West. Thankfully, the man explained. "It's a very old word. It means 'royalty,' but over and above that of the chief. I never heard of it until the chief named this horse himself."

Olonj. No man may read the entirety of the scrolls of the High City in one lifetime, but if Hunter had, then he would have come across an obscure document hidden in the darkest corner of the Seng Grandt archives. Had he been especially interested, he may have read therein of the Olõčon, who ruled over the Desert lands before they became desert. It was a minimal, offhand reference, but it had been the subject of hot debate in ancient years. He had never heard of it before, but thought he could sense the greatness behind it.

Soon he was allowed to ride Olonj, the black horse. Their rides grew longer into the Desert and sometimes even the outer foothills. It was here that the ecstatic moment came, when at last he fell in with the horse's gallop, perfectly suiting his body to the back-and-forth motion. His teacher laughed aloud to see it. "You'll go out alone now!" he cried out as Hunter flew by, the cloak billowing out behind.

But he was brought back to the ground on the ride back, when there came an odd hitch in the stallion's gait, and the Tribesman made him stop and dismount. He held his hand out for the reins and threw a shining steel pick down at his feet. "You picked up a stone out there," he said, and laughed again when at his instruction, Hunter cleaned all four of the horse's hooves, breathing hard at the strain on his arms and legs. This time, Olonj was of no mind to easily submit, and he wore out all the tricks ere his rider was done. He leaned his muzzle on the base of Hunter's neck, kept his legs tense as Hunter tried to hold them, shifted his weight as the pick did its work. Sweat gleamed on Hunter's brow when at last he groaned and stood up straight like a man twice his age. Humbled and sore, the young Sheewa returned to camp.

A great deal of time was spent in walking as well. He did not yet feel confident enough to go everywhere ahorseback, and the long, easy pace of walking appealed to him, fitting with his comfortable Sheewan garments. Each morning, he walked down to the little meadow before his lessons and watched the riding out on the grass. The young bloods would set up races for wagers or the favor of the girls, and nearly kill themselves for profit and pride. The girls sat on the sidelines laughing, Hunter suspected, at the boys' expense. Only then would he ride out himself.

Each day after his ride, he walked back by the same road, past dry river beds and clumps of succulent plants, back to his tent where he would sit until the evening meal, writing notes on what he had learned, as much as anyone can put what a rider knows on paper. Tierna had kept her distance ever since their first uncomfortable encounter, and Hunter was just as glad, albeit regretting the impression he must have given.

This and many other things revolved in his mind as he passed through the arid meadows one hot, cloudy day. His basic research having long been completed, he still enjoyed the horsemanship, and a true student never ceases to learn. He was intoxicated by the excitement of the race. This new animal was a real delight, an embodiment of swift grace, ever in his mind even as he walked, fired all the more by the sweet horsey scent blowing across the sand.

The camp was built against a succession of intertwined gullies, opening out toward the mountains. Generations of invasion upon their tents had driven them to choose this camp, bracketed from the other tribes by its hillocks and ridges. It was a long walk through these little canyons, and as he went Hunter was reminded of the places of his childhood, the seaside mounds, cut off square and round by the tides. The exertion was familiar, this climbing up and down, and once again he rejoiced at being a Sheewa.

A sound stopped him as he passed by the opening of a wide draw, a sound he had first taken for one of the many noises in the wind. Now it was louder and shriller — the high, strident cry of a woman.

It was a peculiar sound, one that sets fire under the feet of a man. His body took over, and instantly he was running along the ravine, staff held at the ready. Three men came into sight, and they were clustered around a girl who struggled against them. Though he had never seen any other tribe, he knew these men were not of the Waileng. The cut of their robes was different, and he had never seen them in camp. Hunter dropped his pouch as he ran, and yelled at the top of his voice.

Instantly, the three heads turned, and the girl broke away, unhindered. She did not run away into the Desert as he had hoped, but crawled partway up the gully wall out of reach and waited to watch. It seemed strange, how little she had struggled, this in a land where the women were, as a rule, as prodigious fighters as the men. Even now, she only watched, though he could not tell which outcome she hoped for.

The young men seemed in no way cowards, and it perplexed him that they should have accosted a young lady so. "You three have a clear choice ahead of you!" His voice rang clear, but without strain. "You can allow her to walk back to the camp in my company, or you can limp home! What say you?"

They saw only a youth about their age, dressed in strange garb, wielding no weapon but a staff (his hook was out of sight behind his cloak). A Tribesman fights from the earliest age, constantly pitted against those as young and as vigorous as he. This stranger from nowhere could never be as deadly. They fanned slowly out on all sides, with the confidence of youth, their long blades balanced and ready.

Hunter covered the ground in three strides, and with a low swing delivered the foremost a crack over the skull that collapsed him, flicking the sword from his limp hand as the staff came around, and with three long strides he moved as swiftly away.

They had not expected Hunter to attack first, but they had been given fair warning, which is more than they had any right to. Indecision stayed them until the girl up the hill laughed. Now their manhood stood in balance, and young manhood is easiest to be offended.

Hunter stood waiting, feet apart, knees bent slightly, very relaxed. It started like any training drill. But Hunter knew better than to be complacent. Suddenly, he moved, and with such efficiency that the tribesmen were completely unprepared, though they watched him carefully. He struck one man's knee with the end of his staff, spun the staff around, and swept another off his feet entirely. They were skilled fighters, it was true, and their slashing blades may well have killed Hunter. But even as one end of his staff struck, the other end turned their attacks aside, and one by one their blades flew across the sand.

He came to rest with the butt of the staff at a young Tribesman's throat. The other hissed vain curses as he lay on his back, clasping his damaged knee while the third lay a little way off, watching without moving.

"You, my friend, can carry on the fight alone, or you can help these two dear fellows back to camp. I take it they are your friends."

The eyes went back and forth between his friends and back to Hunter. "Mark me! In the name of honor, mark me! I cannot bear disgrace!"

The staff did not move. "What honor is there in three preying on one?"

"How can you know so little?" He practically spat the words. "How else are we of the tribes to marry? How else have our mothers and fathers wed for generations? We are above 18 years, all of us! Our brethren have all taken women and married before us! Now mark me, or slay me here and now, I don't care which!"

Hunter put up his staff and knelt, fingering the hilt of his knife. "How — how should I mark you? On the cheek, or—"

"Do you imagine that I care? You've already killed us with your interference! Now make your mark and finish your work!"

Quickly, he made a cut across the boy's face, only deep enough to bleed. Hunter stood back as they went, leaning on one another's shoulders, their eyes never meeting his. He remembered what he had read. Tribal mothers were skilled physicians, and perhaps they could put the knee right. He had given fair warning, and they had outnumbered him, but still the thought of what he had done began to sicken him in the wake of the fight.

They were nearly out of sight as the young man turned, blood streaming down his face and into his light beard. "Soon, my enemy! Soon I will pay this debt!" And they were gone.

He turned to the girl, silent and immobile, nestled in the hillside. She did not seem afraid, only attentive, as though she watched a great drama. Her hair was pale almost to the point of whiteness, the edges adorned in two long braids tucked behind her ears. Hunter sheathed his blade and retrieved his staff. "Are you quite all right?"

With a smile that a more experienced man would find alarming, she stood and walked down to him, moving her braids so that they swayed by her temples. "Will they be waiting for us?" she asked as she took his arm, drawing very near, happy to be led away. Whereas most women of his acquaintance were, of necessity, strong in mind and body, this woman allowed herself to be rescued and led. Was there no woman in the West he need not fear?

"Unlikely." He removed her hand from his and drew away from her. "They will need a while to build up their pride before they try again. Why did you wander alone, inviting capture? Surely nothing in this place could have tempted you so strongly away from camp."

She evaded the question. "Why are you so formal? Who are you?"

"I am a Sheewa. It is our custom to speak this way."

"No, I mean why are you so formal with me? We know each other! I showed you the horses, remember? I put my laundry down for a moment to do that, and I had a little trouble because of it. So, I hope you enjoyed the horses!"

"I am obliged to you for that. I've enjoyed my time learning to ride. Do you ride often?" He already knew the answer, but he felt he should say something.

"We all ride, and pretty often! We all get pretty edgy without enough mounts, and I suppose that's why we're always raiding for them. Really, their horses are all ours. They have nothing they haven't stolen from us. It's really nicer not to have to go with them. That is, if I don't have to. Now that — well, all this has happened, I might not need to. I might be able to stay with — somebody — among the Waileng. Of course, that was why you did it."

"Well, I wanted to save you. Now you can choose a husband from your own tribe."

He felt her draw away, but whether because of his rebuff or a memory of the violence he had just done, who could tell?

They walked back to camp in silence, speaking with not a soul until they arrived. The camp was quiet, with only a few people working in its dusty lanes, it being near to the heat of the day. He broke away from her in the street, and she lost him among the brown tents.

Removing his shoes, Hunter reclined on his bed a while in thought, letting his feet cool. The great problem the Sheewa had always faced was their acquaintance with only one tribe west of the mountains, and one objective of their present mission was to cultivate relations with the Waileng's neighbors. Today's events could only make things difficult.

Byorneth agreed when Hunter told him the story in the cool of the evening, a rising wind rattling the tent back and forth. Though the old man's eyes shone with underlying pride, his tone showed disapproval. "The young man you marked is the son of a chief, to judge by his clothing. They came for women and any horses they could find, and they struck in daylight as though they wanted to achieve some sort of fame. The son of the chief wanted respect as well as a marriage, and mark or no mark, you have humiliated him. It will be difficult for his father and him to command the tribe after such a disgrace. It would have been far better for you to have walked on by. What's one Tribeswoman, more or less?"

"But what of the Waileng? This must have earned us friends among them, and perhaps we could use some of this influence to enforce a peaceful meeting."

"No!" Byorneth came upright in his bed with a suddenness that contorted his face with pain. "We will enforce nothing! The actions of the Sheewa are never to endanger those he studies, you know that! We are and always will be neutral!"

"I only thought that when the time came, we could be a calming influence—"

Byorneth cut in with a laugh and fell back into his covers again. "Calming influence? The sight of you would spark a level of blood feud unheard of between them, and since they've seen your Sheewan garments, I would not fare much better. No, the best we could do would be to accompany the Waileng on their migration, and then study the tribes farther to the south before you manage to antagonize them as well."

Hunter could not seem to relish any travel that took him away from the Kyargh, but Byorneth was right. "I have always been intrigued by the old stories of the Fisherfolk of the farthest West. One day, I would like to travel there, and see what's become of them." Indeed, it had been a minor dream of his to journey into those lands and see those people, learn their own odd dialect of the Western tongue. Their horses were smaller, and tufted about the knees, so they said. They were entirely distinct from their brother tribes, fishing for their living more than they rode.

Byorneth's face relaxed. "I'm inclined that way myself, come to think of it. But no one catches rabbits by chasing two at once. We'll leave them to be studied later. We of the High City are in no hurry."

Hunter got to his feet to make way for Jooenin, who entered with yet another tray of food and insistent inquiries after the health of Byorneth's leg. He left them alone and retired to his tent. It was a cool, sweet wind that fanned the little camp, fresh from the foothills, colored by wild grasses. The world was definitely changing, not least in his own perception of it. For an entire year, the life of a wandering scribe had entranced him, but at this moment he would have given over every tribe of the West, and all the treasures of their knowledge, for one day with his wife among the Hills.

Chapter 19
The Fire

Banat had gone, but he left behind an atmosphere of worry. Of his passing, the woman said nothing to Srstri, and to Srstri's keen mind that fact in itself indicated trouble. If the woolly man had been determined enough to continue his search long after hope and his arm were gone, then a short rebuff could not be expected to hold him off. Of all people in the whole Island, he was the one man she should have expected to see again.

He would be an outcast now, removed from any holding he ever had among the villages. If only he had something to lose by his mad quest, there might be some hope, but she knew him better, understood a little of the state of his life. The thoughts of her restless mind retarded sleep as smoke does bees.

But it was smoke.

Out of half sleep she awakened immediately to the sound of screaming, the rushing of feet back and forth. And her room was awash with red light, though not the light of dawn. The land was burning.

The room was fast filling with smoke, and she began to cough, choking on the poisoned air as she rolled out of bed and crawled toward the open window. When she tried to crawl out through it, a river of scorching air forced her down again. The second time, she crouched and leaped through, hitting the steaming ground heavily and rolling to her hands and knees, then raising to a low crouch. Things were no better outside, and the heat and blowing cinders drove her around the house out of the black world of smoke, lit by the orange and blue light that flickered up over the roof with a heavy growl.

The man of the house was vainly beating back the flames when he saw her figure against the light and called. As she ran to him, he took up an armload of tools and together they fled the land, joining the woman and children where they stood solemnly by the edge of the Trail. The heat of the fire built up as the midnight grew brighter and brighter, until at last it forced them across the road and onto a low knoll, where they stood together to watch the labor of generations burn away. Every ancient tree in the yard, every building, every wooden structure of any kind had its own wreath of flame. No one wept. They simply watched their lives burn away in front of them.

There is a strange power in flame, a fascination that compels even as it destroys. None could take their eyes from the pall of roiling death as it crept across the ground, flowing through the yard on wind of its own handiwork. His family safe, the man of the house was about to go fight the flames again, but horror built upon horror as out of the midst of the fire there walked a man, dark against the light, not running as would any other being. The red tongues leapt around him, playing about his heels, but they made no motion to devour him, their only friend. He walked toward the knoll, but it was not until he crossed the road and began to mount up the incline that Srstri knew the face, and saw the lack of arm among the wool. Even in the hot work of arson, he had discarded none of it.

How he had escaped incineration, how he had been able to set so many things aflame, she could not think. Madness brings its own weird privileges, and smiles through the blisters of its own fire. Pain was always immaterial, and now the joy he had at the sight of his *deesard* was greater than a dozen blazes. The tortured smile broadened as the *deesard* came out of the knot of Hillswine and walked down the hill toward him.

He had her. He knew he had her, and in having her, he had his treasure. Now, one of the Highland pigs stepped between them, a little man in a long nightshirt. He left his children and placed himself between them like a fool, and like a fool he raised a weapon, one of the tools he had taken with him. The woman sent the little ones away, and they scattered like leaves in a storm.

There was no hurry now. Banat stopped short and drew a weapon, a Highland weapon, doubtless stolen. "Give me the woman, she who stands there. Give her to me, or die and I will take her."

The man of the house was chivalrous even for a Hillman, and Srstri knew it. He would die before he let a guest leave against her will. "Banat, I will go with you! Let these people alone, and their children! They've had punishment enough for their kindness to me!" The words were Harniyen, which she had not used for many days, but they came with a freshness that frightened her.

"Oh, it is far easier than that, my slave! I've never wanted you or any Hill vermin, but only the jewel you took away with you! Oh, that was foolishness, *deesard*! I will not be done out of the one thing of value I ever owned! Only just tell me where you hid it, and I may leave you all in peace!" The Hillman stood in confusion between them, still holding fast to his weapon.

"I left the jewel with trusted men in a high city, far away on the edge of the Hills. It was always my burden, never yours." The fire which raged on the other side of the Trail had begun to reach its full fury on the outer edges of the night. The growing tumult of neighbors, risen out of bed to beat out the flames, lifted above its roar.

The girl stood upon the hillside. Though her eyes were wide against the soot on her skin, there was no fear in them. This confused Banat, and he spoke louder. "You had a treasure worth all the villages of the Lowlands in your hands, and you let it go? You left it on the edge of the Lowlands, the only thing that ever made you valuable? I do not believe you!" Then, in Kyarrghnaal to the man between them, "Your life or hers, swine! Which one shall it be?"

"Mine, if it comes to that!"

"It has." Banat's swiftness surprised them all, for despite his bulk, he moved like a squirrel. The weapon would have severed the man's life had he not blocked it, and Banat's second blow was interrupted by the wife, who had moved only a little slower than the Lowlander. With a crushing momentum, she bowled him over, grasping the hand that swung the knife with a powerful grip, and Banat was lost in the swirling fury of her striking fists. By now, Srstri had reached them, but she found she could do nothing against Banat, nor strike through the woman's assault.

In spite of his position, Banat was able to kick the woman away and instantly regain his feet, shoving her back into Srstri. A broad swipe left a deep cut in her right cheek which showered her front with blood. The husband was ready, and he charged forward as Banat raised his blade to meet him. The man was nearly on him when his face changed, and he turned and slipped off into the darkness, the husband and his wife vanishing after him.

Srstri would have followed, but it occurred to her that she had no weapon. She could only wait and look out into the darkness, trying to make sense of the muffled noises.

Out of the darkness behind her, a hand fastened itself over her mouth, and before she could react, it pulled her backward into the ashy night. But she was no longer the slave of the Lowlands, the mark of his status. The lot of lady suited her well, and all her dormant nature awoke and rushed to defend it.

The scratches on Banat's face had healed, but the stump where his arm had been still pained him, and bled a little. Srstri turned on him like a panther and her fingernails tore at him, her flailing fists battering him about the head until it hummed like a water wheel. His hand shot out and wrapped around her throat, squeezing until her breath ceased. "One more move and your throat crackles! I've done it before! Stop struggling, sow, or I will finish you! Where is the jewel?"

Even as she struggled, he dragged her far off into the night, and though she heard the man and woman searching for her, calling to their children to stay hidden, their voices only moved farther away. His grip loosened, but she dared not scream. Not yet.

"I — left it behind," she choked. "It was not mine to keep. I would show you if I had it."

Throwing her to the ground, he struck a blow that loosed a stream of blood from her brow, and would have followed it with another had he not groaned suddenly and staggered a little on his feet, allowing Srstri to break free of him. They had come to rest below a little hill, and at the top there were several children, raining swift stones down upon their enemy. The light from the dying blaze showed them orange against the deep sky, and there were more coming, crying out in triumph.

And then there came out of the night two specters of vengeance, the woman and her husband, disheveled but largely unhurt. Darkly they came, armed with blades and deadly intent, to the rescue of their honored guest. The woman, the voice of their collective will, positively growled as she approached, the man in wool caught between them and the children with their stinging stones.

Her weapon was a long-handled sickle, and she carried it in both hands. "Why do you come here? This lady carries nothing precious with her but her life! What are you? Thief? Murderer? Or both?"

"I am neither!" Srstri thought his voice strained upward a notch or two, and was astonished to see him in fear. "I seek only what is mine. This — this woman brought a certain treasure out of the Lowlands, out of my hands and into the hands of strangers!"

"She brought no treasure but herself and he who is now her husband!"

"And who is her husband?"

"A man, one whose duty took him away westward! For that reason only do you remain safe from him!"

The fear left Banat in that moment, and he was the adamant Lowlander once more. He looked away to the west, then back to his accusers, and an almost noble smile enveloped his face.

And with the sigh of one who has come to the end of his life, he bowed low. "Excuse me for burning your property and slaughtering several of your servants. I'll be away now."

The face of the woman twisted with anger, a rage her children had learned to dread.

But he was gone, and they could find no trace of his presence. Every child swore upon sacred life that no one had passed, and there was nothing save memory to testify of his existence.

For the first time, Srstri felt out of place among the little family, left with nothing but cinders and the memory of their oldest trees. Some part of their hillsides would be saved, the neighbors would see to that, and the husband went himself to help them, but the rare and ancient plants that lined the yard were gone. The wife stayed behind with the children, still wielding her sickle, watching the glowing scene with dry eyes. Turning, she smiled at Srstri.

"At least there is nothing like the chance to start over."

The girl wanted to apologize, but any words she thought of were inadequate. "I never suspected he would still be after me."

"Forget him. He has no reason to stay here in the Hills anymore. There is nothing more he can do to us." Srstri remembered the change she had seen in Banat at the last, before he vanished.

The woman must have remembered it too. "You should go. Go now, if you love your man. Find someone to help you across before the storm finds him." She reached into her clothing and pulled out a skin full of gold, tipping about half out into her hand. Then the bag flew across and Srstri caught it. There was a knife as well and that was given her, of plain construction, but an honest blade. "My husband and I do not like to seem inhospitable. You have been welcome here, and we wish you health and safety, and the life of your husband."

The woman did not see the girl leave, had barely taken her gaze from her ruined property even when she spoke to her. But she thought of her. There was a little resentment, but only a little, and that passed when she reflected upon Srstri's husband, away across the Kyargh. He had taken his wife away from her masters in the Lowlands, an unprecedented feat. The old friend that came with them, Byorneth, terse though he was in speech and manner, set great store by the lad. There was a tide of legend which somehow followed these people, and they were spoken of long after they had passed. There was something new on the wind, and if it was what she felt it to be, then her family's home might be a small price to pay.

Srstri followed the trail to the south, passing no one but a man and woman who stood together in the road, staring at the smoke in dismay. There would be a great deal of dismay all around, she knew, as the news spread. Soon the road branched off, splitting to the right in an upward trail to the high country. She walked with her hand on the dirk in her waistband, jumping at every sound. Though she knew her enemy had ceased to care about her, his coming had shattered her peace of mind. The wind was at her back, sweet and full, carrying all the pleasant sounds of a summer morning, as well as the touch of smoke.

She did not look back at the narrow black pall reaching up among the lower clouds behind her, but she felt it, a towering, accusing witness.

The couple she had passed soon came to the plantation, which now crawled with men and women, putting out the flames. As neighbors, the two newcomers lent a hand as well, and soon they too were black with soot. There were few flames left, for the summer had been wet, and the workers stood exhausted, looking at the extent of the damage for the first time.

It appeared that much of the hillside had been saved, and though the house had been destroyed and the ancient plants damaged, there was still living wood there. They would care for those plants in desperate hope for a long time, nursing them, watching each day for signs of fresh growth. The woman of the house was as tired as the rest, and for the first time her children could remember, it showed. She took a long draught of water and moved the hair back from her sweaty brow.

Now she joined her husband in the latter part of the work — the work of thanking their neighbors for their help. They knew each of their neighbors well, and in each face they could see a sorrow almost equal to their own. Then they came to a man and woman who stood at the remains of the old trees, a man and woman their age or older. "Our thanks to you both. You must have come from far. What brought you out on the roads so early?"

"We've been on our way for some days' walk, from the other side of the Caldera." The man spoke first, and she could hear the slight difference in his speech that marked him as one of the Eastern Hillmen. "We have been looking for the holding with the ancient trees, with the fat woman. This is it?"

"Yes."

"We got word that Srstri was staying here, that she had been away for some years. Is this true?" The woman of the house could see the resemblance now — the frank, handsome features, the honest expression. The woman could have been Srstri herself in 30 years.

Looking at her husband, who had known about the message, she replied. "Yes, I sent it." She felt the tears coming up, and she turned away for a moment. "I sent her away into danger, to find her husband."

They stood in silence for a long time, staring all around them at the smoking landscape. The morning was brightening the clouds in the East, illuminating the Western mountains against the sky.

— ⌒ ⌒ —

The broth was steaming, and Tierna lifted the pot from the fire and laid it on the table, watching her guest fill a bowl from it and sip delicately. Tierna and Kaia had been bosom friends since their earliest years. Every week, sometimes every day, would find them visiting over cooking, laundry or the horses, but it was a rare occurrence when they found the leisure to do nothing but talk.

Kaia was concluding her story. "And the Laiopej boys were about to carry me away when that Sheewa, the young one, happened along. He just used that big staff of his as if they were rats or something! I've never seen fighting like it! Then he took me by the arm just as nice and gentle as you please, and walked me back to camp!"

The sentence ended as she took a breath, and Tierna cut in quickly between sips. "I've heard old stories about how the Longfarers fought, but I never quite believed it. And he never drew his sword?"

"No, never did. Didn't even kill any of them." Another sip. "Thank-you for the broth. I wish I could make it like this!"

The Tribes of the West reserve strong drink for great occasions, preferring broth for ordinary fellowship. Tierna acknowledged the compliment with a smile. "He must be the strangest boy I've ever met. Do you remember how I took care of him after he was found? All the time when he slept he talked about the strangest things — dragons and tea and a beast that carried grain. When he woke up, I tried to talk with him, perfectly ordinary conversation, but he was afraid to be in the same tent with me. Finally, he told me all about his wife, and then he left, just like that!"

Kaia spilled a little out of her cup, and quickly steadied it with both hands. "Oh, is he married?"

"Yes, he told me he had to leave her the day after the wedding. I couldn't help but feel sorry for the bride, being left all alone like that in the cold Highlands." It was widely accepted in the West that the Hillfolk were reclusive creatures, roaming about in skins among the icy peaks. "You're not aiming your arrows at him, are you?"

"Of course not!" A little more broth tipped out of the cup, which she hurried to soak up with the edge of her garment. "There are plenty of boys for me without falling back on common adventurers like him! I'd far rather allow myself to be kidnapped by some Laiopej, or even Ayafet!" Kaia downed the dregs out of her cup. "Thank-you again for the visit. I should get back to my mending."

Tierna frowned at her departing friend and took the pot away, her mind racing as she cleaned up, troubled by the exchange. She knew her friend well, knew how her mind worked when strangely affected. Nearly every boy in the tribe had unwittingly tormented Kaia. Tierna wiped her hands and hurried out into the street.

Hunter was not in his tent, nor was he in Byorneth's, and none had seen him out among the riders since the morning. Finally, one of the boys mentioned that he often took a ride out beyond the pickets in the Desert, and she wrapped her shawl around her and set out over the dunes to meet him.

A man is often better alone than in company, and Hunter was glad to be a lonely man. He had taken the black horse as his favorite, and it was his only company in an ocean of bleak dunes, the sand wisping from their tops and gathering around each clump of tortured plants. He stood absently breaking sticks of dried grass between his fingers, watching his horse as it stood hitched to a small bush.

His heart pained him just as much as ever when there was no one to see him, but the pain was so much more evocative in solitude. There are no sadder songs than those of the Sheewa away from home, and it was these he employed in giving voice to his pain, even writing new ones in his hours alone. It was thus that Tierna found him, in the company of rocks and desiccated plants, singing softly to himself. She watched him for a time, sitting and drawing in the sand with his staff, before she dismounted, tied her horse, and came down the dune toward him. When he saw her, he stood, clasping his staff in both hands.

"I must talk to you!" she called out, as if to ensure against him running away.

Hunter stood still. "Go back! I'll talk to you in camp!"

But she did not go back, and all he could do was meet those frightening, flashing eyes as they drew nearer.

"You needn't fear me. I've not come to compromise your honor. Something more important is afoot."

"Oh, yes?" Hunter was glad for a way out. Even in combat, he had never felt the fear that had him now.

"Kaia came to me, and as we talked, it came out that she fancies you. She's not one to give up when first she sinks her teeth into a thing."

Hunter was confused. "Kaia? Who is she?"

"The girl! The one you saved yesterday and walked back to camp! You may not know it, my nervous friend, but an experience like that changes a girl, and you mustn't be surprised if she has her thoughts on you now. And she has, believe me."

"But — you told her that I was married? Surely she cannot still be bent upon me!"

Tierna shook her head so the honey tresses swayed in the breeze. "No, it is ten times worse now. She is indebted to you, and you are a stranger from a strange land. This has happened before." Hunter jerked the slipknot from his horse's reins and mounted. It annoyed her to have to talk up to him, so she returned and mounted her own mare as he rode slowly behind her.

"Surely she's not of an age to seek a husband! She cannot be very much older than you!"

"Well, thank-you so much! Actually, I happen to be fully 23 years old, and that's three years older than Kaia. But I'm so glad you appreciate my help!" With a touch of her heels, the slim horse carried her at a smooth trot out across the dunes toward home.

His own horse snorted as he galloped to catch her, and she had to rein back as Hunter came up before her on the trail. "If I've given offense, it was in ignorance, not malice. Please forgive me!"

She had not been really offended, but thought it not good to tolerate familiarities from this stranger. They walked together again. "Tierna Doe, I've made enemies already in one tribe, and I need none in yours. Please, tell me how I can make this right. You know her and I do not."

The horses had an easy time of it as they were walked back to camp and their pickets. The people who rode them talked a long time, but their conversation was probably trivial. They were only people, after all.

⁓⋏⋏〜

Srstri could not bear to continue the way she had intended. It was too public, too connected with what had happened. Instead, she set her course directly toward the distant Kyargh, shunning the frequented trails in favor of the wilder places of untended scrub and the outermost reaches of tea. Before the wild trees ceased, she stopped to cut herself a staff. Bitter tears came, and she let them fall, burning her as though they boiled across her cheeks. On she went, with no way of lighting her path, and so when the darkness came at its thickest, she bedded down in the most comfortable place she could find.

The morning came and found her sleeping on a hillside, in a patch of grass in the middle of a coarse thicket of brambles. The sun was on her and took part of the chill away before she was conscious, and when she awoke, she needed a moment to remember what had transpired the day before. The new day was green and bright, and the wind tasted clean. It was incredible to her that she had so quickly put the smoke behind, that a few brief kaind of Hill country could banish such doings, if not their memories. Now she walked out among the bushes, her only companion the low ache of yesterday's pain.

It all came back to her again as she stopped to break her fast and remembered the provisions the woman had packed. She ate, but the taste was bitter, flavored with uncried tears and remembered smoke. *It is better for me to remain in the barren land of the West*, she thought as she chewed. Banat could only kill her there. He could not burn a land already scorched with wind and sun. Of her family in the Hills she had long since ceased to think, and since she had seen the look in

Banat's eyes, turned greedily toward the Kyargh, her thoughts had been only for the safety of her husband.

Slowly, the massive mountain twins grew larger among their brethren, changing shape against the patch of sky between them. Now, she began to meet people — not the ordinary farmers, blacksmiths and tea growers of the trails, but strange, skulking creatures who either avoided her as she passed or gave her such looks that she avoided them. Hands remained on weapons and every eye was averted, with the occasional stare that mingled fear with its challenge. The staff felt better and better in her hands as she went, the weight of her dirk more and more comfortable.

She was far past the tea trees now, beyond the bounds of the farthest plantation. Now there was nothing but tangled pine punctuated by dark stone slabs that jutted out of the thin dirt and menaced passing feet. At last, she came out of the scrub and looked down into a wide clearing which marked the end of one of the main trails of the Caldera, overhung by a brooding giant of gray stone.

A rough building entirely dominated the trailhead, built of stripped tree trunks arranged upright, except for the rear walls, which were of an old rockslide. All around the door there was a wide porch, upon which several men lounged about rolling dice, while one sat off by himself flipping a knife into the wood by his feet. None moved when they saw her, or otherwise acknowledged her beyond guarded or greedy looks. A rough board was tacked up beside the door, proclaiming in hewn letters, "The Wolf's Head."

Srstri had never seen such a place outside the villages, where travelers sojourned in a common structure and imposed no one. With the horrible feeling of being right at home, she entered.

Above all, it smelled very strongly of fresh tar and old sweat. A long sideboard flanked the room upon one side, and far off in the shadows were long benches arranged haphazardly against the wall. Her eyes needed a moment to pierce the gloom and see several other travelers, unsavory by their looks, already sleeping in all the available spaces. Slowly, she walked the room and stood at the counter, waiting until finally a slovenly, stubby creature came forward out of the shadows and stared as though she were a fish in a glass.

"We give no lodging to women alone." His mouth hardly moved with his words, and at first she was not sure he had really spoken. "You have no champion. I will have no confusion in my place."

The night was falling quickly. The world had darkened even since she came in, and there was no shelter anywhere near, no dwelling where she could rest the night. The man behind the counter showed no sympathy, only chuckling greasily and looking her up and down again.

"Where would you go tomorrow? Why are you here and not somewhere in the Caldera with a respectable family? And especially without a champion to keep your dainty self from the cold?"

Such a remark would in the past times have earned the man a blade through his throat. Srstri only flushed slightly and shifted her feet, her mouth hardening into a straight line. "I would journey across the Kyargh, and anything else is not your affair. I must stay here or sleep out in the cold, but I will care for myself."

The man's eyes changed ever so slightly at her tone, and he spared a glance at her weapons, another at her ring. A voice came out of a far corner. "I am here for her. Give her a place, and feed her what passes for a meal on my account." The speaker did not move, never left the obscuring dark. The man behind the counter grunted and set a plate full of cold bread and dry venison in front of her. A gold coin arced across the building and landed dully on the counter, and the man pocketed it quickly before it rolled off.

The food was not much, and she had some of her own left, but it would have been base rudeness to refuse the gift. She ate it bravely with a thank-you over her shoulder and a brief suspicious glance. As she finished, the proprietor motioned toward the corner, where lay a straw tick and pile of blankets. She negotiated her way through the prone bodies which had watched her as she ate, ruffians all, by the look of them, banded together because no one else would stand their company. The corner where her benefactor had been sitting was now empty. Likely, he was one of the men who stared hungrily up at her from the floor, expecting a return for his gold.

Srstri lay down and threw the blankets over herself, hoping the mattress was not inhabited, occupied as it had been with countless visiting bodies. Between this lively concern and the raucous snoring that steadily grew around her, she slept but little. The one time that sleep did find her, she was jolted back awake by a brief, loud scuffle, and then a thud and labored breathing. Gone from this place was the legendary hospitality of the Highlands. Here there was only violence and ill-will.

She finally awoke to the loudness of awakening sleepers. Many drank together in lieu of breakfast, some chewed blandly at thick slices of resilient black bread. One of the benches along the side, evidently reserved for favored guests, was now occupied only by a sharp-faced young man who scratched slowly at his black stubble, and flashed a rim of raw flesh on his knuckles as he did so. His gear was already packed and lay beside him in a tight bundle, and his attention was subtly divided between her and a man at the bar, who ate with hairy elbows heavy on the thick board. When he turned, she saw his upper lip extended redly out beyond the lower. The men's eyes met in a brief instant, and Fat Lip swaggered out after a final leer at the woman, wiping a shine of grease from his mouth.

"You paid for my accommodation last night?" This to the dark stranger, who nodded, lifting the little bundle to his back. He walked past and was nearly outside when he suddenly turned.

"Why do you travel alone in such a bad place?"

Srstri saw no need to lie. "My husband has gone westward over the Hills, and I go to join him."

The stranger saw many questions in this story, but refrained from asking. "Everything has changed in the past few months. The scum of the land has gravitated to the Kyargh, and some have gone over to the West as mercenaries. You should not go through alone."

Somehow, she felt this man was not like the others, and she had known even before that she would be ill-advised to cross the mountains without a guide. By the look of these fellows around them, she might not even make it out of the Caldera. She spoke on impulse. "Do you know a safe way across?"

"Yes. Five times I have made the journey. It is not an easy passage." Then, with a look around on the floor, "Do you have any bags? Any warmer clothing?"

"No, only what I wear. Will I be able to manage as I am?"

"You'd freeze before you reached the Kyargh."

Throwing an involuntary look back toward the north, she thought furiously. The past year of her life ran by in her mind, and then for the first time in months, one face came out of everything, as clear as life. And the face pointed toward the west. She turned back toward the stranger and asked boldly, "Will you help me?"

It seemed hardly right to burden a stranger with such a journey, and she would have gone alone, but she was a practical woman, and would rather have died with her husband than alone and cold among the rocks. The dark stranger squinted and looked from her to the west wall of the inn, beyond which was death a hundred times over. At last, he hoisted her bag and motioned her toward the door.

"Hold, you two!"

They halted, and her young companion turned toward the innkeeper, who had resumed his place behind the bar. "Two for one night, that comes to four gold pieces."

The young man's look darkened. "She is with me. If you do not give lodging to women, you cannot accept gold from them."

"You paid for yourself, not for her. But you will pay before you leave here. This is a valuable floor, and her space on it cost me a great sum. Whether by gold or by blood, you will pay." He looked Srstri up and down. "I do have need of someone to do chores, keep my inn clean. Three months and I will forgive the debt."

As she looked into the sharp face of the young man, it smiled, and Srstri wondered at the change. He turned around and sidled up to the counter, and the host backed up a little. Slowly, the young man removed a pair of dice from his coat, set them on the counter between them, and said something Srstri could not make out.

The man behind the bar shook his head stolidly. "No. If I lose, I'll be out a night's lodging." Drawing nearer, he smiled and said, "I have a far better idea. What would you say to a little tournament? I will hold the bets, and you will fight. It will more than pay for your lady's lodging, and you can both be on your way."

There followed a period of muttered haggling back and forth at which the greasy proprietor seemed to fare better than his young opponent. When he finally joined Srstri in the corner, it was with a tight little smile which at first she could not place. "Come along. We have a fight to lose."

She had hoped for another beautiful sunny day, but found the sun obscured behind a slate-gray banner of clouds, lowly threatening rain. The innkeeper followed them out and jerked his thumb toward a little grove of trees beside the building where the leaves were starting to turn, and a few yellow branches overhung a large open space where men had already begun to gather.

Chapter 20

The West

ONLY IN BATTLE MAY THE EDGE OF A BLADE BE PROVED.

~Maxims of the First Kings~

They were all idle men except for the few murders and rob-beries they committed to make ends meet. When no active entertainment was available, the role of spectator suited them just as well. Word had already gone out, and they set up a terrific yell as the sharp-faced young man, Thorn by name, walked out, stripped out of his long black overcoat, vaulted the high board fence and looked steadily around the arena. Srstri worried at the sight of his arms, which, hard though they may have been, seemed altogether too small to fight with. But he had only to lose.

The crowd grew quickly as the word spread, and another hoarse shout went up as it split and vomited out a monster, a huge side of beef with nearly as many scars as he had hairs. Head and shoulders above anyone else, he stepped over the fence one leg at a time like an insect, and his hands, when he raised them to show himself to the crowd, brushed the lower branches of the trees. Turning around very slowly to give them clear view of him, he began to growl deep down in his throat. He leered at Thorn with a broken mouth. "Come along, my buck! Come and do your best!"

If the display caused Thorn any fear, he did not show it, seeming to stifle a yawn as he watched. Srstri did not feel as confident, for as ignorant as she may have been in these matters, she knew the host could never profit by such a match, arranging for a favorite to win. At last, Thorn gave a little laugh and threw a punch straight from the shoulder into the hard belly, producing no effect.

The response, however, was immediate — a powerful lunge that ended in an iron grip on Thorn's throat. The giant reached back and struck Thorn heavily with his backhand, and then a heavier forehand. Even above the bloodthirsty shouting of the crowd, Srstri could hear the vast, dry impact of the blow and turned sick.

Thorn fell back into the dirt. It was all clear now. With Thorn out of the way, the landlord would be free to hold Srstri for as long as he liked. The giant stood smirking in the center of the ring and waited, allowing Thorn to regain his feet. His weight rested on his rear foot, and Thorn took full advantage of it as he dove into the man, catching him in the ribs and driving him backward into the rough boards. Thorn pummeled him hard and fast about the head and ribs, until someone from the crowd seized him roughly and threw him to the ground.

The enemy stood and swayed to and fro, laboredly breathing through several rivers of blood that ran down his face. Both were on their feet again, circling around slowly. Finally, the enemy lunged with a cocked fist, and Thorn stepped to the left so the giant had to turn, seize him, and twist him to the ground. A brawny hand grasped the entire breadth of Thorn's face as the other reached around for the back of his head, intent on breaking the neck below. Thorn grasped him by the forearms, jerking a vicious knee into his groin.

The giant let out a heavy gasp, and Thorn used the time to squirm away and regain his feet. But the recovery was quick, and the man was once again the block of granite he had been before. Bull head lowered, he advanced slower this time, with a fresh caution. Thorn did not hesitate as he gathered himself one final time and took two long strides, launching upward for an overhanging branch. He caught it with both hands and his swinging feet hammered the rushing man upward beneath the chin. The monster rocked backward and then toppled forward into the dust, his head cocked backward like a crowing rooster's. Thorn only barely scrambled out of the way before the great weight fell.

Silence hung in the air along with the dust the impact had thrown. Each face hung awestricken in the cloud, and Thorn spoke out breathlessly before the moment was broken, wiping streaming blood away, and rocking back and forth from heel to toe. "I have fought this man for the freedom of that woman!" He pointed to Srstri, and the men took notice. "Have I beaten him?"

Some muttered, others nodded solemnly. One even called out in agreement. They were men who admired a good fight, and low though they may have sunk, a bout fairly won was won entirely.

Together, they walked out of the crowd, which split to give them passage. Their coarse host sat on his veranda and watched in silence as they walked toward the Kyargh, soaking in the sudden gray curtain of rain.

—⁓⌃⁓—

"Kaia is not as other women are. In many ways, she is younger than her 20 years. If you tell her immediately, you will stab her to the heart." Tierna sat in the saddle easily, tall like a willow in the wind. "Let it out slowly. Starve her of your attention little by little. Then, when you reject her, she will half expect it."

All the way back to the camp, Tierna had described to Hunter a girl of consistent jest, shallow and changing moods. It was strange to him that a lady should speak so about a dearest friend. Hunter took all she said just as he heard it, earnest and wise. It is an impression which the young work hard to convey.

He shuddered as the little camp came into sight over the dusty dune. His experience of women, limited as it was to an escape and a wedding, had never prepared him for such matters as this. The thought filled him with the same fear as had Leen d'Arns, the Great Bear of the Lowlands. When they passed the tent where Byorneth lay, he let Tierna go past before he lifted the tent flap and told his old friend everything.

Byorneth grinned wider and wider as the tale progressed, finally indulging himself in a generous chuckle. Hunter stood looking on, the color mounting higher and higher in his cheeks. Finally, Byorneth lay still, a tired smirk his only evidence of mirth.

Hunter unclenched his jaw. "Not forgetting that you are recovering from an injury, I would appreciate it if you would explain to me in which way this situation could be construed as lighthearted."

"Oho! None to you, truly. It takes years. I'd always wondered when this manner of trouble might befall you. Even in getting yourself married, you stayed clear. At last it's come, and you had to venture beyond the mountains to find it!" He chuckled to himself again, and the noise brought Jooenin, fearful he would disturb his splints. But he was quiet again when she peered through the doorway.

"Persuader, Hunter. Who laughed?"

Still smiling, Byorneth lay back in bed, his hands clasped behind his neck. "My young friend has ensnared the heart of one of your desert flowers. Now she's intent on taking him for herself, turning him into a Tribesman. By the looks of him, he'd not have far to go!" Hunter flushed again to hear his young secrets exposed to public view. But Grandmother heard it more seriously.

With a scowl of shame, Hunter asked, "Now that this is out, what advice?" But his elders fell silent, and Byorneth shook his whitening head.

"There is none," said Grandmother. "It's different every time. I think it's best if you go right up to her and tell the truth. If she can't accept, so be it. At least you'll be in the right. But as to the words, I really can't say."

Hunter left the tent, then leaned inside to speak to them again. "Tierna, who is of my age, gave me a full half hour of sage advice. How is it that you, who are so much richer in experience than both of us, have only this pittance to give me?"

Byorneth answered, staring at the ceiling. "I think you will often find it so, my son."

Kaia lived with her family as did most unmarried people. Before he could call at her tent, he saw her at the nearby pickets brushing a tall, gray horse with long strokes, speaking softly into its rotating ears.Swallowing hard several times he hailed her from a distance, and she smiled unreadably when she saw him.

"Bright good day to you!" He had left his Sheewan accoutrements behind, and so he stood bareheaded. It were best if he spoke as himself. "Where have you been this afternoon?"

"Oh, I took a walk and watched riding, and visited some people. I was just going to work on my weaving after I was finished here. Do you know about grooming?"

He ran his hand along the beast's neck, and it turned its head with a low snort, but she was a temperate mare, and soon grunted amiably at his touch. "Yes, I've cared for mules all my life."

"What are mules like?"

"They are offspring of horse and donkey."

"I've heard of them, but I've never seen one. A funny creature, I suppose?"

"They are very steady, and they can carry heavy loads nearly forever. They fight too, when the occasion arises, which may help or hinder their driver."

She had heard little of the customs of Outlanders, and the intent manner in which she listened told Hunter his situation could not have much improved. He must change the burden of conversation, and quickly.

"Kaia, how do you feel about me?"

"I like you, very much."

"It's been told to me, Kaia, that there is a more — potent attraction on your part." He would not make Tierna's involvement known, though doubtless Kaia guessed at it. "I must tell you that it is not reciprocated. I am married, and heartily in love with my wife."

She looked at him strangely. "I don't know what you mean."

He opened and shut his mouth once or twice like a turtle, and then kept it shut. Could Tierna have been mistaken? Kaia's face was resolute, and her look baffled him. She turned with a shake of the head and walked away among the tents.

Hunter's mind still reeled, and he leaned on the horse's shoulders. The animal turned her head and fixed him with a large stare.

"My friend," he scratched her velvet ears, "I think you understand better than I do."

When once she was out of sight, Kaia collapsed into a convenient dune and began to cry. But none of her sobs were loud enough for any in the camp to hear. She had too much practise for that.

As the evening sun cast its long shadows across the land and cooled the air, Hunter found his way back to his tent. It was long before he slept, and when he did, he was made busy with dreams of great creatures, now monstrous, filling the very air with evil deeds, and now small as mice to crawl up the legs of their victims. And then they were even more fierce, vanishing even as Hunter would have pierced them, until at last they surrounded him in voluminous masses of shifting black and gray curtains. Then suddenly, they parted, and Srstri stood before him with her old familiar smile, except that she had honey-brown hair that reached all the way down to her feet, wrapping around them like lustrous snakes. She leaned forward, lips pursed, but as he would have kissed her, he was wakened out of unwholesome sleep by the sound of shouts and screams in the night.

He still heard it when he opened his eyes. His sword was ready to hand, and he took it from its place at his bedside and ran out into the dark.

Men on horses filled the camp. Some had women on their saddlebows, kicking and screaming, and others led strings of horses out into the dark. Still others, Waileng men and women, brought horses back, and all around the edges of camp, where the raiders retreated, there were noises of battle. Several who had fought to defend their property lay groaning on the red ground. Soon, the haze and noise cleared, and a certain set of hoofbeats increased in volume and quickness, until at last they resolved into one horse and rider, weapon waving above his head, in the full regalia of a chief's son.

No time for fear, Hunter stood his ground until the man was about ten paces away, and then he stepped in front of the horse with a great cry, throwing his arms wide.

The beast whinnied sharply and reared. When the man fell, his sword flew clear, but he came up quickly and locked eyes with his enemy. Hunter had expected to see anger in the prince's face, fear, excitement even, but he had not expected what he saw now. The boy was sickened.

The wide eyes gazed around him at the work his Laiopej had done, the dark looks of those who stood around, and still he could not comprehend it. The night raids he had heard of, the heady stories from the old Tribesmen of warriors fighting warriors, all were gone in a sheer, hurtling reality, and all he had left was the blood and lives of Tribesmen, both his and those of his brother tribe.

Hunter stood with his blade on guard. The rest of the world had slowed, as if all else had slipped into the night with the captured horses. Inch by inch, his opponent pulled a long, curved dagger from his upper garments, and spread his arms. Hunter yielded to the challenge.

The chief's son made his first thrust toward Hunter's chest, which was easily parried. Again and again, his deadliest blows were turned aside, for Hunter had no wish for blood, and knew what a fresh feud the killing would start. Finally, when he saw an opening, he fetched the lad's hand a sharp blow with the flat of his blade. The dagger fell, and the boy stooped to pick it up again, but Hunter kicked it away in a shower of sand. The prince braced himself up to his full height and threw his head up to its haughtiest angle. "Well, come ahead! Dispatch me!"

Hunter scowled in distaste. The camp was now quiet but for the sounds of mourning, and some stood nearby watching their exchange. As Tribesmen, none interfered between the enemies. Their presence brought a flush to the young man's face, and suddenly it occurred to Hunter what he must do. "Go back to your father's tent. Tell him, if you dare, what has transpired here. If not, then lie, but know that when next we clash, the quarrel cannot but end in blood. Now go!"

The prince's lower lip trembled, and when he spoke, his voice wavered. "I swear to you by my father's name and the name of our tribe that it will be you who bleeds into the dust!" Then he turned on his heel and walked from camp to find his horse, which had run the moment its rider was unseated. Soon, all that remained of the Laiopej was a haze of dust and the great dagger that still lay where it had fallen.

The death toll was light by the standards of earlier times, but earlier times were far gone. Now there was blood, and the same children who had thrilled to tales of the deeds of their fathers saw the red reality of violence touch their very homes. This was far different from the occasional night raid, by which many of their mothers had been won, or single combat for the sake of honor. The sound of weeping prevailed in the camp as Hunter walked through it, as solemn as though he were one of their number. Stepping over a red mark where a Laiopej raider had been dragged, he turned toward a certain tent.

Hunter found Byorneth upright for the first time in weeks, leaning palely against the wall of the tent, still clutching his blade. Grandmother stood by and steadied him, and together she and Hunter coaxed him back into bed, gingerly handling his leg. It was practically healed now, and Byorneth said so, but in the end, he bowed to the old woman's insistence and lay back, muttering under his breath.

"Hunter," he said, after his complaints had subsided. "Were you hurt?"

Hunter only shook his head, and his attention was drawn toward a body lying in the corner. Grandmother said, "He came in and Byorneth killed him from the bed."

With the toe of his shoe, Hunter turned the dead man over onto its back. There was a knife buried in the center of the chest up to the hilt. "Well, a clean shot!" he said, as though he were surprised. "You've rather interfered yourself now, haven't you?"

"They interfered first. Did you settle any?"

"No. I had a little set-to with my friend again, but no blood spilled."

"He vowed to kill you next time, I heard."

"Yes. I doubt he will, though. He seems to have started something beyond his scope with this raid. Why should he bring more trouble down on himself?"

Grimly, Byorneth replied, "This is no small matter. I suppose you've forgotten that among these people blood is the only payment for that kind of dishonor. One of you must die."

An unprofitable tradition, it seemed to Hunter, and more than ever he wished himself away from the trouble. He had, at the very least, looked forward to peace in his time in the West, but the burden of his life had followed him, leaving his sole compensation behind. And then, because he had never felt less like doing it, he smiled broadly as he looked out across the moonlit Desert.

"We have not come to alter things, Hunter, but merely to record them. But if you shrink from confrontation, it will be another 30 years before the Sheewa are again welcomed here.

They will trust a thief with their records before they will trust a coward." Suddenly, he took Hunter's arm in a frightening grip. "You have never been a coward, Hunter. Kill him or let him kill you."

In the cool light of earliest morning, Hunter walked out toward the enemy camp. He had clothed himself, not in the close-fitting garb of the Sheewa, but in the flowing robes and kerchief of a Tribesman. His observation was keen, and he had imitated exactly the odd fit of the robes of his young enemy, all but for the blue trimmings that signified tribal royalty. He bore with him the weapon left behind by his young foe, having left his own hooked dagger behind with his cloak and staff. He wanted no connection to either Waileng or Sheewa, not even in weaponry.

At last, he could see the Laiopej camp through the dust, and soon he was walking down the main avenue. This camp and that of the Waileng were as alike as brothers, but hatred can blossom fastest between siblings.

Visitors were rare, and often unwelcome. Perhaps if he had gone as a Sheewa, or even as a Waileng Tribesman, he would have had a warmer welcome, but his Laiopej clothing and dark color set him apart from all else, making him a usurper. He wished there could have been another way, but he wished to absolve his hosts of any blame for his private quarrel. So, he walked the gauntlet of suspicious looks and casual bad language, never turning his steadfast gaze on his revilers.

The chief's tent was clearly marked by his emblem, that of a man on the back of a great mountain leopard. He swallowed hard and called out in the most elegant Huaynił, "There is one who would speak with you, my master."

"Who desires audience?"

"One from afar, bearing friendship with him."

A voice bade him enter, and he found not one man alone, but fully 15 men seated about in a circle. As his eyes became accustomed to the gloom, he saw they were all over two score years, their weapons all ready to their practised hands. Eldest of all was the chief, facing the door in his red chair, a white-headed man with a frame that seemed to collapse into itself. Darkness surrounded him, so that one might have thought him a woodwork goblin, carved into the back of the chair as a curiosity.

One face he did know in that tent as his eyes pierced the gloom — that of the young man who stood back from the circle, nearly hidden in the shadows of the chief's chair. His eyes burned coldly, and Hunter addressed himself respectfully to the chief.

"May all blessings attend you, worthy warrior. I would beg leave to render unto you my burden freely and without reserve."

The voice of the Laiopej chief was thin and wasted, slurred by the passage of long and weary years. "We will hear you, young stranger. Attend ye, my brothers, and may it be known what a courteous hospitality we extend to our guests."

"Laiopej Chief, I have come unto you out of the tribe Waileng, a Sheewa by training. Today I am of no tribe, a father-less stranger to all, dropped as out of the sky. I have seen here a people divided, clan jealous of clan and greedy of their goods. You rob one another of women and horses, of pride and dignity, making yourselves poor, one and all.

"I stand before you this day and tell you that so long as such discord exists, you and your offspring will be weak, and in spite of all records and chronicles (for you are far famed as skillful writers), you will all be forgotten. Then, when other people set eyes on this land to take it for their own, they will wade through as one who crosses a brook. Thus has it been, and thus shall it be again.

"It is not for this purpose that I come to your tent, and I beg pardon of you for presuming to teach the sage ones of an ancient race. There is a debt of blood between a man of your tribe and myself. Your son, Great Chief, has sworn to kill me, and I am come that he might have the chance."

All eyes went to the shadows behind the wizened chief, and the young man stepped out into the light. His hand was on his hilt, but a weapon may never be drawn in a chief's tent except to defend it. "This is the man, Father Chief. It was him."

The old man's eyes enlivened. "My son, several other good men were injured with you. You barely escape with your lives, and yet all of you could not have claimed that one Waileng girl." He spoke as one repeating himself.

"We forged a pact!" the son replied brashly. "We would claim wives together, each man fighting for the others as well as himself!"

"When I was young, we claimed women alone. It did not need three of us. If the woman fought too bitterly, she did not desire marriage, and there was enough for us."

His son fell silent, jaw clenched tight as the counselors around him kept their eyes strictly on the floor. Finally, the chief spoke again, with the air of one who has come to a decision.

"My son, your years are but few. The young never know the end from the beginning. I know what is in your mind, and that you have made a blood vow which cannot be undone. You must settle this with blood, as would any other Horseman. Go out into the open and finish this."

They turned to leave, but Hunter stopped at the chief's bidding and drew nearer. "I hope with all my heart that you will die in this conflict, stranger. But if you prove more cunning than I hope you to be, then consider an old man's love for his only son."

Hunter inclined his head and backed from the tent. Turning, he saw the chief's son across the dusty way, removing his outer garments and piling them beside a tent. But Hunter kept his robes on, leaving his weapon sheathed while the other drew his and moved out into the street to meet him.

⌒⋏⌒

The air was bitter cold as two bundled figures made their way over the bleak ridges and ice that covered the mountains. They were entirely muffled with furs from head to foot, but the clothing was well made, and did not impede movement. As they mounted a rough crest, they stopped to breathe. The woman was winded from her time in the lower Caldera, but Thorn could see she would rather have died walking than stop before he did.

It had been long since Thorn's last journey, and so he no longer had his warm clothing. They had their garments from a furrier who lived at the mouth of the Pass, who had become rich from those who traveled through. To be an Arlingan furrier was a noble profession, providing travelers with the clothing they needed to get through the mountains alive. But Thorn wondered when he saw the furrier's place of business, a hole underneath an overhang of rock. The only indication of the place's purpose was a board above the doorway on which someone had painted a man dressed in a Hilltiger skin, the bright markings faded by the weather.

When they stepped in, the smell of leather nearly over-powered them. They looked around the shop for a long time, fingering the skins spread on the rocks of the walls before the furrier came out. He seemed more weasel than man, with bags below his heavy, suspicious eyes. He did not speak to them, but stared until Thorn spoke.

"We've seen all this stock. Where is the clothing fit to wear?" Without a word, the man vanished into a dark recess at the rear of the place and returned burdened down. He piled the great mass of animal skins on the table, and stared as his patrons sorted through them.

Srstri and Thorn had a bearskin stretched between them when her champion looked up. "How much for all this?"

"Forty pieces."

Thorn snorted and laughed, then laid the skin out on top of all the other items. "You are quite a riotous sort of man, my little furrier! To set such a price upon such unfinished and moth-eaten stuff as this. Subtly done, little hrnyi! Now fetch the real thing. And something dry to change for these." The furrier slunk away into the darkness of his back rooms, and returned with a load of stuff draped across his shoulders, with two fur caps on top, of the type that covered nearly the whole face. Srstri could see this lot was far superior, each hide lush and whole, sewn sturdily together, almost without seam. The cost was greater, but now the merchandise warranted it, and Thorn paid it readily enough, to Srstri's surprise. They fitted themselves out quickly.

As they were about to leave, a man burst in, panting and sweating, and spat onto the dirt floor. His fear was evident, and so great that he made no masculine effort to conceal it. "They're all dead!" The words came between great sucking breaths. "Everyone at the inn! The host! The other men left in the inn after the fight! Something — something with one arm! I never saw it but once, walking through the door like a man! It asked for clothing, and when the host did not answer, it reached across and killed him! Then there were the screams, the — the cutting! I fought! I escaped to tell you!"

"We should go," Thorn said without hesitation, and Srstri followed him into the cloudy day. They had everything they might have needed in the way of clothing and food. Thorn would have preferred to have purchased at least two mules to bear their belongings with them, but he dared not with the nameless, one-armed fear that followed behind. What could possibly have slain so many men, and who would ever want to? Who could say? Srstri was remarkably silent on this score, but Thorn pondered it all the way through the first part of the Pass.

He set a vigorous pace that Srstri, unused to mountains, strained to follow. The country soon broke into mounds which grew ever smaller until they were walking among thousands of standing stones. The journey had not even the consolation of being interesting, for the stones along the road held small fascination for her, and there was little to keep her thoughts away from her former master. That he had been touched with madness was now clear, for however cruel he may have been in the Lowlands, there had always been a sane reason to his cruelty. No man would so revel in death if his mind had still been his, and she had begun to wonder whether she would ever be free of him. They were both silent for a long time, focusing their energies on the road.

Thorn's eyes never rested, scanning the field at every step, sparing frequent looks for the Trail behind. Those at the inn, friends and enemies, were dead. The messenger was well known to him, a brutal man who been at the forefront of a good many desperate acts of pillage and even murder, when he could be. But this thing of darkness which killed out of the daylight was something else entirely. There was something of a curse about it, and there is nothing brutality fears more.

Srstri knew better than Thorn how badly they needed to be away, and quickly before the day was far spent. She craned to see the new country, the ever-changing rocks and profiles of distant peaks. Whenever the wind blew from a certain quarter the Hills talked to them, perhaps asking who these intruders were, or whispering of their births in the fires of ancient times. The sad, sweet music made their journey a dream, only a few steps ahead of a nightmare.

They topped a round hill, a younger brother to the stones around them. For the first time they had a view of the Trail farther ahead, as well as the high saddle of the Kyargh, dim with distant snowfall.

"Does no one live in this region?" she asked at last, feeling a chill for the first time.

"No, nothing grows here." Then his eyes narrowed. "Why is it you ask?"

"I feel as though someone were watching us."

Thorn had felt it for some time, that old feeling that had kept him alive where so many others would have died. Without warning, he led off in a new direction, not on the main path, but weaving through the field toward the north. At one of the larger stones, they stopped and looked behind, but still there was nothing save the silent shroud that had become a malicious companion. When dusk fell hours later, they were among the scraggly cedars farther up on the ridge, and they made cold camp, lying under one blanket, wrapped in their furs.

Srstri huddled against the chill and dozed by stages into a fitful sleep. Trouble followed her wherever she went, and any who helped her were taken by the avenging spirit she had offended in the Plain. She was visited by dreams which troubled her, making even her rest into a trek. The obscuring clouds had dissolved, and the night was bright with moonlight and the stars which spread out in a milky banner across the sky.

At last she awoke and sat up suddenly, throwing her blankets off. Thorn had moved, and she cast about frantically, looking for him.

"Don't move."

The quiet voice came from above. "I'm still here. Act as though you were still asleep. I'm keeping watch for a while."

She was happy he guarded her so carefully, but the implication frightened her. Breathing regularly, she found she could not sleep again with her ears straining to hear the smallest sound in the dark and frosty distance, hand closed around her dagger, determined to sell her life dearly. With the earliest of dawn's light, she arose shivering and ate coldly from her bag, still scouring the landscape through the cedars with wide eyes, but nothing appeared. Just as the sun began to peek through the rocks, they packed up their few belongings and headed off on a long, crooked trail.

The mountains showered ice crystals down upon them, stinging their faces and closing their eyes. The footing changed as more of these missiles accumulated on the ground, and where before their feet had passed easily, here they slid and stuck by turns, until at last they paused to breathe. Mountain gave unto mountain now, she saw, and what had looked like a simple serration from the Caldera now became a vast network of peaks and glaciers, giving into gullies where strange antelope fled at the sight of them. It was Srstri who continued, for now the wild mountains called to her even as the threat from behind seemed to grow.

Thorn walked behind her now, constantly watching the back trail. Partly to distract her own mind, Srstri asked, "Thorn, who are you?"

"We would be safer if we did not talk as we went. Sound can carry across these valleys like the inside of one of your huts."

So she fell to idle supposition. He was dressed as any rover might have been, but there was in his bearing a certain evidence of gentility. Why he had agreed to accompany her, she did not know. There was none of the typical lechery of his kind, besides an initial appraising glance. The ring on her hand may have discouraged him. Only a fool brings the rightful outrage of a jealous husband upon his head.

They walked along the brush-covered ridge for a long way, and as the sun rose above the High Hills, it was summer once again, warm in spite of the nearness of the snow until they descended once again into a valley of stones. The center of the valley with its lush lawn came to them in less than an hour beyond the gravel which lay at the sides, stripped from its parent rocks by wind and weather.

They dominated her mind, the grim rocks and stern horizons of mountains that grew nearer all the time with the unrelenting, ponderous strength of all giants. Her lack of sleep troubled her keenly, and she did her best not to cough away the tickle that had started in her throat. When at last she did, a flock of birds rose before them with a cawing that echoed against the far rocks, and Thorn scorched her with a look that lasted but a moment, but burned for the next hour. Occasionally, she stumbled as the gravel became pebbles, then stones and boulders.

To cross that land took days. Every Hillman, living out his days planting tea, laboring for a friendly living among his neighbors, had wondered what lived beyond the limits of the paternal mountains. Even Srstri, though well traveled, had harbored the idea that only a day or two's walking separated her from the Desert beyond. It had taken that long even to leave the Caldera, and day fell upon day after that. At last, they arrived at the slope of the mountain and began to climb in earnest.

After that, the air grew truly cold, and even through her fur boots, Srstri's toes began to suffer. At Thorn's insistence, she covered her mouth with her scarf, and that helped protect her lungs from the chill, but she could not seem to keep up with the pace Thorn had set. At last, he slowed for her, staying by her side as she stepped across little gorges, holding her along the icy stretches of rock. She was ashamed when she thought of the stories she had heard, tales of women who moved entire households upon their backs, and she pressed on through the cold and pain.

Thorn stopped her suddenly, and she took a moment to regain her balance. "Do you see that dark spot in the snow just there, halfway up that ridge?"

She needed a moment to find it. "Yes, but I can't tell what it is. Could it be some animal?"

"Yes, I think so. Some kind of animal. Be ready to get down if I give the word."

Soon the spot was resolved into a man, seated cross-legged in the snow, an insect huddled in the rocks. He sat on a slab of black lava which protruded from the high hummock, and his body was covered with a worn deerskin. He wore a rather large, confident smirk under a haphazard black beard, a smirk that made thin white lines through the accumulated dirt. Yet even before they saw all this, they began to smell him. Soon they stood on the rocks below the ledge and looked up at him.

With a look of kingly disdain, he spread his arms expansively, sending out a fresh wave of stench. "My friends, you have come a very long way already, and there is such a long way to go. I have been your fellow traveler, a watchful guardian. I trust you are duly honored to have been allowed passage through this, my domain."

He waited in vain for a reply and went on. "Of course, I cannot expect you to recognize your lord and master by sight. However, I do expect that you will show proper gratitude to a friend who has kept you from innumerable evils along a dangerous path."

Thorn smiled thinly and inclined his head. "We are quite grateful, Baron of the Hills. This is quite a fatherly care! Now, we have pressing business on the other side of the Kyargh." Then, looking at the man again, he smiled wider. "Will you consent to our expedition and lend it your blessing?"

The man on the ledge smiled graciously and stood, bundling his filthy garments around him. "Follow me, and I will." He turned away and headed off along the ridge.

He was difficult to follow, for he moved like a goat over ice and snow where even the sure-footed Thorn minced his steps. With an ever-steady speed, he led them across the broad bowl of the Kyargh and into the broken cliff beyond. Once there, he took up his former position on another ledge and waited while his guests hobbled toward him.

Chapter 21
The Blood

To seek after peace
Is to be ever ware of any who would threaten it.

~*The Bôlairrun of Tagrri*~

Two opponents faced each other across the sun-bathed dust of the Laiopej camp. The chief's son had his blade at the ready, but Hunter's was still sheathed, and remained so as the prince menaced with his blade.

Hunter raised his voice enough so the onlookers who had gathered around could hear. "Are we beasts, that we settle that which is private in a place that is public? Come, let us seek out a secluded spot among the sands where we may fight honorably!" His opponent blinked and nodded, picked his outer garments out of the sand, and walked beside Hunter out of camp.

If it were left to the chief's son, they would have walked in silence. But Hunter could still speak. "What is your name, honored enemy?"

"Tempai. It's fitting that a man should put a name to the one who kills him."

"And your epithet?"

"Liaunom."

"Ah, night wind. What does that signify?"

Tempai stopped and faced Hunter, half drawing his weapon. "You would know the meaning of my name, as though we were friends? How is it that you would be familiar with the son of the chief?"

"You said it yourself. With one of us killed, what does it matter?"

After some thought, the weapon was replaced. "My father says that as a young boy I was wild. He never knew where I would come from next."

They walked again in silence for a while. They were not yet out of sight of the camp. "Could it be that you've not changed?" Hunter said. "You still shake the pot, never satisfied with where you are. You had plenty of women to choose from in your own tribe, yet you had to go and steal one of the Waileng, who to my eyes are no less beautiful than those of your own people."

No reply. He tried another tack.

"How old are you, Tempai?"

"22."

"I have only 24 years myself. I was married the day before I left the Hills, and I've not seen my wife since."

For a few moments, there was no reply, and Hunter thought he had failed again, but soon Tempai spoke, and Hunter was surprised at the change. "What was it like to be married?"

"It was the entire sweetness of life for the first day. After I left, it was like death."

"How did you know she was the one?"

"I loved her, and then I found myself trying to win her. It was as bone unto its joint, hair unto its brow. I've spent all my time since that day missing her, longing to be back. Well, this ought to do."

They had come to a broad, flat place between the dunes, and Hunter laid aside his cloak and drew his weapon. "Shall we be at it? It's such a lovely day to die."

Tempai prepared himself as well, with less relish than before.

"Tempai, who is the girl?"

There are secrets deep within every man which are so much a part of his nature, that to tell them makes him less. Hunter hoped for this. "I don't know, my enemy. And that's the awful torture of it."

With a little sigh, Hunter leaned his blade against his shoulder. "Do you suppose that for us, good enemies are better than half-hearted friends?"

"Perhaps." Briefly, Tempai lowered his guard. "What would you do if you were me?"

"Tempai, I did not know myself, and I still don't. Now—" he raised his voice and lifted his blade, "come, let us clash and salve your honor!"

The young man's blade came up, but he remained still.

"Come, Tempai! Come and try to kill me!"

The younger bared his teeth and groaned deep in his chest, finally throwing his weapon down between them. "The sun strike you, villain! You've drawn all the anger out of me!"

With a small smile, Hunter threw his sword down so that it clanged against the other. "What are we to do, then? Neither of us desires violence, yet if we go back as we are, we will both be marked as cowards."

Tempai thought for a moment. "The blood debt cannot be expunged in aught but blood. Do — do you have any pressing need among the Laiopej?"

"No, this was all I came here to do."

"Well then, does anyone need know what happened here? You can return to the Waileng, I to the Laiopej, and no one need ever know that the other is not lying dead in the sand."

Hunter shook his head. "No, there's too great a chance we would be found out in some future raid. You're a chief's son, and for the good of your tribe, we must preserve your arm among them." He paused with a smile. "If we were both to return together, we could shield one another from wagging tongues."

"And the blood? We both swore to shed some, but we never specified how. Do you think one may be as good as the other?"

Hunter smiled widely. A primary object of his study had been the Western tradition of blood brotherhood, so Tempai's meaning was not lost on him. Only in blood could the blood debt be paid.

They retrieved their weapons and, as one, thrust them into the sand, then flicked a little off to each side. Each held his forearm at a right angle with his blade touching the other's skin, a handspan from the wrist, and in perfect unison made long, shallow cuts. The swords were dropped again in the sand, and the forearms came together so that the blood mixed. The left hand was never to be used in the ceremony.

They left the clearing five minutes after their arrival, and five minutes after that they walked side by side into the Laiopej camp, every eye widely on them, two tall men with blood on their arms and firm peace in their eyes. They came into the tent of the chief together, and when the old man in the chair saw them and the blood on their arms, he stood shakily. "Thank-you," he breathed before he fell back into his seat, wiping his eyes.

And so the day's end found Hunter marching back to the Waileng camp, his wound smarting. He awoke the next morning to a chilly dawn and washed himself, strangely tired, though physically he had done nothing out of the ordinary. He thought he would go visiting, first at the tent of the Waileng chief, remembering how he was made welcome before, and indeed he was treated as genially as ever. When he was comfortable, the chief sat back in his hereditary seat and tapped his fingers together. "Well, my young friend. Have you come to compile more history? Or perhaps one or two of our more obscure customs? I'm sure there must be a few we have overlooked."

"No, Waileng Chief, though doubtless I should devote more of my time to them. Today, I operate in my other capacity as Sheewa — that of an adviser."

For the first time, the thin man's eyes turned cold. "I assume that you have consulted with the Persuader before presuming to render your opinion as to the administration of my office."

Inwardly, Hunter cringed. Outwardly, he never changed. His mind raced through possible replies, discarding them one by one. "Honored Chief, please remember my youth. I have been bold, I know, and I have not consulted with Byorneth as perhaps I should have, but these considerations should not overshadow sound advice. Upon your wisdom as chief depends the safety of two tribes."

Waileng's eyebrows lowered even further. "Two tribes? What do you know of the Laiopej? Have you gone to their camp?"

"Yes, I have. I am a Sheewa, belonging to neither tribe, and as a neutral I have the right to visit either camp with impunity, speaking my mind to any leader. You must make peace between you, become one nation. Show your power and wisdom to your people."

At first, there was no reply as the chief struggled for control of himself until at last he stood, and when he spoke, his words were slow and level. "You go back to your friends across the dunes, and you tell them to give back every wife they have stolen from us. You tell them to give back all our horses, that we may regain our former glory. You tell their chief to beg entrance to my tent on his knees and deliver to me his ancestral sword. You tell them this, young colt, or crawl back to your hideaway among the mountains! I've done with all of you!"

He left the tent and stood for a moment in the cool morning air. The day was cloudy, and it smelled as though they might get one of the rare rains that sometimes visited the West, though not a cloud intruded upon the merciless blue sky. It was toward Byorneth's tent that his steps took him, and soon he stood by the bedside of his oldest friend and poured out the whole story. He waited perhaps a half minute for his reply, until at last only one chilly sentence emerged.

"Why did you not consult me?"

"I felt to involve no one but myself, as the trouble was of my own making."

"The Sheewa are meant to operate in tandem! Even then, we never alter politics without first consulting the Keeper of the Slopes at Seng Grandt! You have undertaken to forge an unadvised peace between these tribes, and may have jeopardized our relations with both of them! You had no business giving one chief advice, much less two! And you might have known that!"

Byorneth gave a mighty heave and sat up. "I hope this bone has mended by now. I can't risk lying abed any longer

while you kill us all. I'll talk with Waileng, if he will see me."
He stood shakily, as on new legs, and Hunter held his peace as
he followed Byorneth out into the yard and stopped partway
across to watch the old man make his salutations before the
chief's tent.

Grandmother sat in the sun in front of her tent. Byorneth
was well recovered, and she did not worry. No one could have
stopped him. "What are you doing, just standing there?" she
asked, and Hunter nodded toward the chief's emblem embroidered on his tent.

"Byorneth is angry with me, and I could say nothing. He's
gone to speak with Waileng."

"And why is he angry?"

He had come to love Grandmother, but now her inquisi-
tiveness irked him. "I overstepped my bounds, interfered
with the government of your tribe. Byorneth has gone to
smooth things."

"Well, I wish him luck!" she laughed. "Waileng doesn't like
advice, even from me. Now come with me and we'll make
some more bread. These people stuff themselves like fowl!"

Hunter was up to his wrists in dough when Byorneth tossed
the flap aside and stormed in, cast about furiously for several
seconds, then thrust his hands into a mound and began to
knead furiously. Then he sucked a long, trembling breath
and composed himself as he scraped the fragments from
his fingers one by one back into the pile. His hands seemed
cleaner. "I — have spoken to Waileng Chief, and concluded
after much consideration that he is a mad fool, perhaps even
a lunatic."

Without a word, Grandmother cut a fragrant chunk from
her freshest loaf and watched as Byorneth engulfed it in three
large bites.

Chapter 22
The Horn

THE HEART IS ALWAYS LIFTED ERE IT IS DASHED,
AND DASHED ERE IT IS LIFTED.

~Maxims of the Chief~

The Great Chief of the Waileng sat alone in his tent on the Chair of Office. For 15 years, he had been chief, and although there are some who enjoy immediate power and authority, his inner animal had required more time to rejoice in its full strength. Yet, in the end, it had not been Byorneth, or even Hunter, who had angered him. It had been his own fear. He felt his power slipping away as he softly pounded his hands against the arms of the chair in thought. His outburst had surprised even him, and while it may have been justified toward the younger Sheewa, he knew that he had made a great error in vexing the old man.

Rising, he wandered the length of his tent slowly twice, thumbs hooked into his belt. He stopped as his eyes rested on the wall of the tent where a familiar figure in a broad hat was depicted in faded embroidery, consorting familiarly with a certain of his most esteemed forebears. A horn sounded from beyond the boundaries of the camp, and he caught his breath as he recognized it.

The congress horn had not been sounded in living memory, and had been considered lost, yet he had heard of its sound, bass and shrill. Waileng took his long weapon from its scabbard at the side of the chair, and joined in the growing flood of people that spilled out of the tents and congregated at the north end of the camp.

Shouldering his way through the crowd, he saw that the Desert was thickly speckled with people, gathered like a small forest, foremost of whom was a man with the huge old silver-braced horn held to his lips. Beside him, supported on the right side by his son, was the chief of Laiopej, propped on the other side by a rugged stick. There were horses also, milling about and barely contained by the Horsemen.

Tempai left his father to the assistance of the man with the horn and came forward into the open space. Hunter hesitated, but Waileng Chief remained in place, and so he stepped out toward his brother, where they locked arms over their scars as custom dictates. There were no words, for although they had made themselves brothers, they were not yet friends. They stood apace, bridging the two companies.

With a loud voice, the chief's son addressed the Waileng. "Our brothers Waileng, and all who sojourn with them, hear me!

"For generations, our people have battled yours. We have lived divided in all things but our basic Tribesman souls. The soul is the same, and it is to this soul we appeal, for a third tribe has come out of the West by the sea. In the night they came upon us, and were we not forewarned, our people would now be dead, root and bough. As it stands, we lost several dear comrades who gave their lives to give us warning. Otherwise, the people and records have been saved.

"Now the enemy occupies our camp, and the smoke of our tents still burns in our nostrils." For the first time, Hunter saw the thin column of distant smoldering. "We know that they follow us, and have doubtless slaughtered all other tribes that have come before them. Will you stand with us in conflict against our enemy and yours?"

The distance between camps was not great, and the enemy had not far to go. Waileng stepped out from the company of his people. "Laiopej, we will fight together! Come, let us set the battle! Today we are as one!"

The companies met like two sea swells, and soon the uninitiated could not have told one tribe from another. They stood in a thick line before the entrance of the camp.

Hunter was frightened, more than he had ever been in his life. It was not the new alliance or the coming horde which caused him fear, but the way in which the Tribesmen intended to meet it. The same thing was in Byorneth's mind, and Hunter was glad when his friend called out, "Friend Chiefs, a word!"

Byorneth and the chiefs gathered together, while Hunter remained where he was, listening to what his friend said.

"As a Sheewa, I must protest this arrangement."

Waileng laughed. "Then protest! This war is private tribal business, and an emissary from a dead kingdom—"

"Why must we alter our battle?" Laiopej cut through with his thin, cracked voice.

"You know only strike-and-flee tactics, but this will be a pitched fight. Many will die here, but you can at least bring a good many of them with you. Put your people in my hands, and show your valor."

The old chief addressed the younger. "I have no reason to distrust these men, and I have already seen the courage of the young one. In all things concerning the Laiopej, they've been proved right."

Waileng scowled, but acquiesced. "Sheewa, how would you set the people?"

"Give me charge of them now! There is no time for advising!"

A brief, intense struggle followed within the Waileng chief, the upshot of which was a victory for Byorneth. The chiefs parted and let him address the gathered tribes. "People of the Desert! I am Byorneth, and I have charge of this company! You will now divide into two troops!"

Some looked to their chiefs for guidance, but the matter rested entirely with Byorneth, and in the lack of time he made them all feel his authority. The riders had already mounted their steeds, each with heavy blade ready, and the beasts, sensing the excitement, pawed and snorted in eagerness for the race.

They smelled the dust of the approaching company long before they saw them.

There had been nothing in the scrolls to adequately describe such a horde, marching line upon line, with a noise like that of thunder. At the head of them marched a line of men in blue tunics, bearing with them two streaming banners of black stars on red fields. Each man in the company held a long sword in one hand with a long dagger ready at his side, and underneath each tunic there was a plate of leather armor.

They had started out from their home a ragged lot of young fishermen. Tribe after tribe had fallen under them since, and they had smelled blood and smoke, and come through it all a skilled lot of young murderers. Discipline had been brutally drummed into them, and they kept strictly to their ranks as their next line of victims faced them across the sand. There was no sympathy in their looks, only cold eagerness. They were met with a volley of arrows, which hardly slowed their relentless pace.

A company of archers, men and women, had been assembled at the boundaries of the Waileng camp, and at Byorneth's orders they fired another flight. They were too few to bring much grief to their enemies, and now a man among the advancing number lifted his voice and they came forward faster, drawing their daggers with a unanimous shout. A third flight of arrows flew, and some soldiers in the front ranks fell, only to be replaced just as quickly from the ranks behind. Another loud order was given, and whipped the army into a full run.

Byorneth cried out for the people to flee, and flee they did, racing through the empty camp. Closer and closer on their heels came their enemy, raising an unearthly wail that pierced each ear that heard it, filling the Desert like a swarm of bees.

But the archers were only part of Byorneth's army. As the last line of soldiers charged into the camp, out of the gullies round about there came Horsemen who swept through the tents, raising a desperate din of their own. They engulfed the outer edges of the foreign army, their long crescent swords flashed up, down and across, thirsty for blood. The red flood that quenched them did its work upon the horses as well, and each eye stood huge, each nostril strained outward to its utmost. Squealing sharply, they dove into the fray, unchecked by their masters.

Back and forth they fought upon the red sand, a cutting, slashing, screaming, crashing conflict. Heated with battle, the Huay archers had turned back and faced the army when they heard the cry of the Horsemen, tearing into their enemies with knife and sword. They labored well, though Tribesmen are most at home upon horses. Men and women fought alongside their children, many as young as 13, for all but the infants fought on this day. Blood was no new thing to them, and each drop that fell in their camp did that much more to protect it.

Before the battle, Hunter had thought of his wife, of the many people he had come to know here, and of the danger of death. But now he thought no longer. He became a thing of fury, roaring with each stroke. He had a long sword, and in the other hand there was his Sheewan dagger. His first enemy went down with steel through his throat, and Hunter pierced the next with the heavy knife.

Looking up, he saw another rushing to him, angling his sword backward for a killing swing, and Hunter darted in. Before the swing came around, he had impaled the man's heart through his armor, and pulling out his sword he bellowed and flung himself headlong into a knot of soldiers clustered around Tempai. He fought in a haze that obscured all else. The eyes of his foes widened with terror as they saw his face.

Filled with the rage of battle and animal strength, he skewered a man with the point of his sword. Then he took another and smashed his head against the old oven, for he fought over the fallen tent of Grandmother. A man flew at him screaming, cutting downwards, and Hunter parried with the dagger, and with his sword he slew the man as he fell.

There was a circle around him now of unwilling warriors, quailing from the blood-drenched sight of him. But the fury was still on him, and he roared in a changed voice, "Come at me! Come at me now!"

But even as he spoke he attacked, and as he did so a Tribesman on a black mount rushed in, cutting back and forth, the light of battle blazing in his eyes. Together they felled five men in succession. One man broke free, and this one, desperate for escape, dragged the Horseman from the saddle. Hunter finished him as he tried to mount with a furious cut to his back.

The horse was Olonj, and Hunter swung into the saddle as he had so many times before. Now, he fought from horseback, and the black creature, more by instinct than experience, played the gory game with skill. As soon as one foe was killed, he moved unbidden to find his rider another one. In the corner of his vision, Hunter saw the old chief of Laiopej fall, then a woman he had known in the Waileng camp. He put his heels to Olonj and charged, slaying those who had slain them.

There was an immense disadvantage on the side of the invading army, for they had never lost. Always had the ribes of the West fled or fallen easily before them, had trusted their raiding experience against the deadly rank and file. But this was altogether different, nightmarish. The Horsemen never stopped coming, and the soldiers found themselves using their weapons for defense, not for attack.

Hunter drew his blade out of a body and looked around him at the waning fight. He had killed before, but to be in the midst of such excess of death was something different. Still, they had fought to protect life, and that was enough for him. His face was as wild as that of his horse, and every Waileng and Laiopej looked up at him as the killing stopped. Byorneth hardly knew him.

Hunter sat his horse easily, steadily, his curved sword resting against the saddle in the sudden quiet. For the first time he felt a wound in his leg, the blood drying on his skin, saw the handiwork of the tribes all about him, and he felt weary. He had been a Sheewa, but it was certain he could be one no longer. And yet he was not of the tribes, though he had bled with them in the same cause. These thoughts were temporary, for his mind was still clear in the wake of the tumult of battle and his murderous rage.

Until he saw the fresh dust in the air over to the north. Until he saw the line of fresh soldiers beneath it, and knew that the people could never get away in time.

The day had grown fearfully hot.

⁓ʌʌ⁓

The going through the mountains grew harder when they left the slick bowl of the Kyargh. This path to the West was a rugged trail, but Srstri, who had struggled with each step, now felt her legs strong under her. Her new vigor could not, however, dispel the frightening thought that at some point along the Trail they might stumble upon two cold, stiff bodies in wide-brimmed hats, covered with the accumulated drifts of lonely weeks.

Finally, the end of their journey came, the last crevasse was crossed, the last granite wall climbed, the last pack hauled up at rope's end. They walked down the last slope and stood among the low foothills with the vast expanse of brush and dunes beyond. Their guide, who had alternately dogged and led their steps all the weary way across the Kyargh, turned and faced them suddenly. It had been a blessing that for most of the distance through the Pass, the wind had blown the man's essence away from them. Now the breeze of the steppes covered them with his reeking stench.

"My masters, you see I have delivered you safely. My unique knowledge and careful direction have saved your lives 50 times over. I trust you are grateful enough to grant me a small tribute in return for my extraordinary condescension." As he spoke, he sidled around them, rubbing his hands on his thighs. Thorn kept facing him, always between the man and Srstri. "You, my lord, have a woman, a great boon to any man, especially to men such as we. I live alone in these mountains with only the deer and leopards for company, but if you were to give me that woman, I would at last have something to warm myself with at night. Hand her over and you can be on your way."

Thorn chuckled softly and laid hand to hilt. His voice, when he replied, was cheerfully cold, a paradox that turned Srstri's skin a shade paler. "Well, well, sir. It was good of you to guide our journey. But now the time has come for you to crawl back under the rock where you live and quit our company. By way of payment, I will let your putrid carcass escape whole."

He took his long knife out to enforce his words. Khornang retreated a step, and with flashing speed brought a dirk out of its place in a forehand grip. His face had never lost its smirk, nor his stature its insinuating stoop. He lingered just outside the circle of Thorn's reach, gesturing with his blade. At last, Thorn attacked, and Khornang slipped past him and laid hold of Srstri.

But there had been a change in her in the past months. She had accepted the care of others because she had known no other way. She had taken a champion for the sake of survival across the mountains. But she was a woman, not a slave. When the man laid hands on her, she slashed him across the face with her knife, and he released her.

Gone was the senseless smirk. Now his eyes stood at their widest, his skin at its palest, and he backed away as he would from a wild beast. Her reddened knife was still ready as she advanced upon him. He seemed reluctant to go, but even more reluctant to draw near.

It was a mad act. He tried to dart in past her blade as he had darted past Thorn's, but this time, she snapped her arm around and buried the knife in his shoulder. He screamed, not merely a scream of pain, but one of sudden and unbearable grief. He clasped the wound and stared at the gore on his fingers, then screamed again, lips quivering, and he began to weep, piteously as a child. Looking up at Srstri like a misbehaving boy toward his mother, he covered his face with his good arm and ran away into the Hills. Long after he vanished, they could hear him weeping far off across the wind.

Chapter 23
The Rider

THE COLD WIND BLOWS AND TASTES OF SNOW,
THE ROCKS HOLD NAUGHT BUT DANGER.
MY HEART WOULD FLOAT AND STAY,
ON THE BREAST OF THE COLD, BRIGHT DAY
OUT OF REACH OF MAN'S ANGER
WHERE MY LOVE LIES BELOW.

~The Returning King Away From His Love~

Srstri stood still for a time, looking toward the crest where the madman had disappeared, holding the knife carefully so as to keep the blood from running onto her hand. Her ears sang and her blood ran high, to have made a stand independently for the first time. Thorn had not moved since she first used the blade, and now he stood watching her, a subtle half smile on his lips. "That's the end of him. Come along, then."

The foothills stretched out before them in mounds, like wrinkles in a woollen blanket. The grass, though it looked dead, was alive, cradled on a dense cushion of its yellowed forebears, sporting the occasional brave flower. There were even trees in the hollows between hills, tangled and short, so that they had to cut through a prickly wall with every piece of level ground.

Then, without warning, the land leveled, and they saw the barren kaind stretching out to the under edge of the sky. The air became warmer, and soon they discarded their thick furs in favor of a single layer. Their footing was sure, solid with each long stride as they moved out of the Hills and into the bare sand, which reflected the naked sun and made the air even hotter. Srstri could see nothing, and felt as she had as a child when she would swim in the river near their home, and the world above shimmered with the movement of the water's surface. They went on through this ragged dance for a while, drinking the occasional hot mouthful of water. Soon, the air was like a furnace, and it began to burrow under her skin, tickle in her hair, eat away her strength. At last, they stopped to camp for the night. For the first time since the foothills, she looked at Thorn, and she was surprised to see him in a similar condition — light-headed, hollow-eyed and sick. That sturdy frame, strong against mountain and man, quailed in the face of the all-pervading blast of the Desert.

The day's heat dissipated with the arrival of stars, brighter than any in the populous Hills, and Srstri lay awake in her blankets for a while, staring at them. It was marvelous to her, this common thread of all lands, that wherever one went, the same moon beguiled the night, the same stars danced together in its company. They had agreed Thorn would keep the first watch, but it was only after she lost count of the stars three times that Srstri slept.

She awoke shivering hours later. The air had lost all its warmth. Her furs, which she had thought herself done with, she dragged out again and put on, waiting for relief. It was already well past her watch, but still Thorn watched all alone. "You should have woken me," she said, but he was silent, his presence marked only by his soft breathing. Then she lowered her voice. "Do you think he will follow us?"

"Whom do you mean? The madman of the Pass or the madman of the Crater? Why did you not tell me at the inn that an enemy was chasing you? I could have prepared for him, gone more carefully."

"I thought it would make you afraid, and you would not guide me. I did not know you then." She could see him now in the spare light of the slivered moon. "I am sorry for the danger, and for having mistrusted you. Is there still a very great risk?"

"I do not know. He would not have much cover here in the Desert, but I've seen him move. He may be outside the camp at this moment. What little cover there may be, he will make skillful use of it. Of course, he would have to keep downwind of us. You never know about that type of man. He is a wild beast, not motivated like other men."

There was a bird chattering somewhere off to the south, and they listened to it for a moment. She was unused to the night noises — the low, slow booming of the wind in the rocky Pass, a distant jackal yapping. Each land sounds different in day and night.

"Thorn, why did you consent to come with me?"

"I had nothing to do, and my latest venture cost me what little gold I had. Now I am seeing you safely through to your husband. Let that suffice for all questions."

Dawn found them once again on their journey. The wind came today out of the west, and there was very little of the late morning's half chill that follows nearly all sunrises among the Hills. It was cold when they awoke, and hot with the dawn, and the day only got hotter, smiting the already withered grass and jaded travelers.

A dull lethargy settled over them. Srstri hummed snatches of picking songs to herself as she walked, and that helped a little. She followed Thorn, and that was all she knew, that was all she could hold in her mind. They stopped to rest and drink more often, but spoke little, for there was not the water to waste with speech.

Soon they entered the dunes, and the ceaseless climb and slide was only broken by the occasional stumble through a clump of stunted grass or succulent flowers that hid on the sheltered sides of hillocks.

Suddenly, Thorn pushed her down onto her belly in the dust as they topped another dune. "I smell smoke. Do you see any?" he whispered, hoarse with thirst. She scanned the vivid sky, and pointed off toward the northwest and a slight darkening of the blue near the horizon.

"Of all the places in this wasteland, where is your man most likely to be?"

Before he could stop her, Srstri was off, all fatigue forgotten in a mad flight across the intervening distance.

Thorn was not far behind her, and though they ran for a long time, she never slowed. Soon, they came to a scorched circle in the sand, peppered all around with blowing ashes. The burning had subsided by the time they arrived, and the tents were now so many blackened hulks, alarmingly red at the north with copious blood. All was laid low but for two objects — the thinned and blackened skeleton of a chair, and an iron stove, hanging open.

Scattered all through the camp were burned or mutilated corpses of all ages. Srstri felt her life stop on the hair's edge of grief as she saw it. Her mouth hung open, and she felt no need to close it, or to do anything but kneel there in the sand and sob silently to herself.

"He may not have been here at all," she barely heard Thorn say. "Who knows where a Longfarer goes?"

She walked back and forth through the ashes, following the bare streets, looking for she knew not what, but Thorn walked wider, searching every inch of ground and at last working his way out beyond the camp, away into the outer Desert. At last, he stood in the middle of the central street and addressed Srstri directly, motioning toward the northwest where the thoroughfare ended.

"An attack came from that direction. The defenders fled, but at some signal a second force attacked the invaders on horses from those gullies on each side of camp. But the enemy was still too strong, and they were replenished by another group, hence the dead Tribesmen and women all around us. Many other bodies were dragged away, probably for burial. The invaders led away many Tribesmen, killing any wounded, and still others fled away into the Desert." Srstri stood and looked about her, seeing the battle unfold in the man's words. At the last, she turned and saw him sifting through the ashes of the tents, salvaging gold and any other goods which may have survived.

"Must you do that?" It was a naive question, she knew, but the pain of the dead people around her could still be felt. Thorn only looked at her and turned back to his work. He had found several knives with minimal flame damage and took them for himself. Looking up again, he said absently, "Your husband is Sheewa."

"Yes."

"There is one track outside the village, made with a shoe such as the Sheewa use. I've seen others like them. Perhaps these were your husband's. They led away from camp, with others of the tracks covering some of his. They must have gone just as the battle was ending. There was a horse as well."

They hurried to find the sign and followed. There was very little of it, and had Thorn not been there, Srstri could not have followed. A little way from camp, it became clear. Soon, they came to a place where the grass grew in islands, surrounded by a sea of fine sand, and at this point even Thorn could not find them again.

He set about to search more carefully, but Srstri could not make herself move slowly enough to help him. She walked to and fro restlessly, careful not to disturb Thorn's search, scanning the land before her while her fingers fumbled with her ring. She began to hum as she paced, and it grew louder as her tension mounted, until finally the words came out in a melancholy strain, the song the pickers on those distant hillsides had sung to set the seal on their union.

> "Two lovers stood in the morning air,
> The moon was full, and the stars were fair.
> I would that I were there again!"

With a gasp she heard the refrain continued by a voice in the distance:

> "The wolf was slinking to his lair,
> His hands were lost in her shining hair.
> Oh, I would that I were there again,
> Were there again."

As the song ended with a lilt, a familiar figure skylined itself against the bright blue, a figure in a broad-brimmed hat and long cloak, with a long staff in his hand. In the next moment, the image was blurred with tears, and she was running across the sand and grass. It was toward her husband, her man and no other woman's.

He came stumbling down the grassy platform, dropping his staff in the sand and losing his hat in the wind. She fell to her knees as she ran, but was back on her feet in an instant. They met in the sand, lips locked together, and they stood for a long time in the same footprints. Once they broke their embrace for a frantic, loving examination of one another, a restoration of the memories which in the past months had begun to fade. Then his face went white, and only then did she see the wound in his side, a broad gash near his belt. Byorneth was there. "Steady, lad. Go back and lie down. You can speak later."

They made camp in the shelter of two broad hummocks, lighting no fire, for they had all endured cold nights before, and the army may have been near them yet. In the hours before midnight, Srstri and Hunter talked. She had introduced him to Thorn, and proper thanks had been given. Byorneth had presided as a grim sentinel, watching to see that no harm came to Hunter. She told them the story of her escape, the ruin of her friends, and then she told of their encounter with the Man of the Mountains.

Byorneth and Hunter exchanged a sudden look.

"Have you met him, Hunter?"

"Yes. He is an outcast who has proclaimed himself king over the mountains, and all Arlinga."

"He gave us to know as much when he left us among the foothills. He would have taken me away with him into the mountains. I doubt we will ever see him again."

Hunter had his doubts, but if the illusion gave Srstri some comfort, he would not correct her. It would suffice for him to be cautious. He doubted, besides, that the little man would ever stray far beyond his kingdom, even for a woman. Perhaps. Banat was another matter.

Byorneth told her the story of the battle. Hunter said very little, only staring forward as the story was retold, never moving except to hold his wife closer.

He did move, however, when the talk turned to the latter part of the fight, when the reinforcement of soldiers had come. Absently, he took the hooked dagger out of his belt and buried the steel in the sand. Srstri saw the knuckles whitening around the handle.

He began to tell the rest, and Byorneth let him, leaning back against the bank and staring with evident sympathy. "We heard them shout, and they ran forward like the others, frantically. But this time all our people were in the open. We met the soldiers. The tribes were brave. They fought, but there were too many this time. We made them pay. We killed many. The first lines of men weakened and fell. The final clash was coming, and I was ready for the end."

His head dropped to his chest, and Byorneth spoke again. "I saw him getting ready to charge into the battle again, but there were great numbers arrayed against us, and I went to him. He was wounded, barely able to hold his weapons, so I took them away and seized the bridle of his horse. I led him away into the sands, then went back on foot to hide our tracks. From there I saw the end of the two tribes, the killing of the wounded. The leading away of the ones who could walk. Then I went back and tended his wounds. When he heard you singing, I could not hold him down."

They were silent for a long time, Hunter and Srstri lying in one another's arms, and it was thus that Srstri fell asleep to the night sounds of the wind and jackals. In her slumber, she wrapped Hunter's cloak around her shoulders and nestled deeper into his unwounded side, so that even in the nighttime desert chill they were warm enough together. A pile of clothing lay in the grass across from them, the clothing which Srstri and Thorn had worn in the Caldera. The horse was ground hitched nearby, dozing. He was their watch, and everyone who stayed awake in their little company kept their eyes fixed on the pointed ears.

Hunter looked out over the dark land above which stars had begun to shine, and wondered what had become of the Huay who had not been taken. Tribe had always slaughtered tribe in the Desert, and this happening was not at all unusual. All the same, it had pained him to see what he had seen, the death of those he knew and had fought beside. For some days, every dream would be haunted by the sickening futility of their last battle.

Srstri's head lay on his shoulder, and Hunter wondered vaguely how among all her trials she had managed to remain attractive to him.

As he finally drifted away into sleep, a thought invaded his consciousness for the first time. The man with whom he had forged a bond of brotherhood was taken away along with the other survivors of his tribe.

At the end of some days, four travelers walked through the waving heat toward the east, making for the mountains. All had been accomplished, all were reunited, and yet Hunter could not seem to walk with the same vigor as his companions. They passed the dead fires of the former Waileng camp and he stopped, sifting through the ashes of the chief's tent with his feet, staring at the blackened Chair of Office which stood bleak and thin in the center of the circle. Srstri joined him and clasped his hand.

"I've made the blood tie," he said, so that all could hear. "I cannot abandon my brother."

Byorneth's brow sank as he came and laid his hand on Hunter's shoulder. "You've become involved. The tribal traditions and customs do not apply to you as a Sheewa, and your words mean nothing to me. You will come with us, because we will not allow you to involve yourself further. Come, and make the break!"

"Byorneth, you would not yourself. I must find him or my word means nothing. You've often told me how manhood depends on a man's word."

"I will stay also." Srstri clasped her husband's hand harder. "My home is my husband."

Byorneth sighed with a force that stirred his whiskers. "Do you know who these people were? They are of Ashtranaag."

The name stirred Hunter's memory. "The island of your stories?"

"Yes, the island upon which I was cast in my young life, where I nearly died at the hands of those who would have feasted on me. I have not seen such men since I was first cast away on that miserable rock. The story is true. Its truth was never important until now."

Thorn came forward also, drawn to the mystery of their words and the prospect of fresh enterprise. Byorneth stared across the dunes, then sighed resignedly. "These people have never been outside their little world of bare rock and gulls, and if they have come to the mainland in force, it can only mean they have set up some permanent settlement, a place in which they can feel at home. That is where they would take their captives. We cannot go there easily."

They remained there far into the day, setting up a scheme which they hoped would mean the liberty of Tempai, now Laiopej Chief.

—⌒ʌʌ⌒

"Push that back into line, there!" the man barked and marked the command with a slap of his long whip across the back of the captive. One of his subordinates shoved the old man back into his position in the long column of prisoners and cuffed him again for good measure. It was a weary duty, given only to soldiers of low degree, and they resented it, much as they resented the captives themselves.

They trod along the curling ridge of a huge dune, the hot wind blowing in each face and piling sand around each hair and through each gap of clothing. Every Tribesman had immediately known these men as outsiders, unused to desert living, with thin, cruel beards. The Huay may steal horses or engage in sudden battle, but no prisoner was treated in this fashion, be he lowborn or high.

Already, they had marched for a day and a night. There was little sleep, and only enough water for barest survival, supplemented by a few mouthfuls of foul black bread each day that tasted of cold fish. Those who had been wounded in the battle, many grievously, were marched as hard as the rest until fatigue and bleeding finally killed them. So came merciful death until, when a strange city appeared in the distance, they were about half their original number.

Weak as he was with heat and thirst, Tempai's young mind pondered the city curiously as they drew near it. The Huay have no word for such a place, a broad edifice of many levels, all carved out of stone, creamy and gleaming newly in the midday sun. The large outer wall had only been erect for about six months, and the inner structures were younger even than that. But the Tribesmen cared nothing for that, nor for the genius that had gone into the labor.

Soon, they came through the main gate, stout and austere. The moment they passed through the posts, all manner of little children fell in behind them yelling, and the people they passed spat and threw dirt and garbage in their faces. Their drivers took them through every street of the city before they came to a thick-walled cage of knotted wood.

⌒ʌ ʌ⌒

A man walked in the snow, a man wrapped in wool underneath two layers of furs. The snow reached halfway up his thighs, and he stopped every few steps to blow great clouds of steam into the crisp air. He took no rest beyond these bare moments, and had long since ceased to sleep altogether. For the first time, he was within reach of his prey, and the thought propelled him along, grunting with each push through the unforgiving snow.

"Stop where you are, my lord!" The voice echoed across the mountain range, reverberating from wall to wall. The man stopped, but could see no one, either in the little valley where he stood or in the vast jumble of confused stone toward which he labored. He was accustomed to being alone, preferring his own company, and the sound of another creature's voice raised the hair on his neck even under the three wool scarves he wore.

At last, a little black figure came out of the rocks, bounding across the great pile like a Lowland deer. With a little plume of snow, he landed on the flat, and ran quickly forward to where Banat stood watching, leaping above the snow each time.

"Your grace has been pleased to pass this way, and truly I offer my felicitations on a job well done! To come this way alone is a feat which few attempt, and even fewer emerge at the other end still breathing!"

"What do you want?" Banat, vulgar as he was, was not inclined to be patient at any interruption in his journey. "I have urgent business at the other end."

With a high laugh, the thin fellow threw his arms wide and addressed the heavens. "What an auspicious land this land of the West must be, that so many have such urgent business across the Pass! And what may be your business, pray?"

"That is my affair. Now stand to one side and let me through before I pluck your stinking head off your body."

Khornang had been condescended to, humored, defied and laughed at, but it had been years since he had heard such rudeness. Regally, he surveyed Banat down his long nose and said, "I will not. You will never leave these mountains, for I will now kill you. I am going to kill you as you have never been killed before. I will begin my work at this moment, and I am now going to kill you."

Before Banat had fully comprehended his words, uttered in a low half chant reminiscent of the music of the Hills, Khornang drew a blade from beneath his belt. Leaping almost quicker than sight, he inserted the blade under Banat's collar and, with five violent wrenches, sliced the coat from his back. Next, he made a shallow cut down the pale skin and drove him forward into the rocks like a wounded animal. Every time Banat slowed in his climb, the man cut him again, until his back and legs left a streak of crimson wherever they scraped against the sharp black stones. His stump began to bleed again. Shivering from the cold and his fear, he tried to draw his own weapon, but with a deft stroke Khornang sheared the sheath away and gave him a cut across the arm for his trouble. Terror mounted with every stroke, every obstacle, until he no longer regarded the cuts, but only the wild, inhuman fury that drove him on.

———∧∧◡—

There was a wind, smelling faintly of salt, which brought to Hunter's mind all manner of forgotten images of home. Home, and a far-off, filthy city at the end of a long Trail. But this city, crouched on a low hill in the middle of an arid plain, seemed clean. It was within plain view of distant foothills, yet still many kaind away. The high walls of the city gleamed in the sinking light, and though he could see no movement except on the narrow parapets, the call of the watch rang clearly even to the dune behind which he lay.

He slid and walked down to where the others waited with Olonj. The horse was busy with the already-harried grass, but as always, his head jerked up when Hunter appeared, and his nostrils flared. He only settled when his rider came near, running his hand down the shining neck and whispering, "Not yet, my friend."

Thorn sat on a hummock a few paces away, honing one of his knives and testing it against the light. "The city is well founded. The watch is well set, vigilant." He looked up at the other young man from under his black brows. He did not know this Lowlander, and he was curious. "We might wait until they've lost their fine edge. Slip in secret."

Byorneth was pointedly silent, waiting for the young man's decision.

Hunter stood still, his hand on the horse's shoulders and staring toward the Hills. "No, we cannot wait. These are unkind men, and their prisoners will be unkindly treated. If he's to survive, we must act now." His eyes contracted in thought, and then they fell on Byorneth by long habit.

"He's your blood brother." Byorneth's eyebrow raised, and he crossed his arms. "Do not look to me for answers."

Srstri watched all this, silent, seeing everything. Her husband stood long in thought, and the others never moved. With a final look she walked up the dune in her husband's footsteps and looked over its edge toward the city.

The wind picked up and blew a cloud of dust into her eyes, and she blinked it away and shook it out of her hair. When she could see again, the gates of the city were open, and one by one, three riders emerged, small and black against the road. By the time she had called softly for the others to come look, two riders had branched out to the north, with the other continuing straight on toward the Hills to the east.

⌒ʌ⌒

He had a good horse under him, and there was a reward waiting for him upon his return, so he sang to himself as he rode. He was lightly loaded, and there was no need for spurs, for the horse was a brave one, and would run long if given his head. But he was also a small beast, and every time he slowed to a trot, he hammered the man down into the saddle.

There was a band of high dunes, the prelude to the foothills, just ahead of him. He was glad of the excuse to rein his mount back into a walk. As the ground went by underneath him, his eyes fell into the easy gaze of the long rider between his horse's ears, fixed on a point far away. The horse walked down an incline and into a thicket of bushes, high-stepping through it and up onto the high ground again, then slipping into a gap between the dunes.

It was cool and shady, and the rhythm of the horse under him and the sounds of the moaning wind threw his mind into a strange calm. He was not asleep, but still he woke with a shrill cry as a strange creature hit him from the side and threw him into a hollow beside the road. The horse galloped away into the sands.

It was a dark beast that crouched above him, like a man except that he had dark hair, and his skin was the color of a dreadful twilight. His features were very sharp, unmarred by anger, though his tone could not have been colder. A knife lay on the rider's throat.

"Tell me where you ride, and why you ride there. Tell me, and no harm comes."

The language of the Hills seemed hardly human to this man from Ashtranaag. As he stared up in blank confusion, he could see others walking down the high slope. There was a woman and a young man, dressed strangely. With them walked one old and bearded man who called out a greeting he had learned in Seng Grandt, recorded in the Lowlands not five years before.

"All hail the man from the West!"

The rider's eyes widened, then he lay back in the sand, his jaw clenched tight.

The eagle soared broadly on the cold air, minding neither weather nor height. It was well used to the pressure beneath its wings, the infinitesimal adjustments which altered its course and maintained its trim. No longer was it a glorious realm, for the vast space in which it rode was its home, as comfortable as a man's fields and fireside. Every particle of its attention was focused on the ground far below, and nothing moved, however small, that escaped its notice. Every fiber, every feather was poised for sudden headlong flight toward the ground, eager for the sudden spread of wings which would hold it up from impact, the satisfying squirm of helpless life between its talons. Flying was its life and the life of its young.

At last the eagle's heart leaped, and with a backward folding of its great wings, the sleek body fell into a plummeting dive.

Banat saw the eagle coming even from where he was bound by his one remaining hand against the side of a mountain. Somewhere in the rocks, he knew, Khornang watched him, viewing death as other men view the sunset, inevitable and beautiful. There was a certain dignity to be had in death, in meeting it with honor. But not for Banat.

He did not want to squirm, desiring above all else to rob his enemy of even the smallest morsel of entertainment, but he could not help it. The bird drew nearer and nearer, unbelievably huge and grim. His bloody back stuck to the stone behind him, and when the eagle came to him at last, it picked him off the mountain like a berry from a tree.

He shrieked as the great claws enclosed him, and then again at the vicious pull of the rope which bound his wrist. Perhaps it was the blood he had lost, perhaps the cold wind, maybe the dizzying swing of the sudden distance between him and earth that separated him from his senses as the bird took him away.

Khornang watched as huntress and prey became lost in the white shroud which had rolled in from the north.

Characters

Algorneth   Keeper of the Slopes and eldest living
Sheewa, welcomed Hunter to Seng Grandt

Allend   a Reiver, or royal thief in the times of the
Last Kings, who founded Allend's End

Anandaans   sons of wealthy Lowland landowners,
treated as aristocracy nearer to the Sky Line

Arn   a Lowland murderer, rumored to have
transfered his spirit to the bear Leen d'Arns
with his death

Arron   a Highland blacksmith who married Hunter
and Srstri

Arneth   young Sheewa who saved Byorneth, Hunter
and Srstri from the Kaarnaan in the Swamps

Ayafet   Western tribe

Banat   Srstri's master, who pursued her after
her rescue

Byorneth	Hunter's oldest friend, companion on his travels
Chadeyzdeer	slave traders of the Marsh, of Harniyen extraction
Children of Ambalyeth	the royal family of the original Pengdyam settlers who, with few interruptions, ruled from the date of their founding of Seng Grandt until the last Great War
Elnaan	young Lowlander and brother to Teidin, Ellarn, Iblar and Merna, joined in the pursuit of Hunter
Ellarn	younger brother to Elnaan, Iblar, Teidin and Merna
Hambaak	one of the Harniyen leaders of the search for Srstri
Harn	driver who led the mule train after Hunter was injured
Harniyen	people and language of the Lowlands, which takes in all dialects from the Chadeyzdeer and the speech of the Upper Trail to that of Pown d'Rith on the Coast
Hastraneth	Sheewa who went with Hunter into the mountains after game and was accosted by robbers
Hinas Ablî	nobleman and warrior of the Old Kingdom, wrote *The Precepts of War*

Hinas Bòrainu nobleman and adviser of the Old Kingdom, whose sayings were written down during his brief stewardship

Huay Western word for the Tribesmen

Hunter young mule driver and Sheewa

Iblar elder brother to Elnaan, Teidin, Ellarn and Merna

Jooenin Gueykikh mother to Waileng Chief

Kaarnaan Great Lizard of the Swamps

Kaia young Tribeswoman of the Waileng

Kerny Chadeyzdeer who found out about the jewel Srstri carried and tried to claim it

Khornang madman exiled into the wilderness of the Hills, the Man of the Mountains

Kistûleth Hunter's name among the Sheewa, taken from their word for "hunter" — "kistûl," and the suffix of every Sheewan name, "-eth"

Laiopej Western tribe, chief rival of the Waileng

Laiopej Chief aged hereditary chieftain of the Laiopej, succeeded upon his death by Tempai, his son

Leen d'Arns the Great Bear which for some years terrorized several villages of the Lowlands

Merna sister to Elnaan, Teidin, Iblar and Ellarn

364 | Roan Clay

Ordo   young friend of Teidin and Elnaan who stayed behind in Allend's End

Pagrâi   the king for whose arrival the Sheewa of Seng Grandt are dedicated to waiting

Pengdyam   the people of the Lowlands and Highlands before the last Great War, of whom the people of the Caldera are descendants

Sheewa   traveling scribes of Arlinga, descended from the scribes and advisers of the Last Kings

Srstri   young slave girl owned by Banat, who escaped captivity in the company of Byorneth and Hunter

Tagrri   scribe and poet of the Old Kingdom, remembered for his treatise on the virtues of women (*The Arranin*), and his manual of kingship (*The Bôlairrun*)

Teidin   young Lowlander and brother to Elnaan, Iblar, Ellarn and Merna, joined in the pursuit of Hunter

Tempai Liaunom   son of Laiopej Chief

Thorn   young man, formerly of the banditry of the Western Caldera, who guided Srstri through the Pass over the Kyargh

Tierna Doe   daughter of Waileng Chief

Treasurer	keeper of a forgotten treasure of the ancient kings, successor to many generations of treasurers, forgotten by the Sheewa
Waileng	tribe of the West, foremost in the knowledge of the Sheewa, bitter rivals of the Laiopej
Waileng Chief	hereditary chieftain of the Waileng, father to Tierna Doe

Glossary

barraakang	Literally "leaf vision," the images of leaves that sometimes haunt tea pickers after long hours of work.
bear	The Arlingan bear can grow to an immense size, though it rarely seeks confrontation with human beings. Its tail is long, and its ears are pointed, giving rise to the alternate term "horned bear."
braaykast	General term for any liquor of the Hills.
deesard	Particularly beautiful female slave who, in the traditions of the southern villages, is owned by the richest man in the community, as a symbol of purity and prosperity.
deeyaz	Slave in the language of the Swamps. Among the southern villages, this translates as "deez." Suffixes change "deeyaz" to "daz."

eagle These creatures reside in the high cliffs of the Western mountain ranges. Many are large enough to carry fully grown human beings to their nests high among the rocks, although they rarely bother with anything but the wild goats that scale the heights.

eestranaah Resting place along the upper parts of the Great Trail.

epithet Part of every personal name among some of the Western tribes, which references some personal trait or circumstance surrounding that person's birth.

feeleuenakh Western heraldic term for the image of a horse and rider at full gallop.

hinai Nocturnal creatures, often the only sign of their presence is the occasional hole in a field and pair of flashing eyes in the night. They inhabit their underground cities in Lowlands and Highlands, and are thus the sworn enemies of every farmer in Arlinga. Often hunted, their thin skins are extraordinarily tough, and often used for shoes.

horse These creatures are well known in every land from the rocky Western shore to the Thicket east of the Trail, and all through the Caldera. They are mainly considered valuable only for the breeding of mules, for they are unattractive, albeit tough and strong, qualities which are easily passed to their offspring, the finest mules a workman could ask for. The Western horse is a different beast entirely, treated by their tribal masters with an incalculable pride, and bred with the utmost care — fleet, elegant and royal.

hrnyi Kyarrghnaal word for "hinai."

hual 1/2 of a kand (1.3 miles/2.09 kilometers).

kaarn A small brown lizard with or without a neck fringe, that lives in the fields of the Lowlands. When they have had a prolific year, the farmers see them fleeing like autumn leaves ahead of their footsteps as they walk through the grass. They prefer meat, and so the farmers bless them for eating the hinai and insects that attack the plants.

kand (Kaind plural) 2.6 miles (4.18 kilometers), or the distance between two ancient markers on the Great Trail.

kual (Kuail plural) 1/4 of a kand (0.65 of a mile/1 kilometer).

leedh Wild plant of the Western foothills, whose flowers are gathered and dried for culinary purposes.

líoš 9.75 inches (25 centimeters), or the width of a column of writing on a Sheewan scroll.

ngyaarban   Ancient gesture of lovers, known from
                  the chivalric writings of the early
                  Calderan culture.

prashkah   Far-off, wistful feeling inspired by certain
                  undefinable musical qualities.

rashi   Homemade liquor of varying strengths
                  and qualities.

rophoil   3.25 feet/1 meter, or the length of a long
                  Sheewan stride.

rover wolves Hardly ever found on their own, packs of
                  these creatures roam the lands to the north
                  of the Death Fields, killing easy prey where
                  they can find it. In hungry years, children
                  and even adults have been known to
                  go missing.

tsalokh   Tea planters' or Hill farmers' moving
                  celebration of success, gaining and losing
                  members as it travels a wide circuit along
                  one of the hill roads.

tusaia   Seed of a wild plant that grows along old
                  riverbeds in the Western Desert.

The Arlingan Way of Speaking

The speech of Arlinga varies from land to land and from group to group, as with any country, especially since there is a different language spoken in each area. This need not greatly concern you, but for those who are interested in the "proper" way of pronouncing the names in the story, here is a brief guide.

The Lowlands

The Lowlanders are perceived as being an abrupt people, and this is to a certain extent evident in their language Harniyen. The names, if you will notice, are largely uncomplicated.

r	always rolled, as in Russian
o	as in "old," without any rounding of the lips
u	as in "blue"
ee	as in "bleed," pronounced as a long "e" in some areas
i	long vowel, as in "beets"
a	as in "jaw"
aa	a lengthened "a"
e	as in "bet"

Seng Grandt

The inhabitants of the High City speak many tongues, words from which are scattered through their language Sheewan. However, basic Sheewan is very basic indeed in terms of pronunciation.

vowels	same as in the Lowlands, except that there are two accent marks.
	$\hat{a}$ — lengthens a vowel or cluster of vowels
	$\grave{a}$ — indicates a tightening of the throat
th	may be pronounced either as in "bath," or as an aspirated "t" (a "t" with a puff of air after it). Either way is correct.
dt	an archaic sound missing from most modern names. Many pronounce it as "t," but certain of the older Sheewa use the classical pronunciation, which is to stop the voice and give this dead letter its own place in the word, aspirating it very strongly.

The Highlands

The people of the Great Crater, or Caldera, speak the language known as Kyarrghnaal. It has many dialects, but the one spoken in the book is the dialect of those who live near the Sky Line and around the western rim of the mountains.

r	pronounced as in North American English, may be used as a vowel
rr	rolled, sometimes heavily, may be used as a vowel
gh	rolled at the back of the throat, as though you were gargling in the morning
kh	rough, like the German "ch"
a	short, like the "u" in "but"
aa	long, like the "a" in "all"
u	as in "rule"
i	short, as in "bit"
ee	long, as in "keen"

The Tribes of the West

The language (Huaynił) of the tribes differs, sometimes greatly, from tribe to tribe. The dialect in this book is shared by the Huaynił and Laiopej, who regularly intermarry. The sound system is actually quite simple, and makes sense to the English speaker except for one sound:

ł	like the Navajo ł or the Welsh ll. A puff of air forced through the cheek (the sound "thl" ought to suffice).

CPSIA information can be obtained
at www.ICGtesting.com
Printed in the USA
LVOW12s1000191017
552858LV00002B/1/P